Margaret Oliphant

The Makers of Venice

Doges, Conquerors, Painters, and Men of Letters

Margaret Oliphant

The Makers of Venice
Doges, Conquerors, Painters, and Men of Letters

ISBN/EAN: 9783744770453

Printed in Europe, USA, Canada, Australia, Japan

Cover: Foto ©Andreas Hilbeck / pixelio.de

More available books at **www.hansebooks.com**

See page 265.

LEONARDO LOREDANO.

THE
MAKERS OF VENICE

DOGES, CONQUERORS, PAINTERS,

AND

MEN OF LETTERS

BY

MRS. OLIPHANT

AUTHOR OF "THE MAKERS OF FLORENCE"

WITH ILLUSTRATIONS BY R. R. HOLMES, F.S.A.

Sia benedeta sta Venezia mia
E sto popolo quieto, alegro e san.
Me sento un vodo in cuor se stago via,
Sento el solito mal de l'isolan
Benedeto Samarco e le putele
Che zira in piazza a ingelosir le stele,
Benedeto el sirocco che ne afana,
E la nostra flacona veneziana.
Rime Veneziane—SARFATTI.

London
MACMILLAN AND CO.
AND NEW YORK
1887

TO

Elizabeth Lady Cloncurry

AND

Emma Fitzmaurice,

KIND AND DEAR COMPANIONS

OF MANY A VENETIAN RAMBLE,

THIS BOOK IS INSCRIBED.

CONTENTS.

PART I.— THE DOGES.

CHAPTER I.

CHAPTER II.

CHAPTER III.

CHAPTER IV.

CHAPTER V.

PART II.—BY SEA AND BY LAND.

PART III.—THE PAINTERS.

PART .IV.—MEN OF LETTERS.

LIST OF ILLUSTRATIONS.

The Makers of Venice.

INTRODUCTION.

ENICE has long borne in the imagination of the world a distinctive position, something of the character of a great enchantress, a magician of the seas. Her growth between the water and the sky; her great palaces, solid and splendid, built, so to speak, on nothing; the wonderful glory of light and reflection about her; the glimmer of incessant brightness and movement; the absence of all those harsh, artificial sounds which vex the air in other towns, but which in her are replaced by harmonics of human voices, and by the liquid tinkle of the waves—all these unusual characteristics combine to make of her a wonder and a prodigy. While there are scarcely any who are unmoved by her special charm, there are some who are entirely subdued by it, to whom the sight of her is a continual enchantment, and who never get beyond the sense of something miraculous, the rapture of the first vision. Not only does she "shine where she stands," which even the poorest cluster of human habitations will do in the light of love: but all those walls, with the mist of ages like a bloom of eternal youth upon them—all those delicate pinnacles and carven-stones, the arches and the pillars and the balconies, the fretted outlines that strike against the sky—shine too as with a light within that radiates into the clear sea-air; and every

B

ripple on the great water-way, and every wave on the lagoon, and each little rivulet of a canal, like a line of light between the piles of masonry, which are themselves built of pearl and tints of ocean shells, shines too with an ever-varied, fantastic, enchanting glimmer of responsive brightness. In the light of summer mornings, in the glow of winter sunsets, Venice stands out upon the blue background, the sea that brims upwards to her very doors, the sky that sweeps in widening circles all around, radiant with an answering tone of light. She is all wonder, enchantment, the brightness and the glory of a dream. Her own children cannot enough paint her, praise her, celebrate her splendours: and to outdo if possible that patriotic enthusiasm has been the effort of many a stranger from afar.

When the present writer ventured to put upon record some of the impressions which mediæval Florence has left upon history, in the lives and deeds of great men, the work was comparatively an easy one—for Florence is a city full of shadows of the great figures of the past. The traveller cannot pass along her streets without treading in the very traces of Dante, without stepping upon soil made memorable by footprints never to be effaced. We meet them in the crowded ways—the cheerful painters singing at their work, the prophet-monk going to torture and execution, the wild gallants with their Carnival ditties, the crafty and splendid statesmen who subjugated the fierce Republic. Faces start out from the crowd wherever we turn our eyes. The greatness of the surroundings, the palaces, churches, frowning mediæval castles in the midst of the city, are all thrown into the background by the greatness, the individuality, the living power and vigour of the men who are their originators, and, at the same time, their inspiring soul.

But when we turn to Venice the effect is very different. After the bewitchment of the first vision, a chill falls upon the inquirer. Where is the poet, where the prophet, the princes, the scholars, the men whom, could we see, we should recognise wherever we met them, with whom the whole world is acquainted? They are not here. In the sunshine of the Piazza, in the glorious gloom of San Marco, in the great council-chambers and offices of state, once so full of busy statesmen, and great interests, there is scarcely a figure recognisable of all, to be met with in the spirit—no one whom we look for as we walk, whose individual footsteps are traceable wherever we turn. Instead of the men who made her what she is, who ruled her with so high a hand, who filled her archives with the most detailed narratives, and gleaned throughout the world every particular of universal history which could enlighten and guide her, we find everywhere the great image—an idealisation more wonderful than any in poetry—of Venice herself, the crowned and reigning city, the centre of all their aspirations, the mistress of their affections, for whom those haughty patricians of an older day, with a proud self-abnegation which has no humility or sacrifice in it, effaced themselves, thinking of nothing but her glory. It is a singular tribute to pay to any race, especially to a race so strong, so full of life and energy, loving power, luxury, and pleasantness as few other races have done; yet it is true. When Byron swept with superficial, yet brilliant eyes the roll of Venetian history, what did he find for the uses of his verse? Nothing but two old men, one condemned for his own fault, the other for his son's, remarkable chiefly for their misfortunes—symbols of the wrath and the feebleness of age, and of ingratitude and bitter fate. This was all which the rapid observer could find in the story of a power which was once supreme in the seas, the arbiter of peace or war through all the difficult and dangerous East, the first defender of Christendom against the Turk, the first merchant, banker, carrier, whose emissaries were busy in all the councils and all the markets of the world. In her records the city is everything—the Republic, the worshipped ideal of a community in which every man for the common glory seems to have been willing to sink his own. Her sons toiled for her, each in his vocation, not without personal glory, far from indifferent to personal gain, yet determined above all that Venice should be great, that she should be beautiful above all the

B 2

thoughts of other races, that her power and her splendour should outdo every rival. The impression grows upon the student, whether he penetrates no further than the door-ways of those endless collections of historic documents which make the archives of Venice important to all the world, and in which lie the records of immeasurable toil, the investigations of a succession of the keenest observers, the most subtle politicians and statesmen; or whether he endeavours to trace more closely the growth and development of the Republic, the extension of her rule, the perfection of her economy. In all of these, men of the noblest talents, the most intense vigour and energy, have laboured. The records give forth the very hum of a crowd; they glow with life, with ambition, with strength, with every virile and potent quality : but all directed to one aim. Venice is the outcome—not great names of individual men.

The Tuscans also loved their great and beautiful city, but they loved her after a different sort. Perhaps the absence of all those outlets to the seas and traffic with the wider world which moulded Venetian character, gave the strain of a more violent personality and fiercer passions to their blood. They loved their Florence for themselves, desiring an absolute sway over her, and to make her their own—unable to tolerate any rivalry in respect to her, turning out upon the world every competitor, fighting to be first in the city, whatever might happen. The Venetians, with what seems a finer purpose in a race less grave, put Venice first in everything. Few were the *fuori-usciti*, the political exiles, sent out from the city of the sea. Now and then a general who had lost a battle—in order that all generals might be thus sharply reminded that the Republic tolerated no failures—would be thrust forth into the wilderness of that dark world which was not Venice; but no feud so great as that which banished Dante ever tore the city asunder, no such vicissitudes of sway ever tormented her peace. A grand and steady aim, never abandoned, never even lost sight of, runs through every page of her story as long as it remains the story of a living and independent power.

Perhaps the comparative equality of the great houses which figure on the pages of the golden book of Venice may have had something to do with this result. Their continual poise and balance of power, and all the wonderful system of checks and restraints so skilfully combined to prevent all possibility of the predominance of one family over the other, would thus have attained a success which suspicion and jealousy have seldom secured, and which, perhaps, may be allowed to obliterate the memory of such sentiments, and make us think of them as wisdom and honourable care. As in most human affairs, no doubt both the greater and the lesser motives were present, and the determination of each man that his neighbour should have no chance of stepping on to a higher level than himself, combined with, and gave a keen edge of personal feeling to his conviction of the advantages of the oligarchical-democratic government which suited the genius of the people, and made the Republic so great. Among the Contarinis, Morosinis, Tiepolos, Dandolos, the Corners and Loredans, and a host of others whose names recur with endless persistency from first to last through all the vicissitudes of the national career, alternating in all the highest offices of state, there was none which was ever permitted to elevate itself permanently, or come within sight of a supreme position. They kept each other down, even while raising each other to the fullness of an aristocratic sway which has never been equalled in Christendom. And the ambition which could never hope for such predominance as the Medici, the Visconti, the Scaligeri attained in their respective cities, was thus entirely devoted to the advancement of the community, the greater power and glory of the state. What no man could secure for himself or his own house, all men could do, securing their share in the benefit, for Venice. And in generous minds this ambition, taking a finer flight than is possible when personal aggrandisement lies at the heart of the effort, became a passion—the inspiring principle of the race. For this they coursed the seas, quenching the pirate tribes that threatened their trade, less laudably seizing the towns of the

coast, the islands of the sea which interfered with their access
to their markets in the East. For this they carried fire and
flame to the mainland, and snatched from amid the fertile
fields the supremacy of Padua and Treviso, and many a landward city, making their seaborn nest into the governing head
of a great province; an object which was impersonal giving
licence as well as force to their purpose, and relieving their
consciences from the guilt of turning crusades and missionary
enterprises alike into wars of conquest. Whatever their
tyrannies, as whatever their hard-won glories might be, they
were all for Venice, and only in a secondary and subsidiary
sense for themselves.

The same principle has checked in other ways that flow of
individual story with which Florence has enriched the records
of the world. Nature at first, no doubt, must bear the
blame, who gave no Dante to the state which perhaps might
have prized him more highly than his own ; but the same
paramount attraction of the idealised and sovereign city, in
which lay all their pride, turned the early writers of Venice into
chroniclers, historians, diarists, occupied in collecting and recording everything that concerned their city, and indifferent to
individuals, devoted only to the glory and the story of the state.
In later days this peculiarity indeed gave way, and a hundred
piping voices rise to celebrate the decadence of the great
Republic ; but by that time she has ceased to be a noble
spectacle, and luxury and vice have come in to degrade the tale
into one of endless pageantry deprived of all meaning—no longer
the proud occasional triumphs of a conquering race, but the
perpetual occupation of a debased and corrupted people. To
the everlasting loss of the city and mankind there was no Vasari
in Venice. Messer Giorgio, with his kindly humorous eyes,
peered across the peninsula, through clouds of battle and conflict
always going on, and perhaps not without a mist of neighbourly
depreciation in themselves, perceived far off the Venetian men
and their works who were thought great painters—a rival school
in competition with his own. He was not near enough to

discover what manner of men the two long-lived brothers Bellini, or the silent Carpaccio, with his beautiful thoughts, or the rest of the busy citizens who filled churches and chambers with a splendour as of their own resplendent air and glowing suns, might be. An infinite loss to us and to the state, yet completing the sentiment of the consistent story, which demands all for Venice : but for the individual whose works are left behind him to her glory, his name inscribed upon her records as a faithful servant, and no more.

Yet when we enter more closely into the often-repeated narrative, transmitted from one hand to another till each chronicler, with sharp incisive touches, or rambling in garrulous details, has brought it down to his own time and personal knowledge, this severity relaxes somewhat. The actors in the drama break into groups, and with more or less difficulty it becomes possible to discover here and there how a change came about, how a great conquest was made, how the people gathered to listen, and how a doge, an orator, a suppliant, stood up and spoke. We begin to discern, after long gazing, how a popular tumult would spring up, and all Venice dart into fire and flame ; and how the laws and institutions grew which controlled that possibility, and gradually, with the enforced assent of the populace, bound them more securely than ever democracy was bound before, in the name of freedom. And among the fire and smoke, and through the mists, we come to perceive here and there a noble figure—a blind old doge, with white locks streaming, with sightless eyes aflame, running his galley ashore, a mark for all the arrows; or another standing, a gentler, less prominent image between the pope and the emperor; or with deep eyes, all hollowed with age and thought, and close-shut mouth, as in that portrait Bellini has made for us, facing a league of monarchs undaunted, for Venice against the world. And though there is no record of that time when Dante stood within the red walls of the arsenal, and saw the galleys making and mending, and the pitch fuming up to heaven—as all the world may still see them through his eyes—yet a milder scholarly image, a round smooth face, with cowl and garland, looks down upon us from the gallery, all blazing with crimson and gold, between the horses of San Marco, a friendly visitor, the best we could have, since Dante left no sign behind him, and probably was never heard of by the magnificent Signoria. Petrarch stands there, to be seen by the side of the historian-doge, as long as Venice lasts: but not much of him, only a glimpse, as is the Venetian way, lest in contemplation of the poet we should for a moment forget the Republic, his hostess and protector—Venice, the all-glorious mistress of the seas, the first object, the unrivalled sovereign of her children's thoughts and hearts.

PART I.—THE DOGES.

CHAPTER I.

THE ORSEOLI.

THE names of the doges, though so important in the old chronicles of the Republic, which are in many cases little more than a succession of *Vitæ Ducum*, possess individually few associations and little significance to the minds of the strangers who gaze upon the long line of portraits under the cornice of the Hall of the Great Council, without pausing with special interest on any of them, save perhaps on that corner where, conspicuous by its absence, the head of Marino Faliero ought to be. The easy adoption of one figure, by no means particularly striking or characteristic, but which served the occasion of the poet without giving him too much trouble, has helped to throw the genuine historical importance of a very remarkable succession of rulers into obscurity. But this long line of sovereigns, sometimes the guides, often the victims, of the popular will, stretching back with a clearer title and more comprehensible history than that of most dynasties, into the vague distances of old time, is full of interest; and contains many a tragic episode as striking and more significant than that of the aged prince whose picturesque story is the one most generally known. There are, indeed, few among them who have been publicly branded with the name

of traitor; but, at least in the earlier chapters of the great
civic history, there are as many examples of a popular struggle
and a violent death as there are of the quiet ending and
serene magnificence which seem fitted to the age and services of
most of those who have risen to that dignity. They have been
in many cases old men, already worn in the service of their
country, most of them tried by land and sea—mariners, generals,
legislators, fully equipped for all the various needs of a
sovereignty whose dominion was the sea, yet which was at
the same time weighted with all the vexations and dangers of a
continental rule. Their elevation was, in later times, a crowning
honour, a sort of dignified retirement from the ruder labours
of civic use; but, in the earlier ages of the Republic this was
not so, and at all times it was a most dangerous post, and one
whose occupant was most likely to pay for popular disappoint-
ments, to run the risk of all the conspiracies, and to be
hampered and hindered by jealous counsellors, and the continual
inspection of suspicious spectators. To change the doge was
always an expedient by which Venice could propitiate fate and
turn the course of fortune; and the greatest misfortunes recorded
in her chronicles are those of her princes, whose names were
to-day acclaimed to all the echoes, their paths strewed with
flowers and carpeted with cloth of gold, but to-morrow insulted
and reviled, and themselves exiled or murdered, all services to
the state notwithstanding. Sometimes, no doubt, the overthrow
was well deserved : but in other instances it can be set down
to nothing but popular caprice. To the latter category belongs
the story of the family of the Orseoli, which, at the very out-
set of authentic history, sets before us at a touch the early
economy of Venice, the relations of the princes and the people,
the enthusiasms, the tumults, the gusts of popular caprice, as
well as the already evident predominance of a vigorous
aristocracy, natural leaders of the people. The history of this
noble family has the advantage of being set before us by the
first distinct contemporary narrative, that of Giovanni Sagornino
—John the Deacon, John of Venice, as he is fondly termed by

a recent historian. The incidents of this period of power, or at least of that of the two first princes of the name, incidents full of importance in the history of the rising Republic, are the first that stand forth, out of the mist of nameless chronicles, as facts which were seen and recorded by a trustworthy witness.

The first Orseolo came into power after a popular tumult of the most violent description, which took the throne and his life from the previous doge, Pietro Candiano. This event occurred in the year 976, when such scenes were not unusual even in regions less excitable. Candiano was the fourth doge of his name, and had been in his youth associated with his father in the supreme authority—but in consequence of his rebellion and evil behaviour had been displaced and exiled, his life saved only at the prayer of the old doge. On the death of his father, however, the young prodigal had been acclaimed doge by the rabble. In this capacity he had done much to disgust and alarm the sensitive and proud Republic. Chief among his offences was the fact that he had acquired, through his wife, continental domains which required to be kept in subjection by means of a body of armed retainers, dangerous for Venice: and he was *superbissimo* from his youth up, and had given frequent offence by his arrogance and exactions. Upon what occasion it was that the popular patience failed at last we are not told, but only that a sudden tumult arose against him, a rush of general fury. When the enraged mob hurried to the ducal palace they found that the doge had fortified himself there, upon which they adopted the primitive method of setting fire to the surrounding buildings. Tradition asserts that it was from the house of Pietro Orseolo that the fire was kindled, and some say by his suggestion. It would seem that the crowd intended only to burn some of the surrounding houses to frighten or smoke out the doge: but the wind was high, and the ducal palace, with the greater part of San Marco, which was then merely the ducal chapel, was consumed, along with all the houses stretching upward along the course of the Grand Canal as far as Santa Maria Zobenigo. This sudden conflagration lights up, in the

darkness of that distant age, a savage scene. The doge seized
in his arms his young child, whether with the hope of saving
it or of saving himself by means of that shield of innocence,
and made his way out of his burning house, through the
church which was also burning, though better able, probably,
to resist the flames. But when he emerged from the secret
passages of San Marco he found that the crowd had anticipated
him, and that his way was barred on every side by armed
men. The desperate fugitive confronted the multitude, and
resorted to that method so often and sometimes so un-
expectedly successful with the masses. In the midst of the
fire and smoke, surrounded by those threatening fierce countenances, with red reflections glittering in every sword and
lance point, reflected over again in the sullen water, he made
a last appeal. They had banished him in his youth, yet had
relented and recalled him and made him doge. Would they
burn him out now, drive him into a corner, kill him like a
wild beast? And supposing even that he was worthy of
death, what had the child done, an infant who had never sinned
against them? This scene, so full of fierce and terrible elements, the angry roar of the multitude, the blazing of the fire
behind that circle of tumult and agitation, the wild glare in the
sky, and amid all, the one soft infantine figure held up in the
father's despairing arms—might afford a subject for a powerful
picture in the long succession of Venetian records made by art.

When this tragedy had ended, by the murder of both father
and child, the choice of the city fell upon Pietro Orseolo as the
new doge. An ecclesiastical historian of the time speaks of his
" wicked ambition " as instrumental in the downfall of his predecessor and of his future works of charity as dictated by remorse ; but we are disposed to hope that this is merely said, as
is not uncommon in religious story, to enhance the merits of his
conversion. The secular chroniclers are unanimous in respect
to his excellence. He was a man in everything the contrary
of the late doge—a man *laudato di tutti*, approved of all men
—and of whom nothing but good was known. Perhaps if he

To face page 13.

S. PETER'S CHAIR: SAN PIETRO IN CASTELLO.

had any share in the tumult which ended in the murder of
Candiano, his conscience may have made a crime of it when the
hour of conversion came; but certainly in Venice there would
seem to have been no accuser to say a word against him. In
the confusion of the great fire and the disorganisation of the
city, "contaminated" by the murder of the prince, and all
the disorders involved, Orseolo was forced into the uneasy seat
whose occupant was sure to be the first victim if the affairs
of Venice went wrong. His first act was to remove the insignia
of his office out of the ruins of the doge's palace to his own
house, which was situated upon the Riva beyond and adjacent
to the home of the doges. It is difficult to form to ourselves
an idea of the aspect of the city at this early period. Venice,
though already great, was in comparison with its after appearance a mere village, or rather a cluster of villages, straggling
along the sides of each muddy, marshy island, keeping the line
of the broad and navigable water-way, in dots of building and
groups of houses and churches, from the olive-covered isle where
San Pietro, the first great church of the city, shone white among
its trees, along the curve of the Canaluccio to the Rialto—Rive-
Alto, what Mr. Ruskin calls the deep stream, where the church
of San Giacomo, another central spot, stood, with its group of
dwellings round—no bridge then dreamed of, but a ferry con-
necting the two sides of the Grand Canal. Already the stir of
commerce was in the air, and the big sea-going galleys, with
their high bulwarks, lay at the rude wharfs, to take in outward-
bound cargoes of salt, salt-fish, wooden furniture, bowls, and
boxes of home manufacture, as well as the goods brought
from northern nations, of which they were the merchants
and carriers—and come back laden with the riches of the
East—with wonderful tissues and carpets, and marbles and
relics of the saints. The palace and its chapel, the shrine
of San Marco, stood where they still stand, but there were no
columns on the Piazzetta, and the Great Piazza was a piece of
waste land belonging to the nuns at San Zaccaria, which was,
as one might say, the parish church. Most probably this

vacant space in the days of the first Orseolo, was little more
than a waste of salt-water grasses, and sharp and acrid plants
like those that now flourish in such rough luxuriance on the Lido
—or perhaps boasted a tree or two, a patch of cultivated ground.
Such was the scene—very different from the Venice of the
earliest pictures, still more different from that we know. But
already the lagoon was full of boats, and the streets of commotion,
and Venice grew like a young plant, like the quick-spreading
vegetation of her own warm, wet marshes, day by day.

The new doge proceeded at once to rebuild both the palace and
the shrine. The energy and vigour of the man who, with that
desolate and smoking mass of ruin around him—three hundred
houses burned to the ground and all their forlorn inhabitants to
house and care for—could yet address himself without a pause to
the reconstruction on the noblest scale of the great twin edifices,
the glorious dwelling of the saint, the scarcely less cared-for
palace of the governor, the representative of law and order in
Venice, has something wonderful in it. He was not rich, and
neither was the city, which had in the midst of this disaster to
pay the dower of the Princess Valdrada, the widow of Candiano,
whose claims were backed by the Emperor Otto, and would if
refused have brought upon the Republic all the horrors of war.
Orseolo gave up a great part of his own patrimony, however, to
the rebuilding of the church and palace ; eight thousand ducats a
year for eighty years (the time which elapsed before its completion), say the old records, he devoted to this noble and pious
purpose, and sought far and near for the best workmen, some
of whom came as far as from Constantinople, the metropolis of
all the arts. How far the walls had risen in his day, or how
much he saw accomplished, or heard of before the end of his
life, it is impossible to tell. But one may fancy how, amid all
the toils of the troubled state, while he laboured and pondered
how to get that money together for Valdrada, and pacify the
emperor and her other powerful friends, and how to reconcile
all factions, and heal all wounds, and house more humbly his
poor burned-out citizens, the sight from his windows of those

fair solid walls, rising out of the ruins, must have comforted his
soul. Let us hope he saw the round of some lower arch, the
rearing of some pillar, a pearly marble slab laid on, or at least
the carved work on the basement of a column before he went
away.

The historian tells us that it was Orseolo also who ordered from
Constantinople the famous *Pala d'oro*, the wonderful gold and
silver work which still on high days and festas is disclosed to
the eyes of the faithful on the great altar, one of the most magnificent ornaments of San Marco. It is a pity that inquisitive
artists and antiquaries with their investigations have determined this work to be at least two centuries later, but
Sagornino, who was the doge's contemporary, could not have
foreseen the work of a later age, so that he must certainly refer
to some former *tabulam miro opere ex argento et auro*, which
Orseolo in his magnificence added to his other gifts. Nor did
the doge confine his bounty to these great and beautiful works.
If the beauty of Venice was dear to him, divine charity was still
more dear. Opposite the rising palace, where now stands the
Libreria Vecchia, Orseolo, taking advantage of a site cleared by
the fire, built a hospital, still standing in the time of Sabellico,
who speaks of it as the " *Spedale, il quale è sopra la Piazza
dirimpetto al Palazzo,*" and where, according to the tale, he
constantly visited and cared for the sick poor.

It must have been while still in the beginning of all these
great works, but already full of many cares, the Candiano faction
working against him, and perhaps but little response coming
from the people to whom he was sacrificing his comfort and his
life, that Orseolo received a visit which changed the course of
his existence. Among the pilgrims who came from all quarters
to the shrine of the evangelist, a certain French abbot, Carinus
or Guarino, of the monastery of St. Michael de Cusano, in
Aquitaine, arrived in Venice. It was Orseolo's custom to have all
such pious visitors brought to his house and entertained there
during their stay, and he found in Abbot Guarino a congenial
soul. They talked together of all things in heaven and earth,

and of this wonderful new Venice rising from the sea, with all her
half-built churches and palaces ; and of the holy relics brought
from every coast for her enrichment and sanctification, the
bodies of the saints which made almost every church a sacred
shrine.   And no doubt the cares of the doge's troubled life, the
burdens laid on him daily, the threats of murder and assassination, with which, instead of gratitude, his self-devotion was
received, were poured into the sympathetic ear of the priest,
who on his side drew such pictures of the holy peace of monastic
life, the tranquillity and blessed privations of the cloister, as made
the heart of the doge to burn within him.   "If thou wouldst
be perfect"—said the abbot, as on another occasion a greater
voice had said.   "Oh, benefactor of my soul!" cried the doge,
beholding a vista of new hope opening before him, a halcyon
world of quiet, a life of sacrifice and prayer.   He had already
for years lived like a monk, putting all the indulgences of wealth
and even affection aside.   For the moment, however, he had
too many occupations on his hands to make retirement possible.
He asked for a year in which to arrange his affairs ; to put order
in the Republic and liberate himself.   With this agreement the
abbot left him, but true to his engagement, when the heats of
September were once more blazing on the lagoon, came back to
his penitent.   The doge in the meantime had made all his
arrangements.   No doubt it was in this solemn year, which no
one knew was to be the end of his life in the world, that he set
aside so large a part of his possessions for the prosecution of
the buildings which now he could no longer hope to see completed.   When all these preliminaries were settled, and everything done, Orseolo, with a chosen friend or two, one of them
his son-in-law, the sharer of his thoughts and his prayers, took
boat silently one night across the still lagoon to Fusina, where
horses awaited them, and so flying in the darkness over the mainland abandoned the cares of the princedom and the world.

Of the chaos that was left behind, the consternation of the
family, the confusion of the state, the record says nothing.   This
was not the view of the matter which occurred to the primitive

mind. We are apt to think with reprobation, perhaps too strongly expressed, of the cowardice of duties abandoned, and the cruelty of ties broken. But in the early ages no one seems to have taken this view. The sacrifice made by a prince, who gave up power and freedom, and all the advantages of an exalted position, in order to accept privation and poverty for the love of God, was more perceptible then to the general intelligence than the higher self-denial of supporting, for the love of God, the labours and miseries of his exalted but dangerous office. The tumult and commotion which followed the flight of Orseolo were not mingled with blame or reproach. The doge, in the eyes of his generation, chose the better part, and offered a sacrifice with which God Himself could not but be well pleased.

He was but fifty when he left Venice, having reigned a little over two years. Guarino placed his friend under the spiritual rule of a certain stern and holy man, the saintly Romoaldo, in whose life and legend we find the only record of Pietro Orseolo's latter days. St. Romoaldo was the founder of the order of the Camaldolites, practising in his own person the greatest austerity of life, and imposing it upon his monks, to whom he refused even the usual relaxation of better fare on Sunday, which had been their privilege. The noble Venetians, taken from the midst of their liberal and splendid life, were set to work at the humble labours of husbandmen upon this impoverished diet. He who had been the Doge Pietro presently found that he was incapable of supporting so austere a rule. "Wherefore he humbly laid himself at the feet of the blessed Romoaldo, and being bidden to rise, with shame confessed his weakness. 'Father,' he said, 'as I have a great body, I cannot for my sins sustain my strength with this morsel of hard bread.' Romoaldo, having compassion on the frailty of his body, added another portion of biscuit to the usual measure, and thus held out the hand of pity to the sinking brother." The comic pathos of the complaint of the big Venetian, bred amid the freedom of the seas, and expected to live and work upon half a biscuit, is beyond comment.

C

He lived many years in the humility of conventual subjection, and died, apparently without any advancement in religious
life, in the far distance of France, never seeing his Venice again.
In after years, his son, who was only fifteen at the period of the
doge's flight, and who was destined in his turn to do so much
for Venice, visited his father in his obscure retirement.   The
meeting between the almost too generous father, who had given
so much to Venice, and had completed the offering by giving up
himself at last to the hard labours and humility of monastic
life—and the ambitious youth full of the highest projects of
patriotism and courage, must have been a remarkable scene.
The elder Pietro in his cloister had no doubt pondered much on
Venice and on the career of the boy whom he had left behind
him there, and whose character and qualities must have already
shown themselves: and much was said between them on this
engrossing subject.   Orseolo, "whether by the spirit of prophecy
or by special revelation, predicted to him all that was to happen.
'I know,' he said, 'my son, that they will make you doge, and
that you will prosper.   Take care to preserve the rights of the
Church, and those of your subjects.   Be not drawn aside from
doing justice, either by love or by hate.'"   Better counsel could
no fallen monarch give—and Orseolo was happier than many
fathers in a son worthy of him.

The city deprived of such a prince was very sad, but still
more full of longing: "*Molto trista ma piu desiderosa,*" says
Sabellico; and his family remained dear to Venice—for as long
as popular favour usually lasts.   Pietro died nineteen years after
in the odour of sanctity, and was canonised, to the glory of
his city.   His *breve*, the inscription under his portrait in the
great hall, attributes to him the building of San Marco, as well
as many miracles and wonderful works.   The miracles, however, were performed far from Venice, and have no place in her
records, except those deeds of charity and tenderness which he
accomplished among his people before he left them.   These the
existing corporation of Venice, never unwilling to chronicle either
a new or antique glory, have lately celebrated by an inscription,

which the traveller will see from the little bay in which the canal terminates, just behind the upper end of the Piazza. This little triangular opening among the tall houses is called the Bacino Orseolo, and bears a marble tablet to the honour of the first Pietro of this name, "*il santo*", high up upon the wall.

In the agitation and trouble caused by Orseolo's unexpected disappearance, a period of discord and disaster began. A member of the Candiano party was placed in the doge's seat for a short and agitated reign, and he was succeeded by a rich but feeble prince in whose time occurred almost the worst disorders that have ever been known in Venice—a bloody struggle between two families, one of which had the unexampled baseness of seeking the aid against their native city of foreign arms. The only incident which we need mention of this disturbed period is that the Doge Memmo bestowed upon Giovanni Morosini, Orseolo's companion and son-in-law, who had returned a monk to his native city—perhaps called back by the misfortunes of his family—a certain " beautiful little island covered with olives and cypresses," which lay opposite the doge's palace, and is known now to every visitor of Venice as St. Georgio Maggiore. There was already a chapel dedicated to St. George among the trees.

Better things, however, were now in store for the Republic. After the incapable Memmo, young Pietro was called, according to his father's prophecy, to the ducal throne. "When the future historian of Venice comes to the deeds of this great doge he will feel his soul enlarged," says Sagredo, the author of a valuable study of Italian law and economics; "it is no more a new-born people of whom he will have to speak, but an adult nation, rich, conquering, full of traffic and wealth." The new prince had all the qualities which were wanted for the consolidation and development of the Republic. He had known something of that bitter but effectual training of necessity which works so nobly in generous natures. His father's brief career in Venice, and his counsels from his cell, were before him, both as example and encouragement. He had been in

c 2

France; he had seen the world. He had an eye to mark that the moment had come for larger action and bolder self-assertion, and he had strength of mind to carry his conceptions out. And he had that touching advantage—the stepping-stone of a previous life sacrificed and unfulfilled—upon which to raise the completeness of his own. In short, he was the man of the time, prepared to carry out the wishes and realise the hopes of his age; and when he became, at the age of thirty, in the fullness of youthful strength, the first magistrate of Venice, a new chapter of her history began.

It was in the year 991, on the eve of a new century, sixteen years after his father's abdication, that the second Pietro Orseolo began to reign. The brawls of civil contention disappeared on his accession, and the presence of a prince who was at the same time a strong man and fully determined to defend and extend his dominion, became instantly apparent to the world. His first acts were directed to secure the privileges of Venice by treaty with the emperors of the East and West, establishing her position by written charter under the golden seal of Constantinople, and with not less efficacy from the imperial chancellorship of the German Otto. On both sides an extension of privilege and the remission of certain tributes were secured. Having settled this, Pietro turned his attention to the great necessity of the moment, upon which the very existence of the Republic depended. Up to this time Venice, to free herself from the necessity of holding the rudder in one hand and the sword in the other, had paid a certain blackmail, such as was exacted till recent times by the corsairs of Africa, to the pirate tribes, who were the scourge of the seas, sometimes called Narentani, sometimes Schiavoni and Croats, by the chroniclers, allied bands of sea-robbers who infested the Adriatic. The time had come, however, when it was no longer seemly that the proud city, growing daily in power and wealth, should stoop to secure her safety by such means. The payment was accordingly stopped, and an encounter followed, in which the pirates were defeated. Enraged but impotent, not daring to attack

Venice, or risk their galleys in the intricate channels of the
lagoons, they set upon the unoffending towns of Dalmatia, and
made a raid along the coast, robbing and ravaging. The result
was that from all the neighbouring seaboard ambassadors
arrived in haste, asking the help of the Venetians. The
cruelties of the corsairs had already, more than once, reduced the
seaports and prosperous cities of this coast to the point of desperation, and they caught at the only practicable help with the
precipitancy of suffering. The doge thus found the opportunity
he sought, and took advantage of it without a moment's delay.
At once the arsenal was set to work, and a great *armata* decided
upon. The appeal thus made by the old to the new, the ancient
cities which had been in existence while she was but a collection
of swamp and salt-water marshes seeking deliverance from the
new-born miraculous city of the sea, is the most striking testimony to the growing importance of Venice. It was at the same
time her opportunity and the beginning of her conquests and
victories.

When the great expedition was ready to set out, the doge
went in solemn state to the cathedral church of San Pietro in
Castello, and received from the hands of the bishop the standard
of San Marco, with which he went on board. It was spring
when the galleys sailed, and Dandolo tells us that they were
blown by contrary winds to Grado, where Vitale Candiano
was now peacefully occupying his see as patriarch. Perhaps
something of the old feud still subsisting made Orseolo
unwilling to enter the port in which the son of the murdered
doge, whom his own father had succeeded, was supreme. But
if this had been the case, his doubts must have soon been set
at rest by the patriarch's welcome. He came out to meet the
storm-driven fleet with his clergy and his people, and added
to the armament not only his blessing, but the standard of
S. Hermagora to bring them victory. Thus endowed, with
the two blessed banners blowing over them, the expedition set
sail once more. The account of the voyage that follows is for
some time that of a kind of royal progress by sea, the galleys

passing in triumph from one port to another, anticipated by processions coming out to meet them, bishops with their clergy streaming forth, and all the citizens, private and public, hurrying to offer their allegiance to their defenders. Wherever holy relics were enshrined, the doge landed to visit them and pay his devotions : and everywhere he was met by ambassadors tendering the submission of another and another town or village, declaring themselves "willingly" subjects of the Republic, and enrolling their young men among its soldiers. That this submission was not so real as it appeared is proved by the subsequent course of events and the perpetual rebellions of those very cities; but in their moment of need nothing but enthusiasm and delight were apparent to the deliverers. At Trau a brother of the Sclavonian king fell into the hands of the doge and sought his protection, giving up his son Stefano as a hostage into the hands of the conquering prince.

At last, having cleared the seas, the expedition came to the nest of robbers itself, the impregnable city of Lagosta. "It is said," Sabellico reports with a certain awe, "that its position was pointed out by the precipices on each side rising up in the midst of the sea. The Narentani trusted in its strength, and here all the corsairs took refuge, when need was, as in a secure fortress." The doge summoned the garrison to surrender, which they would gladly have done, the same historian informs us, had they not feared the destruction of their city ; but on that account, "for love of their country, than which there is nothing more dear to men," they made a stubborn defence. Dandolo adds that the doge required the destruction of this place as a condition of peace. After a desperate struggle the fortress was taken, notwithstanding the natural strength of the rocky heights—the *asprezza de' luoghi nell' ascendere difficile*—and of the *Rocca* or great tower that crowned the whole. The object of the expedition was fully accomplished when the pirates' nest and stronghold was destroyed. "For nearly a hundred and sixty years the possession of the sea had been contested with varying fortune," now once for all the matter was settled. "The army returned victorious to the ships. The prince had purged the sea of robbers, and all the maritime parts of Istria, of Liburnia and of Dalmatia, were brought under the power of Venice." With what swelling sails, *con vento prospero*, the fleet must have swept back to the anxious city which, with no post nor despatch boat to carry her tidings, gazed silent, waiting in that inconceivable patience of old times, with anxious eyes watching the horizon! How the crowds must have gathered on the old primitive quays when the first faint rumour flew from Malamocco and the other sentinel isles of sails at hand! How many boats must have darted forth, their rowers half distracted with haste and suspense, to meet the returning *armata* and know 'the worst! Who can doubt that then, as always, there were some to whom the good news brought anguish and sorrow; but of that the chroniclers tell us nothing. And among all our supposed quickening of life in modern times, can we imagine a moment of living more intense, or sensations more acute, than those with which the whole city must have watched, one by one, the galleys bearing along with their tokens of victory, threading their way, slow even with the most prosperous wind, through the windings of the narrow channels, until the first man could leap on shore and the wonderful news be told?

"There was then no custom of triumphs," says the record, "but the doge entered the city triumphant, surrounded by the grateful people; and there made public declaration of all the things he had done—how all Istria and the sea coast to the furthest confines of Dalmatia with all the neighbouring islands, by the clemency of God and the success of the expedition, were made subject to the Venetian dominion. With magnificent words he was applauded by the great council, which ordained that not only of Venice but of Dalmatia he and his successors should be proclaimed doge."

Thus the first great conquest of the Venetians was accomplished, and the infant city made mistress of the seas.

It was on the return of Pietro Orseolo from this triumphant

expedition, and in celebration of his conquests, that the great
national festivity, called in after days the espousal of the
sea, the Feast of La Sensa, Ascension Day, was first instituted. The original ceremony was simpler but little less imposing than its later development. The clergy in a barge all
covered with cloth of gold, and in all possible glory of vestments
and sacred ornaments, set out from among the olive woods of
San Pietro in Castello, and met the doge in his still more splendid
barge at the Lido: where, after litanies and psalms, the bishop
rose and prayed aloud in the hearing of all the people, gathered
in boat and barge and every skiff that would hold water, in a far-
extending crowd along the sandy line of the flat shore. "Grant,
O Lord, that this sea may be to us and to all who sail upon it
tranquil and quiet. To this end we pray. Hear us, good Lord."
Then the boat of the ecclesiastics approached closely the boat of
the doge, and while the singers intoned "*Aspergi me, O Signor*,"
the bishop sprinkled the doge and his court with holy water,
pouring what remained into the sea. A very touching ceremonial, more primitive and simple, perhaps more real and likely
to go to the hearts of the seafaring population all gathered
round, than the more elaborate and triumphant histrionic
spectacle of the Sposalizio. It had been on Ascension Day that
Orseolo's expedition had set forth, and no day could be more
suitable than this victorious day of early summer, when Nature
is at her sweetest, for the great festival of the lagoons.

These victories and successes must have spread the name of
the Venetians and their doge far and wide; and it is evident
that they had moved the imagination of the young Emperor
Otto II., between whom and Orseolo a link of union had already
been formed through the doge's third son, who had been sent to
the court at Verona to receive there the *sacramento della
chrisma*, the rite of confirmation, under the auspices of the emperor, who changed the boy's name from Pietro to Otto, in sign
of high favour and affection. When the news of the conquest
of Dalmatia, the extinction of the pirates, and all the doge's
great achievements reached the emperor's ears, his desire to

know so remarkable a man grew so strong that an anonymous visit was planned between them. Under the pretext of taking sea-baths at an obscure island, Otto made a sudden and secret dash across the sea and reached the convent of San Servolo, on the island which still bears that name, and which is now one of the two melancholy asylums for the insane which stand on either side of the water-way opposite Venice. The doge hurried across the water as soon as night had come, to see his imperial visitor, and brought him back to pay his devotions, "according to Otto's habit," at the shrine of San Marco. Let us hope the moon was resplendent, as she knows how to be over these waters, when the doge brought the emperor over the shining lagoon in what primitive form of gondola was then in fashion, with the dark forms of the rowers standing out against the silvery background of sea and sky, and the little waves in a thousand ripples of light reflecting the glory of the heavens. One can imagine the nocturnal visit, the hasty preparations: and the great darkness of San Marco, half built, with all its scaffoldings ghostly in the silence of the night, and one bright illuminated spot, the hasty blaze of the candles flaring about the shrine. When the emperor had said his prayers before the sacred spot which contained the body of the evangelist, the patron of Venice, he was taken into the palace, which filled him with wonder and admiration, so beautiful was the house which out of the burning and ruins of twenty years before had now apparently been completed. It is said by Sagornino (the best authority) that Otto was secretly lodged in the eastern tower, and from thence made private expeditions into the city, and saw everything; but later chroniclers, probably deriving these details from traditional sources, increase the romance of the visit by describing him as recrossing to San Servolo, whither the doge would steal off privately every night to sup *domesticamente* with his guest. In one of the night visits to San Marco the doge's little daughter, newly born, was christened, the emperor himself holding her at the font. Perhaps this little domestic circumstance, which disabled her Serenity the Dogaressa, had something

to do with the secrecy of the visit, which does not seem sufficiently accounted for, unless, as some opine, the emperor wanted
secretly to consult Orseolo on great plans which he did not live
to carry out.   Three days after Otto's departure the doge called
the people together, and informed them of the visit he had
received, and further concessions and privileges which he had
secured for Venice.   "Which things," says the record, "were
pleasant to them, and they applauded the industry of Orseolo
in concealing the presence of so great a lord."   Here it is a
little difficult to follow the narrator.   It would be more natural
to suppose that the Venetians, always fond of a show, might
have shown a little disappointment at being deprived of the
sight of such a fine visitor.   It is said by some, however, that
to celebrate the great event, and perhaps make up to the
people for not having seen the emperor, a tournament of several
days' duration was held by Orseolo in the waste ground which
is now the Piazza.   At all events the incident only increased
his popularity.

Nor was this the only honour which came to his house.
Some time after the city of Bari was saved by Orseolo's arms
and valour from an invasion of the Saracens; and the grateful
emperors of the East, Basil and Constantine, by way of
testifying their thanks, invited the doge's eldest son Giovanni
to Constantinople, where he was received with a princely
welcome, and shortly after married to a princess of the
imperial house.   When the young couple returned to Venice,
they were received with extraordinary honours, festivities, and
delight, the doge going to meet them with a splendid train of
vessels, and such rejoicing as had never before been beheld in
Venice.   And permission was given to Orseolo to associate his
son with him in his authority—a favour only granted to those
whom Venice most delighted to honour, and which was the
highest expression of popular confidence and trust.

"But since there is no human happiness which is not disturbed
by some adversity," says the sympathetic chronicle, trouble
and sorrow now burst upon this happy and prosperous reign.

First came a great pestilence, by which the young Giovanni, the hope of the house, the newly-appointed coadjutor, was carried off, along with his wife and infant child, and which carried dismay and loss throughout the city. Famine followed naturally upon the epidemic and the accompanying panic, which paralysed all exertion—and mourning and misery prevailed. His domestic grief and the public misfortune would seem to have broken the heart of the great doge. After Giovanni's death he was permitted to take his younger son Otto as his coadjutor, but even this did not avail to comfort him. He made a remarkable will, dividing his goods into two parts, one for his children, another for the poor, "for the use and solace of all in our Republic"—a curious phrase, by some supposed to mean entertainments and public pleasures, by others relief from taxes and public burdens. When he died his body was carried to San Zaccaria, *per la trista città e lachrimosa,* with all kinds of magnificence and honour. And Otto his son reigned in his stead.

Otto, it is evident, must have appeared up to this time the favourite of fortune, the flower of the Orseoli. He had been half adopted by the emperor; he had made a magnificent marriage with a princess of Hungary; he had been sent on embassies and foreign missions; and finally, when his elder brother died, he had been associated with his father as his coadjutor and successor. He was still young when Pietro's death gave him the full authority (though his age can scarcely have been, as Sabellico says, nineteen). His character is said to have been as perfect as his position. "He was Catholic in faith, calm in virtue, strong in justice, eminent in religion, decorous in his way of living, great in riches, and so full of all kinds of goodness, that by his merits he was judged of all to be the most fit successor of his excellent father and blessed grandfather," says Doge Dandolo. But perhaps these abstract virtues were not of the kind to fit a man for the difficult position of doge, in the midst of a jealous multitude of his equals, all as eligible for that throne as he, and keenly on the watch to stop any succession which looked like the beginning of a dynasty. Otto had been much about courts; he had learned how emperors were served; and his habits, perhaps, had been formed at that ductile time of life when he was caressed as the godson of the imperial Otto, and as a near connection of the still more splendid emperors of the East. And it was not only he, whose preferment was a direct proof of national gratitude to his noble father, against whom a jealous rival, a (perhaps) anxious nationalist, had to guard. His brother Orso, who during his father's lifetime had been made Bishop of Torcello, was elevated to the higher office of patriarch and transferred to Grado some years after his brother's accession, so that the highest power and place, both secular and sacred, were in the hands of one family—a fact which would give occasion for many an insinuation, and leaven the popular mind with suspicion and alarm.

It was through the priestly brother Orso that the first attack upon the family of the Orseoli came. Otto had reigned for some fifteen or sixteen years with advantage and honour to the Republic, showing himself a worthy son of his father, and keeping the authority of Venice paramount along the unruly Dalmatian coast, where rebellions were things of yearly occurrence, when trouble first appeared. Of Orso, the patriarch, up to this time, little has been heard, save that it was he who rebuilt, or restored, out of the remains of the earlier church, the cathedral of Torcello, still the admiration of all beholders. His grandfather had begun, his father had carried on, the great buildings of Venice, the church and the palace, which the Emperor Otto had come secretly to see, and which he had found beautiful beyond all imagination. It would be difficult now to determine what corner of antique work may still remain in that glorious group which is theirs. But Orso's cathedral still stands distinct, lifting its lofty walls over the low edge of green, which is all that separates it from the sea. His foot has trod the broken mosaics of the floor; his voice has intoned canticle and litany under that lofty roof. The knowledge that framed the present edifice,

To face page 28.

INTERIOR OF THE CATHEDRAL OF TORCELLO.

the reverence which preserved for its decoration all those lovely relics of earlier times, the delicate Greek columns, the enrichments of eastern art—were, if not his, fostered and protected by him. Behind the high altar, on the bishop's high cold marble throne overlooking the great temple, he must have sat among his presbyters, and controlled the counsels and led the decisions of a community then active and wealthy, which has now disappeared as completely as the hierarchy of priests which once filled

BISHOP'S THRONE, TORCELLO.

these rows of stony benches. The ruins of the old Torcello are now but mounds under the damp grass; but Bishop Orso's work stands fast, as his name, in faithful brotherly allegiance and magnanimous truth to his trust, ought to stand.

The attack came from a certain Poppo, Patriarch of Aquileia, an ecclesiastic of the most warlike mediæval type, of German extraction or race, who, perhaps with the desire of reasserting

the old supremacy of his See over that of Grado, perhaps
stirred up by the factions in Venice, which were beginning to
conspire against the Orseoli, began to threaten the seat of
Bishop Orso. The records are very vague as to the means
employed by this episcopal warrior. He accused Orso before
the pope as an intruder not properly elected; but without
waiting for any decision on that point, assailed him in his See.
Possibly Poppo's attack on Grado coincided with tumults in the
city—"great discord between the people of Venice and the
doge"—so that both the brothers were threatened at once.
However that may be, the next event in the history is the flight
of both doge and patriarch to Istria—an extraordinary event of
which no explanation is given by any of the authorities. They
were both in the prime of life, and had still a great party in
their favour, so that it seems impossible not to conjecture some
weakness, most likely on the part of the Doge Otto, to account
for this abandonment of the position to their enemies. That
there was great anarchy and misery in Venice during the
interval of the prince's absence is evident, but how long it
lasted, or how it came about, we are not informed. All that
the chroniclers say (for by this time the guidance of Sagornino
has failed us, and there is no contemporary chronicle to refer
to) concerns Grado, which, in the absence of its bishop, was
taken by the lawless Poppo. He swore "by his eight oaths,"
says Sanudo, that he meant nothing but good to that hapless
city; but as soon as he got within the gates gave it up to the
horrors of a sack, outraging its population and removing the
treasure from its churches. Venice, alarmed by this unmask-
ing of the designs of the clerical invader, repented her own
hasty folly, and recalled her doge, who recovered Grado for her
with a promptitude and courage which makes his flight, without apparently striking a blow for himself, more remarkable
still. But this renewed prosperity was of short duration. The
factions that had risen against him were but temporarily
quieted, and as soon as Grado and peace were restored, broke
out again. The second time Otto would seem not to have

had time to fly. He was seized by his enemies, his beard shaven off, whether as a sign of contempt, or by way of consigning him to the cloister—that asylum for dethroned princes—we are not told: and his reign thus ignominiously and suddenly brought to an end.

The last chapter in the history of the Orseoli is, however, the most touching of all. Whatever faults Otto may have had (and the chroniclers will allow none), he at least possessed the tender love of his family. The patriarch, Orso, once more followed him into exile; but coming back as soon as safety permitted, would seem to have addressed himself to the task of righting his brother. Venice had not thriven upon her ingratitude and disorder. A certain Domenico Centranico, the enemy of the Orseoli, had been hastily raised to the doge's seat, but could not restore harmony. Things went badly on all sides for the agitated and insubordinate city. The new emperor, Conrad, refused to ratify the usual grant of privileges, perhaps because he had no faith in the revolutionary government. Poppo renewed his attacks, the Dalmatian cities seized, as they invariably did, the occasion to rebel. And the new doge was evidently, like so many other revolutionists, stronger in rebellion than in defence of his country. What with these griefs and agitations, which contrasted strongly with the benefits of peace at home and an assured government, what with the pleadings of the patriarch, the Venetians once more recognised their mistake. The changing of the popular mind in those days always required a victim, and Doge Centranico was in his turn seized, shaven, and banished. The crisis recalls the primitive chapters of Venetian history, when almost every reign ended in tumult and murder. But Venice had learned the advantages of law and order, and the party of the Orseoli recovered power in the revulsion of popular feeling. The dishonoured but rightful doge was in Constantinople, hiding his misfortunes in some cloister or other resort of the exile. The provisional rulers of the Republic, whoever they might be—probably the chief supporters of the

Orseoli—found nothing so advantageous to still the tempest as to implore the Patriarch Orso to fill his brother's place while they sent a commission to Constantinople to find Otto and bring him home. The faithful priest who had worked so loyally for the exile accepted the charge, and leaving his bishopric and its administration to his deputies, established himself in the palace where he had been born, and took the government of Venice into his hands. It was work to the routine of which he had been used all his life, and probably no man living was so well able to perform it; and it might be supposed that the natural ambition of a Venetian and a member of a family which had reigned over Venice for three generations would stir even in a churchman's veins, when he found the government of his native state in his hands; for the consecration of the priesthood, however it may extinguish all other passions, has never been known altogether to quench that last infirmity of noble minds.

Peace and order followed the advent of the bishop-prince to power. And meanwhile the embassy set out, with a third brother, Vitale, the Bishop of Torcello at its head, to prove to the banished Otto that Venice meant well by him, and that the ambassadors intended no treachery. Whether they were detained by the hazards of the sea, or whether their time was employed in searching out the retirement where the deposed doge had withdrawn to die, the voyage of the embassy occupied more than a year, coming and going. During these long months Orso reigned in peace. Though he was only vice-doge, says Sanudo, for the justice of his government he was placed by the Venetians in the catalogue of the doges. Not a word of censure is recorded of his peaceful sway. The storm seems changed to a calm under the rule of this faithful priest. In the splendour of those halls which his fathers had built he watched— over Venice on one hand, and on the other for the ships sailing back across the lagoons, bringing the banished Otto home. How many a morning must he have looked out, before he said his mass, upon the rising dawn and watched the blueness of the skies and seas grow clear in the east, where lay his bishopric, his flock, his cathedral, and all the duties that were his ; and with anxious eyes swept the winding of the level waters still and gray, the metallic glimmer of the *acqua morta*, the navigable channels that gleamed between. When a sail came in sight between those lines, stealing up from Malamocco, what expectations must have moved his heart ! He was, it would appear, a little older than Otto, his next brother, perhaps his early childish caretaker before thrones episcopal or secular were dreamt of for the boys : and a priest, who has neither wife nor children of his own, has double room in his heart for the passion of fraternity. It would not seem that Orso took more power upon him than was needful for the interests of the people ; there is no record of war in his brief sway. He struck a small coin, *una moneta piccola d'argento*, called *ursiolo*, but did nothing else save keep peace, and preserve his brother's place for him. But when the ships came back, their drooping banners and mourning array must have told the news long before they cast anchor in the lagoon. Otto was dead in exile. There is nothing said to intimate that they had brought back even his body to lay it with his fathers in San Zaccaria. The banished prince had found an exile's grave.

After this sad end to his hopes the noble Orso showed how magnanimous and disinterested had been his inspiration. Not for himself, but for Otto, he had held that trust. He laid down at once those honours which were not his, and returned to his own charge and duties. His withdrawal closes the story of the family with a dignity and decorum worthy of a great race. His disappointment, the failure of all the hopes of the family, all the anticipations of brotherly affection, have no record, but who can doubt that they were bitter ? Misfortune more undeserved never fell upon an honourable house, and it is hard to tell which is most sad—the death of the deposed prince in the solitude of that eastern world where all was alien to him, or, after a brief resurrection of hope, the withdrawal of the faithful brother, his heart sick with all the wistful vicissitudes

D

of a baffled expectation, to resume his bishopric and his life
as best he could. It is a pathetic ending to a noble and
glorious day.

Many years after this Orso still held his patriarchate in
peace and honour, and the name of the younger brother Vitale,
his successor at Torcello, appears as a member along with him

STONE SHUTTERS, CATHEDRAL, TORCELLO.

of an ecclesiastical council for the reform of discipline and
doctrine in the Church; while their sister Felicia is mentioned
as abbess of one of the convents at Torcello. But the day of
the Orseoli was over. A member of the family, Domenico, "a
near relation," made an audacious attempt in the agitation that
followed the withdrawal of Orso to seize the supreme power, and

was favoured by many, the chroniclers say. But his attempt
was unsuccessful, and his usurpation lasted only a day. The
leader of the opposing party, Flabenico, was elected doge in the
reaction, which doubtless this foolish effort of ambition stimu-
lated greatly. And perhaps it was this reason also which moved
the people, startled into a new scare by their favourite bugbear
of dynastic succession, to consent to the cruel and most ungrateful condemnation of the Orseoli family which followed;
and by which the race was sentenced to be denuded of all rights,
and pronounced incapable henceforward of holding any office
under the Republic. The prohibition would seem to have been
of little practical importance, since of the children of Pietro
Orseolo the Great there remained none except priests and nuns,
whose indignation when the news reached them must have been
as great as it was impotent. We may imagine with what swelling hearts they must have met, in the shadow of that great
sanctuary which they had built, the two bishops, one of whom
had been doge in Venice, and the abbess in her convent, with
perhaps a humbler nun or two of the same blood behind,
separated only by the still levels of the lagoon from where the
towers and spires of Venice rose from the bosom of the waters
—Venice, their birthplace, the home of their glory, from which
their race was now shut out. If any curse of Rome trembled
from their lips, if any appeal for anathema and excommunication, who could have wondered? But, like other wrongs, that
great popular ingratitude faded away, and the burning of the
hearts of the injured found no expression. The three consecrated
members of the doomed family, perhaps sad enough once at the
failure of the succession, must have found a certain bitter satisfaction then, in the thought that their Otto, deposed and dead,
had left no child behind him.

But the voice of history has taken up the cause of this ill-
rewarded race. The chroniclers with one voice proclaim the
honour of the Orseoli, with a visionary partisanship in which
the present writer cannot but share, though eight centuries
have come and gone since Venice abjured the family which had

served her so well.   Sabellico tells with indignant satisfaction
that he can find nothing to record that is worth the trouble,
of Flabenico, their enemy, except that he grew old and died.
Non ragionam di lor.   The insignificant and envious rival, who
brings ruin to the last survivors of a great race, is unworthy
further comment.

Such proscriptions, however, are rarely so successful.   The
Orseoli disappear altogether from history, and their name during
all the historic ages scarcely once is heard again in Venice.
Domenico, the audacious usurper of a day, died at Ravenna very
shortly after.   Even their great buildings, with the exception of
Torcello, have disappeared under the splendour of later ornament, or more recent construction.   Their story has the completeness of an epic—they lived, and ruled, and conquered,
and made Venice great.   Under their sway she became the
mistress of the sea.   And then it was evident that they had
completed their mission, and the race came to an end, receiving
its dismissal in the course of nature from those whom it had
best served.   Few families thus recognise the logic of circumstances; they linger out in paltry efforts—in attempts to reverse
the sentence pronounced by the ingratitude of the fickle mob,
or any other tyrant with whom they may have to do.   But
whether with their own will or against it, the Orseoli made no
struggle.   They allowed their story to be completed in one
chapter, and to come to a picturesque and effective end.

It will be recognised, however, that Torcello is a powerful
exception to the extinction of all relics of the race.   The
traveller as he stands with something of the sad respect of pity
mingling in his admiration of that great and noble cathedral,
built for the use of a populous and powerful community, but
now left to a few rough fishermen and pallid women, amid the
low and marshy fields, a poor standing-ground among the floods
—takes little thought of him who reared its lofty walls, and combined new and old together in so marvellous a conjunction.
Even the greatest of all the modern adorers who have idealised
old Venice, and sung litanies to some chosen figures among her

sons, has not a word for Orso, or his race. And no tradition remains to celebrate his name. But the story of this tender brother, the banished doge's defender, champion, substitute, and mourner—he who reigned for Otto, and for himself neither sought nor accepted anything—is worthy of the scene. Greatness has faded from the ancient commune as it faded from the family of their bishop, and Torcello, like the Orseoli, may seem to a fantastic eye to look, through all the round of endless days, wistfully yet with no grudge, across the level waste of the salt sea water to that great line of Venice against the western sky which has carried her life away. The church, with its marbles and forgotten inscriptions, its mournful great Madonna holding out her arms to all her children, its profound loneliness and sentinelship through all the ages, acquires yet another not uncongenial association when we think of the noble and unfortunate race which here died out in the silence of the cloister, amid murmurs of solemn psalms, and whispering amens from the winds and from the sea.

SHRINE OF ORSEOLI "IL SANTO."

CHAPTER II

THE MICHIELI.

IT is of course impossible to give here a continuous history of the doges. To trace the first appearance of one after another of the historic names so familiar to our ears would be a task full of interest, but far too extensive for the present undertaking. All that we can attempt to do is to take up a prominent figure here and there, to mark the successive crises and developments of history and the growth of the Venetian constitution, involved as it is in the action and influence of successive princes, or to follow the fortunes of one or other of the family groups which add an individual interest to the general story. Among these, less for the importance of the house than for the greatness of one of its members, the Michieli find a prominent place. The first doge of the name was the grandfather, the third the son, of the great Domenico Michieli, who made the name illustrious. Vitale Michiel the first (the concluding vowel is cut off according to familiar use in many Venetian names—Cornaro being pronounced Corner; Loredano, Loredan; and so forth) came to the dignity of doge in 1096, more than a century later than the accession of the Orseoli to power. In the meantime there had been much progress in Venice. We reach the limits within which general history begins to become clear. Every day the great Republic, though still in infancy, emerges more and more distinct from

the morning mists. And the accession of Vitale Michieli brings us abreast of information from other sources. He came to the chief magistracy at the time when all Europe was thrilling with the excitement of the first crusade, and the great maritime towns of Italy began to vie with each other in offering the means of transit to the pilgrims. How it happens that the Venetian chroniclers have left this part of their history in darkness, and gathered so few details of a period so important, is the standing wonder of historical students. But so it is. A wave of new life must have swept through the city, with all its wealth of galleys, which lay so directly in the way between the east and west, and trade must have quickened and prosperity increased. All that we hear, however, from Venetian sources is vague and general; and it was not until after the taking of Jerusalem that the doge felt himself impelled to join " that holy and praiseworthy undertaking": and assembling the people proposed to them the formation of an Armada, not only for the primary object of the crusade, but in order that Venice might not show herself backward where the Pisans and Genoese had both acquired reputation and wealth.

The expedition thus fitted out was commanded by his son Giovanni, with the aid of a spiritual coadjutor in the person of Enrico Contarini, Bishop of Castello: but does not seem to have accomplished much except in the search for relics, which were then the great object of Venetian ambition. A curious story is told of this expedition and of the bishop-commodore, who, performing his devotions before his departure at the church on the Lido, dedicated to San Niccolo, made it the special object of his prayers that he might find, when on his travels, the body of the saint. Whether the determination to have this prayer granted operated in other methods more practical cannot be told: but certain it is that Bishop Contarini one fine morning suddenly called upon the fleet to stop in front of a little town which was visible on the top of the cliffs near the city of Mira. The squadron paused in full career, no doubt with many an inquiry from the gazing crowds in the other vessels not near enough to see what the admiral would be at, or what was the meaning of the sudden landing of a little band of explorers on the peaceful coast. The little town, *una città*, a place without a name, was found almost abandoned of its inhabitants, having been ravaged by some recent corsair, Turk or Croat. The explorers, joined by many a boat's crew as soon as the other vessels saw that some adventure was on hand, found a church dedicated also to San Niccolo, which they immediately began to examine not too gently, pulling down walls and altars to find the sacred booty of which they were in search, and even putting to torture the guardians of the church who would not betray its secrets. Finding nothing better to be done, they took at last two bodies of saints of lesser importance, St. Theodore to wit, and a second San Niccolo, uncle of the greater saint—and prepared, though with little satisfaction, to regain their ships. The bishop, however, lingered, praying and weeping behind, with no compunction apparently as to the tortured guardians of St. Nicholas, but much dislike to be balked in his own ardent desire: when lo! all at once there arose a fragrance as of all the flowers of June, and the pilgrims, hastily crowding back to see what wonderful thing was about to take place, found themselves drawn towards a certain altar, apparently overlooked before, where St. Nicholas really lay. One wonders whether the saint was flattered by the violence of his abductors, as women are said to be—yet cannot but feel that it was hard upon the poor tortured custodians, the old and faithful servants who would not betray their trust, to see the object of their devotion thus favour the invaders. This story Romanin assures us is told by a contemporary. Dandolo gives another very similar, adding that his own ancestor, a Dandolo, was captain of the ship which carried back the prize.

This would seem to have been the chief glory, though but at second hand, of Vitale Michieli's reign. The *due corpi di San Niccolo*, the great and small, were placed with great joy in San Niccolo del Lido, and that of St. Theodore deposited in the Church of San Salvatore. The brief account of the Crusade given by

Sanudo reveals to us a hungry search for relics on the part of the Venetian contingent, varied by quarrels, which speedily came to blows, with the Pisans and Genoese, their rivals at sea, but little more. Nor is it apparent that the life of the Doge Vitale was more distinguished at home. He died, after a reign of about five years, in the end of the first year of the twelfth century, and for a generation we hear of the family no more.

His successor, Ordelafo, first of the Falieri, was a man of great energy and character. He was the founder of the great arsenal, which has always been of so much importance to Venice, not less now with its great miraculous scientific prodigies of ironclads, and its hosts of workmen, than when the pitch boiled and the hammers rang for smaller craft on more primitive designs. Ordelafo, however, came to a violent end fighting for the possession of the continually rebellious city of Zara, which from generation to generation gave untold trouble to its conquerors. His fall carried dismay and defeat to the very hearts of his followers. The Venetians were not accustomed to disaster, and they were completely cowed and broken down by the loss at once of their leader and of the battle. For a time it seems to have been felt that the Republic had lost her hold upon Dalmatia, and that the empire of the seas was in danger: and the dismayed leaders came home, bringing grief and despondency with them. The city was so cast down that ambassadors were sent off to the King of Hungary to sue for a truce of five years, and mourning and alarm filled all hearts. It was at this time of discomfiture and humiliation, in the year 1118, that Domenico Michieli, the second of his name to bear that honour, was elected doge. In these dismal circumstances there seems little augury of the splendour and success he was to bring to Venice. His first authentic appearance shows him to us in the act of preparing another expedition for the East, for the succour of Baldwin, the second King of Jerusalem, who, the first flush of success being by this time over, had in his straits appealed to the pope and to the Republic. The pope sent on Baldwin's letters to Venice, and with them a standard bearing the image of St. Peter, to be carried by the doge to battle. Michiel immediately prepared a *possente armata*—a strong expedition. "*Then* the people were called to counsel," the narrative goes on, without any ironical meaning: and, after solemn service in St. Mark's, the prince addressed the assembly. The primitive constitution of the Republic, in which every man felt himself the arbiter of his country's fate, could not be better exemplified. The matter was already decided, and all that was needful to carry out the undertaking was that popular movement of sympathy which a skilled orator has so little difficulty in calling forth. The people pressed in to the church, where, with all the solemnity of a ritual against which no heretical voice had ever been raised, the patriarch and his clergy, in pomp and splendour, celebrated, at the great altar blazing with light, the sacred ceremonies. San Marco, in its dark splendour, with that subtle charm of colour which makes it unique among churches, was probably then more like what it is now than was any other part of Venice—especially when filled with that surging sea of eager faces all turned towards the brilliant glow of the altar. And those who have seen the great Venetian temple of to-day, full of the swaying movement and breath of a crowd, may be permitted to form for themselves an image, probably very like the original, of that assembly, where patricians, townsmen, artisans—the mariners who would be the first to bear their part, and those sons of the people who are the natural recruits of every army, all met together eager for news, ready to be moved by the eloquence, and wrought to enthusiasm by the sentiment, of their doge. It is not to be supposed that the speech of Michieli, given by Sabellico in detail, is the actual oration of the doge, verbally reported in the first half of the twelfth century: but it has no doubt some actual truth of language, handed down by fragments of tradition and anonymous chronicle, and it is very characteristic, and worthy of the occasion. "From you, noble Venetians, these things are not hid," he says, "which were done partly by your-selves, and partly by the other peoples of Europe, to recover the

To face page 42.

BRONZE HORSES ON THE FAÇADE OF S. MARCO.

Holy Land." Then, after a brief review of the circumstances, of the great necessity and the appeal made to Rome, he addresses himself thus to the popular ear :—

"Moved by so great a peril, the Roman pontiff has judged the Venetians alone worthy of such an undertaking, and that he might securely confide it to them. Wherefore he has sent commissions to your prince, and to you, Venetian citizens, praying and supplicating you that in such a time of need you should not desert the Christian cause. Which demand your prince has determined to refer to you. Make up your minds then, and command that a strong force should be prepared. Which thing not only religion and our care for the Church and all Christians enjoins, but also the inheritance of our fathers, from whom we have received it as a charge : which fulfilling we can also enlarge our own dominion. It is very worthy of the religion of which we make profession, to defend with our arms from the injuries of cruel men that country in which Christ our King chose to be born, to traverse weeping, in which to be betrayed, taken, put upon the Cross, and that His most holy body should have sepulture therein : in which place, as testifies Holy Writ, as the great Judge yet once more He must come to judge the human race. What sacred place dedicated to His service, what monastery, what altar, can we imagine will be so grateful to Him as this holy undertaking? by which He will see the home of His childhood, His grave, and, finally, all the surroundings of His humanity, made free from unworthy bondage. But since human nature is so constituted that there is scarcely any public piety without a mixture of ambition, you, perhaps, while I speak, begin to ask yourselves silently, what honour, what glory, what reward may follow such an enterprise? Great and notable will be the glory to the Venetian name, since our forces will appear to all Europe alone sufficient to be opposed to the strength of Asia. The furthermost parts of the West will hear of the valour of the Venetians, Africa will talk of it, Europe will wonder at it, and our name will be great and honoured in everybody's mouth. Yours will be the victory in such a war, and yours will be the glory. . . . .

"Besides, I doubt not that you are all of one will in the desire that our domain should grow and increase. In what way, and by what method, think you, is this to be done? Perhaps here seated, or in our boats upon the lagoons? Those who think so deceive themselves. The old Romans, of whom it is your glory to be thought the descendants, and whom you desire to emulate, did not gain the empire of the world by cowardice or idleness ; but adding one undertaking to another, and war to war, put their yoke upon all people, and with incredible fighting increased their strength. . . . And yet again, if neither the glory, nor the rewards, nor the ancient

and general devotion of our city for the Christian name should move
you, this certainly will move you, that we are bound to deliver from
the oppression of the unbeliever that land in which we shall stand at last
before the tribunal of the great Judge, and where what we have done shall
not be hidden, but made manifest and clear. Go, then, and prepare the
armaments, and may it be well with you and with the Venetian name."

This skilful mingling of motives, sacred and secular; the
melting touch with which that land which was the "place of
His childhood"— *il luogo della sua fanciullezza* — is presented
to their sight; the desire for glory, which is so sweet to all;
the great civic ambition to make Venice great and hear her
praise; the keen sting of the taunt to those who suppose
that fame is to be got by sitting still or by idle exercises upon
the surrounding waters—returning again with the force of a
final argument to "that land" where the final judgment is to be
held, and where those who have fought for the Cross will not
be hidden, great or small—forms an admirable example
of the kind of oration which an eloquent doge might deliver
to the impetuous and easily-moved populace, who had, after all,
a terrible dominant power of veto if they chanced to take
another turn from that which was desired. The speaker, however, who had this theme and knew so well how to set it forth,
must have felt that he had the heart of the people in his hand
and could play upon that great instrument as upon a lute.
When he had ended, the church resounded with shouts mingled
with weeping, and there was not one in the city, we are told,
who would not rather have been written down in the lists of
that army than left to stay in peace and idleness at home.

Dandolo, the most authentic and trustworthy authority,
describes this expedition as one of two hundred ships, large
and small, but other authorities reckon them as less numerous.
They shone with pictures and various colours, the French historian of the Crusades informs us, and were a delightful sight as
they made their way across the brilliant eastern sea. Whether
the painted sails that still linger about the lagoons and give
so much brilliancy and character to the scene were already

adopted by these glorious galleys seems unknown : their high prows, however, were richly decorated with gilding and colour, and it is apparently this ornamentation to which the historian alludes. But though they were beautiful to behold, their pro- gress was not rapid. The doge stopped on his way to besiege and take Corfu, where the squadron passed the winter, as was the custom of the time. Even when they set sail again they lingered among the islands, carrying fire and sword for no par- ticular reason, so far as appears, into Rhodes and other places; until at last evil news from Palestine, and the information that the enemy's fleet lay in front of Joppa, blockading that port, quickened their steps. Michieli divided his squadron, and beguiled the hostile ships out to sea with the hopes of an easy triumph ; then falling upon them with the stronger portion of his force won so terrible and complete a victory that the water and the air were tainted with blood, and many of the Venetians, according to Sanudo, fell sick in consequence.

It is difficult to decide whether it was after this first incident of the war, or at a later period, that the doge found himself like so many generals before and after him, in want of money for the payment of his men. The idea of bank-notes had not then occurred even to the merchant princes. But Michieli did what our own valiant Gordon had to do, and with as great a strain no doubt on the faith of the mediæval mariners to whom the device was entirely new. He caused a coinage to be struck in leather, stamped with his own family arms, and had it published throughout the fleet, upon his personal warrant, that these should be considered as lawful money, and should be exchanged for gold zecchins on the return of the ships to Venice. "And so it was done, and the promise was kept." In memory of this first *assignat* the Ca' Michieli, still happily existing in Venice, bears till this day, and has borne through all the intervening centuries, the symbol of these leathern coins upon the cheerful blue and white of their ancestral coat.

On the arrival of the Venetians at Acre they found the assembled Christians full of uncertain counsels, as was

unfortunately too common, doubtful even with which city, Tyre
or Ascalon, they should begin their operations. The doge
proposed an appeal to God under the shape of drawing lots.
always a favourite idea with the Venetians, and the two
names were written on pieces of paper, and placed in the pyx
on the altar, from which one was drawn by a child, after mass
had been said. On this appeared the name of Tyre, and the
question was decided. Before, however, the expedition set out
again, the prudent Venetian, well aware that gratitude is less
to be calculated upon after than before the benefit is received,
made his conditions with "the Barons" who represented the
imprisoned King Baldwin. These conditions were, that in every
city of the Christian kingdom the Venetians should have
secured to them a church, a street, an open square, a bath, and
a bakehouse, to be held free from taxes as if they were the property of the king : that they should be free from all tolls on entering or leaving these cities, as free as if in their own dominion,
unless when conveying freight, in which case they were to pay
the ordinary dues. Further, the authorities of Baldwin's kingdom pledged themselves to pay to the doge in every recurring
year, on the feast of SS. Peter and Paul, 300 bezants ; and
consented that all legal differences between Venetian residents
or visitors should be settled by their own courts, and that in
cases of shipwreck or death at sea the property of dead
Venetians should be carefully preserved and conveyed to Venice
for distribution to the lawful heirs. Finally, the third parts of the
cities of Tyre and Ascalon, if conquered by the help of the
Venetians—in so far at least as these conquered places belonged
to the Saracens and not to the Franks—were to be given to the
Venetians, to be held by them as freely as the king held the
rest. These conditions are taken from the confirmatory charter
afterwards granted by Baldwin. The reader will perceive that
the doge drove an excellent bargain, and did not, though so
great and good a man, disdain to exact the best terms possible
from his friends' necessities.

These important preliminaries settled, the expedition set out

for Tyre, which, being very strong, was assailed at once by land and
by sea. The siege had continued for some time without any
important result, and the Crusaders were greatly discouraged
by rumours of an attack that was being planned against
Jerusalem, when it began to be whispered in the host that the
Venetians, who were so handy with their galleys, would, in case
of the arrival of the army of the King of Damascus, who was
known to be on his way to the relief of the city, think only of
their own safety, and getting up all sail abandon their allies and
make off to sea. This suggestion made a great commotion in
the camp, where the knowledge that a portion of the force had
escape within their power, made danger doubly bitter to the
others who had no such possibility. The doge heard the
rumour, which filled him with trouble and indignation.
Dandolo says that he took a plank from each of the galleys
to make them unseaworthy. "Others write," says Sabellico,
"that the sails, oars, and other things needed for navigation
were what Michieli removed from his ships." These articles
were carried into the presence of Varimondo or Guarimondo,
the patriarch, and all the assembly of the leaders. The
astonishment of the council of war, half composed of priests,
when these cumbrous articles, smelling of pitch and salt water,
were thrown down before them, may be imagined. The doge
made them an indignant speech, asking how they could have
supposed the Venetians to be so light of faith; and, with a touch
of ironical contempt, informed them that he took this means to
set them at their ease, and show that the men of Venice meant
to take Tyre, and not to run away.

Another picturesque incident recorded is one which Sabellico
allows may be fabulous, but which Sanudo repeats, from two
different sources—the story of a carrier pigeon sent by the relieving army to encourage the people of Tyre in their manful
resistance, which the Christian army caught, and to which they
attached a message of quite opposite purport, upon the receipt of
which the much tried and famished garrison lost heart, and at
length, though with all the honours of war, capitulated, and

threw open their gates; upon which the besiegers took possession, not without much grumbling on the part of the disappointed soldiers who looked for nothing less than the sacking of the wealthy city. The royal standard of Jerusalem was immediately erected on the highest tower, those of St. Mark and of the Count of Tripoli waving beside it. The siege lasted, according to Dandolo, nearly four months. The doge had spent Christmas solemnly at Jerusalem, and it was in July that the city was entered by the allies: but all the authorities are chary of dates, and even Romanin is not too clear on this point. It was, however, in July, 1123, that the victory was gained.

In the portion of the city which fell to the share of the Venetians, true to their instincts, a scheme of government was at once set up. The doge put in a *balio chi facesse ragione*—a deputy who should do right—seek good and ensue it. Mr. Ruskin, in his eloquent account of this great enterprise (which it would be great temerity on our part to attempt to repeat, were it not necessary to the story of the doges) quotes the oath taken by inferior magistrates under the *balio*, which is a stringent promise to act justly by all men and "according to the ancient use and law of the city." The Venetians took possession at once of their third of the newly acquired town, with all the privileges accorded to them, and set up their bakeries, their exclusive weights and measures, their laws, their churches, of which three were built without delay, and along with all these secured an extension of trade, which was the highest benefit of all.

It is asserted by an anonymous commentator upon the manuscript of Dandolo, that it was proposed by the Crusaders, after this great success of their arms, to elect the doge king of Jerusalem, in place of the imprisoned Baldwin: but of this there seems no confirmation. Michieli was called from the scene of his victories by information of renewed troubles on the Dalmatian coast, and departed, carrying along with him many of the fine things for which Tyre was famous—the purple and the goldsmiths' work, and many treasures. But among others, one on which Dandolo and Sanudo both agree, a certain great stone

which had stood near one of the gates of Tyre since the time
when our Lord, weary after a journey, sat down to rest upon it.
Such a treasure was not likely to escape the keen scent of the
Venetians, so eager for relics. The doge carried it away, a
somewhat cumbrous addition to his plunder, and when he
reached home placed it in San Marco, where it is still to be seen,
in the Baptistery, a chapel not built in Michieli's day, where it
forms the altar, *un enorme mossetto de granito*—as says the last
guide-book. The guide-book, however (the excellent one published by Signori Falin and Molmenti, from the notes of Lazari,
and worth a dozen Murrays), says that it was Vitale Michieli,
and not Domenico, who brought over this stone from Tyre; just
as Mr. Ruskin assures us that it was Domenico who brought
home the two famous columns on the Piazzetta, of which the
chronicles do not say a word. Who is to decide when doctors
disagree ?

The homeward journey of the Venetians was full of adventure
and conflict. Their first pause was made at Rhodes, where the
inhabitants, possibly encouraged by the Greek emperor in their
insolence to the Venetians, refused to furnish them with provisions : whereupon the doge disembarked his army, and took, and
sacked the city. After this swift and summary vengeance the
fleet went on to Chios, which not only was treated as Rhodes
had been, but was robbed of a valuable piece of saintly plunder,
the body of St. Isidore. The other isles of the Archipelago fell
in succession before the victorious fleet, which passed with a
swelling sail and all the exhilaration of success from one to
another. At Cephalonia the body of San Donato was discovered
and carried away. Nearer home the expedition executed those
continually required re-adjustments of the Dalmatian towns
which almost every doge in succession, since they were first
annexed, had been compelled to take in hand. Trau, Spalatro,
and Zara were re-taken from the Hungarians, and the latter city,
called by Sanudo Belgrado (*Belgrado, cioè Zara vecchia*), from
which the Venetian governor had been banished, and which had
cost much blood and trouble to the Republic, the doge is said

E

to have caused to be destroyed, " that its ruin might be an example to the others," a fact which, however, does not prevent it
from reappearing a source of trouble and conflict to many a subsequent doge.   Here, too, Michieli paused and distributed the spoil,
setting apart a portion for God, and dividing the rest among the
army.   Then, with great triumph and victory, after an absence
of nearly three years, the conquerors made their way home.

A more triumphant voyage had never been made.   The Venetians had, as the doge predicted, covered their name with glory,
and at the same time extended and increased their realm.   They
had acquired the third part of Tyre and settled a strong colony
there, to push their trade and afford an outlet for the superfluous
energies of the race.   They had impressed the terror of their
name and arms upon the Grecian isles.   The doge himself
had performed some of those magnanimous deeds which take
hold upon the imagination of a people, and outlive for centuries
all violent victories and acquisitions.   The story of the leather
coinage and of the disabled galleys are such as make those
traditions which are the very life of a people.   And Michieli
.had served his country by seizing upon the imagination and
sympathies of other lands.   He had almost been made king in
Jerusalem.   When he passed by Sicily he had again been
offered a kingdom.   There was nothing wanting to the perfection of his glory.   And when he came home triumphant,
and told his story of danger and successes in the same glowing
area of St. Mark's, to the same fervent multitude whose sanction he had asked to the undertaking, it is easy to imagine
what his welcome must have been.   He had brought with him
treasures of cunning workmanship, the jewels of gold and silver,
the wonderful embroideries and carpets of the East; perhaps also
the secret of the glass-workers creating a new trade among the
existing guilds, things to make all Venice beside itself with
delight and admiration.   And when the two saintly corpses
were carried reverentially on shore—one for Murano, to con-
secrate the newly-erected church, one to remain in Venice—and
the shapeless mass of the great stone upon which our Lord had

sat in His weariness, or which, as another story says, had served
Him as a platform from which to address the wondering crowd
—with what looks of awe and reverential ecstasy must these
sacred relics have been regarded, the crown of all the victor's
spoil! The enlightened, or even partially enlightened spectator
in Venice, as well as in other places, has ceased to feel any
strong veneration for dead men's bones, except under the decent
coverings of the tomb; but we confess, for our own part, that
the stone which stood at the gate of Tyre all those ages, and
which the valorous doge haled over the seas to make an altar of
—the stone on which, tradition says, our Lord rested when He
passed by those coasts of Tyre and Sidon, where perhaps that
anxious woman who would not take an answer first saw Him
seated, and conceived the hope that so great a prophet might
give healing to her child—has an interest for us as strong as
if we had lived in the twelfth century, and seen the doge come
home. The Baptistery of St. Mark's is well worthy examination. There is a beautiful description of it in the second
volume of Mr. Ruskin's *Stones of Venice*, to read which is the
next best thing to visiting the solemn quiet of the place; but
there is no allusion there to this one veracious relic, Doge
Domenico's trophy—the mighty bit of Syrian stone.

The doge lived but a few years after his return. Mr. Ruskin,
following the chroniclers, says that he was the first who lighted
the streets of Venice by the uncertain and not very effectual
method, though so much better than nothing, of lamps before
the shrines which abounded at every corner; so that the
traveller, if he pleases, may find a token of our doge at every
Traghetto where a faint little light twinkles before the shrine
enclosing the dim print or lithograph which represents the
Madonna. Mr. Ruskin would have us believe that he for one
would like Venice better if this were the only illumination of
the city; but we may be allowed to imagine that this is only a
fond exaggeration on the part of that master. The Venetians
were at the same time prohibited from wearing beards according
to the fashion of the Greeks—a rule which must surely apply to

some particular form of beard, and not to that manly ornament itself, on which it is evident the men of Venice had set great store.

In the year 1129, having reigned only eleven years, though he had accomplished so much, and achieved so great a reputation, the doge, being old and weary, resigned his crown and retired to San Giorgio Maggiore, though whether with the intention of joining the brotherhood there, or only for repose, we are not told. It would have been a touching and grand retirement for an old prince who had spent his strength for Venice, to pass his latter days in the island convent, where all day long, and by the lovely moonlight nights that glorify the lagoons, he could have watched across the gleaming waters his old home and all the busy scenes in which he had so lately taken the chief part, and might have received in many an anxious moment the visit of the reigning doge, and given his counsel, and become the best adviser of the city which in active service he could aid no more. But this ideal position was not realised for Doge Domenico. He had been but a few months in San Giorgio when he died, full of years and honours, and was buried in the refuge he had chosen. "The place of his grave," says Mr. Ruskin, "you find by going down the steps on your right hand behind the altar leading into what was yet a monastery before the last Italian revolution, but is now a finally deserted loneliness. On his grave there is a heap of frightful modern upholsterer's work (Longhena's), his first tomb being removed as too modest and time-worn for the vulgar Venetian of the seventeenth century. The old inscription was copied on the rotten black slate which is breaking away in thin flakes dimmed by destroying salt." It is scarcely decipherable, but it is given at length by Sanudo : " Here lies the terror of the Greeks, and the glory of the Venetians," says the epitaph ; " the man whom Emmanuel feared, and all the world still honours. The capture of Tyre, the destruction of Syria, the desolation of Hungary, proclaim his strength. He made the Venetians to dwell in peace and quiet, for while he flourished the country was safe." We add

the concluding lines in the translation given by Mr. Ruskin :
" Whosoever thou art who comest to behold this tomb of his,
bow thyself down before God because of him."

It was probably from an idea of humility that the great
doge had himself buried, not in the high places of the church,
but in the humble corridor which led to the monastery. All
that Mr. Ruskin says with his accustomed force about the
hideousness of the tomb is sufficiently just ; yet though nothing
may excuse the vulgar Venetian of the seventeenth century for
his bad taste in architecture, it is still morally in his favour
that he desired in his offensive way to do honour to the great
dead—a good intention which perhaps our great autocrat in art
does not sufficiently appreciate.

After Domenico Michieli there intervened two doges, one his
son-in-law Polani, another a Morosini, before it came to the
turn of his son Vitale II. to ascend the throne. What may be
called the ordinary of Venetian history, the continual conflict on the Dalmatian coasts, went on during both these
reigns with unfailing pertinacity : and there had arisen a new
enemy, the Norman, who had got possession of Naples, and
whose hand was by turns against every man. These fightings
came to little, and probably did less harm than appears ;
otherwise, if war meant all that it means now, life on
the Dalmatian coast, and among the Greek isles, must
have been little worth the living. In the time of Vitale
Michieli's predecessor, Sabellico says, the Campanile of San
Marco was built, " a work truly beautiful and admirable.
The summit of this is of pure and resplendent gold, and rises
to such a height that not only can you see all the city, but
towards the west and the south can behold great stretches of
the sea, in such a manner that those who sail from hence to
Istria and Dalmatia, two hundred stadii away and more, are
guided by this splendour as by a faithful star." This was the
first of the several erections which have ended in the grand
and simple lines of the Campanile we know so well, rising
straight out of the earth with a self-reliant force which makes

its very bareness impressive. Rising out of the earth however is the last phrase to use in speaking of this wonderful tower, which, as Sabellico reports, wondering, is so deeply founded in mysterious intricacies of piles and props below, that almost as much is hidden as that which is visible.

Vitale Michieli II. has this distinction, that he was the last of the doges elected by that curious version of universal suffrage which is to be found in this primitive age in most republics—that is to say, the system by which the few who pull the strings in every human community make it apparent to the masses that the potent suggestion whispered in their ear is their own inspiration. Such had been, up to this period, the manner of electing the doge. The few who were instinctively and by nature at the head of affairs—men themselves elected by nobody, the first by natural right, or because their fathers had been so, or because they were richer, bolder, more enterprising, more audacious, than the rest—settled among themselves which of them was to be the ruler; then calling together the people in San Marco, gave them, but with more skill and less frankness than the thing is done in ecclesiastical matters among ourselves, their *congé d'elire*. The doge elected by this method reigned with the help of these unofficial counsellors—of whom two only seem to have borne that name—and he was as easily ruined when reverses came as he had been promoted. But the time of more formal institutions was near, and the primitive order had ceased to be enough for the rising intelligence, or at least demands, of the people. The third Michieli had, however, the enormous advantage of being the son of the most distinguished of recent doges, and no doubt was received with those shouts of "*Provato ! Provato !*" (that is, *approvato*) which was the form of the popular fiat. One of the first incidents of his reign was a brief but sharp struggle for the independence of the metropolitan church of Grado, once more attacked by the Patriarch of Aquileia. The Venetians overcame the assailants, and brought the belligerent prelate and twelve of his canons as prisoners to Venice, whence after a while they were sent home, having promised to meddle with Grado no more, and to pay a somewhat humiliating tribute yearly—in the exaction of which there is a grim humour. Every year before Lent, in the heat of what we should call the Carnival, a great bull and twelve pigs were to be sent to Venice, representing the patriarch and his twelve canons. On the Thursday, when the mirth was at its height, the bull was hunted in the Piazza, and the pigs decapitated in memory of the priestly captives. This curious ironical celebration lasted till the days of Sabellico and Sanudo, the latter of whom entitles it the *giobba di Carnevale*. It shows, notwithstanding all the reverential sentiments of these ages of faith, how a certain contempt for the priest as an adversary tempered the respect of the most pious for all the aids and appurtenances of religion.[1]

This, however, was the only victory in the life of a doge so much less fortunate than his father. Italy was in great commotion throughout his reign, all the great northern cities, with Venice at their head, being bound in what was called the Lombard League against the Emperor Frederick Barbarossa. But the Venetians were more exposed to attacks from the other side, from the smouldering enmity of the Greeks than from anything Barbarossa could do: and it was from this direction that ruin came upon the third Michieli. Not only were conspiracies continually fostered in the cities of the Adriatic; but the Greek Emperor Emmanuel seized the opportunity while Venice seemed otherwise occupied to issue a sudden edict by which all the Venetian traders in his realm were seized upon a certain day, their goods confiscated, themselves thrown into prison. His reckoning, however, was premature; for the excitement in Venice when this news reached the astonished and enraged Republic was furious: and with cries of "War! war!" the indignant populace rushed together, offering themselves and

---

[1] Romanin considers the bull to have had nothing to do with this commemoration, the twelve pigs accompanied by twelve cakes being, he says, the tribute exacted.

everything they could contribute, to the avenging of this injury.

The great preparations which were at once set on foot demanded, however, a larger outlay than could be provided for by voluntary offerings, and the necessity of the moment originated a new movement of the greatest importance to the world. The best expedient which occurred to the Venetian statesmen was to raise a national loan, bearing interest, to collect which officers were appointed in every district of Venice with all the machinery of an income-tax, assessing every family according to its means. These contributions, the first, or almost the first, directly levied in Venice, and all the inquisitorial demands necessary to regulate them, passed without offence in the excitement of the great national indignation, but told afterwards upon the fate of the doge. Vitale Michieli set out in September, 1171, six months after the outrage, at the head of a great fleet, to avenge it; but misfortune pursued this unlucky prince. He was beguiled by his wily adversary into waiting for explanations and receiving embassies, only intended to gain time, or worse, to expose to the dangers of inaction and the chances of pestilence the great and powerful expedition which the Greeks were not able to encounter in a more legitimate way. These miserable tactics succeeded fully; lingering about the islands, at Chios, or elsewhere, disease completed what discontent and idleness had begun. The Greek emperor, all the chroniclers unite in saying, poisoned the wells so that everybody who drank of them fell ill. The idea that poison is the cause of every such outbreak of pestilence is still, as the reader knows, a rooted belief of the primitive mind—one of those original intuitions gone astray, and confused by want of understanding, which perhaps the progress of knowledge may set right; for it is very likely the waters were poisoned, though not by the emperor. The great epidemic which followed was of the most disastrous and fatal character; not only decimating the fleet, but when it returned to Venice broken and discouraged, spreading throughout the city.

This great national misfortune gave rise to a curious and romantic incident. The family Giustinian, one of the greatest in Venice, was, according to the story, so strongly represented in the armada that the race became virtually extinct by the deaths, one after another, of its members, in the disastrous voyage homewards. The only man left was a young monk, or rather novice not yet professed, in the convent of San Niccolo, on the Lido. When the plague-stricken crews got home, and this misfortune among so many others was made apparent, the doge sent messengers to the pope, asking that young Niccolo might be liberated from his vows. The old Giustiniani fathers, in the noble houses which were not as yet the palaces we know, must have waited among their weeping women—with an anxiety no doubt tempered by the determination, if the pope should refuse, to take the matter into their own hands—for the decision of Rome. And it is wonderful that no dramatist or modern Italian romancer, touched by the prevalent passion for moral dissection, should have thought of taking for his hero this young monk upon the silent shores of the Lido, amid all the wonderful dramas of light and shade that go on upon the low horizon sweeping round on every side, a true globe of level long reflections, of breadth and space and solitude, so apt for thought. Had he known, perhaps, before he thought of dedication to the Church, young Anna Michieli, between whose eyes and his, from her windows in the doge's palace to the green line of the Lido, there was nothing but the dazzle of the sunshine and the ripple of the sea? Was there a simple romance of this natural kind, waiting to be turned into joyful fulfilment by the pope's favourable answer? Or had the novice to give up his dreams of holy seclusion, or those highest, all-engrossing visions of ambition, which were to no man more open than to a bold and able priest? These are questions which might well furnish forth pages of delicate description and discussion. Naturally the old chronicler has no thought of any such refinement. The pope consented, and the doge gave his daughter to young Niccolo, "which thing procured the continuance in the city of the Casa Giustinian, in

which afterwards flourished men of the highest intellect and
great orators," is all the record says. The resuscitated race gave
many notable servants to the state, although no doge until well on
in the seventeenth century. When the pair thus united had done
their duty to the state, Niccolo Giustinian re-dedicated himself
in his old convent and resumed his religious profession ; while
Anna, his wife, proceeded to her chosen nunnery, and there
lived a life so holy as to add to the fame of her family by
attaining that partial canonisation which is represented by the
title of Beata. This, one cannot but feel, was an admirable
way of making the best of both worlds.

"In this year," says Sanudo, "there were brought to Venice
from Constantinople, in three great ships, three mighty columns,"
one of which in the course of disembarkation fell into the sea,
and remains there, it is to be supposed, till this day ; the others
are the two well-known pillars of the Piazzetta. We need not
repeat the story, so often told, of how it was that, no one being
able to raise them to their place, a certain Lombard, Niccolo of
the Barterers, succeeded in doing so with wetted ropes, and
asked in return for permission to establish a gambling-table in
the space between them. Sabellico says that the privilege granted
went so far "that every kind of deception" was permitted to
be practised there : but it can scarcely be supposed that even
a sharp Lombard money-changer would ask so much. This
permission, given because they could not help it, having fool-
ishly pledged their word, like Herod, was, by the doge and his
counsellors, made as odious as possible by the further law that
all public executions should take place between the columns. It
was a fatal place to land at, and brought disaster, as was afterwards seen ; but its evil augury seems to have disappeared
along with the gaming-tables, as half the gondolas in Venice
lie at its margin now. The columns would seem to have been
erected in the year 1172, but whether by Doge Vitale or his
successor is uncertain.

Other improvements were done under this doge besides the
elevation of the columns in the Piazzetta. He filled up the canal

which crossed the broad space of the Piazza, still a green and open ground, partly orchards, and enlivened by this line of water—and thus prepared the way for the work of his successor, who first began to pave it, and surrounded it with buildings and lines of porticoes, suggesting, no doubt, its present form. There must, however, have been a charm in the greenness and trees and sparkling waters—grass growing and foliage waving at the foot of the great golden-crowned Campanile, and adding a brightness of nature to the Byzantine splendour of the church and palace. The *Camera degli Imprestidi*, or great Public Loan Office, however—the first National Bank of Europe—is more important to history than even the ceaseless improvements of the city. The first loan is said to have carried interest at the rate of four per cent.—a high rate for a public debt —and the organisation necessary to arrange and regulate it seems to have come into being with wonderful speed and completeness. The time was beginning when the constitution, or rather want of constitution, of the ancient Republic, full of the accidents and hasty expedients of an infant state, would no longer suffice for the gradually rising and developing city.

None of these things, however, stood the doge in stead when he came back beaten and humiliated, with the plague in his ships, to face his judges in solemn conclave in San Marco—a tumultuous assembly of alarmed and half maddened men, trembling for their lives and for the lives of those dear to them, and stung by that sense of failure which was intolerable to the haughty Republic. This was in the month of May, 1172. From the first the meeting must have borne an air dangerous to the doge, against whom there began to rise a cry that he was the occasion of all their evils—of the war, of enforced military service and compulsory contributions, and, last and greatest, of the pestilence which he had brought back with him. The men who had virtually elected him, who were his friends, and had shared the councils of his reign, would no doubt stand by him so far as their fears permitted : but the harmless assembly called together

to give its sanction to the election of a new and popular doge is
very different from the same crowd in the traditionary power of
its general parliament, assembling angry and alarmed, its pride
wounded and its fears excited, to pronounce whose fault these
misfortunes were, and what should be done to the offender.
The loud outcry of *traditore*, so ready to the lips of the populace
in such circumstances, resounded through San Marco, and there
were ominous murmurs that the doge's head was in danger.
He tried to clear himself by a touching oration, *con piangente
parole*, says one: then hastily going out of the church and from
the presence of the excited assembly took his way towards San
Zaccaria, along the Riva, by what would seem to have been a
little-frequented way. As he passed through one of the little
calli, or lanes, called now, tradition says, Calle delle Rasse, some
one who had, or thought he had, a special grievance, sprang out
upon him and stabbed him. He was able to drag himself to
San Zaccaria and make his confession, but no more: and there
died and was buried. The people, horror-stricken perhaps by
the sudden execution of a doom which had only been threatened,
gave him a great funeral, and his sudden end so emphasised
the necessity of a relation more guarded and less personal between the chief ruler and the city, that the leading minds in
Venice proceeded at once to take order for elections more formal
and a constitution more exact. There had been, according to
primitive rule, two counsellors of permanent character, and an
indefinite number of *pregadi*, or men "prayed" to help the
doge—a sort of informal council; but these were called together
at the doge's pleasure, and were responsible only to him. The
steps which were now taken introduced the principle of elective
assemblies, and added many new precautions for the choice and
for the safety of the doge. The fact which we have already
remarked, that all the names [1] given belong to families already

---

[1] Romanin informs us that a few names of the people appear in early
documents as Stefano Tinctor (dyer), Vitale Staniario (tin-worker), &c.,
but these are so few as to prove rather than confute the almost invariable
aristocratic rule.

THE CEMETERY ISLAND.

To face page 60.

conspicuous in Venice, continued with equal force under the new rule. No doubt the elections would be made on the primitive principle, one man suggesting another, all of the same class as those who, without the forms of election, had hitherto suggested the successive princes, for the sanction of the people. But the mass of the Venetians probably thought with enthusiasm that they had taken a great step towards the consolidation of their liberties when they elected these Dandolos, Faliers, Morosinis, and the rest, to be their representatives, and do authoritatively what they had done all along in more subtle ways.

Thus ended the Doges Michieli: but not the family, which is one of the few which has outlived all vicissitudes, and still has a habitation and a name in Venice. And the new *régime* of elective government began.

ARMS OF THE MICHIELI.

CHAPTER III

ENRICO DANDOLO.

THE first beginnings of a more formal mode of government thus followed close upon the murder of Vitale Michieli. The troubles of the state under his rule, as well as the prompt vengeance taken upon him by the infuriated multitude, combined to make it apparent that it was not for the safety or dignity of Venice either to remain so entirely in the hands of her chief magistrate, or to bring the whole business of the state to a standstill, and impair her reputation among foreign countries by his murder. The Republic had thus arrived at a comprehension of the idea which governments of much later date have also had impressed upon them painfully, that the person of the head of the state ought to be *sacrosanto*, sacred from violence. And no doubt the rising complications of public life, the growth of the rich and powerful community in which personal character was so strong, and so many interests existed, now demanded established institutions, and a rule less primitive than that of a prince with both the legislative and executive power in his hands, even when kept in check by a counsellor or two, and the vague mass of the people by whom his proceedings had to be approved or non-approved after an oration skilfully prepared to move the popular mind. The Consiglio Maggiore, the great Venetian Parliament, afterwards so curiously limited, came into being at this crisis in the national history. The mode of its first selection reads like the description of a Chinese puzzle ; and perhaps the subtle, yet artless complication of elections ending at last in the doge, may be taken as a sort of appeal to the fates, by a community not very confident in their own powers, and bent upon outwitting destiny itself. Two men were first chosen by each sestiere or district (a division which had been made only a short time before for the convenience of raising funds for Doge Vitale's fatal expedition), each of whom nominated forty of the best citizens, thus forming the Great Council, who, in their turn, elected eleven representatives who elected the doge. The latter arrangement was changed on several occasions before that which commended itself as the best, and which was more artificial and childishly elaborate still, was chosen at last.

The people were little satisfied at first with this constitutional change, and there were tumults and threatened insurrections in anticipation of the new body of electors, and of the choice of a prince otherwise than by acclamation of the whole community assembled in San Marco. " It was in consequence ordained," says Romanin, " that the new doge should be presented to the multitude with these words : ' This is your doge, if it pleases you,' and by this means the tumult was stilled." So easy is it to deceive the multitude ! What difference the new rules made in reality it would be difficult to say. The council was made up of the same men who had always ruled Venice. A larger number no doubt had actual power, but there was no change of hands. The same fact we have already noted as evident through all the history of the Republic. New names rarely rise out of the crowd. The families from among whom all functionaries were chosen at the beginning of all things still held power at the end.

The power of the doge was greatly limited by these new laws, but at least his person was safe. He might be relieved from his office, as happened sometimes, but save in one memorable instance he was no longer liable to violence. And he was

surrounded by greater state and received all the semi-oriental
honours which could adorn a pageant. Sebastiano Ziani, the
first doge chosen under the new order, was carried in triumph
round the Piazza, throwing money to the crowd from his un-
steady seat. Whether this was his own idea (for he was very
rich and liberal), or whether it was suggested to him as a way
of increasing his popularity, we are not told; but the jealous
aristocrats about him, who had just got hold of the power of law-
making, and evidently thought there could not be too detailed
a code, seized upon the idea, perceiving at once its picturesque and attractive possibilities and its dangers, and decided
that this largesse should always be given by a new doge, but
settled the sum, not less than a hundred, nor more than a
hundred and fifty ducats, with jealous determination that no
wealthy potentate should steal the hearts of the populace with
gifts. There came to be in later times a special coinage for the
purpose, called Oselle, of which specimens are still to be found,
and which antiquarians, or rather those lovers of the curious
who have swamped the true antiquarian, "pick up" wherever
they appear.

Sebastiano Ziani, according to some of our chroniclers, was
not the man upon whom the eleven electors first fixed their
choice, who was, it is said, Aurio, or Orio Mastropiero, the
companion of Ziani in a recent ambassage, and his friend—who
pointed out that Ziani was much older and richer than himself,
and that it would be to the greater advantage of Venice that he
should be chosen, a magnanimous piece of advice. This story,
unfortunately, is not authenticated; neither is the much more
important one of the romantic circumstances touching the
encounter of Pope Alexander III. and the Emperor Barbarossa
at Venice, which the too conscientious historian, Romanin (not
to speak of his authorities) will not hear of, notwithstanding the
assertions of Sanudo, Sabellico, and the rest, and the popular
faith and the pictures in the ducal palace, all of which maintain
it strongly. The popular tale is as follows. It is painted in the
hall of the Maggiore Consiglio, where all the world may see.

The pope, driven from Rome by the enmity of the emperor, after many wanderings about the world took refuge in Venice, where he concealed himself in the humble habit of a friar, acting, some say, as cook to the brethren in the convent of La Carità. The doge, hearing how great a personage was in the city, hurried to visit him, and to give him a lodging worthy of his dignity; then sent ambassadors to intercede with Barbarossa on his behalf. He of the red beard received benignly the orators of the great Republic; but when he heard their errand, changed countenance, and bade them tell the doge that unless he delivered up the fugitive pope it would be the worse for him—that the eagle should fly into the church of San Marco, and that its foundation should be made as a ploughed field. Such words as these were not apt to Venetian ears. The whole city rose as one man, and an *armata* was immediately prepared to resist any that might be sent against Venice. The doge himself, though an old man over seventy, led the fleet. Mass was said solemnly in San Marco by the pontiff himself, who girded his loyal defender with a golden sword, and blessed him as he went forth to battle. There were seventy-five galleys on the opposite side, commanded by young Prince Otto, the son of Barbarossa, and but thirty on that of Venice. It was once more the Day of the Ascension—that fortunate day for the Republic—when the two fleets met in the Adriatic. The encounter ended in complete defeat to the imperial ships, of which forty were taken, along with the commander, Otto, and many of his most distinguished followers. The Venetians went home with natural exultation, sending before them the glorious news, which was so unexpected, and so speedy, that the whole city rushed to the Riva with half incredulous wonder and joy to see the victors disembark with their prisoners, among them the son of the great German prince who had set out with the intention of planting his eagles in San Marco. The pope himself came down to the Riva to meet the victorious doge, and drawing a ring from his finger gave it to his deliverer, hailing him as the lord and master of the sea. It was on Ascension Day that

F

Pietro Orseolo had set out from Venice on the triumphant
expedition which ended in the extermination of the pirates,
and the extension of the Venetian sway over all the coast of the
Adriatic—and then it was, according to our chroniclers, that the
feast of the *Sposalizio*, the wedding of the sea, had been first
established.   But by this time they have forgotten that early hint,
and here we have once more, and with more detailed authorities,
the institution of this great and picturesque ceremony.

Prince Otto was nobly treated by his captors, and after a
while undertook to be their ambassador to his father, and was
sent on parole to Rome to the emperor.   The result was that
Frederick yielded to his son's representations and the Venetian
prowess, and consented to go to Venice and there be reconciled to
the pope.   The meeting took place before the gates of San Marco,
where His Holiness, in all his splendour, seated in a great chair
(*grande e honoratissima sedia*), awaited the coming of his rival.
Popular tradition never imagined a more striking scene : the
Piazza outside thronged, every window, balcony, and housetop,
with eager spectators, used to form part of every public event
and spectacle, and knowing exactly every coign of vantage, and
how to see a pageant best.   The great Frederick, the story goes,
approached the seat where the vicar of Christ awaited him, and
subduing his pride to necessity, knelt and kissed the pope's foot.
Alexander, on his part, as proud and elated with his victory,
raised his foot and planted it on Barbarossa's neck, intoning as
he did so, as Sabellico says, that Psalm of David, " *Super aspidem
et basilicum ambulabis.*"   The emperor, with a suppressed roar
of defiance in his red beard, exclaimed, " Not thee, but Peter ! "
To which the pope, like one enraged, planting his foot more
firmly, replied, " Both I and Peter."   One can imagine this
brief colloquy carried on, under their breath, fierce and terse,
when the two enemies, greatest in all the western hemisphere,
met in forced amity; and how the good doge, amiable peace-
maker and master of the ceremonies, and all the alarmed
nobles, and the crowds of spectators ripe for any wonder,
must have looked on, marvelling what words of blessing they

were saying to each other, while all the lesser greatnesses had to wait.

But the later historians refuse their affirmation to this exceedingly circumstantial, most picturesque, and, it must be added, most natural story. Romanin assures us, on the faith of all the documents, that the meeting was a stately ceremonial, arranged by pope and emperor, without either passion or humiliation in it; that the pope was not a fugitive in Venice, and that the emperor never threatened to fly his eagles into San Marco; that Prince Otto never was made prisoner, and that the pontiff received with nothing less satisfactory than a kiss of peace the formal homage of the emperor. The facts are hard to deny, and no doubt Romanin is right. But there is a depth of human nature in the fable, which the facts do not reveal. It is impossible to imagine anything more likely to be true than that brief interchange of words, the churchman's triumph, and the statesman's unwilling submission.

The story goes on to tell how Doge Ziani escorted his two splendid guests to Ancona, where the pope and the emperor were presented with umbrellas—a tribute apparently made to their exalted rank; whereupon the pope requested that a third might be brought: "*Manca la terza pel Doge de Venezia chi ben lo merita,*" from which incident arose the use of this royal, if unimposing, article by the doges ever after. The pope had previously granted the privilege of sealing with lead instead of wax—another imperial attribute. To all this picturesque narrative Romanin again presents an array of chilling facts, proving that the pope and emperor left Venice singly on different dates, and that the Doges of Venice had carried the umbrella and used the leaden *bollo* long before Ziani—all which is very disconcerting. It seems to be true, however, that during the stay of the pope in Venice the feast of the *Sensa*—Ascension Day—was held with special solemnity, and its pageant fully recorded for the first time. The doge went forth in the Bucintoro, which here suddenly springs into knowledge, all decorated and glorious, with his umbrella over his head, a white flag which the pope had given him flying beside the standard of St. Mark, the silver trumpets sounding, the clergy with him and all the great potentates of the city, and Venice following, small and great, in every kind of barge or skiff which could venture on the lagoon.   It is said to have been with a ring which the pope had given him that old Ziani wedded the sea.   Whether the ceremony had fallen into disuse, or if our chroniclers merely forgot that they had assigned it to an earlier date, or if this was the moment when the simpler primitive rite was changed into its later form, it is difficult to say.   It must be added that the strange travesty of history thus put together is regarded with a certain doubt by the chroniclers themselves.   Sabellico for one falters over it.   He would not have ventured to record it, he says, if he had not found the account confirmed by every writer, both Venetian and foreign.   And, says Sanudo, " Is it not depicted in the hall of the great council ?   *Se non fosse stata vera i nostri buoni Venetiani noll avrebbero mai fatta depingere :* if it had not been true our good Venetians never would have had it painted."

It was during the stormy reign of Vitale Michieli, in the midst of the bitter and violent quarrel between the Greek Emperor Emmanuel and the Venetians, when ambassadors were continually coming and going, that an outrage, which cannot be called other than historical, and yet can be supported by no valid proof, is said to have been inflicted upon one of the messengers of Venice.   This was the noble Arrigo or Enrico Dandolo, afterwards one of the most distinguished of the doges, and the avenger of all Venetian wrongs upon the Greeks.   The story is that in the course of some supposed diplomatic consultation he was seized and had his eyes put out by red-hot irons—according to a pleasant custom which the Greeks of that day indulged in largely.   It is unlikely that this could be true, since it is impossible to believe that the Venetians would have resumed peaceable negotiations after such an outrage ; but it is a fact that Dandolo has always been called the blind doge, and even the scrupulous Romanin finds reason to suppose that some injury had been inflicted upon the ambassadors. Dandolo's blindness, however, must have been only comparative. The French chronicler, Villehardouin, describes him as having fine eyes, which scarcely saw anything, and attributes this to the fact that he had lost his sight from a wound in the head. Dandolo's descendant, successor, and historian, however, says only that he was of weak vision, and as he was at the time eighty-four, there would be nothing remarkable in that. Enrico Dandolo was elected doge in 1193, after the death of Orio Mastropietro, who succeeded Ziani, and whose reign was not marked by any special incident.

Dandolo was the first doge, if not to sign the *promissione,* or solemn ducal oath of fidelity to all the laws and customs of the Republic, at least to reach the period of history when such documents began to be preserved. His oath is full of details, which show the jealousy of the new *régime* in defining and limiting the doge's powers. He vows not only to rule justly, to accept no bribes, to show no favouritism, to subordinate his own affairs and all others to the interests of the city, but also not to write letters on his own account to the pope or any other prince; to submit his own affairs to the arbitrament of the common tribunals, and to maintain two ships of war at his own expense—stipulations which must have required no small amount of self-control on the part of men scarcely as yet educated to the duties of constitutional princes. The beginning of Dandolo's reign was distinguished by the usual expeditions to clear the Adriatic and re-confirm Venetian supremacy on the Dalmatian coast; also, by what was beginning to be equally common, certain conflicts with the Pisans, who began to rival Venice in the empire of the seas. These smaller commotions, however, were dwarfed and thrown into the shade by the great expedition, known in history as the Fourth Crusade, which ended in the destruction of Constantinople and great aggrandisement of the Republic, but, so far as the objects of the Crusade were concerned, in nothing.

The setting out of this expedition affords one of the most

picturesque and striking scenes in Venetian history, though its
details come to us rather from the chronicles of the Crusade
than from the ancient historians of Venice, who record them
briefly with a certain indifference and at the same time with a
frankness which sounds cynical. Perhaps the conviction of a
later age that the part played by Venice was not a very noble
one, may have here restrained the record. "In those days a
great occasion presented itself to the Venetians to increase their
dominion," Sabellico says, calmly putting aside all pretence at
more generous motives. Villehardouin, however, has left a
succession of pictures which could not be surpassed in graphic
force, and which place all the preliminaries before us in the
most brilliant daylight. He describes how the French princes
who had taken the cross sent an embassy to Venice in order to
arrange if possible for means of transport to the Holy Land—
six noble Frenchmen, in all their bravery and fine manners,
and fortunately with that one among them who carried a pen
as well as a sword. It is evident that this proposal was considered on either side as highly important, and was far from
being made or received as merely a matter of business. The
French messengers threw themselves at once upon the generosity,
the Christian feeling, of the masters of the sea. Money and
men they had in plenty; but only Venice, so powerful on the
seas, so rich, and at peace with all her neighbours, could give
them ships. From the beginning their application is an entreaty,
and their prayers supported by every argument that earnestness
could suggest. The doge received them in the same solemn
manner, submitting their petition to the council, and requiring
again and again certain days of delay in order that the matter
should be fully debated. It was at last settled with royal
magnificence not only that the ships should be granted, but that
the Republic should fit out fifty galleys of her own to increase
the force of the expedition : after which, everything being settled
(which again throws a curious side-light upon popular government), the doge called the Venetians together in San Marco—
ten thousand of them in the most beautiful church that ever

To face page 70.

HIGH ALTAR OF S. MARCO.

was, says the Frenchman—and bade the strangers plead their
own cause before the people. When we consider that everything was arranged beforehand, it takes something from the
effect of the scene, and suggests uncomfortable ideas of solemn
deceits practised upon the populace in all such circumstances—
but in itself the picture is magnificent.

Mass being celebrated, the doge called the ambassadors, and
told them to ask humbly of the people whether the proposed
arrangement should be carried into effect. Godfrey de Villehardouin then stood forth to speak in the name of all, with the
following result :—

"Messieurs, the noblest and most powerful barons of France have sent us
to you, to pray you to have pity upon Jerusalem in bondage to the Turk,
and for the love of God to accompany us to avenge the shame of Christ ;
and knowing that no nation is so powerful on the seas as you, they have
charged us to implore your aid and not to rise from our knees till you have
consented to have pity upon the Holy Land."

"With this the six ambassadors knelt down weeping. The doge and all
the people then cried out with one voice, raising their hands to heaven,
'We grant it, we grant it !' And so great was the sound that nothing ever
equalled it. The good doge of Venice, who was most wise and brave, then
ascended the pulpit and spoke to the people. 'Signori,' he said, 'you see
the honour which God has done you that the greatest nation on earth has
left all other peoples in order to ask your company, that you should share
with them this great undertaking which is the re-conquest of Jerusalem.'
Many other fine and wise things were said by the doge which I cannot
here recount. And thus the matter was concluded."

It must have been a strange and imposing sight for these
feudal lords to see the crowd that filled San Marco and over-
flowed in the Piazza, the vast trading seafaring multitude tanned
with the sunshine and the sea, full of their own importance,
listening like men who had to do it, no submissive crowd of
vassals, but each conscious (though, as we have seen, with but
little reason) that he individually was appealed to, while those
splendid petitioners knelt and wept—moved no doubt on their
side by that wonderful sea of faces, by the strange circumstances, and the rising wave of enthusiasm which began to move

the crowd. The old doge, rising up in the pulpit, looking with dim eyes across the heads of the multitude, with the great clamour of the "*Conceediamo*" still echoing under the dome, the shout of an enthusiastic nation, gives the last touch of pictorial effect. His eyes still glowed, though there was so little vision in them ; pride and policy and religious enthusiasm all mingled in his words and looks. The greatest nation of the world had come as a suppliant—who could refuse her petition ? This was in the winter, early in the year 1201. It is not difficult to imagine the wintry afternoon, the dim glories of the choir going off into a golden gloom behind, the lights glimmering upon the altars, the confused movement and emotion of the countless crowd, indistinct under the great arches, extending into every corner—while all the light there was concentrated in the white hair and cloth of gold of the venerable figure to which every eye was turned, standing up against the screen at the foot of the great cross.

The Republic by this bargain was pledged to provide transport for four thousand five hundred cavaliers, and nearly thirty thousand men on foot : along with provisions for a year for this multitude ; for which the Frenchmen pledged themselves to pay eighty-five thousand silver marks " according to the weight of Cologne," in four different instalments. The contingent of Venice, apart from this, was to consist of fifty galleys. The ships were to be ready at the feast of SS. Peter and Paul in the same year, when the first instalment of the money was to be paid.

In the meantime, however, while the workmen in the arsenal were busily at work, and trade must have quickened throughout Venice, various misfortunes happened to the other parties to the engagement. Young Thibaut of Champagne died in the flower of his youth, and many small parties of Crusaders went off from other quarters in other vessels than those of Venice : so that when at last the expedition arrived it was considerably diminished in numbers, and, what was still more disastrous, the leaders found themselves unable to pay the first instalment of the appointed price. The knights denuded themselves of all

their valuables, but this was still insufficient. In these circumstances an arrangement was resorted to which produced many
and great complications, and changed altogether the character
of the expedition. Venice has been in consequence reproached
with the worldliness and selfishness of her intentions. It has
been made to appear that her religious fervour was altogether
false, and her desire to push her own interests her sole motive.
No one will attempt to deny that this kind of selfishness, which
in other words is often called patriotism, was very strong in
her. But on the other side it would be hard to say that it was
with any far-seeing plan of self-aggrandisement that the
Republic began this great campaign, or that Dandolo and his
counsellors perceived how far they should go before their enterprise was brought to an end. They were led on from point to
point like those whom they influenced, and were themselves
betrayed by circumstances and a crowd of secondary motives, as
well as the allies whom they are believed to have betrayed.

The arrangement proposed was, since the Crusaders could not
pay the price agreed for their ships, that they should delay
their voyage to the Holy Land long enough to help the
Venetians in subduing Zara, which turbulent city had again,
as on every possible occasion, rebelled. The greater part of the
Frenchmen accepted the proposal with alacrity; though some
objected that to turn their arms against Christians, however
rebellious, was not the object of the soldiers of the cross. In
the long run, however, and notwithstanding the remonstrances
of Pope Innocent, of which the independent Venetians made
light, the bargain was accepted on all hands, and all the
preliminaries concluded at last. Another of the wonderful
scenic displays with which almost every important step was
accompanied in Venice took place before the final start.

"One day, upon a Sunday, all the people of the city, and the greater
part of the barons and pilgrims, met in San Marco. Before mass began,
the doge rose in the pulpit and spoke to the people in this manner :—
'Signori, you are associated with the greatest nation in the world in the
most important matter which can be undertaken by men. I am old and

weak and need rest, having many troubles in the body, but I perceive that none can so well guide and govern you as I who am your lord. If you will consent that I should take the sign of the cross to care for you and direct you, and that my son should, in my stead, regulate the affairs of the city, I will go to live and die with you and the pilgrims.'

" When they heard this, they cried with one voice, 'Yes ! we pray you, in the name of God, take it and come with us.'

" Then the people of the country and the pilgrims were greatly moved and shed many tears, because this heroic man had so many reasons for remaining at home, being old. But he was strong and of a great heart. He then descended from the pulpit and knelt before the altar weeping, and the cross was sewn upon the front of his great cap, so that all might see it. And the Venetians that day in great numbers took the cross."

It was in October, 1202, that the expedition finally sailed, a great fleet of nearly three hundred ships : the Frenchmen in their shining mail with their great war-horses furnishing a wonderful spectacle for the Venetians, to whom these noble creatures, led unwillingly on board the galleys, were so little familiar. The whole city watched the embarkation with excitement and high commotion, no doubt with many a woman's tears and wistful looks, anguish of the old, and more impassioned grief of the young, as the fifty galleys which contained the Venetian contingent slowly filled with all the best in the Republic, the old doge at their head. Bound for the Holy Land, to deliver it from the infidel !—that no doubt was what the people believed who had granted with acclamation their aid to the barons in San Marco. And to watch the great fleet which streamed along with all its sails against the sunshine through the tortuous narrow channels that thread the lagoon, line after line of high beaked painted galleys, with their endless oars, and all their bravery, it must have seemed as if the very sea had become populous, and such a host must carry all before them. Days must have passed in bustle and commotion ere, with the rude appliances of their time, three hundred vessels could have been got under weigh. They streamed down the Adriatic, a maritime army rather than a fleet, imposing to behold, frightening the turbulent towns along the coast which were so ready when the Venetian galleys were out of sight to rebel—and arrived before Zara in crushing strength. The citizens closed the harbour with a chain, and with a garrison of Hungarians to help them, made a brave attempt to defend themselves. But against such an overwhelming force their efforts were in vain, and after a resistance of five days, the city surrendered. It was by this time the middle of November, and to tempt the wintry sea at that season was contrary to the habits of the time. The expedition accordingly remained at Zara, where many things took place which decided the course of its after movements. It was not a peaceful pause. The French and the Venetians quarrelled in the first place over their booty or their privileges in the sacked and miserable city. When that uproar was calmed, which took the leaders some time, another trouble arrived in the shape of letters from Pope Innocent, which disturbed the French chiefs greatly, though the old doge and his counsellors paid but little attention. Innocent called the Crusaders to account for shedding Christian blood when they ought to have been shedding pagan, and for sacking a city which belonged to their brethren in the faith, to whom he commanded them to make restitution and reparation. Whether the penitent barons gave up their share of the booty is not told us, but they wrote humble letters asking pardon, and declaring that to take Zara was a necessity which they had no power to resist. The pope was moved by their submission, but commanded them to proceed to Syria with all possible speed, "neither turning to the right hand nor to the left," and as soon as they had disembarked on the Syrian shores to separate themselves from the Venetians, who seem to have been excommunicated (which did not greatly disturb them) for their indifference to the papal commands.

This correspondence with Rome must have given a certain amount of variety, if not of a very agreeable kind, to the winter sojourn on the Adriatic, confused with tumults of the soldiery and incessant alarms lest their quarrels should break out afresh, quarrels which—carried on in the midst of a hostile people bitterly rejoicing to see their conquerors at enmity among themselves, and encouraged by the knowledge that the pope had interfered on their behalf—must have made the invaders doubly uncomfortable. From the Venetian side there is not a word of the excommunication levelled against themselves, and generally so terrible a weapon. Such punishments perhaps were more easily borne abroad than at home, and the Republic already stoutly held its independence from all external interference.

While Pope Innocent's letters were thus occupying all minds, and the French Crusaders chafing at the delay, and perhaps also at the absence of all excitement and occupation in the Dalmatian town, another incident occurred of the most picturesque character, as well as of the profoundest importance. This was—first, the arrival of ambassadors from the Emperor Philip of Swabia with letters recommending the young Alexius, the son of Isaac, dethroned emperor of the Greeks, to the Crusaders : and secondly that young prince himself, an exile and wanderer, with all the recommendations of injured helplessness and youth in his favour. The ambassadors brought letters telling such a story as was most fit to move the chivalrous leaders of the Christian host. The youth for whom their appeal was made was the true heir of the great house of Comnenus, born in the purple, a young Hamlet whose father had been, not killed, but overthrown, blinded, and imprisoned by his own brother, and now lay miserable in a dungeon at Constantinople while the usurper reigned in his stead. What tale so likely to move the pity of the knights and barons of France ? And, the suppliants added, what enterprise so fit to promote and facilitate the object of the Crusaders ? For Constantinople had always been a difficulty in the way of the conquest of Syria, and now more than ever, when a false and cruel usurper was on the throne ; whereas if old Isaac and his young son were restored, the Crusaders would secure a firm footing, a stronghold of moral as well as physical support in the East, which would make their work easy. One can imagine the high excitement, the keen discussions, the eagerness of some, the reluctance of others, the heat of debate and diverse opinion which arose in the camp. There were some among the pilgrims upon whom the pope's disapproval lay heavy, and who longed for nothing so much as to get away, to have the wearisome preliminaries of the voyage over, and to find themselves upon the holy soil which they had set out to deliver; while there were some, perhaps more generous than devout, to whom the story of the poor young prince, errant through the world in search of succour, and the blind imperial prisoner in the dungeon, was touching beyond description, calling forth every sentiment of knighthood. The Venetians had still another most moving motive; it seems scarcely possible to believe that they did not at once perceive the immense and incalculable interests involved. They were men of strictly practical vision, and Constantinople was their market-place at once and their harvest ground. To establish a permanent footing there by all the laws of honour and gratitude, what a thing for Venice! It is not necessary to conclude that they were untouched by other inducements. They, better than any, knew how many hindrances Constantinople could throw in the way, how treacherous her support was, how cunning her enmity, and what an advantage it would be to all future enterprises if a power bound to the west by solid obligations could be established on the Bosphorus. Nor is it to be supposed that as men they were inaccessible to the pleas of humanity and justice urged by Philip. But at the same time the dazzle of the extraordinary advantages thus set before themselves must have been as a glamour in their eyes.

It was while the whole immense tumultuous band, the Frenchmen and knights of Flanders, the barons of the Low Country, the sailor princes of the Republic, were in full agitation over this momentous question, and all was uncertainty and confusion, that the young Alexius arrived at Zara. There was a momentary lull in the agitation to receive, as was his due, this imperial wanderer, so young, so high-born, so unfortunate. The Marquis of Montserrato was his near kinsman, his rank was undoubted, and his misfortunes, the highest claim of all, were known to every one. The troops were turned out to receive him with all the pomp of military display, the doge's silver trumpets sounding, and all that the Crusaders could boast of in music and magnificence. The monks who had been pressing hotly from band to band urging Pope Innocent's commands and the woes of Jerusalem; the warlike leaders who had been anxiously attempting to reconcile their declared purpose with the strong temptations of such a chivalrous undertaking—all for the moment arrested their arguments, their self-reasonings, their mutual upbraidings, to hear what their young guest had to say. And Alexius had everything to say that extreme necessity could suggest. He would give subsidies unlimited—two hundred thousand marks of silver, all the costs of the expedition, as much as it pleased them to require. He would himself accompany the expedition, he would furnish two thousand men at once, and for all his life maintain five hundred knights for the defence of Jerusalem. Last of all, and greatest, he vowed—a bait for Innocent himself, an inducement which must have stopped the words of remonstrance on the lips of the priests and made their eyes glow—to renounce for ever the Greek heresy and bring the Eastern Church to the supremacy of Rome!

Whether it was this last motive, or simply a rush of sudden enthusiasm, such as was, and still is, apt to seize upon a multitude, the scruples and the doubts of the Crusaders melted like wax before the arguments of the young prince, and his cause seems to have been taken up by general consent. A few pilgrims of note indeed left the expedition and attempted to find another way to the Holy Land, but it was with very slightly diminished numbers that the expedition set sail in April, 1203, for Constantinople. Zara celebrated their departure by an immediate rising, once more asserting its independence, and necessitating a new expedition sent by Renier Dandolo, the doge's son and deputy, to do all the work of subjugation over again. But that was an occurrence of every day.

The Crusaders went to Corfu first, where they were received

with acclamation, the islanders offering at once their homage
to Alexius: and lingered thereabouts until the eve of Pentecost,
when they set sail directly for Constantinople. Over these
summer seas the crowd of ships made their way with ensigns
waving and lances glittering in the sun, like an army afloat, as
indeed they were, making the air resound with their trumpets
and warlike songs. The lovely islands, the tranquil waters,
the golden shores, filled these northmen with enthusiasm—
nothing so beautiful, so luxuriant, so wealthy and fair had
ever been seen. Where was the coward who would not dare to
strike a blow for such a land? The islands, as they passed,
received Alexius with joy, all was festal and splendid in the
advance. It was the 24th of June, the full glory of midsummer,
when the fleet passed close under the walls of Constantinople.
We need not enter into a detailed description of the siege.
The Venetians would seem to have carried off the honours of
the day. The French soldiers having failed in their first assault
by land, the Venetians, linking a number of galleys together
by ropes, ran them ashore, and seem to have gained possession,
almost without pausing to draw breath, of a portion of the city.
We will quote from Gibbon, whose classical splendour of style
is so different from the graphic simplicity of our chroniclers, a
description of this extraordinary attack. He is not a historian
generally favourable to the Venetians, so that his testimony
may be taken as an impartial one.

"On the side of the harbour the attack was more successfully conducted
by the Venetians; and that industrious people employed every resource
that was known and practised before the invention of gunpowder. A
double line, three bowshots in front, was formed by the galleys and ships;
and the swift motion of the former was supported by the weight and
loftiness of the latter, whose decks and poops and turrets were the plat-
forms of military engines that discharged their shot over the heads of the
first line. The soldiers who leaped from the galleys on shore immediately
planted and ascended their scaling ladders, while the large ships, advancing
more slowly into the intervals and lowering a drawbridge, opened a way
through the air from their masts to the rampart. In the midst of the
conflict the doge's venerable and conspicuous form stood aloft in complete

armour on the prow of his galley. The great standard of St. Mark was displayed before him ; his threats, promises, and exhortations urged the diligence of the rowers ; his vessel was the first that struck ; and Dandolo was the first warrior on shore. The nations admired the magnanimity of the blind old man, without reflecting that his age and infirmities diminished the price of life and enhanced the value of immortal glory. On a sudden, by an invisible hand (for the standard-bearer was probably slain), the banner of the Republic was fixed on the rampart, twenty-five towers were rapidly occupied, and, by the cruel expedient of fire, the Greeks were driven from the adjacent quarter."

A finer battle-picture than this—of the galleys fiercely driven in shore, the aged prince high on the prow, the Venetians rushing on the dizzy bridge from the rigging to the ramparts, and suddenly, miraculously, the lion of St. Mark unfolding in the darkened air full of smoke and fire and bristling showers of arrows—could scarcely be. The chroniclers of Venice say nothing of it all. For once they fail to see the pictorial effect, the force of the dramatic situation. Andrea Dandolo's moderate description of his ancestor's great deed is all we have to replace the glowing narrative in which the Venetians have recorded other facts in their history. "While they (the French) were," he says, " pressed hard, on account of their small numbers, the doge with the Venetians burst into the city, and he, though old and infirm of vision, yet being brave and eager of spirit, joined himself to the French warriors, and all of them together, fighting with great bravery, their strength reviving and their courage rising, forced the enemy to retire, and at last the Greeks yielding on every side, the city was taken."

The results of the victory were decisive, if not lasting. The old blind emperor, Isaac, was taken from his dungeon—his usurping brother having fled—and replaced upon his throne ; and the young wanderer, Alexius, the favourite and plaything of the crusading nobles, the *fanciullo*, as the Venetians persist in calling him, was crowned in St. Sophia as his father's coadjutor with great pomp and rejoicing. But this moment of glory was shortlived. As soon as the work was done, when there began to be talk of the payment, and of all the wonderful things

which had been promised, these brilliant skies were clouded over.
It appeared that Alexius had neither authority to make such
promises, nor any power of fulfilling them. Not even the
money could be paid without provoking new rebellions ; and
as for placing the Greek Church under the power of Rome, that
was more than any emperor could do. Nor was this all; for it
very soon appeared that the throne set up by foreign arms was
anything but secure. The Crusaders, who had intended to push
on at once to their destination, the Holy Land, were again
arrested, partly by a desire to secure the recompence promised
for their exertions, partly because the young prince, whom his
own countrymen disliked for his close alliance with the strangers,
implored them to remain till his throne should be more firmly
established. But that throne was not worth a year's purchase
to its young and unfortunate tenant. Notwithstanding the
great camp of the invaders at Galata, and the Venetian galleys
in the Bosphorus, another sudden revolution undid everything
that had been done. The first assault had been made in June,
1203. So early as March of the next year, the barons and the
doge were taking grim counsel together as to what was to be
done with the spoil—such spoil as was not to be found in any
town in Europe—when they should have seized the city, in
which young Alexius lay murdered, and his old father dead of
misery and grief.

The second siege was longer and more difficult than the first,
for the new emperor, Marzoufle, he of the shaggy eyebrows, was
bolder and more determined than the former usurper. But at
last the unhappy city was taken, and sacked with every circumstance of horror that belongs to such an event. The
chivalrous Crusaders, the brave Venetians, the best men of
their age, either did not think it necessary or were unable to
restrain the lowest instincts of an excited army. And what was
terrible everywhere was worse in Constantinople, the richest
of all existing cities, full of everything that was most exquisite
in art and able in invention. "The Venetians only, who were of
gentler soul," says Romanin, "took thought for the preservation

G

of those marvellous works of human genius, transporting them
afterwards to Venice, as they did the four famous horses
which now stand on the façade of the great Basilica, along with
many columns, jewels and precious stones, with which they
decorated the *Pala d'oro* and the treasury of San Marco." This
proof of gentler soul was equally demonstrated by Napoleon when
he carried off those same bronze horses to Paris in the beginning
of the century, but it was not appreciated either by Italy or the
world. Altogether this chapter in the history of the Venetian
armaments, as in that of the Crusaders and Western Christendom
in general, is a terrible and painful one. The pilgrims had got
into a false and miserable vortex from which they could not
clear their feet. All that followed is like some feverish and
horrible dream, through which the wild attempts to bring some
kind of order, and to establish a new rule, and to convince themselves that they were doing right and not wrong, make the
ruinous complications only more apparent. During the whole
period of their lingering, of their besieging, of their elections of
Latin emperors and archbishops—futile and shortlived attempts
to make something of their conquest—letters from Pope Innocent were raining upon them, full of indignant remonstrances,
appeals, and reproaches; and little groups of knights were
wandering off towards their proper destination sick at heart,
while the rest appointed themselves lords and suzerains, mar-
shals and constables of a country which they neither understood
nor could rule.

In less than a year there followed the disastrous defeat of
Adrianople, in which the ranks of the Crusaders were broken,
and the unfortunate newly-elected emperor, Baldwin, disappeared, and was heard of no more. The old doge, Enrico
Dandolo, died shortly after, having both in success and defeat
performed prodigies of valour which his great age (ninety-seven
according to the chroniclers) make almost incredible, and
keeping to the last a keen eye upon the interests of Venice,
which alone were forwarded by all that had happened. But
he never saw Venice again. He died in June, 1205—two

To face page 34.

DOORWAY, SAN MARCO.

years after the first attack upon Constantinople, three years after his departure from Venice—and was buried in St. Sophia. Notwithstanding the royal honours that we are told attended his funeral, one cannot but feel that the dim eyes of the old warrior must have turned with longing to the rest that ought to have been his in his own San Marco, and that there must have echoed in his aged heart something of the pang that went through that of a later pilgrim whose last fear it was that he should lay his bones far from the Tweed.

We read with a keen perception of the rapidity with which comedy dogs the steps of tragedy everywhere, that one Marino Zeno, hastily appointed after Dandolo as the head of the Venetians, assumed at once as marks of his dignity " a rose-coloured silk stocking on his right foot and a white silk stocking on his left, along with the imperial boots and purse." This was one outcome of all the blood and misery, the dethronements, the sack, the general ruin. The doges of Venice added another to their long list of titles—they were now lords of Croatia, Dalmatia, and of the fourth part and the half of the Roman (or Romanian) empire. *Dominus quartæ partis cum dimidio totius Imperi Romaniæ.* And all the isles, those dangerous and vexatious little communities that had been wont to harbour pirates and interrupt traders, fell really or nominally into the hands of Venice. They were a troublesome possession, constantly in rebellion, difficult to secure, still more difficult to keep, as the Venetian conquests in Dalmatia had already proved: but they were no less splendid possessions. Candia alone was a jewel for any emperor. The Republic could not hold these islands, putting garrisons into them at her own expense and risk. She took the wiser way of granting them to colonists on a feudal tenure, so that any noble Venetian who had the courage and the means might set himself up with a little sea-borne principality in due subjection to his native state, but with the privilege of hunting out its pirates and subduing its rebellions for himself. " To divide," says Sabellico, " the public forces of Venice into so many parts would have been very unsafe. The best thing, therefore, seemed that those who were rich should fit out, according to their capabilities, one or more galleys, and other ships of the kind required. And there being no doubt that many would find it to their private advantage to do this, it followed that the Republic in time of need would secure the aid of these armed vessels, and that each place acquired could be defended by them with the aid of the state—a thing which by itself the Republic could not have accomplished except with much expense and trouble. It was therefore ordained that they (who undertook this), with their wives and children and all they possessed, might settle in these islands, and that as colonists sent by the city their safety would be under the care and guarantee of the Republic." Many private persons, he adds, armed for this undertaking.

The rambling chronicle of Sanudo gives us here a romantic story of the conquest of Candia by his own ancestor Marco Sanudo, who, according to this narrative, having swept from the seas a certain corsair called Arrigo or Enrico of Malta, became master of the island. The inhabitants, as a matter of course, resisted and rebelled, but not in the usual way. "Accept the kingdom as our sovereign," their envoys said, "or in three hours you must leave Candia." This flattering but embarrassing alternative confounded the Venetian leader. But he accepted the honour thrust upon him, writing at once, however, to the doge, telling the choice that had been given him, and how he had accepted it from necessity and devotion to the Republic, in whose name he meant to hold the island. The Venetians at once sent twelve ships of war, on pretence of congratulating him, whom he received with a royal welcome; then, handing over his government to the commander of the squadron, took to his ships and left the dangerous glory of the insecure throne behind him. It is a pity that the documents do not bear out this pleasant story. But if a man's own descendant does not know the rights of his ancestor's actions, who should? Sanudo goes on to relate how, as a reward for this magnanimous renunciation, his forefather was allowed the command of the fleet for a year, and with this scoured the sea and secured island after island, placing his own kinsmen in possession ; but at last, being outnumbered, was taken prisoner in a naval engagement by the admirals of the Emperor of Constantinople (which emperor is not specified). "But," says his descendant, "when the said emperor saw his valorosity and beauty, he set him free, and gave him one of his sisters in marriage, from which lady are descended almost all the members of the Ca' Sanudo." The historian allows with dignified candour that this story is not mentioned by Marc Antonio Sabellico, but it is to be found, he says, in the other chroniclers. We regret to add that the austere Romanin gives a quite different account of the exploits of Marco Sanudo, the lord of Naxos. It would have been pleasant to have associated so magnanimous a seaman with the name of the chronicler of the Crusades, and the indefatigable diarist to whom later Venetian history is so deeply indebted.

These splendid conquests brought enormous increase of wealth, of trade, of care, and endless occupation to the Republic. Gained and lost, and regained and lost again, fairly fought for, strenuously held, a source perhaps at all times of more weakness than strength, they had all faded out of the tiara of the Republic long before she was herself discrowned. But there still remains in Venice one striking evidence of the splendid disastrous expedition, the unexampled conquests and victories yet dismal end, of what is called the Fourth Crusade. And that is the four great bronze horses, curious, inappropriate bizarre ornaments that stand above the doorways of San Marco. This was the blind doge's lasting piece of spoil.

The four doges of the Dandolo family who appear at intervals in the list of princes of the Republic are too far apart to be followed here. Francesco Dandolo, 1328–1339, the third of the name, was called *Cane*, according to tradition, because when ambassador to Pope Clement V. this noble Venetian, for the love of Venice, humbled himself, and with a chain round his

neck and on his knees, approached the pontiff, imploring
that the interdict might be raised, and Venice delivered from
the pains of excommunication.   If this had been to show
that men of his race thought nothing too much for the
service of their city, whether it were pride or humility, defiance
or submission, the circle which included blind Enrico and
Francesco the Dog, could scarcely be more complete.   The last
of the Dandolo doges was Andrea, 1342-1354, a man of letters
as well as of practical genius, and the historian of his
predecessors and of the city; whom at a later period and in
gentler company we shall find again.

DANDOLO

CHAPTER IV.

E have endeavoured up to this time to trace the development of the Venetian government and territory, not continuously, but from point to point according to the great conquests which increased the latter, and the growth of system and political order in the former, which became necessary as the community increased and the primitive rule was outgrown. But at the end of the thirteenth century a great revolution took place in the Republic which had risen to such prosperity, and had extended its enterprises to every quarter of the known world. It was under the Doge Gradenigo, a new type among the rulers of the State, neither a soldier nor a conqueror but a politician, that this change took place—a change antagonistic to the entire sentiment of the early Venetian institutions, but embodying all with which the world is familiar in the later forms of that great oligarchy, the proudest type of republic known to history. The election of Pietro Gradenigo was not a popular one. It is evident that a new feeling of class antagonism had been gathering during the last reign, that of Giovanni Dandolo; and that both sides were on the alert to seize an advantage. Whether the proposals for the limitation of the Consiglio Maggiore which were already in the air, and the sensation of an approaching attack upon their rights, were sufficiently clear to the populace to stimulate them to an

attempt to regain the ancient privilege of electing the Doge by acclamation: or whether it was this attempt which drove the other party to more determined action, it is impossible to judge. But at the death of Gradenigo's predecessor there was a rush of the people to the Piazza with " Voci e parole pungentissime " in a wild and sudden endeavour to push off the yoke of the regular (and most elaborate) laws which had now been in operation for many generations and to reclaim their ancient custom. The crowd coming together from all quarters of the city proclaimed the name of Jacopo Tiepolo, the son or nephew of a former doge and a man of great popularity, while still the solemn officers of state were busy in arranging the obsequies of the dead doge and preparing the multitudinous ballot-boxes for the election of his successor. Had Tiepolo been a less excellent citizen, Romanin says, civil war would almost certainly have been the issue, but he was "a man of prudence and singular goodness," a *huomo da bene*, who " despising the madness of the crowd " and to avoid the discord which must have followed, left the town secretly, in the midst of the tumult, and took refuge in his villa on the Brenta, the favourite retreat of Venetian nobles. The people were apparently not ripe for anything greater than this sudden and easily baffled effort, and when their favourite stole away, permitted the usual wire-pullers, the class which had so long originated and regulated everything, to proceed to the new election in the usual way.

No more elaborate machinery than that employed in this solemn transaction could be imagined. The almost ludicrous multiplicity of its appeals to Providence or fate, developed and increasing from age to age, the continually repeated drawing of lots, and double and triple elections, seem to evidence the most jealous determination to secure impartiality and unbiassed judgment. The order of the proceedings is recorded at length by Martin da Canale in his chronicle, which is of undoubted authority, and repeated by later writers. The six counsellors (augmented from the two of the early reigns) of the doge, according to this historian, called a meeting of the Consiglio Maggiore,

having first provided a number of balls of wax, the same
number as the members of the council, in thirty of which was
inclosed a little label of parchment inscribed with the word
LECTOR. The thirty who drew these balls were separated from
the assembly in another chamber of the palace, first being made
to swear to perform their office justly and impartially. There
were then produced thirty more waxen balls, in nine of which
was the same inscription. The chosen, who were thus reduced
to nine, the number of completeness, varied the process by
electing forty citizens, whether members or not of the Consiglio
Maggiore being left to their discretion. Each of these, however, required to secure the suffrages of seven electors. The
reader will hope that by this time at last he has come to the
electors of the doge; but not so. The forty thus chosen were
sent for from their houses by the six original counsellors who
had the management of the election; and forty waxen pellets
with the mystic word LECTOR, this time inclosed in twelve of
them, were again provided. These were put into a hat, and,
apparently for the first time, a child of eleven was called in
to act as the instrument of fate. Another writer describes
how one of the permanent counsellors going out at this point,
probably in the interval while the forty new electors were being
sent for from their houses, heard mass in San Marco, and taking
hold of the first boy he met on coming out, led him into the
palace to draw the balls. The twelve thus drawn were once
more sworn, and elected twenty-five, each of whom required
eight votes to make his election valid. The twenty-five were
reduced once more by the operation of the ballot, to nine, who
were taken into another room and again sworn, after which they
elected forty-five, reduced by ballot to eleven, who finally
elected forty-one, who at the end of all things elected the doge.
The childish elaboration of this mode of procedure is scarcely
more strange than the absolute absence of novelty in the result
produced. No plebeian Tribune ever stole into power by these
means, no new man, mounted on the shoulders of the people,
or of some theorist or partisan, ever surprised the reigning

families with a new name. The elections ran in the established
lines without a break or misadventure. If any popular interference disturbed the serenity and self-importance of the endless
series of electors it was only to turn the current in the direction
of one powerful race instead of another. Even the populace in the
Piazza proclaimed no Lanifizio or Tintorio, wool-worker or dyer,
but a Tiepolo, when they attempted to take the election into
their own hands. Neither from without or within was there a
suggestion of any new name.

The doge elected on this occasion was Pietro, called Perazzo
(a corruption of the name not given in a complimentary sense)
Gradenigo, who was at the time governor of Capo d'Istria, an
ambitious man of strongly aristocratic views and no favourite
with the people. It can scarcely be supposed that he was individually responsible for the change worked by his agency in the
constitution of the Consiglio Maggiore. It was a period of constitutional development when new officers, new agencies, an
entire civil service was coming into being, and the great council
had not only all the affairs of the State passing through its hands,
but a large amount of patronage increasing every day. Although,
as has been pointed out repeatedly, the sovereignty of Venice
under whatever system carried on, had always been in the hands
of a certain number of families, who kept their place with almost
dynastic regularity undisturbed by any intruders from below—
the system of the Consiglio Maggiore was still professedly a representative system of the widest kind ; and it would seem at the
first glance as if every honest man, all who were *da bene* and
respected by their fellows, must one time or other have been
secure of gaining admission to that popular parliament.
Romanin, strongly partisan, like all Venetians, of the institution
under which Venice flourished, takes pains to point out here
and there one or two exceptional names which show that at
long intervals such elections did happen : but they were very
rare, and the exceptional persons thus elevated never seem to
have made themselves notable. However, as the city grew and
developed, it is evident that the families who had always ruled

over her began to feel that the danger of having her courts invaded by the democracy was becoming a real one. The mode
of electing the great council was very informal and variable, and
it had recently fallen more and more into the hands of the in-
triguers of the Broglio, the lobbyists as the Americans would
say : which doubtless gave a pretext for the radical change
which was to alter its character altogether. Sometimes its
members were chosen by delegates from each sestiere or district
of the city, sometimes, which was the original idea, by four indi·
viduals, "two from this side of the canal, two from that;"
sometimes they were elected for six months, sometimes for a
year. The whole system was uncertain and wanted regulation.
But this curious combination of chances which was something
like putting into a lottery for their rulers, pleased the imagination of the people in their primitive state, and perhaps flattered
the minds of the masses with a continual possibility that upon
some of their own order the happy lot might fall. It had been
proposed in the previous reign not only that these irregularities
should be remedied, which was highly expedient, but also that a
certain hereditary principle should be adopted, which was, in
theory, a new thing and strange to the constitution of Venice :
the suggestion being that those whose fathers had sat in the
council should have a right to election, though without
altogether excluding others whom the doge or his counsellors
should consider worthy of being added to it.

When Gradenigo came to power he was probably, like a
new prime minister, pledged to carry out this policy : and
within a few years of his accession the experiment was tried,
but very cautiously, in a tentative way. Venice was profoundly
occupied at the time with one of her great wars with her rival
Genoa, a war in which she had much the worst, though certain
victories from time to time in Eastern waters encouraged her to
pursue the struggle ; and it was under cover of this conflict
which engaged men's thoughts that the new experiment was
made. Instead of the ordinary periodical election of the council,
nominally open to all, the four chosen electors to whom this

duty ordinarily fell, nominated only—in the first place—such
members of the existing Consiglio Maggiore as had in their own
persons or in those of their fathers sat in the council during
the last four years, who were then re-elected by ballot, taken
for each man individually by the Forty, a recently constituted
body; to whom a further number of names from outside were
then proposed, and voted for in the same way. Thus the
majority of members elected was not only confined to those
possessing a hereditary claim, but the election was taken out
of the hands of the traditional electors, and transferred to those
of the existing rulers of the city. The new method was first

ARMS OF GRADENIGO.

tried for a year, and then established as the fundamental law
of the Republic, with the further exclusion of the one popular
and traditional element, the nominal four electors, whose work
was now transferred to the officials of the State. The change
thus carried out was great in principle, though perhaps not
much different in practice from that which had become the use
and wont of the city. "The citizens," says Romanin, " were
thus divided into three classes—1st, Those who neither in their
own persons nor through their ancestors had ever formed part
of the great council; 2nd, Those whose progenitors had been

members of it; 3rd, Those who were themselves members of the council, both they and their fathers. The first were called New men, and were never admitted save by special grace; the second class were included from time to time; finally, the third were elected by full right."

This was the law which under the name of the *Serrata del Consiglio Maggiore* caused two rebellions in Venice and confirmed for ever beyond dispute her oligarchical government. Her parliament, so fondly supposed to be that of the people, was no more closed to the New men than is our House of Lords. Now and then an exceptional individual might be nominated, and by means of great services, wealth, or other superior qualities, obtain admission. It was indeed the privilege and reward henceforward zealously striven for by the plebeian class, and unfortunately more often bestowed in recompence for the betrayal of political secrets, and especially of popular conspiracies, than for better reasons. But the right was with those whose fathers had held the position before them, whose rank was already secure and ascertained, the nobles and patrician classes. The hereditary legislator thus arose in the bosom of the State which considered itself the most free in Christendom, in his most marked and distinct form. Romanin tells us that the famous Libro d'Oro, the book of nobility, was formed in order to keep clear the descent and legitimacy of all claimants, bastards, and even the sons of a wife not noble, being rigorously excluded. The law itself was strengthened by successive additions so as to confine the electors exclusively to the patrician class.

The war with Genoa was still filling all minds when this silent revolution was accomplished. How could Venice give her attention to what was going on in the gilded chambers of the Palazzo, when day by day the city was convulsed by bad news or deluded by faint gleams of better hope? Once and again the Venetian fleets were defeated, and mournful galleys came drifting up, six or seven out of a hundred, to tell the tale of destruction and humiliation; and ever with renewed efforts, in a rage of despairing energy, the workmen toiling in the arsenal, the boatmen giving up their tranquil traffic upon the lagoons to man the new-appointed ships, and every family, great and small, offering its dearest to sustain the honour of the Republic, the energies of the city were strained to the utmost. In the autumn of 1298, just when the Serrata had been confirmed in the statute-book, the great fleet, commanded by Admiral Andrea Dandolo, sailed from the port, with all the aspect of a squadron invincible, to punish the Genoese and end the war. In one of the ships was a certain Marco Polo, from his home near San Giovanni Chrisostomo, Marco of the Millions, a great travelling merchant, whose stories had been as fables in his countrymen's ears. This great expedition did indeed for the time end the war; but not by victory. It was cruelly defeated on the Dalmatian coasts after a stubborn and bloody struggle. The Admiral Andrea dashed his head against his mast and died rather than be taken to Genoa in chains; while the humbler sailor Marco Polo with crowds of his countrymen was carried off to prison there, to his advantage and ours, as it turned out. But Venice was plunged into mourning and woe, her resources exhausted, her captains lost. Genoa, who had bought the victory dear, was in little less unhappy condition; and in the following year the rival Republics were glad to make peace under every pledge of mutual forbearance and friendship, for as long as it could last. It was only after this conclusion of the more exciting interests abroad that the Venetians at home, recovering tranquillity, began to look within and see in the meantime what the unpopular doge and his myrmidons, while nobody had been looking, had been engaged about.

It is difficult to tell what the mass of the people thought of the new position of affairs: for all the chroniclers are on the winning side, and even the careful Romanin has little sympathy with the revolutionaries. The Venetian populace had long been pleasantly deceived as to their own power. They had been asked to approve what their masters had decided upon and made to believe it was their own doing. They had given a picturesque and impressive background as of a unanimous people to the decisions of the doge and his counsellors, the sight of their immense assembly making the noble French envoys weep like women. But whether they had begun to see through those fine pretences of consulting them, and to perceive how little they had really to do with it all, no one tells us. Their attempt to elect their own doge without waiting for the authorities, looks as if they had become suspicious of their masters. And at the same time the arbitrary closing of the avenues of power, to all men whose fortune was not made or their position secure, and the establishment in the council of that hereditary principle so strenuously opposed in the election of the doges, were sufficiently distinct changes to catch the popular eye and disturb the imagination. Accordingly when the smoke of war cleared off and the people came to consider internal politics, discontent and excitement arose. This found vent in a sudden and evidently natural outburst of popular feeling. The leader of the malcontents was "a certain Marino whose surname was Bocconio," says Sabellico, "a man who was not noble, nor of the baser sort, but of moderate fortune, bold and ready for any evil," precisely of that class of new men to whom political privileges are most dear, one on the verge of a higher position, and doubtless hoping to push his way into parliament, and secure for his sons an entry into the class of patricians. "He was much followed for his wealth," says another writer. Sanudo gives an account of Bocconio's (or Bocco's) rebellion, which the too well informed Romanin summarily dismisses as a fable, but which as an expression of popular feeling, and the aspect which the new state of affairs bore to the masses, has a certain value. The matter of fact legend of shutting out and casting forth embodies in the most forcible way the sense of an exclusion which was more complete than could be effected by the closing of any palace doors. Bocconio and his friends, according to Sanudo, indignant and enraged to be shut out from the council, crowded into the

Piazza with many followers, at the time when they supposed the elections to be going on, and found the gates closed and the Gentilhuomini assembled within.

"Then beating at the door they called out that they desired to form part of the Council, and would not be excluded : upon which the Doge sent messengers to tell them that the Council was not engaged upon the election, but was discussing other business. As they continued, however, to insist upon coming in, the Doge seeing that he made no advance, but that the tumult kept increasing in the piazza, deliberated with the Council how to entrap these seditious persons, to call forth against them *ultimum de potentia*, the severest penalty of the law. Accordingly he sent to tell them that they should be called in separately in parties of five, and that those who succeeded in the ballot should remain as members of the Council, on condition that those who failed should disperse and go away. The first called were Marino Bocco, Jacopo Boldo, and three others. The doors were then closed and a good guard set, after which the five were stripped and thrown into a pit, the Trabucco della Toresella, and so killed ; and the others being called in, in succession, and treated in the same way, the chief men and ringleaders were thus disposed of to the number of a hundred and fifty or sixty men. The crowd remaining in the piazza persuaded themselves that all those who were called in, of whom none came back, had been made nobles of the Great Council. And when it was late in the evening the members of the Council came down armed into the piazza, and a proclamation was made by order of the Doge that all should return to their homes on pain of punishment ; hearing which the crowd, struck with terror, had the grace to disperse in silence. Then the corpses of those who were dead were brought out and laid in the piazza, with the command that if any one touched them it should be at the risk of his head. And when it was seen that no one was bold enough to approach, the rulers perceived that the people were obedient. And some days after, as they could not tolerate the stench, the bodies were buried. And in this manner ended that sedition, so that no one afterwards ventured to open his mouth on such matters."

This legend Sanudo takes, as he tells us, from the chronicles of a certain Zaccaria da Pozzo; and it does not interfere with his faith in the narrative that he himself has recorded on a previous page the execution of Bocco and his fellow conspirators "between the columns" in the usual way. Perhaps he too felt that this wild yet matter of fact version of the incident, the closed doors, and the mysterious slaughter of the intruders

in the hidden courts within, was an effective and natural way of
representing the action of a constitutional change so important.
The names of the conspirators who died with Bocconio are
almost all unknown and obscure names, yet there was a
sprinkling of patricians, upholders of the popular party, such
as are always to be found on similar occasions, and which
reappear in the more formidable insurrection that followed.
For the moment however the summary extinction of Bocconio's
ill-planned rebellion intimidated and silenced the people, while,
on the other side, it was made an occasion of tightening the
bonds of the *Serrata*, and making the admission of the *homo
novus* more difficult than ever.

This little rebellion, so soon brought to a conclusion, took
place in the spring of the year 1300, the year of the jubilee,
when all the world was crowding to Rome, and Dante standing
on the bridge of St. Angelo, watching the streams of the
pilgrims coming and going, bethought himself, like a true
penitent, of his own moral condition, and in the musings of his
supreme imagination found himself astray in evil paths, and,
began to seek through hell and heaven the *verace via*, the right
way which he had lost. This great scene of religious fervour,
in which so many penitents from all quarters of the world
renewed the vows of their youth and pledged over again their
devotion to the Church and the Faith, comes strangely into the
midst of the fierce strife between Guelf and Ghibelline, which
then rent asunder the troubled Continent, and especially Italy,
where every city took part in the struggle. Venice, in the
earlier ages as well as in later times when she maintained her
independence against papal interference, has usually shown
much indifference to the authority of the pope. But in the
beginning of the fourteenth century this was impossible,
especially when the great Republic of the Sea meddled, as she
had no right to do, with the internal policy of that Terra Firma,
the fat land of corn and vine, after which she had always a
longing. And there now fell upon her in the midst of all other
contentions, the most terrible of all the catastrophes to which

H

mediæval States were subject, the curse of Rome. It was, no
doubt, rather with that keen eye to her own advantage which
never failed her, than from any distinct bias towards the side of
the Ghibelline, that Venice had interposed in the question of
succession which agitated the city of Ferrara, and finally made
an attempt to establish her own authority in that distracted
place. Indeed it seems little more than an accidental appeal
on the part of the other faction to the protection of the pope
which brought upon her the terrible punishment of the excommunication which Pope Clement launched from Avignon, and
which ruined her trade, reduced her wealth, put all her
wandering merchants and sailors in danger of their lives, and
almost threatened with complete destruction the proud city
which had held her head so high. It would have been entirely
contrary to the habits of Venice as of every other republican
community, not to have visited this great calamity more or less
upon the head of the State. And it gave occasion to the
hostile families who from the time of Gradenigo's accession had
been seeking an opportunity against him, the house of Tiepolo
and its allies, the Quirini who had opposed the war of Ferrara
all through and had suffered severely in it, and others, in one
way or another adverse to the existing Government. The
Tiepoli do not seem to have been generally of the mild and
noble character of him who had refused to be elected doge
by the clamour of the Piazza. They had formed all through
a bitter opposition party to the doge who had displaced their
kinsman. Perhaps even Jacopo Tiepolo himself while retiring
from the strife to save the peace of the Republic, had a natural
expectation that the acclamation of the populace would be
confirmed by the votes of the electors. At all events his
family had throughout maintained a constitutional feud, keeping
a keen eye upon all proceedings of the government and eager
to find a sufficient cause for interference more practical.

It would seem a proof that the popular mind had not fully
awakened to the consequences of the change of laws at the
moment of Bocconio's insurrection that the patrician opposition

did not seize that opportunity. The occasion they sought came later, when the disastrous war and the horrors of the Interdict, events more immediately perceptible than any change of constitution, had excited all minds and opened the eyes of the people to their internal wrongs by the light of those tremendous misfortunes which the ambition or the unskilfulness of their doge and his advisers had brought upon them. The rebellious faction took advantage of all possible means to fan the flame of discontent, stimulating the stormy debates of the Consiglio Maggiore, which was not more but less easy to manage since it had been restricted to the gentry, while at the same time stirring up the people to a sense of the profound injury of exclusion from its ranks. The Quirini, the Badoeri, and various others, connected by blood and friendship with the Tiepoli, among whom were hosts of young gallants always ready for a brawl, and ready to follow any warlike lead, to quicken the action of their seniors, increased the tension on all sides. How the excitement grew in force and passion day by day—how one incident after another raised the growing wrath, how scuffles arose in the city and troubles multiplied, it is not difficult to imagine. On one occasion a Dandolo took the wall of a Tiepolo and a fight ensued; on another, "the devil, who desires the destruction of all government," put it into the head of Marco Morosini, one of the Signori di Notte (or night magistrates) to inquire whether Pietro Quirini of the elder branch (della Ca' Grande) was armed, and to order him to be searched: on which Quirini, enraged, tripped up the said Morisini with his foot, and all Rialto was forthwith in an uproar. The houses of the chiefs of the party, both Tiepoli and Quirini, were in the quarter of the Rialto, and close to the bridge.

At length the gathering fire burst into flame. No doubt driven beyond patience by some incident, trifling in itself, Marco Quirini, one of the heads of his house, a man who had suffered much in the war with Ferrara, called his friends and neighbours round him in his palace, and addressed the assembled party, attacking the doge as the cause of all the troubles of the country, the chief instrument in changing the constitution, in closing the Great Council to the people, in carrying on the fatal war with Ferrara, and bringing down upon the city the horrors of the excommunication. To raise a party against the doge for private reasons, however valid, would not be, he said, the part of a good citizen. But how could they stand cold spectators of the ruin of their beloved and injured country, or shut their eyes to the fact that the evil passions of one man were the chief cause of their misery, and that it was he who had not only brought disaster from without, but, by the closing of the council, shut out from public affairs so many of the worthiest citizens? He was followed by a younger and still more ardent speaker in the person of Bajamonte Tiepolo, the son of Jacopo, with whose name henceforward this historical incident is chiefly connected, at that time one of the most prominent figures in Venice, the *Gran Cavaliero* of the people, who loved him, and among whom he had inherited his father's popularity. "Let us leave words and take to action," he said, "nor pause till we have placed on the throne a good prince, who will restore the ancient laws, and preserve and increase the public freedom." The struggle was probably in its essence much more a family feud than a popular outbreak, but it is a sign of the excitement of the time that the wrongs of the people were at every turn appealed to as the one unquestionable argument.

Never had there been a more apt moment for a popular rising. "In the first place," says Caroldo, "the city was very ill content with the illustrious Pietro Gradenigo, who in the beginning of his reign had the boldness to reform the Consiglio Maggiore, admitting a larger number of families who were noble, and few of those who ought to have been the principal and most respected of the city, taking from the citizens and populace the ancient mode of admission into the council: the root of this change being the hatred he bore to the people, who, before his election, had proclaimed Jacopo Tiepolo doge, and afterwards had shown little satisfaction with the choice made of

himself. And not only did he bear rancour against Jacopo
Tiepolo but against the whole of his family."

Notwithstanding this rancour Jacopo Tiepolo himself, the
good citizen, was the only one who now raised his voice for
peace and endeavoured to calm the excitement of his family and
their adherents. But the voice of reason was not listened to.
On the night of the 14th of June, 1310, ten years after Bocconio's brief and ill-fated struggle, the fires of insurrection were
again lighted up in Venice. The conspirators gathered during
the night in the Quirini Palace, meeting under cover of the
darkness in order to burst forth with the early dawn, and with
an *impeto*, a sudden rush from the Rialto to the Piazza, to gain
possession of the centre of the city and seize and kill the doge.
The night, however, was not one of those lovely nights of June
which make Venice a paradise. It was a fit night for such a
bloody and fatal undertaking as that on which these muffled
conspirators were bound. A great storm of thunder and lightning,
such as has nowhere more magnificent force than on the lagoons,
burst forth while their bands were assembling, and torrents of
rain poured from the gloomy skies. It was in the midst of this
tempest, which favoured while it cowed them, the peals of the
thunder making their cries of " Death to the Doge " and " Freedom to the people " inaudible, and muffling the tramp of their
feet, that the insurrectionists set forth. One half of the little
army, under Marco Quirini, kept the nearer way along the canal
by bridge and fondamenta ; the other, led by Bajamonte himself,
threaded their course by the narrow streets of the Merceria to
the same central point. The sounds of the march were lost in
the commotion of nature, and the dawn for which they waited
was blurred in the stormy tumult of the elements. The dark
line of the rebels pushed on, however, spite of storm and rain,
secure, it would seem, that their secret had been kept and that
their way was clear before them.

But in the meantime the doge, who, whatever were his faults,
seems to have been a man of energy and spirit, had heard, as
the authorities always heard, of the intended rising ; and taking

his measures as swiftly and silently as if he had been the conspirator, called together all the officers of state, with their retainers and servants, and sending off messengers to Chioggia, Torcello, and Murano for succour, ranged his little forces in the Piazza under the flashing of the lightning and the pouring of the rain, and silently awaited the arrival of the rebels. A more dramatic scene could not be conceived. The two lines of armed men stumbling on in the darkness, waiting for a flash to show them the steps of a bridge or the sharp corner of a narrow *calle*, pressed on in mutual emulation, their hearts hot for the attack, and all the points of the assault decided upon. When lo! as the first detachment, that led by Quirini, debouched into the great square, a sudden wild flash, lighting up earth and heaven, showed them the gleaming swords and dark files of the defenders of San Marco, awaiting their arrival. The surprise would seem to have been complete: but it was not the doge who was surprised. This unexpected revelation precipitated the fight, which very shortly, the leaders being killed in the first rush, turned into a rout. Bajamonte appearing with his men by the side of the Merceria made a better stand, but the advantage remained with the doge's party, who knew what they had to expect and had the superior confidence of law and authority on their side.

By this time the noise of the human tumult surmounted that of the skies, and the peaceful citizens who had slept through the storm woke to the sound of the cries and curses, the clash of swords and armour, and rushed to their windows to see what the disturbance was. One woman, looking out, in the mad passion of terror seized the first thing that came to hand, a stone vase or mortar on her window-sill, and flung it down at hazard into the midst of the tumult. This trifling incident would seem to have been the turning-point of the struggle. The heavy flower-pot or mortar descended upon the head of the standard-bearer who carried Bajamonte's flag with its inscription of LIBERTA, and struck him to the ground. When the rebels, in the gray of the stormy dawn, saw their banner waver and fall, a panic seized them. They thought it was taken by the enemy, and

To face page 102.

PONTE DEL PARADISO.

even the leader himself, the Gran Cavaliero, turned with the panic-stricken crowd and fled. Pursued and flying, fighting, making here and there a stand, they hurried through the tortuous ways to the Rialto, which, being then no more than a bridge of wood, they cut down behind them, taking refuge on the other side, where their headquarters were, in the palace of the Quirini, the remains of which, turned to ignoble use as a poulterer's shop, still exist in the Beccaria. The other half of the insurrectionists, that which had been thrown into confusion and flight by the death of its leader, Marco Quirini, met on its disastrous backward course a band hastily collected by the head of the Scuola della Carità, and increased by a number of painters living about that centre of their art—in the Campo San Luca, where the rebels were cut to pieces.

Bajamonte and his men, however, arrived safely at their stronghold, having on their way sacked and burnt the office of the customs on that side of the river, thus covering their retreat with smoke and flame. Once there they closed their gates, entrenching their broken strength in the great mediæval house which was of itself a fortress and defensible place. And after all that had happened the fate of Venice still hung in the balance, and such was the gravity of the revolt that it still seemed possible for the knot of desperate men entrenched on the other side of the Rive Alto, the deep stream which sweeps profound and strong round that curve of the bank, to gain, did Badoer come back in time with the aid he had been sent to seek in Padua, the upper hand. Even when Badoer was cut off by Giustinian and his men from Chioggia, the doge and his party, though strong and confident, do not seem to have ventured to attack the headquarters of the rebels. On the contrary, envoys were sent to offer an amnesty, and even pardon, should they submit. Three times these envoys were rowed across the canal, the ruined bridge lying black before their eyes, fretting the glittering waves, which no doubt by this time leaped and dashed against the unaccustomed obstacle in all the brightness of June, the thunderstorm over, though not the greater tempest of human passion. From the other bank over the charred ruins of the houses they had destroyed, the rebel Venetians, looking out in their rage, disappointment, and despair, to see embassy after embassy conducted to the edge of the ferry, must have felt still a certain fierce satisfaction in their importance, and in the alarm to which these successive messengers testified. At last, however, there came alone a venerable counsellor, Filippo Belegno, "moved by love of his country" to attempt once more the impossible task of moving these obstinate and desperate men. No doubt he put before them the agitated state of the city, the strange sight it was with the ruins still smoking, the streets still full of the wounded and dying; torn in two, the peaceful bridge lying a great wreck in mid-stream. "And such was his venerable aspect and the force of his eloquence" that he won the rebels at last to submission. Bajamonte and his immediate followers were banished for life from Venice and its vicinity to the distant lands of Slavonia beyond Zara; others less prominent were allowed to hope that in a few years they might be recalled; and the least guilty, on making compensation for what they had helped to destroy, were pardoned. Thus ended the most serious revolt that had ever happened in Venice. One cannot help feeling that it was hard upon Badoer and several others who were taken fighting to be beheaded, while Bajamonte was thus able to make terms for himself and escape, with his head at least.

The lives thus spared, however, were but little to be envied. The banishment to the East was a penalty which the Republic could not enforce. She could put the rebels forth from her territory, but even her power was unable in those wild days to secure a certain place of banishment for the exiles. Those who are familiar with the life of Dante will remember what was the existence of a *fuor-uscito* banished from the beloved walls of Florence. Bajamonte Tiepolo was a personage of greater social importance than Dante, with friends and allies no doubt in all the neighbouring cities, as it was natural a man should have who belonged to one of the greatest Venetian families. The records

of the State are full of signs and tokens of his passage through
the Italian mainland, and his long wanderings afterwards on the
Dalmatian coasts. He was scarcely well got rid of out of Venice
before the doge is visible in the records making a great speech
in the council, in which he gives a lively picture of the state
of affairs, and of the contumacy of Bajamonte and his companions, their visits to Padua and Rovigo, their parleys with
the turbulent spirits of the Marshes, and even of Lombardy—
their perpetual attempts to raise again the standard of revolt
in Venice. It may be supposed even that the doge died of
this revolt and its consequences, in the passion and endless
harassment consequent upon the constant machinations of his
opponent, whom indeed he had got the better of, but who
would not yield.

Romance has scarcely taken hold, except in obscure attempts,
upon the juxtaposition of these two men : but nothing seems
more likely than that some profounder personal tragedy lay at
the bottom of this historical episode. At all events the cha-
racters of the two opponents, the doge and the rebel, are
strongly contrasted, and fit for all the uses of tragedy. Had
Venice possessed a Dante, or had Bajamonte been gifted with a
poet's utterance, who can tell in what dark cave of the Inferno
the reader of those distant ages might not have found the dark
unfriendly doge, sternly determined to carry through his plans,
to shut out contemptuously from his patrician circle every low-
born aspirant, and to betray the beloved city, whose boast had
always been of freedom, into the tremendous fetters of a system
more terrible than any despotism ? Gradenigo, so far as he can
be identified personally, would seem to have been an excellent
type of the haughty aristocrat, scornful of the new men who
formed the rising tide of Venetian life, and determined to keep
in the place in which they were born the inferior populace.
He had been employed in distant dependencies of the Republic,
where a state of revolt was chronic, and where the most heroic
measures were necessary : and it was clear to him that there
must be no hesitation, no trifling with the forces below. When

he became doge, Venice was still to some extent governed by
her old traditions, and it was yet possible that the democracy
might have largely invaded her sacred ranks of patrician
power.   She was ruled by an intricate and shifting magistracy
of councils, sages, pregadi (the simplest primitive title, men
"prayed" to come and help the doge with their advice),
among whom it is difficult to tell which was which, or how
many there were, or how long any one man held his share of
power.   But when Perazzo, proud Peter, the man whom the
commons did not love, of whom no doubt they had many a story
to tell, ended his reign in Venice, the Great Council had become
hereditary, the old possibilities were all ended, and the Council
of Ten sat supreme—an institution altogether new, and as terrible as unknown—a sort of shifting but permanent Council
of Public Safety endowed with supreme and irresponsible power.
A greater political revolution could not be.   The armed revolutionaries who carried sword and flame throughout the city could
not, had they been successful in their conjectured purpose of
making Bajamonte lord of Venice, have accomplished a greater
change in the state than was done silently by this determined
man.

That he was determined and prompt and bold is evident from
all his acts.   The rapidity and silence of his preparations to
rout the insurgents; the trap in which he caught them when,
marching under cover of the thunder to surprise him in his
palace, they were themselves surprised in the Piazza by a
little army more strong because forewarned than their own ;
the brave face he showed at another period, even in front of the
pope's excommunication, proclaiming loudly to his distant
envoys "We are determined to do all that is in us, manfully
and promptly, to preserve our rights and our honour;" the
boldness of his tremendous innovations upon the very fabric of
the State; and that final test of success which forcible character
and determination are more apt than justice or mercy to win—
leave no doubt as to his intrinsic qualities.   He was successful,
and his rival was unfortunate: he was hated, and the other

was beloved. Neither of these two figures stand prominent in picturesque personal detail out of the pages of history. We see them only by their acts, and only in so far as those acts affected the great all-absorbing story of their city. But the influence of Perazzo upon that history is perhaps more remarkable than that of any other individual so far as law and sovereignty is concerned.

The rebel leader was a very different man. The noble youth whom Venice called the Gran Cavaliero—the young Cavalier, as one might say, like our own Prince Charlie—fiery and swift, bidding his kinsman not talk but act—the hope of the elder men, put forth by Marco Quirini as most worthy of all to be heard when the malcontents first gathered in the palace near the Rialto, and ventured to tell each other what was in their hearts—could have been no common gallant, and yet would seem to have had the faults and weaknesses as well as the noble qualities of the careless foolhardy cavalier. No doubt he held his life as lightly as any knight errant of the time : yet when his kinsman fell in the narrow entrance of the Merceria in the wild dawning when foes and friends were scarcely to be distinguished, Bajamonte, too, was carried away by the quick imaginary panic and retreated, dragged along in the flight of his discouraged followers. He had not that proof of earnestness which success gives, and he had the ill-fortune to escape when other men perished. The narrative which Romanin has collected, out of the unpublished records, of his after life, presents a picture of restless exile, never satisfied, full of conspiracies, hopeless plots, everlasting spyings and treacheries, which make the heart sick. We can only remember that Bajamonte was no worse in this respect than his great contemporary, Dante. And perhaps the two exiles may have met, if not on those stairs which the poet found so hard to climb, yet somewhere in the wild roaming which occupied both their lives, full of a hundred fruitless schemes to get back, this to Florence, that to Venice. Romanin ever severe to the rebel, argues that all circumstances and all documents prove the hero of the Venetian tragedy to have been "a man of excessive ambition, a subverter of law and order ; in fact, a traitor"—most terrible of all reproaches. But as a matter of fact it was not he but his adversary who subverted the civil order of the Republic, and whether the young Tiepolo had a true sense of patriotism at his heart, and of patriotic indignation against these innovations, or was merely one of the many ambitious adventurers of the day struck with the idea of making himself lord of Venice as the Scaligeri were lords in Padua on no better title—there seems no evidence, and probably never will be any evidence to show.

When Bajamonte left Venice he proceeded anywhere but to the distant countries to which he was nominally banished. Evidently all that was done in the way of carrying out such a sentence was to drive the banished men out of the confines of the Republic, leaving them free to obey the further orders of the authorities if they chose. In this case the exiles lingered about secretly for some time in neighbouring cities, watched by spies who reported all their actions, and especially those of Bajamonte, to the doge. When at last he did proceed to Dalmatia, he became, according to Romanin, a centre of conspiracy and treason, and at the bottom of the endless rebellions of Zara, which, however, had rebelled on every possible occasion long before Bajamonte was born. It is curious to find that all the chroniclers, and even a writer so recent and so enlightened as Romanin, should remain pitiless towards all rebels against the authority of the Republic. The picture this historian gives of Bajamonte's obscure and troubled career, pursued from one city to another by the spies and letters of the Signoria warning all and sundry to have nothing to do with the rebel, and making his attempts to re-enter life impossible—is a very sad one ; but no pity for the exile ever moves the mind of the narrator. For with the Venetian historian, as with all other members of this wonderful commonwealth, Venice is everything, and the individual nothing : nor are any man's wrongs or suffering of any importance in comparison with the peace and prosperity of the adored city.

The traces of this insurrection have in the long progress of years almost entirely disappeared, though at the time many commemorative monuments bore witness to the greatest popular convulsion which ever moved Venice. The Tiepolo Palace, inhabited by Bajamonte, was razed to the ground, and a pillar, *una colonna d'infamia*, was placed on the spot with the following inscription:—

> " Di Baiamonte fo questo terreno,
> E mo [1] per lo so Iniquo tradimento
> S'è posto in Chomun per l'altrui spavento
> E per mostrar a tutti sempre seno."

" This was the dwelling of Bajamonte : for his wicked treason this stone is set up, that others may fear and that it may be a sign to all. " The column was broken, Tassini tells us in his curious and valuable work upon the *Streets of Venice*, soon after it was set up, by one of the followers of Tiepolo who had shared in the amnesty, but whose fidelity to his ancient chief was still too warm to endure this public mark of infamy. It was then removed to the close neighbourhood of the parish church of S. Agostino, probably for greater safety ; afterwards it was transferred, no longer as a mark of shame but as a mere antiquity, from one patrician's garden to another, till it was finally lost. In later times, when the question was seriously discussed whether Bajamonte was not a patriot leader rather than a traitor, proposals were made to raise again the column of shame as a testimony of glory misunderstood. But the convictions of the rehabilitators of the Gran Cavaliero have not been strong enough to come to any practical issue. All that remains of him is (or was) a white stone let into the pavement behind the now suppressed church of S. Agostino with the inscription—" Col : Bai : The : MCCCX.," marking the site of his house : but whether a relic of his own age or the work of some more recent sympathiser we are not told. On the other side of the canal in the

---

[1] " *Quel* MO *del secondo verso*," says Tassini, *spiegasi per* ORA, *e quel* SENO *dell' ultimo per* SIENO *sott' intendendovi, queste parole.*

campo of San Luca stood till very recent times a flagstaff,
ornamented on gala days with the standard of the Scuola of
the Carità, in remembrance of their victory over one party of
the insurrectionists: and in the Merceria, not far from the
Piazza, there still exists, or lately existed, a shop with the
sign "*Della grazia del morter,*" being the same out of which
Giustina Rossi threw forth the flower-pot, to the destruction
of the failing cause.

Another singular sign of disgrace and punishment was the
condemnation of the families of Quirini and Tiepolo to a change
of armorial bearings. Had they been compelled to wear their arms
reversed or to bear any other understood heraldic symbol of
shame this would have been comprehensible: but all that seems to
have been demanded of them was a change of their bearings,
not any ignominious sign. The authorities went so far as to
change the arms upon the shields of the two defunct Tiepoli
doges, a most senseless piece of vengeance, since it obliterated
the shame which it was intended to enhance. The palaces still
standing along the course of the Grand Canal which carry
rising from their roofs the two obelisks erected upon all
the houses of the Tiepoli for some reason unknown to us—prove
that in latter days the race was little injured or diminished
by its disgrace and punishment.

A much greater memorial of this foiled rebellion, however,
still remains to be noticed. This was the institution of the far-
famed Council of Ten, the great tribunal which henceforward
reigned over the Republic with a sway which was in sober
reality tremendous and appalling, but which is still further
enhanced by the mystery in which all its proceedings were
wrapped, and the impression made upon an imaginative people
by the shadow of this great secret voiceless tribunal, every man
of which was sworn to silence, and before which any Venetian
at any moment might find himself arraigned. It was professedly to guard against such a danger as that which the
Republic had just escaped that this new tribunal was instituted,
"Because of the new thing which had happened and to guard

against any repetition of it." Among the many magistratures
of the city this was the greatest, most fatal, and important : it
held the keys of life and death; it was responsible to no
superior authority, permitted no appeal, and was beyond the
reach of public opinion or criticism, its decisions as unquestionable as they were secret. The system of denunciation, the
secret documents dropped into the Bocca di Leone, the mys-
sterious processes by which a man might be condemned before
he knew that he had been accused, have perhaps been ex-
aggerated, and Romanin does his utmost to prove that the
dreaded council was neither so formidable nor so mysterious as
romance has made it out to be. But his arguments are but
poor in comparison with the evident dangers of an institution, whose proceedings were wrapped in secrecy and which was
accountable neither to public opinion nor to any higher tribunal.
Political offences in our own day are judged more leniently
than crime ; in those times they were of deeper dye than anything that originated in private rage or covetousness. And
amid the family jealousies of that limited society the opportunity thus given of cutting off an enemy, undermining the
reputation of any offender, or spoiling the career of a too
prosperous rival, was too tremendous a temptation for human
nature to resist. This formidable court was, in conformity with
the usual Venetian custom, appointed first for a year only, as
an experiment, and with the special purpose of forestalling
further rebellion by the most suspicious and inquisitive vigilance : but once established it was too mighty a power to be
abandoned and soon became an established institution.

Thus the two rebellions did nothing but rivet the chains
which had been woven about the limbs of the Republic. And
though there still remained the boast of freedom, and the City
of the Sea always continued to vaunt her republican severity
and strength, Venice now settled into the tremendous framework of a system which had no room for the plebeian or the
poor, more rigid than any individual despotism, in which there
are always chances for the new man, more autocratic and

irresponsible than the government of any absolute monarch.
The Council of Ten completed the bonds which the *serrata* of
the council had made.   The greatest splendours if not the
greatest triumphs of the State were yet to come, but all
the possibilities of political freedom and expansion were
finally destroyed.

The circumstances which surrounded this new institution
were skilfully, almost theatrically disposed to increase the terror
with which it was soon regarded.   The vow of secrecy exacted
from each member and from all who appeared before them,
the lion's mouth ever open for denunciations—which however
well founded may be Romanin's assertion that those which
were anonymous were rarely acted upon, yet bore an impression of the possibility of a dastardly and secret blow, which
nothing can wipe out—the mysterious manner in which a man
accused was brought before that tribunal in the dark, to answer
to judges only partially seen, with the consciousness of the
torture-room and all its horrors near if his startled wits should
fail him—all were calculated to make the name of the Ten a
name of fear.   Nothing could be more grim than the smile of
that doge who leaving the Council chamber in the early
sunshine after a prolonged meeting, answered the unsuspicious
good morrow of the great soldier whom he had been condemning
with the words, "There has been much talk of you in the
Council."   Horrible greeting, which meant so much more than
met the ear !

The Doge Gradenigo died little more than a year after the
confusion and discomfiture of his adversaries.   He was conveyed
without funeral honours or any of the respect usually shown to
the dead, to S. Cipriano in Murano, where he was buried.   "The
usual funeral of princes was not given to him," says Caroldo,
"perhaps because he was still under the papal excommunication,
perhaps because, hated as he was by the people in his lifetime,
it was feared that some riot would rise around him in his death."
He who had carried out the *serrata*, and established the Council
of Ten, and triumphed over all his personal opponents, had to

skulk over the lagoon, privately, against all precedent, to his grave, leaving the state in unparalleled trouble and dismay. But he had crushed the rebel, whether patriot or conspirator, and revolutionised Venice, which was work enough and success enough for one man. He died in August, 1311, a year and some months after the banishment of Bajamonte and the end of his rebellion.

CHAPTER V.

THE DOGES DISGRACED.

HE history of the two princes to whom Venice has given a lasting place in the annals of the unfortunate, those records which hold a surer spell over the heart than any of the more triumphant chronicles of fame, are of less material import to her own great story than those chapters of self-development and self-construction which we have surveyed. But picturesque in all things and with a dramatic instinct which rarely fails to her race, the republic, even in the height of her vengeance, and by means of the deprivation which has banished his image from among those of her rulers, has made the name of the beheaded doge, Marino Faliero, one of the best known in all her records. We pass the row of pictured faces, many of them representing her greatest sons, till we come to the place where this old man is not, his absence being doubly suggestive and carrying a human interest beyond that of all fulfilled and perfect records. Nor is it without significance in the history of the state, that after having finally suppressed and excluded the popular element from all voice in its councils, the great oligarchy which had achieved its proud position by means of doge and people, should have applied itself to the less dangerous task of making a puppet of its nominal prince, converting him into a mere functionary and ornamental head of the state. Such words have been applied

often enough to the constitutional monarch of our own highly refined and balanced system, and it is usual to applaud the strict and honourable self-restraint of our English sovereign as the brightest of royal qualities : but these were strange to the mediæval imagination, which had little understanding of a prince who was no ruler. Whether it was in accordance with some tremendous principle of action secretly conceived in the minds of the men who had by a series of skilful and cautious movements made the parliament of Venice into an assembly of patricians, and then neutralised that assembly by the still more startling power of the Council of Ten, that this work was accomplished, it is impossible to tell. It is difficult indeed to imagine that such a plan could be carried from generation to generation, though it might well be conceived, like Strafford's "Thorough," in the subtle intellect of some one far-seeing legislator. Probably the Venetian statesmen were but following the current of a tendency such as serves all the purpose of a foregone determination in many conjunctures of human affairs—a tendency which one after another leader caught or was caught by, and which swept towards its logical conclusion innumerable kindred minds with something of the tragic cumulative force of those agencies of nature against which man can do so little. It was however a natural balance to the defeat of the people that the doge also should be defeated and bound. And from the earliest days of recognised statesmanship this had been the subject of continual effort, taking first the form of a jealous terror of dynastic succession, and gradually growing, through oaths more binding and *promissioni* more detailed and stringent, until at length the doge found himself less than the master, a little more than the slave of those fluctuating yet consistent possessors of the actual power of the state, who had by degrees gathered the entire government into their hands.

Marino Faliero had been an active servant of Venice through a long life. He had filled almost all the great offices which were entrusted to her nobles. He had governed her distant colonies, accompanied her armies in that position of proveditore,

omnipotent civilian critic of all the movements of war, which so
much disgusted the generals of the republic. He had been
ambassador at the courts of both Emperor and Pope, and was
serving his country in that capacity at Avignon when the news
of his election reached him. It is thus evident that Faliero
was not a man used to the position of a lay figure, although at
seventy-six the dignified retirement of a throne, even when so
encircled with restrictions, would seem not inappropriate. That
he was of a haughty and hasty temper seems apparent. It
is told of him that after waiting long for a bishop to head
a procession at Treviso where he was podesta, he astonished
the tardy prelate by a box on the ear when he finally appeared, a punishment for keeping the authorities waiting which
the churchman would little expect.

Old age to a statesman, however, is in many cases an advantage rather than a defect, and Faliero was young in vigour and
character and still full of life and strength. He was married a
second time to presumably a beautiful wife much younger than
himself, though the chroniclers are not agreed even on the
subject of her name, whether she was a Gradenigo or a Contarini.
The well-known story of young Steno's insult to this lady and
to her old husband has found a place in all subsequent histories
—but there is no trace of it in the unpublished documents of the
state. The story goes, that Michel Steno, one of those young
and insubordinate gallants who are a danger to every aristocratic
state, having been turned out of the presence of the dogaressa
for some unseemly freedom of behaviour, wrote upon the chair
of the doge, in boyish petulance, an insulting taunt, such as
might well rouse a high-tempered old man to fury. According
to Sanudo, the young man on being brought before the Forty,
confessed that he had thus avenged himself in a fit of passion:
and regard having been had to his age and the "heat of love"
which had been the cause of his original misdemeanour (a
reason seldom taken into account by the tribunals of the state)
he was condemned to prison for two months, and afterwards to
be banished for a year from Venice. The doge took this light

punishment greatly amiss, considering it indeed as a further insult. Sabellico says not a word of Michel Steno, or of this definite cause of offence, and Romanin quotes the contemporary records to show that though *"Alcuni zovanelli, fioli de genti-luomini di Venetia"* are supposed to have affronted the doge, no such story finds a place in any of them. But the old man thus translated from active life and power, soon became bitterly sensible in his new position that he was *senza parentado*, with few relations, and flouted by the *giovinastri*, the dissolute young gentlemen who swaggered about the Broglio in their finery, strong in the support of fathers and uncles among the Forty or the Ten. That he found himself at the same time shelved in his new rank, powerless, and regarded as a nobody in the state where hitherto he had been a potent signior—mastered in every action by the Secret Tribunal, and presiding nominally in councils where his opinion was of little consequence—is evident. And a man so well acquainted and so long, with all the pro-ceedings of the state, who had been entering middle age in the days of Bajamonte, who had seen consummated the shutting out of the people, and since had watched through election after election a gradual tightening of the bonds round the feet of the doge, would naturally have many thoughts when he found himself the wearer of that restricted and diminished crown. He could not be unconscious of how the stream was going, nor unaware of that gradual sapping of privilege and decreasing of power which even in his own case had gone further than with his predecessor. Perhaps he had noted with an indignant mind the new limits of the *promissione*, a narrower charter than ever, when he was called upon to sign it. He had no mind, we may well believe, to retire thus from the administration of affairs. And when these *giovinastri*, other people's boys, the scum of the gay world, flung their unsavoury jests in the face of the old man, who had no son to come after him, the silly insults so lightly uttered, so little thought of, the natural scoff of youth at old age, stung him to the quick.

And it so happened that various complaints were at this

moment presented to the doge in which his own cause of
offence was repeated. A certain Barbaro, one of the reigning
class, asking something at the arsenal of an old sailor, an
admiral high in rank and in the love of the people, but not a
patrician, who was not of his opinion, struck the officer on the
cheek, and wounded him with a great ring he wore. A similar
incident occurred between a Dandolo and another sea captain,
Bertuccio Isarello ; and in both cases the injured men, old
comrades very probably of Faliero, men whom he had seen representing the republic on stormy seas or boarding the Genoese
galleys, carried their complaints to the doge. "Such evil beasts
should be bound, and when they cannot be bound they are
killed!" cried one of the irritated seamen. Such words were
not unknown to the Venetian echoes. Not long before, a
wealthy citizen, who in his youth had been of Bajamonte's
insurrection, had breathed a similar sentiment in the ears of
another rich plebeian, after both had expressed their indignation that the Consiglio was shut against them. The second
man in this case betrayed the first, and got the much-coveted
admission in consequence, he and his : while his friend made
that fatal journey to the Piazzetta between the columns, from
which no man ever came back.

Old Faliero's heart burned within him at his own injuries and
those of his old comrades. How he was induced to head the
conspiracy, and put his crown, his life, and honour on the cast,
there is no further information. His fierce temper, and the
fact that he had no powerful house behind him to help to
support his case, probably made him reckless. It was in the
April of 1355, only six months after his arrival in Venice as doge,
that the smouldering fire broke out. As happened always, two
of the conspirators were seized with a compunction on the eve
of the catastrophe and betrayed the plot—one with a merciful
motive to serve a patrician he loved, the other with perhaps
less noble intentions; and without a blow struck the conspiracy collapsed. There was no real heart in it, nothing to
give it consistence: the hot passion of a few men insulted,

the variable gaseous excitement of those wronged commoners who were not strong enough or strenuous enough to make the cause triumph under Bajamonte; and the ambition, if it was ambition, of one enraged and affronted old man, without an heir to follow him or anything that could make it worth his while to conquer.

Did Faliero ever expect to conquer, one wonders, when he embarked at seventy-seven on such an enterprise? And if he had, what good could it have done him save vengeance upon his enemies? An enterprise more wild was never undertaken. It was the passionate stand of despair against a force so overwhelming as to make mad the helpless yet not submissive victims. The doge, who no doubt in former days had felt it to be a mere affair of the populace, a thing with which a noble ambassador and proveditore had nothing to do, a struggle beneath his notice, found himself at last, with fury and amazement, to be a fellow-sufferer caught in the same toils. There seems no reason to believe that Faliero consciously staked the remnant of his life on the forlorn hope of overcoming that awful and pitiless power, with any real hope of establishing his own supremacy. His aspect is rather that of a man betrayed by passion, and wildly forgetful of all possibility in his fierce attempt to free himself and get the upper hand. One cannot but feel, in that passion of helpless age and unfriendedness, something of the terrible disappointment of one to whom the real situation of affairs had never been revealed before; who had come home triumphant to reign like the doges of old, and only after the ducal cap was on his head and the palace of the state had-become his home, found out that the doge, like the unconsidered plebeian, had been reduced to bondage, his judgment and experience put aside in favour of the deliberations of a secret tribunal, and the very boys, when they were nobles, at liberty to jeer at his declining years.

The lesser conspirators, all men of the humbler sort—Calendario, the architect, who was then at work upon the palace, a number of seamen, and other little-known persons—were hung,

not, like greater criminals, beheaded between the columns,
but strung up, a horrible fringe along the side of the palazzo,
beginning at the two red pillars now forming part of the loggia,
then apparently supporting the arches over a window from
which the doge was accustomed to behold the performances in
the Piazza. The fate of Faliero himself is too generally known
to demand description. Calmed by the tragic touch of fate, the
doge bore all the humiliations of his doom with dignity, and
was beheaded at the head of the stairs where he had sworn the
promissione on first assuming the office of doge. (Not, however, it need hardly be said, at the head of the Giants' Staircase,
which was not then in being.) What a contrast from that triumphant day when probably he felt that his reward had come to
him after the long and faithful service of years!

Death stills disappointment as well as rage : and Faliero is
said to have acknowledged the justice of his sentence. He had
never made any attempt to justify or defend himself, but frankly
and at once avowed his guilt, and made no attempt to escape
from its penalties.

His body was conveyed privately to the church of SS. Giovanni and Paolo, the great "Zanipolo" with which all visitors
to Venice are so familiar, and was buried in secrecy and silence
in the *atrio* of a little chapel behind the great church ; where·
no doubt for centuries the pavement was worn by many feet
with little thought of who lay below. Even from that refuge
in the course of these centuries his bones have been driven
forth ; but his name remains in that corner of the Hall of the
Great Council which everybody has seen or heard of, and
where, with a certain dramatic affectation, the painter-historians
have painted a black veil across the vacant place. "This is the
place of Marino Faliero, beheaded for his crimes," is all the
record left of the doge disgraced.

Was it a crime? The question is one which it is difficult to
discuss with any certainty. That Faliero desired to establish,
as so many had done in other cities, an independent despotism
in Venice, seems entirely unproved. It was the prevailing fear,

To face page 120.

NEAR THE SANTI APOSTOLI.

the one suggestion which alarmed everybody, and made sentiment unanimous. But one of the special points which are
recorded by the chroniclers as working in him to madness,
was that he was *senza parentado*, without any backing of rela-
tionship or allies—sonless, with no one to come after him.
How little likely, then, was an old man to embark on such a
desperate venture for self-aggrandisement merely! He had,
indeed, a nephew who was involved in his fate, but apparently
not so deeply as to expose him to the last penalty of the law.

ARMS OF FALIERO.

The incident altogether points more to a sudden outbreak of
the rage and disappointment of an old public servant coming
back from his weary labours for the state, in triumph and
satisfaction to what seemed the supreme reward: and finding
himself no more than a puppet in the hands of remorseless
masters, subject to the scoffs of the younger generation—
supreme in no sense of the word, and with his eyes opened
by his own suffering, perceiving for the first time what justice
there was in the oft-repeated protest of the people, and how

they and he alike were crushed under the iron heel of that
oligarchy to which the power of the people and that of the
prince was equally obnoxious. The chroniclers of his time were
so much at a loss to find any reason for such an attempt on the
part of a man *non abbiando alcun propinquo* that they agree in
attributing it to diabolical inspiration. It was more probably
that fury which springs from a sense of wrong, which the sight
of the wrongs of others raised to frenzy, and that intolerable
impatience of the impotent which is more rash in its hopeless-
ness than the greatest hardihood. He could not but die for it;
but there seems no more reason to characterise this impossible
attempt as deliberate treason than to give the same name to
many an alliance formed between prince and people in other
regions—the King and Commons of our early Stuarts for one
—against the intolerable exactions and cruelty of an aristocracy
too powerful to be faced by either alone.

FRANCESCO FOSCARI was a more innocent sufferer, and his
story is a most pathetic and moving tale. Seventy years had
elapsed since the dethronement and execution of Faliero, the
fifteenth century was in its first quarter, and all the complications and crimes of that wonderful period were in full operation
when the old Doge Tommaso Mocenigo on his death-bed
reviewed the probable competitors for his office, and warned the
republic specially against Foscari. The others were all men
da bene, but Foscari was proud and deceitful, grasping and
prodigal, and if they elected him they would have nothing but
wars. He was at the same time, gravely adds one of the
electors in the severe contest for his election, a man with a
large family, and a young wife who added another to the
number once a year; and therefore was likely to be grasping
and covetous so far as money was concerned.

Notwithstanding these evil prognostications the reign of
Foscari was a great one and full of important events. He fulfilled the prophecy of his predecessor in so far that war was
perpetual in his time, and the republic under him involved
itself in all the contentions which tore Italy asunder, and,

joining with the Florentines against the victorious Lord of Milan, Filippo Maria Visconti, and having the good fortune to secure Carmagnola for its general, became in its turn aggressive, and conquered town after town, losing, retaking, and in one or two instances securing permanently the sovereignty of great historic cities. The story of the great soldiers of fortune, which is to a large extent the story of the time, will be told in another chapter, and we need not attempt to discover what was the part of the doge in the tragedy of Carmagnola.

From the limitations of the prince's power which we have indicated, it will, however, be evident enough that neither in making war nor in the remorseless punishment of treachery, whether real or supposed, could the responsibility rest with the doge, who could scarcely be called even the most important member of the courts over which he presided. It is not until the end of his brilliant career that Francesco Foscari separates himself from the roll of his peers in that tragic distinction of great suffering which impresses an image upon the popular memory more deeply than the greatest deeds can do. Notwithstanding the reference quoted above to the alarming increase of his family, there was left within a few years, of his five sons, but one, Jacopo, who was no soldier nor statesman, but an elegant young man of his time, full of all the finery, both external and internal, of the Renaissance, a Greek scholar and collector of manuscripts, a dilettante and leader of the golden youth of Venice, who were no longer as in the stout days of the republic trained to encounter the clang of arms and the uncertainties of the sea. The battles of *Terra Firma* were conducted by mercenaries, under generals who made of war a costly and long-drawn-out game ; and the young nobles of the day haunted the Broglio under the arches of the palazzo, or schemed and chattered in the ante-chambers, or spread their gay plumes to the sun in festas and endless parties of pleasure. When Jacopo Foscari was married the splendour of his marriage feast was such that even the gravest of historians, amid all the crowding

incidents of the time, pauses to describe the wedding procession.
A bridge was thrown across the canal opposite the Foscari
Palace, over which passed a hundred splendid young cavaliers
on horseback, making such a show as must have held all Venice
breathless, caracolling cautiously over the temporary pathway not
adapted for such passengers, and making their way, one does
not quite understand how, clanging and sliding along the stony
ways, up and down the steps of the bridges to the Piazza, where
a tournament was held in honour of the occasion. They were all
in the finest of clothes, velvets and satins and cloth of gold,
with wonderful *calze*, one leg white and the other red, and
various braveries more fine than had ever been seen before.
The bride went in all her splendour, silver brocade and jewels
sparkling in the sun, in a more beautiful and graceful procession
of boats to San Marco. She was a Contarini, a neighbour from
one of the great palaces on the same side. The palace of
the Foscari as it now stands in the turn of the canal ascending
towards the Rialto, had just been rebuilt by Doge Francesco in
its present form, and was the centre of all these festivities,
the house of the bride being near, in the neighbourhood of
San Barnaba. No doubt the hearts of the Foscari and all their
retainers must have been uplifted by the glories of a festa
more splendid than had ever been given in Venice on such an
occasion.

But this brilliant sky soon clouded over. Only three years
after Jacopo fell under suspicion of having taken bribes to promote the interests of various suitors, and to have obtained
offices and pensions for them *per broglio:* that is to say in the
endless schemes, consultations, exchanges, and social conspiracies of the general meeting-place, the Broglio, a name
which stood for all the jobbing and backstairs influences which
flourish not less in republics than in despotisms. Against this
offence when found out the laws were very severe, and Jacopo was
sentenced to banishment to Naples, where he was to present
himself daily to the representative of the Republic there—a
curious kind of penalty according to our present ideas. Jacopo,

however, fled to Trieste, where, happily for himself, he fell ill, and after some months was allowed to change his place of exile to Treviso, and finally on a pathetic appeal from the doge was pardoned and allowed to return to Venice.

Three years, afterwards, however, a fatal event occurred, the assassination of one of the Council of Ten who had condemned Jacopo, Ermolao Donato, who was stabbed as he left the palace after one of its meetings. The evidence which connected Jacopo with this murder seems of the slightest. One of his servants, a certain Olivïeri, met on the road to Mestre almost immediately after one of the house of Gritti, and being asked "what news" replied by an account of this assassination, a fact which it was barely possible he could have heard of by common report before he left Venice. This was considered sufficient to justify the man's arrest and examination by torture, which made him confess everything, Sanudo tells us. Jacopo, too, was exposed to this method of extorting the truth, but "because of his bodily weakness, and of *some words of incantation employed by him*, the truth could not be obtained from his mouth, as he only murmured between his teeth certain unintelligible words when undergoing the torture of the rack." In these circumstances he had a mild sentence and was banished to the island of Candia. Here the exile, separated from all he loved and from all the refinements of the life he loved, was not long at rest. He took, according to one account, a singular and complicated method of further criminating himself and thus procuring his return to Venice, if even to fresh examination and torture—by writing a letter to the Duke of Milan, against whom the Republic had fought so long, asking his intercession with the Signoria, a letter which he never intended to reach the person to whom it was addressed, but only to induce the jealous Council to whom it was artfully betrayed, to recall him for further question : which at least in the middle of whatever sufferings would give his impatient heart a sight of those from whom he had been separated. That it should have been possible even to invent such a story of him conveys a kind of revelation of the foolish, hot-headed yet tender-hearted being, vainly struggling among natures so much too strong for him—which sheds the light of many another domestic tragedy upon this.

The matter would seem, however, to have been more serious, though Romanin's best investigations bring but very scanty proof of the graver accusation brought against the banished man: which was that of an attempt on Jacopo's part to gain his freedom by means of the Sultan and the Genoese, the enemies of the republic. The sole document given in proof of this is a letter written by the Council to the Governor of Candia, in which the account of the attempt, given in his own communication to them, is repeated in detail, of itself a somewhat doubtful proceeding. To say " You told us so and so," is seldom received as independent proof of alleged facts. There are, however, letters in cipher referred to, which may have given authentication to these accusations. Romanin, however, is so manifestly anxious to justify the authorities of Venice and to sweep away the romance which he declares to have gathered about these terrible incidents, that the reader can scarcely avoid a certain reaction of suspicion against the too great warmth of the defence. Some personal touches may no doubt have been added by adverse historians to heighten the picture. But it would be wiser for even the patriotic Venetian to admit that, at least three times in that cruel century—in the case of the Carrari murdered in their prison, in that of Carmagnola beguiled into the cell from which he came out only to die, and in that of the unfortunate Foscari—that remorseless and all-powerful Council of Ten, responsible to no man, without any safeguard even of publicity, who were too much feared to be resisted and all whose proceedings were wrapped in seeming impenetrability, stands beyond the possibility of defence. There are few historians who do not find it necessary to acknowledge at some points that the most perfect of human governments has failed: but this the Venetian enthusiast—and all Venetians are enthusiasts—is extremely reluctant to do.

Poor Jacopo, with his weak mind and his weak body, and the lightness of nature which both friends and foes admitted, perhaps rejoicing in the success of his stratagem, perhaps

troubled in the consciousness of guilt, but yet with a sort
of foolish happiness anyhow in coming home, and hoping,
as such sanguine people do, in some happy chance that might
make all right, was brought back in custody of one of the Ten,
a Loredano, the enemy of his house, who had been sent to fetch
him. It would seem that when the unfortunate prisoner was
brought before this awful tribunal, he confessed everything,
de plano, says Sanudo, *spontaneamente* adds Romanin, probably
forgetting the horrible torture-chamber next door, which Jacopo
had too good reason to remember, and to avoid which, this
easy-going and light-minded sinner, intent only upon seeing
once again those whom he loved, would be ready enough to say
whatever their illustrious worships pleased. The stern Loredano would have had him beheaded between the columns; but
even the Ten and their coadjutors were not severe enough for
that: and his sentence was only after all to be re-transported
to Candia and to spend a year in prison there—a sentence which
makes any real and dangerous conspiracy on his part very unlikely. When the sentence was given, his prayer—to make
which he had, as some say, thus risked his head—that he might
see his family, was laid before the court. The doge and all
other relations had been during the proceedings against him
excluded, according to the law, from the sittings of the Council:
so that the statement that he was sentenced by his father is
pure romance. His petition was granted, and father and
mother, wife and children were permitted to visit the unfortunate.
When the moment of farewell came, it was not in his prison,
but in the apartments of the doge, that the last meeting took
place. Poor Jacopo, always light minded, never able apparently
to persuade himself that all this misery was in earnest, and
could not be put aside by the exertions of somebody, made yet
one more appeal to his father in the midst of the sobs and kisses
of the unhappy family. "Father, I beseech you make them let me
go home," said he to the poor old doge, who knew too well how
little he could do to help or succour. "*Padre, vi prego pro-
curé per mi che ritorni a casa mia:*" as if he had been a school-
boy caught in some trifling offence, with that invincible ignor-

ance of the true meaning of things which the Catholic Church
with fine human instinct acknowledges as a ground of salvation.
But it is not an argument which tells with men. "Jacopo, go,
obey the will of the country, and try no more," said the doge
with the simplicity of despair. No romance is needed to enhance
the pathos of this scene.

When the exile had departed pity would seem to have
touched the hearts of various spectators, and by their exertions,
six months later his pardon was obtained. But too late. Before
the news could reach him the unhappy Jacopo had gone beyond
the reach of all human recall.

The aged doge, the father of this unfortunate young man, had
been the head of the Venetian state through one of the
most brilliant and splendid periods of its history. He had been
always at war, as his predecessor had prophesied : but his wars
had been often victorious for the republic, and had added
greatly, for the time at least, to her territories and dominion.
Whether these acquisitions were of any real advantage to Venice
is another question. They involved a constant expenditure of
money such as is ruinous to most states, but the glory and
the triumph were always delightful to her. Foscari had held
the place of a great prince in the estimation of the world,
and his life had been princely at home in every way that can
affect the imagination and stimulate the pride of a nation ;
he had received the greatest personages in Christendom,
the emperors of the east and of the west, and entertained
them royally to the gratification and pride of all Venice ; he
had beautified the city with new buildings and more commo-
dious streets ; he had made feasts and pageants more magnificent than ever had been seen before. But for the last dozen
years of this large, princely, and splendid life a cloud had come
over all its glory and prosperity. There are no lack of parallels
to give the interested spectator an understanding of what a son
such as Jacopo, so reckless, so light-minded, so incapable of any
serious conception of the meaning of life and its risks and
responsibilities, yet with so many claims in his facile, affectionate
nature, upon those who loved him—must have been to the

father, proud of his many gifts, bowed down by his follies, watching his erratic course with sickening terrors, angry, tender, indignant, pitiful, concealing his own disappointment and misery in order to protect and excuse and defend the son who was breaking his heart. The spectacle is always a sad one, but never rare : and the anguish of the father's silent watch, never knowing what folly might come next, acutely feeling the fault and every reproof of the fault, his pride humbled, his name disgraced, his every hope failing, but never the love that underlies all—is one of the deepest which can affect humanity. Foscari was over seventy when this ordeal began. Perhaps he had foreseen it even earlier : but when he made that most splendid of feasts at his son's bridal, and saw him established with his young wife in the magnificent new palace, with his books and his manuscripts, his chivalrous and courtly companions, his Greek, the crown of accomplishment and culture in his time, who could suppose that Jacopo would so soon be a fugitive and an exile ? The years between seventy and eighty are not those in which a man is most apt to brave the effects of prolonged anxiety and sorrow, and Foscari was eighty-four when, after the many vicissitudes of this melancholy story, he bade Jacopo go and bear his sentence and try no more to elude it. When the news came six months after that his only son was dead—dead far away and alone, among strangers, just when a troubled hope had arisen that he might come back, and be wiser another time—the courage of the old doge broke down. He could no longer give his mind to the affairs of the state, or sit, a venerable image of sorrow, patience, and self-control, at the head of the court which had persecuted and hunted to the death his foolish, beloved boy. One can imagine how the very touch of the red robe of Loredano brushing by would burn to the heart of the old man who could not avenge himself, but in whom even the stillness of his age and the habit of self-command could not take away the recollection that there stood the man who had voted death between the columns for poor Jacopo's follies! Who could wonder that he forbore

K

to attend their meetings, and that in the bitterness of his heart it seemed not worth while to go on appearing to fulfil an office, all the real power of which had been taken from his hands?

Thereupon there got up a low fierce murmur among the Ten ; not too rapidly developed. They waited a month or two, marking all his absences and slackness before gathering together to talk of matters *secretissime* concerning Messer lo Doge: they said to each other that it was a great inconvenience to the state to have a doge incapable of attending the councils and looking after the affairs of the republic: and that it was full time they should have a *zonta* or junta of nobles to help them to discuss the question. The law had been that in case of the absence (which often happened on state affairs) or illness of the doge, a vice-doge should be elected in his place ; but of this regulation no heed was taken, and the issue of their deliberations was that a deputation should be sent to the doge to desire him "*spontaneamente e libramente*" to resign his office. Foscari had more than once in his long tenure of office proposed to retire, but his attempt at resignation had never been received by the Council. It is one thing to make such an offer, and quite another to have it proposed from outside: and when the deputation suddenly appeared in the sorrowful chamber where the old man sat retired, he refused to give them any immediate answer. For one thing it was not their business to make such a demand, the law requiring that the Consiglio Maggiore should be consulted, and should at least agree in, if not originate, so important an act. But the Ten had perhaps gone too far to draw back, and when the deputation returned without a definite reply, the ceremonial of waiting for the spontaneous and free dimission of the disgraced prince was thrown aside, and an intimation was made to him that his resignation was a matter of necessity, and that if within eight days he had not left the palace his property would be confiscated. When this arbitrary message was conveyed to him the old man attempted no further resistance. His ducal ring was drawn from his finger and broken to pieces in the presence of the deputation who had brought him these final orders, headed by his enemy Loredano—not, says the apologetic historian, because he was Foscari's enemy, which was a cruelty the noble Ten were incapable of, but because he was, after Foscari himself, the finest orator of the republic and most likely to put things in a good light! The ducal cap with its circlet of gold, the historical *Corno*, was taken from his tremulous old head, and a promise extracted that he would at once leave the palace. The following incident is too touching not to be given in the words quoted by Romanin from the unpublished chronicles of Delfino. As the procession of deputies filed away, the discrowned doge saw one of them, Jacopo Memmo, one of the heads of the Forty, look at him with sympathetic and compassionate eyes. The old man's heart, no doubt, was full, and a longing for human fellowship must have been in him still. He called the man who gave him that friendly look, and took him by the hand.

"[1] Whose son art thou?" (It is the Venetian vernacular that is used, not ceremonious Italian, "Di chi es tu fio.") I answered, "I am the son of Marin Memmo." To which the doge—"He is my dear friend; tell him from me that it would be sweet to me if he would come and pay me a visit, and go with me in my bark for a little pleasure. We might go and visit the monasteries."

It is difficult to read this simple narrative without a sympathetic tear. Despoiled of the vestments of his office which he had worn for thirty-four years, amid all the magnificence of one of the richest and most splendid states in the world, the old man pauses with a tremulous smile more sad than weeping, to make his last gracious invitation, the habit of his past sovereignty exercised once more, at once with sorrowful humour, and that wistful turning to old friends which so often comes with trouble. If it had ever been accomplished, what a touching

---

[1] "Di chi es tu fio? Rispose, Io son figlio di Messere Marin Memmo. Al chi il doxe, L'e mio caro compagno; dilli da mia parte che averó caro ch'el mi vegna a visitar, accio el vegna con mi in barca a solazzo : andaremo a visitare i monastieri."

party of pleasure! the two old men in their *barca* going forth *a solazzo*, making their way across the shining waters to San Giorgio, perhaps as far as San Servolo if the weather were fine : for it was October, and no time to be lost before the winter set in for the two old companions, eighty and more.   But that voyage of pleasure never was made.

The same day the doge left the palace where he had spent so many years of glory and so many of sorrow, accompanied by his old brother Marco, and followed sadly by his household and relations.   " *Serenissimo*," said Marco Foscari, " it is better to go to the boat by the other stair, which is covered."   But the old doge held on in the direction he had first taken.   " I will go down by the same stair which I came up when I was made doge," he said, much as Faliero had done.   And then the mournful procession rowed away along the front of the palace, past all the boats that lay round the dogana, between the lines of great houses on either side of the canal, to the new shining palace scarcely faded from its first splendour where Jacopo sixteen years before had taken his bride.   The house that has seen so many generations since and vicissitudes of life still stands there at its corner, the water sweeping round two sides of it, and the old gateway, *merlato*, in its ancient bravery, on the smaller canal behind.

This was on the 24th October, 1357.   The new doge was elected on the 31st, and on the 1st of November Francesco Foscari died.   The common story goes that the sound of the bell which announced the entry of his successor was the old man's final death blow, but it is unnecessary to add this somewhat coarse touch of popular effect to the pathetic story.   The few days which elapsed between the two events were not too much for the operation of dying, which is seldom accomplished in a moment. When the new prince and his court assembled in San Marco on All Saints' Day to mass, Andrea Donato, the old doge's son-in-law, came in and announced, no doubt with a certain solemn satisfaction and consciousness of putting these conspirators for ever in the wrong, the death of Foscari.   The councillors who had pursued him to his end looked at each other mute, with eyes, let us hope, full of remorse and shame.

And he had a magnificent funeral, which is always so easy to bestow. The *Corno* was taken again from the head of the new doge to be put on the dead brows of the old, and he lay in state in the hall from which he had been expelled a week before, and was carried, with every magnificence the republic could give, to the noble church of the Frari, with tapers burning all the way, and every particular of solemn pomp that custom authorised. There he lies under a weight of sculptured marble, his sufferings all over for five hundred years and more; but never the story of his greatness, his wrongs and sorrows, which last gave him such claims upon the recollection of mankind as no magnificence nor triumph can bestow.

ARMS OF FOSCARI.

DEPARTURE OF MARCO POLO : FROM AN ILLUMINATED
MANUSCRIPT IN THE BODLEIAN.

PART II.- BY SEA AND BY LAND.

CHAPTER I.

THE TRAVELLERS : NICCOLO, MATTEO, AND MARCO POLO.

IN the middle of the thirteenth century, two brothers of the Venetian family of Polo, established for a long time in the parish of San Giovanni Grisostomo, carrying on their business in the midst of all the tumults of the times as if there had been nothing but steady and peaceful commerce in the world, were at the head of a mercantile house at Constantinople, probably the branch establishment of some great counting-house at Venice. These seem prosaic terms to use in a story so full of adventure and romance ; yet no doubt they represent, as adequately as the changed aspect of mercantile life allows, the condition of affairs

under which Niccolo and Matteo Polo exercised their vocation
in the great Eastern capital of the world. Many Venetian
merchants had established their warehouses and pursued the
operations of trade in Constantinople in the security which
the repeated treaties and covenants frequently referred to in
previous chapters had gained for them, and which, under whatsoever risks of convulsion and rebellion, they had held since the
days when first a Venetian *Bailo*—an officer more powerful than
a consul, with something like the rights and privileges of a
governor—was settled in Constantinople. But the ordinary risks
were much increased at the time when the Latin dynasty was
drawing near its last moments, and Paleologus was thundering
at the gates. The Venetians were on the side of the falling
race: their constant rivals the Genoese had taken that of the
rising: and no doubt the position was irksome as well as
dangerous to those who had been the favoured nation, and
once the conquerors and all potent rulers of the great capital
of the East. Many of the bolder spirits would no doubt be
urged to take an active part in the struggle which was going
on: but its effect upon Niccolo and Matteo Polo was different.
The unsatisfactory state of affairs prompted them to carry their
merchandise further East, where they had, it is supposed, already
the standing-ground of a small establishment at Soldachia, on
the Crimean peninsula. Perhaps, however, it is going too far
to suppose that the commotions in Constantinople, and not some
previously arranged expedition with milder motives, determined
the period of their departure. At all events the dates coincide.

The two brothers set out in 1260, when the conflict was at
its height, and all the horrors of siege and sack were near at
hand. They left behind them, it would appear, an elder
brother still at the head of the family counting-house at
Constantinople—and taking with them an easily carried stock
of jewels, went forth upon the unknown but largely inhabited
world of Central Asia, full, as they were aware, of wonders of
primitive manufacture, carpets and rich stuffs, ivory and spices,
furs and leather. The vast dim empires of the East, where

struggles and conquests had been going on, more tremendous
than all the wars of Europe, though under the veil of distance
and barbarism uncomprehended by the civilised world, had
been vaguely revealed by the messengers of Pope Innocent IV.,
and had helped the Crusaders at various points against their
enemies the Saracens.   But neither they nor their countries
were otherwise known when these two merchants set out.   They
plunged into the unknown from Soldachia, crossing the Sea
of Azof, or travelling along its eastern shores and working
their way slowly onward, sometimes lingering in the tents
of a great chief, sometimes arrested by a bloody war
which closed all passage, made their way at last to Bok-
hara, where all further progress seemed at an   end, and
where they remained three years, unable either to advance
or to go back.   Here, however, they had. the good fortune
to be picked up by certain envoys on their way to the court
of "the Great Khan, the lord of all the Tartars in the
world"—sent by the victorious prince who had become master
of the Levant, to that distant and mysterious potentate.
These ambassadors, astonished to see the Frankish travellers
so far out of the usual track, invited the brothers to join
them, assuring them that the Great Khan had never seen any
Latins, and would give them an eager welcome.   With this
escort the two Venetians travelled far into the depths of the
unknown land until they reached the city of Kublai Khan,
that great prince shrouded in distance and mystery, whose
name has been appropriated by poets and dreamers: but who
takes immediate form and shape in the brief and abrupt
narrative of his visitors, as a most courteous and gentle human
being, full of endless curiosity and interest in all the wonders
which these sons of Western civilisation could tell him.   The
Great Khan received them with the most royal courtesy, and
questioned them closely about their laws and rulers, and still
more about their religion, which seems to have excited the
imagination and pleased the judgment of this calmly impartial
inquirer. No doubt the manners and demeanour of the

Venetians, devout Catholics in all the fervour habitual to their age and city, recommended their faith. So much interested indeed was the Tartar prince that he determined to seek for himself and his people more authoritative teaching, and to send his merchant visitors back with a petition to this purpose addressed to the pope. No more important mission was ever entrusted to any ambassadors. They were commissioned to ask from the head of the Church a hundred missionaries to convert the Tartar multitudes to Christianity. These were to be wise persons acquainted with "the Seven Arts," well qualified to discuss and convince all men by force of reason that the idols whom they worshipped in their houses were things of the devil, and that the Christian law was better than those, all evil and false, which they followed. And above all, adds the simple narrative, "he charged them to bring back with them some of the oil from the lamp which burns before the sepulchre of Christ at Jerusalem."

The letters which were to be the credentials of this embassy were drawn out "in the Turkish language," in all likelihood by the Venetians themselves: and a Tartar chief, "one of his barons," was commissioned by the Great Khan to accompany them: he, however, soon shrank from the fatigues and perils of the journey. The Poli set out carrying with them a royal warrant, inscribed on a tablet of gold, commanding all men wherever they passed to serve and help them on their way. Notwithstanding this, it took them three years of travel, painful and complicated, before they reached Acre on their homeward—or rather Rome-ward—journey. There they heard, to their consternation, that the pope was dead. This was terrible news for the ambassadors, who doubtless felt the full importance of their mission. In their trouble they appealed to the highest ecclesiastic near, the pontifical legate in Egypt, who heard their story with great interest, but pointed out to them that the only thing they could do was to wait till a new pope was elected. This suggestion seems to have satisfied their judgment, although the conflict over that election must have tried any but a very robust faith. The Poli then concluded—an idea which does not seem to have struck them before—that having thus certain time vacant on their hands, they might as well employ it by going to see their family in Venice. They had quitted their home apparently some fifteen years before, Niccolo having left his wife there, who gave birth to a son after his departure and subsequently died; Colonel Yule suggests that the wife was dead before Niccolo left Venice, which would have given a certain explanation of the slight interest he showed in revisiting his native city. But at all events the brothers went home : and Niccolo found his child, whether born in his absence or left behind an infant, grown into a sprightly and interesting boy, no doubt a delightful discovery. They had abundant time to renew their acquaintance with all their ancient friends and associations, for months went by and still no pope was elected, nor does there seem to have been any ecclesiastical authority to whom they could deliver their letters. Probably, in that time, any enthusiasm the two traders may have had for the great work of converting those wild and wonderful regions of the East had died away. Indeed, the project does not seem to have moved any one save to a passing wonder; and all ecclesiastical enterprises were apparently suspended while conclave after conclave assembled and no result was attained.

At length the brothers began to tire of inaction, and to remember that through all those years of silence Kublai Khan was looking for them, wondering perhaps what delayed their coming, perhaps believing that their return home had driven all their promises from their memory, and that they had forgotten him and his evangelical desires. Stirred by this thought, they determined at last to return to their prince, and setting out, accompanied by young Marco, Niccolo's son, they went to Acre, where they betook themselves once more to the pious legate, Tebaldo di Piacenza, whom they had consulted on their arrival. They first asked his leave to go to Jerusalem to fetch the oil from the holy lamp, the only one of the Great Khan's commissions which it seemed possible to carry out; and then, with some fear apparently that their word might not be believed, asked him to give them letters, certifying that they had done their best to fulfil their errand, and had failed only in consequence of the strange fact that there was no pope to whom their letters could be delivered. Provided with these testimonials they started on their long journey, but had only got as far as Lagos, on the coast of the then kingdom of Armenia, which was their point of entrance upon the wild and immense plains which they had to traverse, when the news followed them that the pope was at last elected, and was no other than their friend, the legate Tebaldo. A messenger, requesting their return to Acre, soon followed, and the brothers and young Marco returned with new hopes of a successful issue to their mission. But the new pope, Gregory X., though he received them with honour and great friendship, had not apparently a hundred wise men to give them, nor the means of sending out a little Christian army to the conquest of heathenism. All that he could do for them was to send with them two brothers of the order of S. Dominic, *frati predicatori*, to do what they could towards that vast work. But when the Dominicans heard that war had broken out in Armenia, and that they had to encounter not only a fatiguing journey but all the perils of perpetual fighting along their route, they went no further than that port of Lagos beyond which lay the unknown. The letters of privilege, indulgences, no doubt, and grants of papal favour to be distributed among the Tartar multitude, they transferred hastily to the sturdy merchants—who were used to fighting as to most other dangerous things, and had no fear—and ·ignominiously took their flight back to the accustomed and known.

It is extraordinary, looking back upon it, to think of the easy relinquishment of such a wonderful chance as this would seem to have been. Pope and priests were all occupied with their own affairs. It was of more importance in their eyes to quell the Ghibellines than to convert and civilise the Tartars. And perhaps, considering that even an infallible pope is but a

man, this was less wonderful than it appears: for Kublai Khan
was a long way off, and very dim and undiscernible in his
unknown steppes and strange primeval cities—whereas the
emperor and his supporters were close at hand and very
sensible thorns in consecrated flesh.   It seems somewhat
extraordinary however that no young monk or eager preacher
caught fire at the suggestion of such an undertaking.   Some
fifty years before Fra Francisco from Assisi, leaving his new
order and all its cares, insisted upon being sent to the Soldan
to see whether he could not forestall the Crusaders and make
all the world one, by converting that noble infidel—which
seemed to him the straightforward and simple thing to do.   If
Francis had but been there with his poor brothers, vowed to
every humiliation, the lovers of poverty, what a mission for
them!—a crusade of the finest kind, with every augury of
success, though all the horrors of the steppes, wild winters and
blazing summers, and swollen streams, and fighting tribes lay in
their way.   And had the hundred wise men ever been gathered
together, what a pilgrimage for minstrel to celebrate and story-
teller to write, a new expedition of the saints, a holier Israel
in the desert!   But nothing of the kind came about.   The two
papal envoys, who had been the first to throw light upon those
kingdoms beyond the desert, had no successors in the later half
of the century.   And with only young Marco added to their
band, the merchant brothers returned, perhaps a little ashamed
of their Christian rulers, perhaps chiefly interested about the
reception they would meet with, and whether the great Kublai
would still remember his luckless ambassadors.

The journey back occupied once more three years and a half.
It gives us a strange glimpse into the long intervals of silence
habitual to primitive life to find that these messengers, without
means of communicating any information of their movements
to their royal patron, were more than eight years altogether
absent on the mission from which they returned with so little
success.   In our own days their very existence would probably
have been forgotten in such a long lapse of interest.   Let us

hope that the holy oil from the sepulchre, the only thing Christianity could send to the inquiring heathen, was safely kept, in
some precious bottle of earliest glass from Murano, or polished
stone less brittle than glass, through all the dangers of the
journey.

Thus the Poli disappeared again into the unknown for many
additional years. Letters were not rife anywhere in those days,
and for them, lost out of the range of civilisation, though in the
midst of another full and busy world, with another civilisation, art,
and philosophy of its own, there was no possibility of any communication with Venice or distant friends. It is evident that they
sat very loose to Venice, having perhaps less personal acquaintance with the city than most of her merchant adventurers.
Niccolo and Matteo must have gone to Constantinople while
still young—and Marco was but fifteen when he left the lagoons.
They had apparently no ties of family tenderness to call them
back, and custom and familiarity had made the strange world
around, and the half savage tribes, and the primitive court with
its barbaric magnificence, pleasant and interesting to them. It
was nearly a quarter of a century before they appeared out of
the unknown again.

By that time the Casa Polo in San Grisostomo had ceased
to think of its absent members. In all likelihood they had no
very near relations left. Father and mother would be dead long
ago : the elder brother lived and died in Constantinople : and
there was no one who looked with any warm expectation for the
arrival of the strangers. When there suddenly appeared at the
gate of the great family house full of cousins and kinsmen one
evening in the year 1295, about twenty-four years after their
departure, three wild and travel-worn figures, in coats of coarse
homespun like those worn by the Tartars, the sheep-skin collars
mingling with the long locks and beards of the wearers, their
complexions dark with exposure, their half-forgotten mother
tongue a little uncertain on their lips—who could believe that
these were Venetian gentlemen, members of an important family
in the city which had forgotten them ? The three unknown

personages arrived suddenly, without any warning, at their ancestral home. One can imagine the commotion in the court-yard, the curious gazers who would come out to the door, the heads that would gather at every window, when it became known through the house that these wild strangers claimed to

DOORWAY, MARCO POLO'S HOUSE.

belong to it, to be in some degree its masters, the long disappeared kinsmen whose portion perhaps by this time had fallen into hands very unwilling to let it go. The doorway which still exists in the Corte délla Sabbionera, in the depths of the cool quadrangle, with its arch of Byzantine work, and the cross above

which every visitor in Venice may still see when he will, behind
San Grisostomo, is, as tradition declares, the very door at
which the travellers knocked and parleyed. The house was
then—according to the most authentic account we have, that of
Ramusio—*un bellissimo e molto alto palazzo*. Absolute authenti-
city it is perhaps impossible to claim for the story. But it was
told to Ramusio, who flourished in the fifteenth century, by an
old man, a distinguished citizen who, and whose race, had been
established for generations in the same parish in the immediate
vicinity of the Casa Polo, and who had heard it from his predecessors there, a very trustworthy source of information. The
family was evidently well off and important, and, in all probability, noble. "In those days," says Colonel Yule, making with
all his learning a mistake for once, "the demarcation between
patrician and non-patrician at Venice, where all classes shared
in commerce, all were (generally speaking) of one race, and
where there were neither castles, domains, nor trains of horsemen, formed no very wide gulf." This is an astounding statement to make in the age of Bajamonte's great conspiracy : but
as Marco Polo is always spoken of as noble, no doubt his family
belonged to the privileged class.

The heads of the house gathered to the door to question the
strange applicants, "for, seeing them so transfigured in countenance and disordered in dress, they could not believe that
these were those of the Ca' Polo who had been believed dead
for so many and so many years." The strangers had great trouble
even to make it understood who they claimed to be. "But at
last these three gentlemen conceived the plan of making a
bargain that in a certain time they should so act as to recover
their identity and the recognition of their relatives, and honour
from all the city." The expedient they adopted again reads
like a scene out of the *Arabian Nights*. They invited all their
relatives to a great banquet which was prepared with much
magnificence "in the same house," says the story-teller : so
that it is evident they must already have gained a certain
credence from their own nearest relations. When the hour

fixed for the banquet came, the following extraordinary scene occurred :—

"The three came out of their chamber dressed in long robes of crimson satin, according to the fashion of the time, which touched the ground. And when water had been offered for their hands, they placed their guests at table, and then taking off their satin robes put on rich damask of the same colour, ordering in the meanwhile that the first should be divided among the servants. Then after eating something (no doubt a first course), they rose from table and again changed their dress, putting on crimson velvet, and giving as before the damask robes to the servants, and at the end of the repast they did the same with the velvet, putting on garments of ordinary cloth such as their guests wore. The persons invited were struck dumb with astonishment at these proceedings. And when the servants had left the hall, Messer Marco, the youngest, rising from the table, went into his chamber and brought out the three coarse cloth surcoats in which they had come home. And immediately the three began with sharp knives to cut open the seams, and tear off the lining, upon which there poured forth a great quantity of precious stones, rubies, sapphires, carbuncles, diamonds, and emeralds, which had been sewed into each coat with great care, so that nobody could have suspected that anything was there. For on parting with the Great Khan they had changed all the wealth he bestowed upon them into precious stones, knowing certainly that if they had done otherwise they never could by so long and difficult a road have brought their property home in safety. The exhibition of such an extraordinary and infinite treasure of jewels and precious stones, which covered the table, once more filled all present with such astonishment that they were dumb and almost beside themselves with surprise : and they at once recognised these honoured and venerated gentlemen of the Ca' Polo, whom at first they had doubted, and received them with the greatest honour and reverence. And when the story was spread abroad in Venice, the entire city, both nobles and people, rushed to the house to embrace them, and to make every demonstration of loving kindness and respect that could be imagined. And Messer Matteo, who was the eldest, was created one of the most honoured magistrates of the city, and all the youth of Venice resorted to the house to visit Messer Marco, who was most humane and gracious, and to put questions to him about Cathay and the Great Khan, to which he made answer with so much benignity and courtesy that they all remained his debtors. And because in the continued repetition of his story of the grandeur of the Great Khan he stated the revenues of that prince to be from ten to fifteen millions in gold, and counted all the other wealth of the country always in millions, the surname was given him of Marco Millione, which may be seen noted in the public books of the republic. And the courtyard of his house from that time to this has been vulgarly called the Corte Millione."

It is scarcely possible to imagine that the narrator of the above wonderful story was not inspired by the keenest humorous view of human nature and perception of the character of his countrymen when he so gravely describes the effectual arguments which lay in the *gioie preciosissime*, the diamonds and sapphires which his travellers had sewed up in their old clothes, · and which according to all the laws of logic were exactly fitted to procure their recognition "as honoured and venerated gentlemen of the Ca' Polo." The scene is of a kind which has always found great acceptance in primitive romance : the cutting asunder of the laden garments, the ripping up of their seams, the drawing forth of one precious little parcel after another amid the wonder and exclamations of the gazing spectators, are all familiar incidents in traditionary story. But in the present case this was a quite reasonable and natural manner of conveying the accumulations of a long period through all the perils of a three years' journey from far Cathay : and there is nothing at all unlikely in the miraculous story, which no doubt would make a great impression upon the crowded surrounding population, and linger, an oft-repeated tale, in the alleys about San Giovanni Grisostomo and along the Rio, where everybody knew the discreet and sensible family which had the wit to recognise and fall upon the necks of their kinsmen, as soon as they knew how rich they were. The other results that ensued—the rush of golden youth to see and visit Marco, who, though no longer young, was the young man of the party, and their questions, and the jeer of the new mocking title Marco Millione—follow the romance with natural human incredulity and satire and laughter. It is true, and proved by at least one public document, that the gibe grew into serious use, and that even the gravest citizens forgot after a time that Marco of the Millions was not the traveller's natural and sober name. There was at least one other house of the Poli in Venice, and perhaps there were other Marcos from whom it was well to distinguish him of San Grisostomo.

L

It would seem clear enough however, from this, that these travellers' tales met with the fate that so often attends the marvellous narratives of an explorer. Marco's Great Khan, far away in the distance as of another world, the barbarian purple and gold of Kublai's court, the great cities out of all mortal ken, as the young men in their mirth supposed, the incredible wonders that peopled that remote and teeming darkness, which the primitive imagination could not believe in as forming part of its own narrow little universe—must. have kept one generation at least in amusement. No doubt the sunbrowned traveller had all that desire to instruct and surprise his hearers which came natural to one who knew so much more than they, and was capable of being endlessly drawn out by any group of young idlers who might seek his company. They would thread their way through the labyrinth of narrow passages with all their mediæval bravery, flashing along in parti-coloured hose and gold-embroidered doublets on their way from the Broglio to get a laugh out of Messer Marco —who was always so ready to commit himself to some new prodigy.

But after a while the laugh died out in the grave troubles that assailed the Republic. The most dreadful war that had ever arisen between Venice and Genoa had raged for some time, through various vicissitudes, when the city at last determined to send out such an expedition as should at once overwhelm all rivalry. This undertaking stirred every energy among the population, and both men and money poured in for the service of the commonwealth. There may not be any authentic proof of Colonel Yule's suggestion, that Marco Polo fitted out, or partially fitted out, one of the boats, and mounted his own flag at the masthead, when it went into action. But the family were assessed at the value of one or more galleys, and he was certainly a volunteer in the fleet, a defender of his country in the terrible warfare which was draining all her resources. The battle of Curzola took place in September, 1298, and it ended in a complete and disastrous defeat for the

Venetians. Of the ninety-seven galleys which sailed so bravely out of Venice, only seventeen miserable wrecks found refuge in the shelter of the lagoons, and the admiral and the greater part of the survivors, men shamed and miserable, were carried prisoners to Genoa with every demonstration of joy and triumph. The admiral, as has already been said, was chained to his own mast in barbarous exultation, but managed to escape from the triumph of his enemies by dashing his head against the timber, and dying thus before they reached port.

Marco Polo was among the rank and file who do not permit themselves such luxuries. Among all the wonderful things he had seen, he could never have seen a sight at once so beautiful and so terrible as the great semicircle of the Bay of Genoa, crowded with the exultant people, gay with every kind of decoration, and resounding with applause and excitement when the victorious galleys with their wretched freight sailed in. No doubt in the Tartar wastes he had longed many a time for intercourse with his fellows, or even to see the face of some compatriot or Christian amid all the dusky faces and barbaric customs of the countries he had described. But now what a revelation to him must have been the wild passion and savage delight of those near neighbours with but the width of a European peninsula between them, and so much hatred, rancour, and fierce antagonism! Probably however Marco, having been born to hate the Genoese, was occupied by none of these sentimental reflections; and knowing how he himself and all his countrymen would have cheered and shouted had Doria been the victim instead of Dandolo, took his dungeon and chains, and the intoxication of triumph with which he and his fellow prisoners were received, as matters of course.

He lay for about a year, as would appear, in this Genoese prison; and here, probably for the first time, his endless tales of the wonders he had seen and known first fulfilled the blessed office of story-telling, and became to the crowded prison a fountain of refreshment and new life. To all these unfortunate groups, wounded, sick, especially sick for home, humiliated and forlorn,

with scarcely anything wanting to complete the round of misery,
what a solace in the tedium of the dreary days, what a help to
get through the lingering time, and forget their troubles for a
moment, must have been this companion, burned to a deeper
brown than even Venetian suns and seas could give, whose
memory was inexhaustible, who day by day had another tale to
tell, who set before them new scenes, new people, a great, noble
open-hearted monarch, and all the quaint habits and modes of
living, not of one, but of a hundred tribes and nations, all
different, endless, original! All the poor expedients to make
the time pass, such games as they might have, such exercises
as were possible, even the quarrels which must have risen to
diversify the flat and tedious hours, could bear no comparison
with this fresh source of entertainment, the continued story
carried on from day to day, to which the cramped and weary
prisoner might look forward as he stretched his limbs and
opened his eyes to a new unwelcome morning. If any one
among these prisoners remembered then the satire of the
golden youth, the laughing nickname of the Millione, he had
learned by that time what a public benefactor a man is who
has something to tell: and the traveller who perhaps had
never found out how he had been laughed at had thus the
noblest revenge.

Among all these wounded, miserable Venetians, however, there
was one whose presence there was of more immediate importance to the world—a certain Pisan, an older inhabitant than
they of these prisons, a penniless derelict, forgotten perhaps
of his own city, with nobody to buy him out—Rusticiano, a
poor poetaster, a rusty brother of the pen, who had written
romances in his day, and learned a little of the craft of
authorship. What a wonderful treasure was this fountain of
strange story for a poor mediæval literary man to find in
his dungeon! The scribbler seems to have seized at once by
instinct upon the man who for once in his life could furnish
him with something worth telling. Rusticiano saw his opportunity in a moment with an exultation which he could not keep

to himself. It was not in his professional nature to refrain from a great fanfare and flourish, calling upon heaven and earth to listen. "*Signori imperatori e re, duchi e marchesi, conti, cavalieri, principi, baroni,*" he cries out, as he did in his romances. "Oh, emperors and kings, oh, dukes, princes, marquises, barons and cavaliers, and all who delight in knowing the different races of the world, and the variety of countries, take this book and read it!" This was the proper way, according to all his rules, to present himself to the public. He makes his bow to them like a showman in front of his menagerie. He knows, too, the language in which to catch the ear of all these fine people, so that every noble may desire to have a copy of this manuscript to cheer his household in the lingering winter, or amuse the poor women at their embroidery while the men are at the wars. For, according to all evidence, what the prisoner of Pisa took down from the lips of the Venetian in the dungeons of Genoa was written by him in curious antique French, corrupted a little by Italian idioms, the most universal of all the languages of the Western world. Nothing can be more unlike than those flourishes of Rusticiano by way of preface, and the simple strain of the unvarnished tale when Messer Marco himself begins to speak. And the circumstance of these two Italians employing another living language in which to tell their wonderful story is so curious that many other theories have been set forth on the subject, though none which are accepted by the best critics as worthy of belief. One of the earliest of these, Ramusio, pronounces strongly in favour of a Latin version. Marco had told his stories over and over again, this historian says, with such effect that "seeing the great desire that everybody had to hear about Cathay and the Great Khan, and being compelled to begin again every day, he was advised that it would be well to commit it to writing"—which was done by the dignified medium of a Genoese gentleman, who took the trouble to procure from Venice all the notes which the three travellers had made of their journeys: and then compiled in

Latin, according to the custom of the learned, a continuous narrative. But the narrative itself and everything that can be discovered about it are wholly opposed to this theory. There is not the slightest appearance of notes worked into a permanent record. The story has evidently been taken down from the lips of a somewhat discursive speaker, with all the breath and air in it of oral discourse. "This is enough upon that matter; now I will tell you of something else." "Now let us leave the nation of Mosul and I will tell you about the great city of Baldoc." So the tale goes on, with interruptions, with natural goings back—"But first I must tell you——" "Now we will go on with the other." While we read we seem to sit, one of the eager circle, listening to the story of these wonderful unknown places, our interest quickened here and there by a legend—some illustration of the prolonged conflict between heathen and Christian, or the story of some prodigy accomplished: now that of a grain of mustard-seed which the Christians were defied to make into a tree, now a curious Eastern version of the story of the Three Magi. These episodes have all the characteristics of the ordinary legend; but the plain and simple story of what Messer Marco saw and heard, and the ways of the unknown populations among whom he spent his youth, are like nothing but what they are—a narrative of facts, with no attempt to throw any fictitious interest or charm about them. No doubt the prisoners liked the legends best, and the circle would draw closer, and the looks become more eager, when the story ran of Prester John and Genghis Khan, of the Old Man of the Mountain, or of how the Calif tested the faith of the Christians. When all this began to be committed to writing, when Rusticiano drew his inkhorn, and pondered his French, with a splendour of learning and wisdom which no doubt appeared miraculous to the spectators, and the easy narrative flowed on a sentence at a time, with half-a-dozen eager critics ready no doubt to remind the *raconteur* if he varied a word of the often told tale, what an interest for that melancholy crowd! How they must have peered over each other's shoulders to see the miraculous manuscript, with a feeling of pleased complacency as of a wonderful thing in which they themselves had a haud! No doubt it was cold in Genoa in those sunless dungeons the weary winter through; but so long as Messer Marco went on with his stories and he of Pisa wrote, with his professional artifices, and his sheet of vellum on his knee, what endless entertainment to beguile dull care away!

The captivity lasted not more than a year, and our traveller returned home, to where the jest still lingered about the man with the millions, and no one mentioned him without a smile. He would not seem to have disturbed himself about this— indeed, after that one appearance as a fighting man, with its painful consequences, he would seem to have retired to his home as a peaceful citizen, and awoke no echoes any more. He might perhaps be discouraged by the reception his tale had met with, even though there is no evidence of it; or perhaps that tacit assent to a foolish and wrong popular verdict, which the instructors of mankind so often drop into, with a certain indulgent contempt as of a thing not worth their while to contend against, was in his mind who knew so much better than his critics. At all events it is evident that he did nothing more to bring himself to the notice of the world. It was in 1299 that he returned to Venice—on the eve of all those great disturbances concerning the *serrata* of the Council, and of the insurrections which shook the Republic to its foundation. But in all this Marco of the Millions makes no appearance. He who had seen so much, and to whom the great Kublai was the finest of imperial images, most likely looked on with an impartiality beyond the reach of most Venetians at the internal strife, knowing that revolutions come and go, while the course of human life runs on much the same. And besides, Marco was noble, and lost no privilege, probably indeed sympathised with the effort to keep the *canaille* down.

He married in these peaceful years, in the obscurity of a quiet life, and had three daughters only—Faustina, Bellela, and Moretta : no son to keep up the tradition of the adventurous race : a thing which happens so often when a family has come to its climax, and can do no more. He seems to have kept up in some degree his commercial character, since there is a record of a law-suit for the recovery of some money of which he had been defrauded by an agent. But only once does he appear in the character of an author responsible for his own story. Attached to two of the earliest manuscript copies of his great book, one preserved in Paris and the other in Berne, are MS. notes, apparently quite authentic, recording the circumstances under which he presented a copy of the work to a noble French cavalier who passed through Venice, while in the service of Charles of Valois in the year 1307. The note is as follows :—

"This is the book of which my Lord Thiebault, Knight and Lord of Cepoy (whom may God assoil !), requested a copy from Sire Marco Polo, citizen and resident in the City of Venice. And the said Sire Marco Polo, being a very honourable person of high character and report in many countries, because of his desire that what he had seen should be heard throughout the world, and also for the honour and reverence he bore to the most excellent and puissant Prince, my Lord Charles, son of the King of France, and Count of Valois, gave and presented to the aforesaid Lord of Cepoy the first copy of his said book that was made after he had written it. And very pleasing it was to him that his book should be carried to the noble country of France by so worthy a gentleman. And from the copy which the said Messire Thiebault, Sire de Cepoy above-named, carried into France, Messire John, who was his eldest son and is the present Sire de Cepoy, had a copy made after his father's death, and the first copy of the book that was made after it was brought to France he presented to his very dear and dread Lord, Monseigneur de Valois ; and afterwards to his friends who wished to have it. . . . . This happened in the year of the Incarnation of our Lord Jesus Christ one thousand three hundred and seven, and in the month of August."

This gives a pleasant opening through the mist of obscurity which had fallen over the Ca' Polo. If Messer Marco was illustrious enough to be sought out by a young stranger of Thiebault's rank and pretensions, then his labours had not been without their reward. It is possible, however, that the noble visitor might have been taken to see one of the amusing per-

sonages of the city, and with the keenness of an unaccustomed
eye might have found out for himself that Messer Marco of
the Millions was no braggard, but a remarkable man with a
unique history. In any case the note is full of interest. One
can imagine how the great traveller's eye and his heart would
brighten, when he saw that the noble Frenchman understood
and believed, and how he would turn from the meaning smile
and mock respect of his own countrymen to the intelligent
interest of the new comer who could discriminate between
truth and falsehood. " *Et moult lui estoit agreable quant par si
preudomme estoit avanciez et portez es nobles parties de France.*"

The final record of his will and dying wishes is the only
other document that belongs to the history of Marco Polo.
He made this will in January, 1323, " finding myself to grow
daily weaker through bodily ailment, but being by the grace of
God of sound mind, and senses and judgment unimpaired," and
distributing his money among his wife and daughters, whom he
constitutes his executors, and various uses of piety and charity.
He was at this time about sixty-nine, and it is to be supposed
that his death took place shortly after—at least that is the last
we know of him. His father, who had died many years before,
had been buried in the atrio of San Lorenzo, where it is to be
supposed Messer Marco also was laid : but there is no certainty
in this respect. He disappears altogether from the time his
will is signed, and all his earthly duties done.

It is needless here to enter into any description of his travels.
Their extent, and the detailed descriptions he gives at once of
the natural features of the countries, and of their manners and
customs, give them, even to us, for whose instruction so many
generations of travellers have laboured since, a remarkable
interest; how much more to those to whom that wonderful new
world was as a dream. The reason why he observed so closely
and took so much pains to remember everything he saw is very
characteristically told in the book itself. The young Venetian
to whom the Great Khan had no doubt been held up during the
three years' long journey as an object of boundless veneration,

whose favour was the sum of existence to his father and uncle, observed that potentate and his ways when they reached their destination with the usual keen inspection of youth. He perceived the secret of the charm which had made these Latin merchants so dear to Prince Kublai, in the warm and eager interest which he took in all the stories that could be told him of other countries and their government, and the habits of their people. The young man remarked that when ambassadors to the neighbouring powers came back after discharging their mission, the prince listened with impatience to the reports which contained a mere account of their several errands and nothing else, saying that it would have pleased him more to have heard news of all they had seen, and a description of unknown or strange customs which had come under their observation. Young Marco laid the lesson to heart, and when he was sent upon an embassy, as soon happened, kept his eyes about him, and told the monarch on his return all the strange things he had seen, and whatever he heard that was marvellous or remarkable; so that all who heard him wondered, and said, "If this youth lives he will be a man of great sense and worth." It is evident throughout the book that the Venetians were no mere mercenaries, but had a profound regard and admiration for the great, liberal, friendly monarch, who had received them so kindly, and lent so ready an ear to all they could tell, and that young Marco had grown up in real affection and sympathy for his new master. Indeed, as we read, we recognise, through all the strangeness and distance, a counten- ance and person entirely human in this half savage Tartar, and find him no mysterious voluptuary like the Kublai Khan of the poet, but a cordial, genial, friendly human being, glad to know about all his fellow creatures, whoever they might be, taking the most wholesome friendly interest in everything, ready to learn and eager to know. One wonders what he thought of the slackness of the Christian powers who would send no men to teach him the way of salvation: of the shrinking of the teachers themselves who were afraid to dare the dangers of the way: and what of that talisman they had brought him, the oil from the holy lamp, which he had received with joy. It was to please him that Marco made his observations, noting everything—or at least, no doubt the young ambassador believed that his sole object was to please his master when he followed the characteristic impulses of his own inquisitive and observant intelligence.

Since his day, the world then unknown has opened up its secrets to many travellers, the geographer, the explorer, and those whose study lies among the differences of race and the varieties of humanity. The curious, the wise, the missionary and the merchant, every kind of visitor has essayed in his turn to lift the veil from those vast spaces and populations and to show us the boundless multitudes and endless deserts, which lay, so to speak, outside the world for centuries, unknown to this active atom of a Europe, which has monopolised civilisation for itself; but none of them, with all the light of centuries of accumulated knowledge, have been able to give Marco Polo the lie. Colonel Yule, his last exponent in England, is no enthusiast for Marco. He speaks, we think without reason, of his "hammering reiteration," his lack of humour, and many other characteristic nineteenth century objections. But when all is done, here is the estimate which this impartial critic makes of him and his work :—

"Surely Marco's real, indisputable, and in their kind unique, claims to glory may suffice. He was the first traveller to trace a route across the whole longitude of Asia, naming and describing kingdom after kingdom which he had seen with his own eyes, the deserts of Persia, the flowering plateaux and wild gorges of Beloochistan, the jade-bearing rivers of Khotan, the Mongolian steppes, cradle of the power which had so lately threatened to swallow up Christendom, the new and brilliant court that had been established at Cambaluc : the first traveller to reveal China in all its wealth and vastness, its mighty ruins, its huge cities, its rich manufactures, its swarming population ; the inconceivably vast fleets that quickened its seas and its inland waters ; to tell us of the nations on its borders, with all their eccentricities of manners and worship : of Thibet with its sordid devotees, of Burmah with its golden pagodas and their tinkling crowns, of Caos, of Siam, of Cochin-China, of Japan, the Eastern Thule, with its rosy pearls

and golden-roofed palaces ; the first to speak of that museum of beauty and
wonder, the Indian Archipelago, source of the aromatics then so prized and
whose origin was so dark : of Java, the pearl of islands : of Sumatra, with
its many kings, its strange costly products, and its cannibal races ; of the
naked savage of Nicobar and Andaman ; of Ceylon, the isle of gems, with
its sacred mountain and its tomb of Adam ; of India the great, not as a
dreamland of Alexandrian fables, but as a country seen and partially
explored, with its virtuous Brahmins, its obscure ascetics, its diamonds and
the strange tales of their acquisition, its seabeds of pearls, and its powerful
sun ; the first in mediæval times to give any distinct account of the
secluded Christian empire of Abyssinia, and the semi-Christian isle of
Socotra ; to speak, though indeed dimly, of Zanzibar with its negroes and
its ivory, and of the vast and distant Madagascar bordering on that dark
ocean of the south, and in a remotely opposite region, of Siberia and the
Arctic Ocean, of dog sledges, white bears, and reindeer-riding Tunguses."

We get to the end of this sentence with a gasp of exhausted
breath. But though it may not be an example of style (in a
writer who has no patience with our Marco's plainer diction)
it is a wonderful *résumé* of one man's work, and that a Venetian
trader of the thirteenth century. His talk of the wonders he
had seen, which amused and pleased the lord of all the Tartars
in the world, and charmed the dreary hours of the prisoners in
the dungeons of Genoa, an audience so different, is here for us
as it came from his lips in what we may well believe to be the
self-same words, with the same breaks and interruptions, the
pauses and digressions which are all so natural. The story is so
wonderful in its simplicity of spoken discourse that it is scarcely
surprising to know that the Venetian gallants jeered at the
Man of the Millions: but it is still full of interest, a book not
to be despised should it ever be the reader's fate to be shut up
in any dungeon, or in a desolate island, or other enforced
seclusion. And not all the flood of light that has been poured
since upon these unknown lands, not the progress of science or
evolution, or any great development of the last six hundred
years, has proved Messer Marco to have been less than
trustworthy and true.

Meanwhile the archway in the Corte della Sabbionera, in its

crowded corner behind San Grisostomo, is all that remains in Venice of Marco Polo. He has his (imaginary) bust in the loggia of the Ducal Palace, along with many another man who has less right to such a distinction: but even his grave is unknown. He lies probably at San Lorenzo among the nameless bones of his fathers, but even the monument his son erected to Niccolo has long ago disappeared. The Casa Polo is no more: the name extinct, the house burnt down except that corner of it. It would be pleasant to see restored to the locality at least the name of the Corte Millione, in remembrance of all the wonders he told, and of the gibe of the laughing youths to whom his marvellous tales were first unfolded: and thus to have Kublai Khan's millions once more associated with his faithful ambassador's name.

INSCRIPTION ON PILLAR IN ARSENAL, THE FIRST ERECTED.

CHAPTER II.

A POPULAR HERO.

BOUT seventy years after the events above recorded, in the later half of the fourteenth century there occurred a crisis in the life of the Venetian Republic of a more alarming and terrible character than had ever been caused before by misfortunes external or internal. Since those early times when the fugitive fathers of the state took refuge in the marshes and began to raise their miraculous city out of the salt pools and mud-banks, that corner of the Adriatic had been safe from all external attacks. A raid from Aquileia, half ecclesiastical, half warlike, had occurred by times in early days, threatening Grado or even Torcello, but nothing which it gave the city any trouble to overcome. The Greek with all his wiles had much ado to keep her conquering galleys from his coasts, and lost island after island without a possibility of reprisals. The Dalmatian tribes kept her in constant irritation and disturbance, yet were constrained over and over again to own her mistress of the sea, and never affected her home sovereignty. The Turk himself, the most appalling of invaders, though his thunders were heard near enough to arouse alarm and rage, never got within sight of the wonderful city. It was reserved for her sister republic, born of the same mother, speaking the same language, moved by the same instincts, Genoa, from the other side of the penin-

sula, the rival from her cradle of the other sea-born state, to
make it possible, if but for one moment, that Venice might
cease to be.   This was during the course of the struggle called
by some of the chroniclers the fourth, by others the seventh,
Genoese war—a struggle as causeless and as profitless as all
the wars between the rivals were, resulting in endless misery
and loss to both, but nothing more.   The war in question
arose nominally, as they all did, from one of the convulsions
which periodically tore the Empire of the East asunder, and in
which the two trading states, the rival merchants, seeking
every pretence to push their traffic, instinctively took different
sides.   On the present occasion it was an Andronicus who had
dethroned and imprisoned his father, as on a former occasion
it had been an Alexius.   Venice was on the side of the injured father, Genoa upon that of the usurping son—an excellent reason for flying at each other's throats wherever that
was practicable, and seizing each other's stray galleys on the
high seas, when there was no bigger fighting on hand.   It
is curious to remark that the balance of success was with
Genoa in the majority of these struggles, although that state
was neither so great nor so consistently independent as that of
Venice.   Our last chapter recorded the complete and ignominious rout of the great Venetian squadron in which Marco
Polo was a volunteer, in the beginning of the century; and
seventy years later (1379) the fortune of war was still the same.
In distant seas the piracies and lesser triumphs of both powers
maintained a sort of wavering equality : but when it came to
a great engagement Genoa had generally the upper hand.

The rival republic was also at this period reinforced by
many allies.   The Carrarese, masters of Padua and all the rich
surrounding plains, the nearest neighbours of Venice, afterwards
her victims, had joined the league against her.   So had the
King of Hungary, a hereditary foe, ever on the watch to
snatch a Dalmatian city out of the grip of Venice : and the
Patriarch of Aquileia, a great ecclesiastical prince, who from
generation to generation never seems to have forgiven the

withdrawal of Venice from his sway and the erection of Grado
into a rival primacy. This strong league against her did not
at first daunt the proud republic, who, collecting all her forces,
sent out a powerful expedition, and so long as the war went
on at a distance regarded it, if not without anxiety, yet with
more wrath than fear. But when Vittore Pisani, the beloved
admiral in whose prowess all Venice believed, was defeated
at Pola, a thrill of alarm ran through the city, shortly to be
raised into the utmost passion of fear. Pisani himself and
a few of his captains escaped from the rout, which was so
complete that the historian records "almost all the Venetian
sea-forces" to have been destroyed. Two thousand prisoners,
Sabellico tells, were taken by the Genoese, and the entire fleet
cut to pieces. When the beaten admiral arrived in Venice
he met what was in those days the usual fate of a defeated
leader, and was thrown into prison; but not on this occasion
with the consent of the populace, who loved him, and believed
that envy on the part of certain powerful persons, and not any
fault of his, was the occasion of his condemnation. After
this a continued succession of misfortunes befell the republic.
What other ships she had were away in eastern seas, and
the authorities seem to have been for the moment paralysed.
Town after town was taken. Grado once more fell into the
power of that pitiless patriarch: and the Genoese held the
mastery of the Adriatic. The Venetians, looking on from the
Lido, saw with eyes that almost refused to believe such a
possibility, with tears of rage and shame, one of their own
merchantmen pursued and taken by the Genoese, and plundered
and burnt while they looked on, within a mile of the shore.
The enemy took Pelestrina; they took part of Chioggia, burning
and sacking everywhere; then sailed off triumphant to the
turbulent Zara, which they had made their own, dragging the
Venetian banners which they had taken at Pola through the
water as they sailed triumphantly away. The Venetian Senate,
stung to the quick, attempted, it would seem, to raise another
fleet: but in vain, the sailors refusing to inscribe themselves

under any leader but Pisani. A few vessels were with difficulty
armed to defend the port and Lido, upon which hasty fortifications, great towers of wood, were raised, with chains drawn
across the navigable channels and barges sunk to make the
watery ways impassable. When, however, the enemy, returning
and finding the coast without defence, recaptured one after
another the Venetian strongholds on the west side of the
Adriatic, and finally took possession in force of Chioggia, the
populace took up the panic of their rulers.

"When the fall of Chioggia was known, which was towards midnight,
the city being taken in the morning, there arose such a terror in the palace
that as soon as day dawned there was a general summons to arms, and from
all quarters the people rushed towards the piazza. The court and square
were crowded with the multitude of citizens. The news of the taking of
Chioggia was then published by order of the Senate, upon which there arose
such a cry and such lamentations as could not have been greater had Venice
itself been lost. The women throughout the city went about weeping, now
raising their arms to heaven, now beating upon their breasts: the men
stood talking together of the public misfortune, and that there was now no
hope of saving the republic, but that the entire dominion would be lost.
They mourned each his private loss, but still more the danger of losing
their freedom. All believed that the Genoese would press on at once, overrun all the territory, and destroy the Venetian name: and they held
consultations how to save their possessions, money, and jewels, whether
they should send them to distant places, or hide them under ground in the
monasteries. All joined in this lamentation and panic, and many believed
that if in this moment of terror the enemy's fleet had pressed on to the
city, either it would have fallen at once, or would have been in the
greatest danger."

"But," adds Sabellico piously, "God does not show everything
to one man. Many know how to win a battle but not how to
follow up the victory." This fact, which has stood the human
race in stead at many moments of alarm, saved Venice. The
Genoese did not venture to push their victory: but their presence at Chioggia, especially in view of their alliance with
Carrara at Padua, was almost as alarming. The Venetian ships
were shut out from the port, the supplies by land equally interrupted; only from Treviso could any provisions reach the city, and

M

the scarcity began at once to be felt. Worse, however, than any of the practical miseries which surrounded Venice was the want of a leader or any one in whom the people could trust. The doge was Andrea Contarini, a name to which much of the fame of the eventual success has been attributed, but it does not seem in this terrible crisis to have inspired the public mind with any confidence. After the pause of panic, and the troubled consultations of this moment of despair, one thought suddenly seized the mind of Venice. "Finally all concluded that in the whole city there was but one Pisani, and that he, who was dear to all, might still secure the public safety in this terrible and dangerous crisis." That he should lie in prison and in darkness, this man whose appearance alone would give new heart to the city! There was a general rush towards the palazzo when this thought first burst into words and flew from one to another. The Senate, unable to resist, notwithstanding "the envy of certain nobles," conceded the prayer of the people. And here for a moment the tumultuous and complicated story pauses to give us a glimpse of the man *che ad ognuno era molto caro*, as the historian, impressed by the universal sentiment, assures us again and again. The whole population had assembled in the piazza to receive him :

"But so great was his modesty that he preferred to remain for this night in the prison, where he begged that a priest might be sent to him, and confessed, and as soon as it was day went out into the court, and to the church of San Niccolo, where he received the precious Sacrament of the Host, in order to show that he had pardoned every injury both public and private : and having done this he made his appearance before the Prince and the Signoria. Having made his reverence to the Senate, not with angry or even troubled looks, but with a countenance glad and joyful, he placed himself at the feet of the Doge, who thus addressed him. 'On a former occasion, Vittore, it was our business to execute justice ; it is now the time to grant grace. It was commanded that you should be imprisoned for the defeat of Pola, now we will that you should be set free. We will not inquire if this is a just thing or not, but leaving the past, desire you to consider the present state of the republic, and the necessity for preserving and defending it, and so to act that your fellow-citizens, who honour you for your great bearing, may owe to you their safety, both public and private.' Pisani made answer in this wise : 'There is no punishment, most serene Prince, which can come to me from you or from the others who govern the republic which I should not bear with a good heart, as a good citizen ought. I know, most serene Prince, that all things are done for the good of the republic, for which I do not doubt all your counsels and regulations are framed. As for private grievances, I am so far from thinking that they should work harm to any one that I have this day received the blessed sacrament, and been present at the holy sacrifice, that nothing may be more evident than that I have for ever forgotten to hate any man. . . . As for what you say inviting me to save the republic, I desire nothing more than to obey it, and will gladly endeavour to defend her, and God grant that I may be he who may deliver her from peril, by whatsoever way, with my best thought and care, for I know that the will shall not be wanting.' With these words he embraced and kissed the Prince with many tears, and so went to his house, passing through the joyful multitude, and accompanied by the entire people."

It may afford some explanation of the low ebb to which Venice had come at this crisis, that not even now was Pisani appointed to the first command, and it was only after another popular rising that the *invidia d'alcuni nobili* was finally defeated, and he was put in his proper place as commander of the fleet. When this was accomplished the sailors enlisted in such numbers that in three days six galleys were fully equipped to sail under the beloved commander, along with a great number of smaller vessels, such as were needful for the narrow channels about Chioggia, only navigable by light flat-bottomed boats and barges. A few successes fell to Pisani's share at first, which raised the spirits of the Venetians : and another fleet of forty galleys was equipped, commanded by the Doge himself, in the hope of complete victory. But it was with the greatest difficulty that the city, once so rich, could get together money enough to prepare these armaments; and poverty and famine were in her streets, deserted by all the able-bodied and left to the fear and melancholy anticipations of the weaker part of the population. To meet this emergency the Senate published a proclamation holding out to all who would furnish money or ships or men, the prize of admission into the Great Council, offering that much-coveted promotion to thirty new families from among the most liberal citizens, and

promising to the less wealthy or less willing interest for their
money, five thousand ducats to be distributed among them yearly.
" Many moved by the hope of such a dignity, some also for love
of their country," says Sabellico, came forward with their offerings, no less than sixty families thus distinguishing themselves:
and many fine deeds were done. Among others there is mention
made of a once rich Chioggiote, Matteo Fasnolo by name, who
having lost everything presented himself and his two sons, all
that was left to him, to give their lives for the republic."

The rout of Pola took place in March, 1379: in August the
Genoese took possession of Chioggia and sat down at the gates
of Venice. It was as if the mouth of the Thames had been in
possession of an assailant of London, with this additional misfortune, that the country behind, the storehouse and supply on
ordinary occasions of the city, was also in the possession of her
enemies. How it came about that Pisani with his galleys and
innumerable barks, and the Doge with his great fleet, did next
to nothing against these bold invaders, it seems impossible to
tell. The showers of arrows with which they harassed each
other, the great wooden towers erected on both sides, for attack
and defence, were no doubt very different from anything
that armies and fleets have trusted in since the days of artillery.
But with all these disadvantages it seems wonderful that this
state of affairs should languish on through the winter months—
then universally considered a time for rest in port and not for
action on the seas—without any result. A continual succession
of little encounters, sallies of the Genoese, assaults of the besiegers, sometimes ending in a trifling victory, sometimes only
adding to the number of the nameless sufferers—the sailors
sweating at the oars, the bowmen on the deck—went on for
month after month. The Doge's fleet, according to one account,
went back every night to Venice, the men sleeping at home and
returning to their hopeless work every day, with it may be
supposed but little heart for it. And not only their enemies but
all the evils of the season, cold and snow and storm fought against
the Venetians. Sometimes they would be driven apart by the

tempestuous weather, losing sight of each other, occasionally even coming to disastrous shipwreck; and lovely as are the lagoons under most aspects, it is impossible to imagine anything more dreary and miserable than the network of slimy passages among the marshes, and the grey wastes of sea around, in the mists and chill of December, and amid the perpetual failures and defeats of an ever unsuccessful conflict. Want grew to famine in Venice, her supplies being stopped and her trade destroyed: and even the rich plebeians who had strained their utmost to benefit their country and gain the promised nobility, began to show signs of exhaustion, and "the one Pisani" in whom the city had placed such entire confidence—though, wonderfully enough, he does not seem to have lost his hold upon the popular affections—had not been able to deliver his country. In these circumstances the eyes of all began to turn with feverish impatience to another captain, distant upon the high seas, after whom the Senate had despatched message after message to call him back with his galleys to the help of the republic. He was the only hope that remained in the dark mid-winter: when all their expedients failed them, and all their efforts proved unsuccessful, there remained still a glimmer of possibility that all might go well if Carlo were but there.

Carlo Zeno, the object of this last hope, at the moment careering over the seas at the head of an active and daring little fleet which had been engaged in making reprisals upon the Genoese coasts, carrying fire and flame along the eastern Riviera—and which was now fighting the battles of Venice against everything that bore the flag of Genoa, great or small— was a man formed on all the ancient traditions of the republic, a soldier, a sailor, a merchant, adventurer, and orator, a born leader of men. Of the house of Zeno, his mother a Dandolo, no better blood is in the golden book (not then, however, in existence) than that which ran in his veins, and his adventurous life and career were most apt to fire the imagination and delight the popular fancy. His father had died a kind of martyr for

the faith in an expedition for the relief of Smyrna, when Carlo
was but seven years old.   He was then sent to the pope at
Avignon, who endowed the orphan with a canonicate at Patras,
apparently a rich benefice.   But the boy was not destined to
live the peaceful life of an ecclesiastical dignitary.   He passed
through the stormy youth which in those days was so often the
beginning of a heroic career—ran wild at Padua, where he was
sent to study, lost all that he had at play, and having sold even
his books, enlisted as would appear in some troop of free lances,
in which for five years he was lost to his friends, but learned the
art of war, to his great after profit and the good of his country.
When, after having roamed all Italy though, he reappeared in
Venice, his family it is probable made little effort to prevent
the young trooper from proceeding to Greece to take up his
canon's stall, for which no doubt these wanderings had curiously
prepared him.   His biography, written by his grandson, Jacopo,
Bishop of Padua, narrates all the incidents of his early life in
full detail.   At Patras, the adventurous youth, then only twenty-
two, was very soon placed in the front during the incessant
wars with the Turks, which kept that remote community in
perpetual turmoil—and managed both the strategy of war and
the arts of statesmanship with such ability, that he obtained
an honourable peace and the withdrawal of the enemy on the
payment of a certain indemnity.   However great may be the
danger which is escaped in this way, there are always objectors
who consider that better terms might have been made.
" Human nature," says Bishop Jacopo, " is a miserable thing,
and virtue always finds enemies, nor was anything ever so
well done but envy found means of spoiling and misrepresenting
it."   Carlo did not escape this common fate, and the Greek
governor, taking part with his adversaries, deprived him of his
canonicate.   Highly indignant at this affront, the angry youth
threw up " various other ecclesiastical dignities," which we are
told he possessed in various parts of Greece ; whereupon his
life took an aspect much more harmonious with his character
and pursuits.   " Fortune," says our bishop, " never forsakes

him who has a great soul. There was in Chiarenza a noble
lady of great wealth, who having heard of Carlo's achievements,
and marvelling at the greatness of his spirit, conceived a desire
to have him for her husband. And Carlo, being now free from
the ecclesiastical yoke, was at liberty to take a wife, and willingly
contracted matrimony with her." This marriage however was
not apparently of very long duration, for scarcely had he cleared
himself of all the intrigues against him, when his wife died,
leaving him as poor as before. " Her death, which as was befitting he lamented duly, did him a double injury, for he lost
his wife and her wealth together, her property consisting entirely
of feoffs, which fell at her death to the Prince of Achaia." This
misfortune changed the current of his life. He returned to
Venice and after a proper interval married again, a lady of the
house of Giustiniani. " Soon after, reflecting that in a maritime
country trade is of the highest utility, and that it was indeed
the chief sustenance of his city, he made up his mind to
adopt the life of a merchant; and leaving Venice with this
intention, remained seven years absent, living partly in a castle
called Tanai on the banks of the river Tanai, and partly in
Constantinople."

Such had been the life, full of variety and experience, of the
man to whom the eyes of Venice turned in her humiliation.
He had been all over Italy in his youth, during that wild
career which carried him out of the view of his family and
friends. He had been even further a-field, in France, Germany,
and England, in a short episode of service under the Emperor
Charles IV. between two visits *alla sua chiesa di Patrasso.*
He had fought the Turks and led the armaments of Achaia
during his residence at his canonicate; and now, all these
tumults over, re-settled into the natural position of a Venetian,
with a Venetian wife and all the traditions of his race to
shape his career, had taken to commerce, peacefully, so far as
the time permitted, in those golden lands of the east where
it was the wont of his countrymen to make their fortunes.
And success it would appear had not forsaken *chi ha*

l'anima grande, the man of great mind—for when he re-appeared in Venice it was with a magnificence of help to the republic which only a man of wealth could give. He was still engaged in peaceful occupations when war broke out between Genoa and Venice. Carlo had already compromised himself by an attempt to free the dethroned emperor, and had been in great danger in Constantinople, accused before the Venetian governor of treasonable practices, and only saved by the arrival of the great convoy from Venice "which reached Constantinople every year," and in which he had friends. Even at this time he is said to have had soldiers in his service, probably for the protection of his trade in the midst of the continual tumults; and his historian declares that no sooner had he escaped from Constantinople than he began to act energetically for the republic, securing to Venice the wavering allegiance of the island of Tenedos, from which the Venetian galleys under his (part) command chased off the emissaries of the emperor, and where a Venetian garrison was installed. His first direct action in the service of the state however would seem to have been that sudden raid upon the Genoese coast at the very beginning of the war, to which we have referred, with the purpose of making a diversion and if possible calling back to the defence of their own city the triumphant armies of Genoa. This intention however was not carried out by the result, though otherwise the expedition was so successful that "the name of Carlo Zeno," says his historian writing more than a hundred years after, "is terrible to that city even to the present day." After this exploit he seems to have returned to the east, *per nettare la mare*, sweeping the sea clear of every Genoese vessel that came in his way, and calling at every rebellious port with much effect.

In the midst of these engagements the news of the defeat at Pola did not reach him till long after the event, and even the messengers despatched by the Senate, one boat after another, failed to find the active and unwearied seaman as he swept the seas. Such a ubiquitous career, now here, now there, darting from one point to another with a celerity which was a marvel in those days of slow sailing and long pauses, and the almost invariable success which seemed to attend him, gave Carlo a singular charm to the popular imagination. No one was more successful at sea, no one half so successful on land as this leader, suddenly improvised by his own great deeds in the very moment of need, whose adventures had given him experience of everything that the mediæval world knew, and who had the special gift of his race in addition to everything else—the power of the orator over a people specially open to that influence. Sanudo says that Carlo at first refused to obey the commands of the Senate, preferring to *nettar la mare* to that more dangerous work of dislodging the Genoese from Chioggia. But there would seem to be no real warrant for this assertion. The messengers were slow to reach him. They arrived when his hands were still full and when it was difficult to give immediate obedience; and when he did set out to obey, a strong temptation fell in his way and for a time delayed his progress. This was a great ship from Genoa, the description of which is like that of the galleons which tempted Drake and his brother mariners. It was *grande oltre misura*, a bigger ship than had ever been seen, quite beyond the habits and dimensions of the time, laden with wealth of every kind, and an enormous crew, "for besides the sailors and the bowmen it carried two hundred Genoese, each of whom was a senator or the son of a senator." It was winter, and the great vessel was more at home on the high seas than the *navigli leggieri* with which our hero had been flying from island to island. The sight of that nimble fleet filled the Genoese commander with alarm; and he set all sail to get out of their way. It was evidently considered a mighty piece of daring to attack such a ship at all, or even to be out at all at such a season instead of in port, as sensible galleys always were in winter. When however the wind dropped and the course of the big vessel was arrested, Carlo's opportunity came. He called his crews together and made them a speech, which seems to have been his habit. The vessels collected in a cluster

round the high prow on which he stood, reaching with his
great voice in the hush of the calm all the listening crews,
must have been such a sight as none of our modern wonders
could parallel: and he was as emphatic as Nelson if much longer
winded. The great *Bichignona*, with her huge sails drooping
and no wind to help her from her pursuers, was no doubt lying
in sight, giving tremendous meaning to his oration. "Men,"
he cried, "*valenti uomini*, if you were ever prompt and ardent
in battle, now is the time to prove yourselves so. You have to
do with the Genoese, your bitter and cruel enemies, whose
whole endeavour is to extinguish the Venetian name. They
have beaten our fleet at Pola, with great bloodshed; they have
occupied Chioggia: and our city itself will soon be assailed by
them to reduce her to nothing, killing your wives and children,
and destroying your property and everything there by fire and
sword. Up then, my brothers, *compagni miei!* despise not the
occasion here offered to you to strike a telling blow; which,
if you do, the enemy shall pay dearly for their madness, as
they well deserve, and you, joyful and full of honour, will
deliver Venice and your wives and children from ruin and
calamity."

When he had ended this speech he caused the trumpets
to sound the signal of attack. The oars swept forth, the
galleys rushed with their high beaked prows like so many
strange birds of prey round the big helpless over-crowded ship.
"They fought with partisans, darts, arrows, and every kind of
arm; but the lances from the ship were more vehement as
reaching from a higher elevation, the form of the ship (*nave*)
being higher than the galleys, which were long and low; nevertheless the courage of the Venetians and their science in warfare
were so great that they overcame every difficulty. Thus,"
goes on the historian, "this ship was taken, which in size
exceeded everything known in that age." Carlo dragged his
prey to Rhodes, "not without difficulty," and there burnt her,
giving up the immense booty to his sailors and soldiers; then
"recalling to his mind his country," with great trouble got his

men together laden with their spoils, and, toiling day and night
without thought of danger or fatigue, at length reached the
Adriatic. Calling at an Italian port on his way to victual his
ships, he found other letters from the Senate still more impera-
tive, and on the 1st day of January, 1380, he arrived before
Chioggia, where lay all the force that remained to Venice, and
where his appearance had been anxiously looked for, for many
a weary day.

The state of the republic would appear to have been all but
desperate at this miserable moment. After endless comings and
goings, partial victories now and then which raised their spirits
for the moment, but a ceaseless course of harassing and fatiguing
conflict in narrow waters where scarcely two galleys could keep
abreast, and where the Venetians were subject to constant
showers of arrows from the Genoese fortifications, the two fleets,
one of them under the Doge, the other under Pisani, seem to
have lost heart simultaneously. In the galleys under the
command of Contarini were many if not all the members of the
Senate, who had from the beginning shown the feeblest heart;
and meetings were held, and timorous and terrified consultations,
unworthy their name and race, as to the possibility of throwing
up the struggle altogether, leaving Venice to her fate, and taking
refuge in Candia or even Constantinople, where these terrified
statesmen, unused to the miseries of a winter campaign on
board ship, and the incessant watchings and fighting in which
they had to take their part, thought it might be possible to
begin again as their fathers had done. While these cowardly
counsels were being whispered in each others' ears, on one hand,
on the other, the crews with greater reason were on the verge
of mutiny.

"The galleys were so riddled with the arrows of the enemy that the
sailors in desperation cried with one voice that the siege must be relin-
quished, that otherwise all that were in the galleys round Chioggia were
dead men. Those also who held the banks, fearing that the squadrons of
Carrara would fall upon them from behind, demanded anxiously to be
liberated, and that the defence of the coast should be abandoned.

Pisani besought them to endure a little longer, since in a few days
Carlo Zeno must arrive, adding both men and ships to the armata, so that
the Genoese in their turn would lose heart. Equal desperation of mind
was in the other division of the fleet, where cold, hunger, and the deadly
shower of arrows which were continually directed against the galleys, had
so broken and worn out all spirit that soldiers and all who were on board
thought rather of flight than combat. The presence of the Doge somewhat
sustained the multitude, and the exhortation he made, showing them what
shame and danger would arise to their country if they raised the siege, since
the Genoese, seeing them depart, would immediately follow them to Venice.
But neither by prayers nor by promises could the spirits of the men be
emboldened to continue the siege. And things had come to such a pitch
that, for two days, one after the other on either side had determined to raise
the siege, when Carlo Zeno, just in time, with fourteen galleys fully equipped
with provisions and men, about noon, as if sent by God, entered the port of
Chioggia."

Carlo turned the balance, and supplied at once the stimulus
needed to encourage these despairing squadrons, unmanned by
continual failure and by all the miseries of sea and war—
troubles to which the greater part were unaccustomed, since in
the failure of fighting men this armada of despair had been
filled up by unaccustomed hands : mostly artisans, says Sabellico
—whose discouragement is more pardonable. Great was the
joy of the Venetians, continues the same authority, "when they
heard what Carlo had done; how he had sunk in the high
seas seventy ships of divers kinds belonging to the enemy, and
the great bark *Bichignona,* and taken three hundred Genoese
merchants, and three hundred thousand ducats of booty, besides
seamen and other prisoners." The new comer passed on to
Pisani after he had cheered the Doge's squadron and spread joy
around, even the contingent upon the coast taking heart; and
another arrival from Candia taking place almost at the same
moment, the Venetians found themselves in possession of fifty-
two galleys, many of them now manned with veterans, and
feared the enemy no more.

It is impossible to follow in detail the after incidents of this
famous siege. Carlo in concert with, and partial subordination to,
Pisani, succeeded in blockading Chioggia so completely that the

enemy began to feel the same stress of famine which they had
inflicted upon the Venetians. But the various attacks and
assaults, the varying fortunes of the besieged and besiegers, are
too many to be recorded, as the painstaking and leisurely
chronicler does, event by event. According to the biographer
of Carlo, that hero was never at a loss, but encountered every
movement of the Genoese, as they too began to get uneasy, and
to perceive that the circle round them was being drawn closer
and closer, with a more able movement on his side, and met
the casualties of storm and accident with the same never-failing
wit and wealth of resource. According to Bishop Jacopo, the
entire work was accomplished by his ancestor, though other
writers give a certain credit to the other commanders. But
as soon as operations of a really important and practical
character had begun, a new danger, specially characteristic of
the age, arose on the Venetian side. Bishop Jacopo Zeno would
have us believe that up to this time the Venetians had hired
no mercenaries, which is an evident mistake, since we have
already heard, even in this very conflict, of forces on shore, a
small and apparently faithful contingent, led by a certain
Giacomo Cavallo, of Verona. But perhaps it was the first time
that a great armament had been collected under the banner of
San Marco. With that daring of despair which is above all calculation as to means of payment or support, the Senate had got
together a force of six thousand men—a little army, which was
to be conducted by the famous English Condottiere, Sir John
Hawkwood, Giovanni Aguto according to the Italian version of
his name. These soldiers assembled at Pelestrina, an island in
the mouth of the lagoons not far from Chioggia. But when the
band was collected and ready for action, the Senate, dismayed,
found the leader wanting. Whether the Genoese had any hand
in this defalcation, or whether the great Condottiere was kept
back by other engagements, it is certain that at the last moment
he failed them; and the new levies, all unknown and strange to
each other, fierce fighting men from every nationality, stranded
on this island without a captain, became an additional care

instead of an aid to the anxious masters of Venice. Fierce discussions arose among them, *una pericolosa contesa*, the Italians against the French and Germans. In this emergency the Senate turned to Carlo Zeno as their only hope. His youthful experiences had made him familiar with the ways of those fierce and dangerous auxiliaries, and he was considered a better leader, Sabellico tells us, by land than by sea. To him accordingly the charge of pacifying the mercenaries was given. " Carlo, receiving this commission to pass from the fleet to the camp, and from war at sea to war on land," put on his armour, and quickly, with a few companions, transferred himself to Pelestrina, where he found everything in a deplorable condition :

"It would be hard to tell the tumult which existed in the army, in which there was nothing but attack and defence, with cries of blood and vengeance, so that the uproar of men and weapons made both shore and sky resound. Carlo announced his arrival by the sound of trumpets, calling upon the soldiers to pause and listen to what their captain had to say. His voice as soon as it was heard so stilled that commotion that the storm seemed in a moment to turn into a calm ; and every one, of whatever grade, rushed to him exposing his grievances, and demanding, one justice, the other revenge. There were many among them who had served under him in other wars, and were familiar with him."

To these excited and threatening men he made a judicious speech, appealing at once to their generosity and their prudence, pointing out the embarrassed circumstances of the Senate, and the ingratitude of those who received its pay yet added to its troubles : and finally succeeded in making a truce until there was time to inquire into all their grievances. When he had soothed them for the moment into calm, he turned to the Senate for the one sole means which his experience taught him could keep these unruly bands in order. He had been told when his commission was given to him that "it appeared to these fathers" (the Senate) "that it was his duty to serve the republic without pay," which was scarcely an encouraging preliminary for a demand on their finances. Carlo, however, did not hesitate. He wrote to the Senate informing them of his temporary success with the soldiery, and suggest-

ing that like medicine in the hands of a doctor money should
be used to heal this wound. To make the proposal less dis-
agreeable to the poverty-stricken state, he offered himself
to undertake the half of the burden, and to give five hundred
ducats to be divided among the soldiers, if the Senate would
do the same; to which the rulers of Venice—partly moved by
the necessities of the case and partly by his arguments, and
that the republic might not seem less liberal than a simple
citizen—consented, and peace was accordingly established among
the always exacting mercenaries. Peace, however, lasted only
for a time; and it gives us a lively impression of the troubles of
mediæval powers with these artificial armies, to trace the violent
scenes which were periodically going on behind all other difficulties, from this cause.

When Carlo finally got his army in motion, and landed
them on the edge of the shore at Chioggia, he found occasion
almost immediately to strike a telling blow. Understanding
by the signals made that the enemy intended to make a
sally from two points at once—from Brondolo on one side,
and from the city of Chioggia on the other—he at once
arranged his order of battle: placing the English, French, and
Germans on the side towards Chioggia, while the Italians faced
the party coming from Brondolo. It would seem from this that
Carlo's confidence in his own countrymen was greater than in
the strangers; for the sallying band from Chioggia had to cross
a bridge over a canal, and therefore lay under a disadvantage
of which he was prompt to avail himself.

The following scene has an interest, independent of the
quaint story, to the English reader:

"When Carlo saw this" (the necessity of crossing the bridge) "he was filled
with great hope of a victory, and adding a number of the middle division
to the Italians, he himself joined the foreign band, and having had experience of the courage and truth of the English captain whose name was
William, called by his countrymen il Coquo" (Cook? or Cock?), "he called
him and consulted with him as to the tactics of the enemy, and how they
were to be met, and finding that he was of the same opinion, Carlo called
the soldiers together" (a parlamento) "and addressed them thus."

Carlo's speeches, it must be allowed, are a little long-winded. Probably the bishop, his grandson, with plenty of leisure on his hands, did not reflect that it must have been a dangerous and useless expedient to keep soldiers *a parlamento*, however energetic the words were, when the enemy was visibly beginning to get over the bridge in face of them. We feel when these orations occur something as spectators occasionally do at an opera, when in defiance of common sense the conspirators pause to roar forth a martial ditty at the moment when any whisper might betray them, or the lovers perform an elaborate *duo* when they ought to be running away with all speed from the villain who is at their heels. Probably the hero's speech was very much shorter than his descendant makes it—just long enough, let us suppose, with William the Cock at his elbow, who would naturally have no faith in speechifying at such a moment, to let the Genoese get completely started upon that bridge which, though *assai largo*, allowed the passage of but a small number abreast. The enemy themselves came on gaily, with the conviction that, taken thus between assailants on two sides, Carlo would lose heart and fly—and had passed a number of their men over the bridge before the Venetian army moved. Then suddenly Carlo flung his forces upon them with a great shouting and sound of trumpets. "The English were the first who with a rush and with loud cries assailed the adversaries, followed by the others with much readiness and noise (*romore.*)" The Genoese, taken by surprise, resisted but faintly from the first, and driven back upon the advancing files already on the bridge, were disastrously and tragically defeated—the crowd, surging up into a mass, those who were coming confused and arrested, those who were flying pushed on by the pursuers behind, until with the unwonted weight the bridge broke, and the whole fighting, flying mass was plunged into the canal. The division which approached from Brondolo was not more fortunate. On seeing the rout of their companions they too broke and fled *con velocissimi corsi*, as it seems to have been the universal habit to do in the face of any great danger—the fact that discretion was the better part of valour being apparently recognised by all without any shame in putting the maxim into practice. This victory would seem to have been decisive. The tables were turned with a rapidity which is strongly in contrast with the lingering character of all military operations in this age. *I Veneziani di vinti diventarono vincitori*, the vanquished becoming victors : and the Genoese lost courage and hope all at once. The greater part of them turned their eyes towards Padua as the nearest place of salvation, and many fled by the marshes and difficult tortuous water passages, in which they were caught by the pursuing barks of the Venetians and those Chioggiotes whom the invaders had driven from their dwellings. Of thirteen thousand combatants who were engaged in the *zuffa* here described, six thousand only, we are told, found safety within the walls of Chioggia. Bishop Jacopo improves the occasion with professional gravity, yet national pride. " And certainly," he says, " there could not have been a greater example of the changeableness of human affairs than that those who a little time before had conquered the fleets, overcome with much slaughter all who opposed them, taken and occupied the city, despised the conditions of peace offered to them, and made all their arrangements for putting Venice to sack, in full confidence of issuing forth in their galleys and leading back their armies by the shore, proud of the hosts which they possessed both by land and sea—now broken and spent, having lost all power and every help, fled miserably, wandering by dead waters and muddy marshes to seek out ferries and hiding-places, nor even in flight finding salvation. Such are the inconstancy and changeableness of human things."

We cannot but sympathise with the profound satisfaction of the bishop in thus pointing his not very original moral by an event so entirely gratifying to his national feelings.

This sudden victory, however, as it proved, was, if decisive, by no means complete, the Genoese who remained still obstinately holding their own within the shelter of their fortifications. It was in February that the above-recorded

N

events occurred, and it was not till June that Chioggia
was finally taken : a delay to be attributed, in great part at
least, to the behaviour of the mercenaries. No sooner was
the first flush of delight in the unaccustomed triumph over,
than the troops who had done their duty so well again turned
upon their masters. On being ordered by sound of trumpet to
put themselves in motion and establish their camp under the
walls of Chioggia, these soldiers of fortune bluntly refused. The
captains of the different bands sought Carlo in his tent, where
two Provveditori, sent by the Senate to congratulate him, and to
urge him to follow up his victory, were still with him. Their
message was a very practical one. They rejoiced that their
victory had been so helpful to the republic, which they regarded
with great reverence and affection, ready at all times to fight
her battles ; but they thought that in the general joy the Senate
might very becomingly cheer the soldiers by a present, *qualche
donativo*—something like double pay, for example, for the month
in which the victory had been won. This would be very grateful and agreeable to all ranks, the captains intimated, and
whatever dangerous work there might be to do afterwards the
authorities should find them always ready to obey orders and
bear themselves valorously : but if not granted, not a step would
they make from the spot where they now stood. To this claim
there was nothing to be said but consent. Once more Carlo had
to use all his powers, *con buone parole di addolcire gli animi
loro*, for he was aware " by long trial and practice of war that
soldiers have hard heads and obstinate spirits." He therefore
addressed himself once more to the republic, urging the prudence
of yielding this *donativo* lest worse should come of it, adding
" that he, according to his custom, would contribute something
from his own means to lighten the burden to the republic."
Such scenes, ever recurring, show how precarious was the hold
of any authority over these lawless bands, and what power to
exact and to harass was in their merciless hands.

Some time later, when the Genoese shut up in Chioggia had
been well nigh driven to desperation, a rescuing fleet of thirty

galleys laden with provisions and men having been driven off
and every issue closed either by sea or land, the mutinous free
lances appear on the scene again—this time in the still more
dangerous guise of traitors. "The mercenaries were not at
all desirous that the Genoese should give themselves up,
being aware that their occupation and pay would be stopped
by the conclusion of the war." This fear led them to open
negotiations with the besieged, and to keep up their courage
with false hopes, the leaders of the conspirators promising so
to act as that they might have at least better conditions of
surrender. A certain Robert of Recanati was at the head of
these unfaithful soldiers. Carlo, who seems to have kept up
a secret intelligence department such as was highly necessary
with such dubious servants, discovered the conspiracy, and
that there was an intention among them of taking advantage
of a parade of the troops for certain mutinous manifestations.
The wisdom and patience of the leader, anxious in all things for
the success of his enterprise and the safety of the republic,
and dealing with the utmost caution with the treacherous and
unreasoning men over whom he held uneasy sway, comes out
conspicuously in these encounters. Carlo forbade the parade,
but finding that the mutineers pretended to be unaware of its
postponement, took advantage of their appearance armed and in
full battle array to remonstrate and reason with them. While
the men in general, overawed by their general's discovery of their
conspiracy and abashed by his dignified reproof, kept silence,
Robert, ferocious in his madness and hot blood, sprang to the
front, and facing Carlo, adroitly pressed once more the ever-
repeated exactions. "We come to you armed and in order of
battle," he said, "as you see, to demand double pay till the end
of the war. We are determined to have it, and have sworn, by
whatsoever means, to obtain it; and if it is denied to us we
warn you that with banners flying, and armed as you see us, we
will go over to Chioggia to the enemy." The much-tried general
was greatly disturbed by this defiance, but had no resource save
to yield.

" Believing it to be better to moderate with prudence the impetuosity of this hot blood, without showing any alarm, with cheerful countenance and soft words Carlo replied that nothing would induce him to believe that these words were spoken in earnest, knowing the good faith and generosity of the speaker's mind, and believing that they were said only to try him ; that he had good reason for believing this, since otherwise Robert would have committed a great villainy and introduced the worst example, such as it was impossible a man of his high reputation could intend to do. Nor could the Senate ever believe it of him, having always expected and thought most highly of him and rewarded him largely according to the faith they had in his trustworthiness and experience in the art of war ; for nothing rendered soldiers more dear to the republic than that good faith which procured them from the said republic and other princes great gifts and donations. If soldiers were indifferent to the failure and violation of this faith, who could confide to their care the safety of the state, of the women and children ? Therefore he adjured them to lay down their arms, and he would watch over their interests and intercede for them with the Senate. While Carlo thus mildly addressed them the multitude renewed their uproar, opposing him furiously and repeating the cry of double pay, which they demanded at the top of their voices, and certain standard-bearers posted among them raised their banners, crying out that those who were of that opinion should follow them ; to whom Carlo turned smiling, and declared 'That he also was on that side, and promised if they were not contented to fight under their ensigns.'"

While this struggle was still going on, the general, with a smile on his lips but speechless anxiety in his heart, facing the excited crowd which any touch might precipitate into open mutiny beyond his control, a sudden diversion occurred which gave an unhoped-for termination to the scene.   The manner in which Carlo seized the occasion, his boldness, promptitude, and rapid comprehension of an occurrence which might under less skilful guidance have turned the balance in the opposite direction, show how well he deserved his reputation.   The Genoese, who had been warned by secret emissaries that on this day the mercenaries intended some effort in their favour, and probably perceiving from their battlements that something unusual was going on in the camp, seized the moment to make a desperate attempt at escape. They had prepared about eighty small vessels, such as were used to navigate the passages among the marshes, and filled them with everything of value they pos-

To face page 181.

FONDAMENTA' ZEN.

sessed in preparation for such an occasion. The propitious moment seeming now to present itself, they embarked hastily, and pushing out into the surrounding waters, seeking the narrowest and least-known passages, stole forth from the beleaguered city. "But vain," cries the pious bishop, "are the designs of miserable man !"

"The boatmen whose attention was fixed upon every movement within the walls had already divined what was going on, and with delight perceiving them issue forth, immediately gave chase in their light barks, giving warning of the escape of the enemy with shouting and a great uproar. And already the cry rose all around, and the struggle between the fugitives and their pursuers had begun, when Carlo, fired by the noise and clash of arms, suddenly turned upon the soldiers, and with stern face and terrible eyes addressed them in another tone. 'What madness is this,' he cried, 'cowards, that keeps you standing still while the enemy pushes forth before your eyes laden with gold and silver and precious things, while you stand and look on chattering like children !' Upon which he ordered the banners to move on, and with a great voice, so that the whole army could hear him, commanded all who kept faith with the republic to follow him against the enemy. Without loss of time, with his flag carried before him, he among the first rushed to the marshes, plunging breast high in the water and mud, and his voice and the impetuosity with which he called them to their senses and rushed forth in their front had so great a power that the whole army, forgetting their complaint, followed their captain, flinging themselves upon the enemy, and thus, with little trouble, almost all fell into Carlo's hands. The booty thus obtained was so great that never had there been greater, nor was anything left that could increase the victory and the fury until night fell upon the work. In this way and by this means was an end made of the controversy of that day."

This accidental settlement, however, was only for the moment. Robert of Recanati was not to be so easily driven from his purpose. The remnant of the imprisoned and discouraged Genoese, greatly diminished by these successive defeats and now at the last point of starvation, were about to send messengers to the Doge with their submission, when he and the other conspirators, seducing the soldiers in increasing numbers to their side, by prophecies of the immediate disbandment which was to be anticipated if the war were thus brought to an end, and promises of continued service in the other case—again hurried their movements to the brink of an outbreak. Carlo, who was advised of all that happened by his spies, at last in alarm informed the Senate of his fears, who sent a deputation of two of their number to address the captains and *mitigare gli animi dei soldati con qualche donativo*, the one motive which had weight with them. This process seemed again so far successful that the captains in general accepted the mollifying gift and undertook to secure the fidelity of their men—all but Robert, who, starting to his feet in the midst of the assembly, protested that nothing would make him consent to the arrangement, and rushed forth into the camp to rouse to open rebellion the men who were disposed to follow him. Carlo, perceiving the imminent danger, rushed forth after him and had him seized, and was about to apply the rapid remedy of a military execution when the deputation from Venice—popular orators perhaps, trembling for their reputation as peacemakers and friends of the soldiers—threw themselves before the angry general and implored mercy for the rebel. Against his better judgment Carlo yielded to their prayers. But it was very soon proved how foolish this clemency was, since the same afternoon, the orators being still in the tents, the sound of cries, *Arme! Arme!* and *Sacco!* resounded through the camp, and it soon became apparent that a rush was about to be made upon Chioggia without discipline or pre-arrangement, a number of the troops following Robert and his fellow conspirators in hope of a sack and plunder, and in spite of all the general could say. When Carlo found it impossible to stop this wild assault, he sent a trusted retainer of his own to mix in the crowd and bring a report of all that went on. This trusty emissary, keeping close to Robert, was a witness of the meeting held by the conspirators with the Genoese leaders under cover of this raid, and heard it planned between them how on that very night, after the Venetian mercenaries had been driven back, a sudden attack should be made by the Genoese on the camp with the assistance of the traitors within it, so that the rout and destruction of the besiegers should be certain and the way of exit from Chioggia be thrown open. The soldiers

streamed back defeated into the camp when the object of the
raid had been thus accomplished, the poor dupes of common men,
spoiled of their arms and even clothes by the desperate garrison,
while Robert and his friends returned "almost naked" to carry
out the deception.   Carlo met them as they came back in broken
parties with every appearance of rout, and in a few strong words
upbraided them with their folly and rashness; but when he
heard the story of his spy, the gravity of the position became
fully apparent.   Night was already falling, and the moment
approaching when the camp unprepared might have to sustain
the last despairing assault of the besieged, for whom life and
freedom hung upon the possibility of success, combined with the
still more alarming danger of treachery within.   The soldiers
were at supper and occupied, those who had come back from
Chioggia probably lamenting their losses, and consoling themselves with hopes of the sack of the town, which Robert had
used as one of his lures—when the captains of the mounted
troops (which is what we imagine to be the meaning of the
expression "*i capi degli uomini d'arme—de fante no, perche
sapeva che tutti erano nella congiura*"), leaving their own meal,
stole towards the general's tent in the quiet of the brief twilight.
Carlo made them a vigorous speech, more brief than his ordinary
addresses, first thanking and congratulating them on their former
exploits and their fidelity to the republic; then laying before
them the discovery he had made, the risk that all they had
done might be lost through the treachery of one among them,
and the desperate necessity of the case.   The captains, startled
by the sudden summons, and by the incidents of the day, sat
round him, with their eyes fixed upon their leader, hearing
with consternation his extraordinary statement, and for the
moment bewildered by the revelation of treachery and by the
suddenness of the peril.   This moment, upon which hung the
safety of the Venetian name and the decisive issue of the long
struggle, must have been one of overwhelming anxiety for the
sole Venetian among them, the only man to whom it was a
question of life or death, the patriot commander unassured of

what reply these dangerous subordinates might make.   But he was not kept long in suspense.

"There was a certain captain among the others called William, of Britannic origin. He, who was a man of great valour and the greatest fidelity, rose to his feet, and looking round upon them all, spoke thus :— 'Your words, oh general (*imperatore*), have first rejoiced and then grieved us. It rejoiced us to hear that you have so much faith in us, and in our love and devotion to your republic, than which we could desire no better— and for this we thank you with all our hearts. We have known you always not only as our general and leader (*imperatore e duce*), but as our father, and it grieves us that there should be among us men so villainous as those of whom you tell us. It appals my soul to hear what you say : and for my own part there is nothing I am not ready to do in view of the hardihood of the offender, of our peril, and the discipline of our army, matters which cannot be treated without shame of the military art. But you are he who have always overcome by your care and vigilance, and, with that genius which almost passes mortal, have always secured the common safety, defended us from ill fortune and from our enemies, and trusted in our good faith. We can never cease to thank you for these things, and God grant that the time may come when we shall do more than thank you. In the meantime we are yours, we are in your power ; we were always yours, and now more than ever ; make of us what pleases you. And now tell us the names of those who have offended you, let us know who are these scoundrels and villains, and you shall see that the faith you have had in us is well-founded.' "

It is satisfactory to find our unknown countryman taking this manly part. Robert was sent for, the entire assembly echoing the Englishman's words; and when the traitor's ex-planations had been summarily stopped by a gag, Carlo and his faithful captains came out of the general's quarters with a shout for the republic, calling their faithful followers round them, and a short but sharp encounter followed, in which the conspirators were entirely subdued. The Genoese meanwhile, watching from their walls for the concerted signal, and perplexed by the sounds of battle, soon learned by flying messengers that the plot was discovered and their allies destroyed. An un-conditional surrender followed, and the invaders, who had for ten months been masters of Chioggia, and for half that time at least had held Venice in terror and had her in their power, driving the mistress of the seas to the most abject despair, were now hurried off ignominiously in every available barge and fisherman's coble, rude precursors of the gondola, to prison in Venice—five thousand of them, Bishop Jacopo says. He adds, that after their long starvation they ate ravenously, and that the greater part of them died in consequence, a statement to be received with much reserve. Sabellico tells us that four thousand men altogether fell into the hands of the republic, three thousand of whom were Genoese. The soldiers among them, mercenaries no doubt and chiefly foreigners, had their arms taken from them and were allowed to go free. The plunder was taken to the church of S. Maria, and there sold by auction, the Venetians fixing the price, which was handed over to the soldiers, the chroniclers say. One wonders if the bargains to be had under these circumstances satisfied the citizens to whom this siege had cost so much.

It would be interesting, though sad, to follow the fate of these prisoners, shut up in dungeons which it is not at all likely were much better than the *pozzi* at present exhibited to shrinking visitors, though these prisons did not then exist. They had no Marco Polo, no chosen scribe among them to make their misery memorable. The war lasted another year, during which there were moments in which their lives were in extreme peril. At one time a rumour rose of cruelties practised by the Genoese upon the Venetian prisoners, many of whom were reported to have died of hunger and their bodies to have been thrown into the sea—news which raised a great uproar in Venice, the people breaking into the prisons and being with difficulty prevented from a general massacre of the prisoners, who were punished for the supposed sin of their compatriots by losing all comforts and conveniences and being reduced to bread and water, the women who had cooked their food "for pity" being ordered away. Afterwards, however, the city, according to ancient custom, had compassion, and restored to them everything of which they had been deprived. On the conclusion of the war, when peace was made and the prisoners exchanged, there is a

little record which shows, however far behind us were these
mediæval ages, that charity to our enemies is not, as some
people think, an invention of the nineteenth century.

"The Venetian ladies (*matrone*) collected among themselves money
enough to supply the Genoese, who were almost naked, with coats, shirts,
shoes, and stockings, and other things necessary for their personal use before
their departure, that they might not have any need to beg by the way,
and also furnished them with provisions for their journey. And those
who were thus sent back to their home were of the number of fifteen
hundred."

Half of the prisoners, it would thus appear, perished within
the year.

The war with Genoa did not end with the restoration of
Chioggia, but it was carried .on henceforward in distant waters
and among the Dalmatian towns and islands. Carlo Zeno himself was sent to take at all hazards a certain Castle of Marano,
against his own will and judgment, and failed, as he had previously assured his masters he must fail; and there were many
troubles on the side of Treviso, which Venice presented to Duke
Leopold of Austria, in order to preserve it from the Carrarese, now
the obstinate enemies of the republic. Here the difficulties with
the Condottieri reappeared again, but in a less serious way. The
soldiers whose pay was in arrears, and who, hearing of the
proposed transfer, felt themselves in danger of falling between
two stools, and getting pay from neither side, confided their cause
to a certain Borato Malaspina, who presented himself before the
Venetian magistrates of Treviso, and set his conditions before
them. "We have decided," he said, "in consideration of the
dignity of the Venetian name and the good faith of the soldiers,
to take our own affairs in hand, and in all love and friendship
to ask for our pay. We have decided to remain each man at his
post until one of you goes to Venice for the money. During this
interval everything shall be faithfully defended and guarded by
us. But we will no longer delay, nor can we permit our business
with the Senate to be conducted by letter. Your presence is
necessary in order that everything may go well. And we will

await the return of him who shall be sent to Venice, with a proper regard to the time necessary for his coming and going. There is no need for further consultation in the case, for what we ask is quite reasonable." The astounded magistrates stared at this bold demand, but found nothing better for it than to obey.

And at last the war was over, and peace, in which to heal her wounds, and restore her half-ruined trade, and put order in her personal affairs, came to Venice. According to the promise made in her darkest hour, thirty families from among those who had served the republic best were added to the number of the nobles. "Before they went to the palazzo they heard the divine mass, then, presenting themselves before the prince and Senate, swore to the republic their faith *and silence.*" The last is a remarkable addition to the oath of allegiance, and curiously characteristic of Venice. "Giacomo Cavallo, Veronese," adds Sabellico, "for his strenuous and faithful service done during this war, obtained the same dignity." It was the highest which the republic could bestow.

The subsequent history of Carlo Zeno we have entirely upon the word of his descendant and biographer, who, like most biographers of that age, is chiefly intent upon putting every remarkable act accomplished in his time to the credit of his hero. At the same time, we have every reason to trust Bishop Jacopo, whose work is described by Foscarini as the most faithful record existing of the war of Chioggia: the author, as that careful critic adds, "being a person of judgment and enlightenment, and living at a period not far removed from these acts." He was indeed born before the death of his grandfather, and must have had full command of all family memorials, as well as the evidence of many living persons, for the facts he records. We may accordingly take his book, with perhaps a little allowance for natural partiality, as a trustworthy record of the many wonderful vicissitudes of Carlo's life. And whether the bold pirate-like countenance which serves as frontispiece to Quirini's translation of the bishop's book be taken from any authentic portrait (which is little likely), there can be at least no doubt of the family tradition, which describes the great soldier-seaman thus :

" He was square-shouldered, broad-chested, solidly and strongly made, with large and speaking eyes, and a manly, great, and full countenance; his stature neither tall nor short, but of a middle size. Nothing was wanting in his appearance which strength, health, decorum, and gravity demanded." With the exception perhaps of the gravity and decorum, which are qualities naturally attributed by a clergyman to his grandfather, the description is true to all our ideas of a naval hero. At the time of the struggle before Chioggia, which he conducted at once so gallantly and so warily, he was forty-five, in the prime of his strength : and that solid and steadfast form which nothing could shake, those eyes which met undaunted the glare of so many mutinous troopers, always full of the keenest observation, letting nothing escape them, stand out as clearly among the crowd as if, forestalling a century, Gentile Bellini had painted him, strongly planted upon those sturdy limbs to which the rock of the high seas had given a sailor's double security of balance, confronting the heavy, furious Germans, the excited Frenchmen, the revengeful Italians of other states, scarcely less alien to his own than the *forestieri* with their strange tongues—whose sole bond of allegiance to their momentary masters was the double pay, or occasional *donativo*, which they exacted as the price of their wavering faith. A truer type of the ideal Venetian, strong, subtle, ready-witted, prompt in action and prepared for everything, the patriot, pirate, admiral, merchant; general, whichever character was most needed at the moment, could not be.

Carlo did not return to his merchandise after this absorbing struggle. He was made captain-general of the forces on the death, not long after, of Vittor Pisani : and when the old Doge Contarini died he was for a time the favourite candidate for that honour. The electors indeed had all but decided in his favour, the bishop tells us, when a certain Zaccaria Contarini, "a man of great authority and full of eloquence and the art of speech," addressed an oration to them on the subject. His argument was a curious one. Against Carlo Zeno, he allowed, not a word could be said : there was no better man, none more worthy, nor of higher virtue in all Venice, none who had served the republic better, or to whom her citizens were more deeply indebted ; but these were the very reasons why he should not be made Doge—for should another war arise with Genoa, who could lead the soldiers of Venice against her rival but he who was the scourge of the Genoese, a man with whom no other could compare for knowledge of things naval and military : for prudence, judgment, fidelity to the country, greatness and good fortune ? "If you should bind such a man to the prince's office, most noble fathers, to stay at home, to live in quiet, to be immersed in the affairs of the city, tell me what other have you ?" Thus Carlo's fame was used against him, "whether with a good intention for the benefit of the republic, or from envy of Carlo," Bishop Jacopo does not undertake to say. Neither does he tell us whether his illustrious ancestor was disappointed by the issue. But when peace was proclaimed, and there was no more work for him nor further promotion possible, Carlo left Venice and went forth upon the world "to see and salute various princes throughout Italy with whom he was united by no common friendship." A man so celebrated was received with open arms everywhere, especially where fighting was going on, and made himself useful to his princely friends in various emergencies. He served Galeazzo Visconti of Milan in this way, and was governor of that city for several years and also of the province of Piedmont, which was under Visconti's sway : and absorbed in such occupations was absent from Venice for ten years, always with increasing honour and reputation. While thus occupied, what seemed a very trifling incident occurred in his career. At Asti he encountered Francesco da Carrara, the son of the lord of Padua, sometime the enemy but at that moment at peace with Venice, an exile and in great straits and trouble ; and finding him sad, anxious and unhappy, and in want of

every comfort, *per non mancare all' ufficio di gentiluomo*, not to
fail in the duty of a gentleman, did his best to encourage and
cheer the exile, and lent him four hundred ducats for his immediate wants. Some years after, when Francesco had been restored to Padua and regained his place, Carlo passed through
that city on his way to Venice, and was repaid the money he
had lent. The incident was a very simple one, but not without
disastrous consequences.

On his return to Venice Carlo was again employed successfully against the Genoese under a French general, that proud
city having fallen under the sway of France—and covered the
Venetian name once more with glory. This to all appearance
was his last independent action as the commander of the forces
of Venice. He was growing old, and civil dignities, though
never the highest, began to be awarded to him. When the war
with the house of Carrara broke out, Carlo Malatesta of Rimini,
one of the great Condottieri of the time, held the chief command, and Carlo Zeno accompanied the army only in the capacity
of Provveditore. A strong military force was by this time in the
pay of the republic; but again as ever it was as hard a task
to keep them from fighting among themselves as to overcome
the enemy. Malatesta threw up his commission in the midst of
the campaign, and Paolo Savello was appointed in his stead;
but either this did not please the mercenaries, or personal feuds
among them breaking out suddenly on the occasion of the
change, the camp was immediately in an uproar, and the different factions began to cut each other in pieces. Carlo forced
his way into the middle of the fight, and when he had succeeded
in calming it for the moment, called before him the chiefs of
the factions, and after his usual custom addressed them. His
speech is no longer that of a general at the head of an army,
but of an old man much experienced and full of serious dignity,
before the restless and ferocious soldiers. "I thought," he said,
"that the uses and customs of war would have moderated your
minds and delivered you from passion; for there is true noble-
ness where prudence is conjoined with courage, and nothing so

becomes a generous man as a tranquil modesty and gravity in military operations. The shedding of blood becomes a sordid business if not conducted and accompanied by a decorous dignity." He then points out to them that their work is nearly accomplished : all the difficulties have been overcome : Padua is closely besieged and famishing, the end is at hand :

" We have come, oh captains, to the conclusion of the war, a fortunate end is near to your toils and watches, and nothing remains but the prize and the victory. What then would you have, oh signori? What do you desire ? What fury moves you ? Why are these arms, which should subdue the enemy, turned against each other ? Will you make your own labours, your vigils, your great efforts, and all the difficulties you have overcome but useless pains, and the hope of success in so hard a fight as vain as they ? And can you endure, oh strong men, to see the work of so many months destroyed in one hour ? I pray you then, generous captains, if any sense of lofty mind, of valour, and of fidelity is in you, come, lay down your arms, calm your rage, conciliate and pacify the offended, make an end of these feuds and conflicts, return to your former brotherliness, and let us condone those injuries done to the republic and to me."

The old warrior was seventy when he made this speech. Yet it was he, if his biographer reports truly, who had explored in his own person the marshes about Padua, sometimes wading, sometimes swimming, pushing his way through bog and mud, to discover a way by which the troops could pass. He had a right to plead that all the labours thus gone through should not be in vain.

When Padua was taken Carlo was made governor of the city. The unfortunate Carrarese were taken to Venice and imprisoned in San Giorgio, where was enacted one of the darkest scenes in Venetian history. But with this Zeno had nothing to do. He left his post soon after, a colleague having been appointed, in the belief that nothing called for his presence, and returned to Venice. The colleague, to whom Bishop Jacopo gives no name, among his other labours, took upon him to examine the expenditure of the city for many years back, and there found a certain strange entry : *To Carlo Zeno, paid four hundred ducats.* No doubt it was one of the highest exercises of

Christian charity on the part of the bishop to keep back this busybody's name. With all haste the register was sent to Venice to be placed before the terrible Ten. "The Ten," says Jacopo, "held in the city of Venice the supreme magistracy, with power to punish whomsoever they pleased ; and from their sentence there is never any appeal permitted for any reason whatever, and all that they determine is final, nor can it be known of any one whether what they do is according to reason or not." Called before this tribunal Carlo gave the simple explanation with which the reader has been already furnished. But before that secret tribunal, his honour, his stainless word, his labours for his country, availed him nothing. Perhaps the men whose hands had strangled Francesco da Carrara and his son in their prison, still thrilling with the horror of that deed, felt a secret pleasure in branding the hero of Chioggia, the deliverer of Venice, her constant defender and guard, as a traitor and miserable stipendiary in foreign pay. The penalty for this crime was the loss of all public place and rank as senator or magistrate, and two years of prison. And to this Carlo Zeno was sentenced as a fitting end to his long and splendid career.

It is unnecessary to tell, though our bishop does it with fine suppressed indignation, how the people, thunderstruck by such an outrage, both in Venice itself and in the other surrounding cities, would have risen against it :

"But Carlo," he adds, "with marvellous moderation of mind and with a strong and constant soul, supported the stroke of envious fortune without uttering a complaint or showing a sign of anxiety, saying solely that he knew the course of human things to be unstable, and that this which had happened to him was nothing new or unknown, since he had long been acquainted with the common fate of men, and how vain was their wisdom, of how little value their honours and dignities, of which he now gave to all a powerful example."

But Venice is not alone in thus rewarding her greatest men.

Bishop Jacopo does not say in so many words that Carlo fulfilled his sentence and passed two years in prison; so we may hope that even the Ten, with all their daring, did not venture to execute the sentence they had pronounced. All we are told is that "as soon as he was free to go where he pleased" he made a pilgrimage to Jerusalem, turning his soul to religion and sacred things. Here a curious incident is recorded, to which it is difficult to say what faith should be given. In the Holy City Carlo, according to his biographer, met and formed a warm friendship with a Scotch prince, "Pietro, son of the King of Scotland," who insisted, out of the love and honour he bore him, on knighting the aged Venetian. We know of no Prince Peter in Scottish history, but he might have been one of the many sons of Robert II., the first Stewart king. The rank of knight, so prized among the Northern races, seems to have been, like other grades, little known among the Venetians, the great distinction between the noble and the plebeian being the only one existing. To be made a knight in peaceful old age, after a warlike career, is a whimsical incident in Carlo's life.

But though he was old, and a peaceful pilgrim on a religious journey, his hand had not forgotten its cunning in affairs of war: and on his way home he lent his powerful aid to the King of Cyprus, and once more, no doubt with much satisfaction to himself, beat the Genoese and saved the island. Returning home the old man, somewhere between seventy and eighty, married for the third time, but very reasonably, a lady of a noble Istrian family, of an age not unsuitable to his own, "for no other reason than to secure good domestic government, and a consort and companion who would take upon herself all internal cares, and leave him free to study philosophy and the sacred writings." Let us hope that the old couple were happy, and that the lady was satisfied with the position assigned her. Having thus provided for the due regulation of all his affairs, the old warrior gave himself up to the enjoyment of his evening of leisure. He made friends with all the doctors and learned men of his day, a list of names *cruditissimi* in their time, but, alas! altogether passed from human recollection: and his house became a second court, a centre of intellectual life in Venice as well as the constant haunt of honest statesmen and good citizens

o

seeking his advice on public questions and material difficulties as they arose. As for Carlo, he loved nothing so much as to spend his time in reading and writing, and every day when he was able heard mass in San Stefano, "nor ever went out," adds the bishop with satisfaction, "that he did not go to church or some other religious place." "In the cold winter (*nell' orrida e gelida invernata*) he had his bed filled with books, so that when he had slept sufficiently he could sit up in bed, and pass the rest of the night in reading, nor would he put down his book save for some great necessity." One wonders what books the noble old seaman had to read. Scholastic treatises on dry points of mediæval philosophy, hair-splitting theological arguments most probably. Let us hope that there blossomed between some saintly legends, some chronicle newly written of the great story of Venice, perhaps some sonnet of Petrarch's, whom Carlo in his early manhood must have met on the Piazza, or seen looking out from the windows on the Riva—or perhaps even some portion of the great work of Dante the Florentine. He forgot himself and the troubles of his old age among his books; but before he had reached the profounder quiet of the grave Carlo had still great sorrows to bear. The worthy wife who took the cares of his household from him grew ill and died, to his great grief: and—a pang still greater—Jacopo, his youngest son, the father of the bishop, died too in the flower of his manhood, at thirty, leaving the old father desolate. Another son, Pietro, survived, and was a good seaman and commander: but it was upon Jacopo that the father's heart was set. At last, in 1418, at the age of eighty-four—in this point too following the best traditions of Venice—Carlo Zeno died, full of honours and of sorrows. He was buried with all imaginable pomp, the entire city joining the funeral procession. One last affecting incident is recorded in proof of the honour in which his countrymen and his profession held the aged hero. The religious orders claimed, as was usual, the right of carrying him to his grave: but against this the seafaring population, *quasi tutti i Veneziani allevati sul mare*, arose as one man, and hastening to the Doge claimed the right of bearing to his last rest the commander who had loved them so well. Their prayer was granted: and with all the ecclesiastical splendours in front of them, and all the pomp of the State behind, the seamen of Venice, *i Veneziani sperimentati nelle cose maritime*, carried him to his grave; each relay watching jealously that every man might have his turn. This band of seamen great and small, forming the centre of the celebration, makes a fitting conclusion to the career of the great captain, who had so often swept the seas, the *alto mare*, of every flag hostile to his city.

But in modern Venice the tomb of Carlo Zeno is known no more. He was buried "in the celebrated church called La Celestia," attached to a convent of Cistercians, but long ago destroyed. Its site and what unknown fragments may remain of its original fabric now form part of the Arsenal, and there perhaps under some forgotten stone lie the bones of the great admiral, the scourge of Genoa—not, after all, an inappropriate spot.

CHAPTER III.

HE history of Venice opens into a totally new chapter when the great republic, somewhat humbled and driven back by the victorious Turk from her possessions beyond sea, and maintaining with difficulty her broken supremacy as a maritime power, begins to turn her eyes towards the green and fat *terra firma*—those low-lying plains that supplied her with bread and beeves, which it was so natural to wish for, but so uneasy to hold. The suggestion that her enemies, if united, could cut her off at any time from her supplies, so nearly accomplished in the struggle for Chioggia, was a most plausible and indeed reasonable ground for acquiring, if possible, the command in her own hands of the rich Lombardy pastures and fields of grain. And when the inhabitants of certain threatened cities hastily threw themselves on her protection in order to escape their assailants, her acceptance was instantaneous, and it would seem to have been with an impulse of delight that she felt her foot upon the mainland, and saw the possibility within her power of establishing a firm standing, perhaps acquiring a permanent empire there. It would be hopeless to enter into the confused and endless politics of Guelph and Ghibelline, which threw a sort of veil over the fact that every man was in reality for his own hand, and

that to establish himself or his leader in the sovereignty of a
wealthy city, by help of either one faction or the other, or in
the name of a faction, or on any other pretext that might be
handy, was the real purpose of the captains who cut and
carved Lombardy, and of the reigning families who had already
established themselves upon the ashes of defunct republics or
subdued municipalities. But of this there was no possibility
in Venice. No Whites and Blacks ever struggled in the canals.
The only rebellions that touched her were those made by men
or parties endeavouring to get a share of the power which by
this time had been gathered tightly beyond all possibility of
moving in patrician hands. Neither the Pope nor the Emperor
was ever the watchword of a party in the supreme and independent city, which dealt on equal terms with both.

There was no reason, however, why Venice should not take
advantage of these endless contentions: and there was one existing in full force which helped to make the wars of the mainland
more easy to the rich Venetians than war had ever been before.
All their previous expeditions of conquest, which had been neither
few nor small, were at the cost of the blood as well as the wealth
of Venice, had carried off the best and bravest, and even, as in
the romantic story of the Giustiniani, swept whole families away.
But this was no longer the case when she strode upon *terra
firma* with an alien general at her elbow, and mercenary
soldiers at her back. Though they might not turn out very
satisfactory in the long run, no doubt there must have been a
certain gratification in hiring, so to speak, a ready-made army,
and punishing one's enemy and doubling one's possessions
without so much as a scratch on one's own person or the loss
even of a retainer. The *Condottieri*, conductors, leaders, captains
of the wild spirits that were to be found all over the world in
that age of strife and warfare, were, if not the special creation
of, at least most specially adapted for the necessities of those
rich towns, always tempting to the ambitious, always by their
very nature exposed to assault, and at once too busy and too
luxurious at this advanced stage of their history to do their

fighting themselves—which divided Italy among them, and which
were each other's rivals, competitors, and enemies, to the sad hind-
rance of all national life, but to the growth, by every stimulus
of competition, of arts and industries and ways of getting
rich—in which methods each endeavoured with the zeal of
personal conflict to outdo the rest. The rights, the liberties
and independence of those cities were always more or less at
the mercy of any adventurous neighbouring prince who had
collected forces enough to assail them, or of the stronger among
their own fellows. We must here add that between the horrors
of the first mercenaries, the *Grande Compagnia*, which carried
fire and sword through Italy, and made Petrarch's blood run
cold, and even the endless turbulence and treachery of the men
whom Carlo Zeno had so much ado to master, and the now fully
organised and re-organised armies, under their own often famous
and sometimes honourable leaders, there was a great difference.
The Free Lances had become a sort of lawful institution,
appropriate and adapted to the necessities of the time.

The profession of soldier of fortune is not one which commends
itself to us nowadays : and yet there was nothing necessarily in it
dishonourable to the generals who carried on their game of
warfare at the expense of the quarrelsome races which employed
them, but at wonderfully little cost of human life. No great
principle lay in the question whether Duke Philip of Milan
or the Republic of Venice should be master of Cremona.
One of them, if they wished it, was bound to have the lesser
city ; and what did it matter to a general who was a Savoyard,
coming down to those rich plains to make his fortune, which
of these wealthy paymasters he should take service under ?
His trade was perhaps as honest as that of the trader who
buys in the cheapest market and sells in the dearest all the
world over. He obeyed the same law of supply and demand.
He acted on the same lively sense of his own interests. If he
transferred himself in the midst of the war from one side to
the other there was nothing very remarkable in it, since neither
of the sides was his side ; and it was a flourishing trade. One

of its chief dangers was the unlucky accident that occurred
now and then, when a general, who failed of being successful,
had his head taken off by the Signoria or Seigneur in whose
employment he was, probably on pretence of treason.   But
fighting of itself was not dangerous, at least to the troops
engaged, and spoils were plentiful and the life a merry one.
Italy, always so rich in the bounties of nature, had never been so
rich as in these days, and the troops had a succession of
villages always at their command, with the larger morsel of a
rich town to sack now and then, prisoners to ransom, and all
the other chances of war.   Their battles were rather exercises
of skill than encounters of personal opponents, and it was not
unusual to achieve a great feat of arms without shedding a
drop of blood.   The bloodshed was among the non-combatants—
the villagers, the harmless townsfolk who were mad enough
to resist them—and not among the fighting men.

Such was the profession, when a wandering Savoyard trooper
—perhaps come home with his spoils in filial piety, or to make
glad the heart of a rustic love with trinkets dragged from the
ears or pulled bloody from the throat of some Lombard maiden
—took note among the fields of a keen-eyed boy, who carried
his shaggy locks with such an *aria fiera*, so proud an air, that
the soldier saw something beyond the common recruit in this
young shepherd lad.   Romance, like nature, is pretty much the
same in all regions; and young Francesco, the peasant's son,
under the big frontier tower of Carmagnola, makes us think
with a smile of young Norval " on the Grampian Hills "—that
noble young hero whose history has unfortunately fallen into
derision.   But in those distant days, when the fifteenth century
had just begun, and through all the Continent there was nothing
heard but the clatter of mail and the tread of the war-horse,
there was nothing ridiculous in the idea that the boy, hearing
of battles, should long " to follow to the field some warlike
lord," or should leave the sheep to shift for themselves, and go
off with the bold companion who had such stories of siege and
fight to tell.   He appears to have entered at once the service of

Facino Cane, one of the greatest generals of the time, under whom he rose, while still quite young, to some distinction. Such, at least, would seem to have been the case, since one of the first notices in history of the young Piedmontese is the record in one of the old chronicles of a question put to Facino —Why did he not promote him ? To which the great Condottiere replied that he could not do so—the rustic arrogance of Francesco being such that if he got one step he would never be satisfied till he was chief of all. For this reason, though his military genius was allowed full scope, he was kept in as much subjection as possible, and had but ten lances under him, and small honour as far as could be seen ; yet was noted of the captains as a man born to be something beyond the ordinary level when his day should come.

The Italian world was as usual in a state of great disturbance in these days. Giovanni or Gian Galeazzo, the Duke of Milan, in his time as masterful an invader as any, had died, leaving two sons—the one who succeeded him, Gian Maria, being a feeble and vicious youth, of whose folly and weakness the usual advantages were soon taken. When the young Duke was found to be unable to restrain them, the cities of Lombardy sprang with wonderful unanimity each into a revolution of its own. The generals who on occasion had served the house of Visconti faithfully enough, found now the opportunity to which these free-lances were always looking forward, and established themselves, each with hopes of founding a new dukedom, and little independent dominion of his own, in the revolted cities. Piacenza, Parma, Cremona, Lodi, all found thus a new sovereign, with an army to back him. The Duke's younger brother, Filippo Maria, had been left by his father in possession of the town of Pavia, a younger son's inheritance : but Facino Cane made light of this previous settlement, and in the new position of affairs with the house of Visconti visibly going downhill, took possession of the city, retaining young Philip as half guest, half prisoner. When matters were in this woeful state, the Duke was assassinated in Milan, and by his death the young captive

in Pavia became the head of the house—to little purpose, however, had things remained as they were. But on the very
same day Facino died in Pavia, and immediately all the prospects
of Philip were altered. There was evidently no one to take the
place of the dead soldier. The troops who had brought him to
that eminence, and the wealth he had acquired, and the wife
who probably mourned but little for the scarred and deaf old
trooper who had won her by his bow and spear, were all left to
be seized by the first adventurer who was strong enough to take
advantage of the position. Whether by his own wit or the
advice of wise counsellors, the young disinherited prince sprang
into the vacant place, and at once a counter revolution began.

It would seem that the death of his leader raised Francesco,
the Savoyard, by an equally sudden leap, into the front of the
captains of that army. He had taken the name of his village,
a well-sounding one and destined to fatal celebrity, perhaps by
reason of the want of a surname which was common to Italian
peasants, and which probably told more among the Condottieri,
whose ranks included many of the best names in Italy, than
it did in art. He was still very young, not more than twenty-
two. But he would seem to have had sufficient sense and
insight to perceive the greatness of the opportunity that lay
before him, and to have at once thrown the weight of his sword
and following upon Philip's side. Probably the two young men
had known each other, perhaps been comrades more or less,
when Carmagnola was a young captain under Facino's orders
and Philip an uneasy loiterer about his noisy court. At all
events Carmagnola at once embraced the prince's cause. He
took Milan for him, killing an illegitimate rival, and overcoming
all rival factions there; and afterwards, as commander-in-chief
of the Duke of Milan's forces, reconquered one by one the
revolted cities. This was a slow process, extending over several
seasons—for those were the days when everything was done by
rule, when the troops retired into winter quarters, and a campaign was a leisurely performance executed at a time of year
favourable for such operations, and attended by little danger

except to the unfortunate inhabitants of the district in which it was carried on.

The services thus rendered were largely and liberally rewarded. A kinswoman of Philip's, a lady of the Visconti family, whose first husband had been high in the Duke's confidence, became Carmagnola's wife, and the privilege of bearing the name of Visconti and the arms of the reigning house was conferred upon him. He was not only the commander-in-chief of the troops, but held a high place at Court, and was one of the chief and most trusted of Philip's counsellors. The Piedmontese soldier was still a young man when all these glories came upon him, with accompanying wealth, due also to Philip's favour, as well as to the booty won in Philip's cause. He seems to have lived in Milan in a state conformable to these high pretensions and to the position of his wife, and was in the act of building himself a great palace, now known as the Broletto, and appropriated to public use, when the usual fate of a favourite began to shadow over him. This was in the year 1424, twelve years after he had thrown in his fate with the prince in Pavia. The difference in Philip's position by this time was wonderful. He had then possessed nothing save a doubtful claim on the city where he was an exile and prisoner. He was now one of the greatest powers in Italy, respected and feared by his neighbours, the master of twenty rich cities, and of all the wealthy Lombard plains. To these Carmagnola had lately added the richest prize of all, in the humiliation and overthrow of Genoa, superbest of northern towns, with her seaboard and trade, and all her proud traditions of independence, the equal and rival of the great Republic of Venice. Perhaps this last feat had unduly exalted the soldier, and made him feel himself as a conqueror something more than the Duke's humble kinsman and counsellor: at all events, the eve of the change had come.

The tenure of a favourite's favour is always uncertain and precarious. In those days there were many who rose to the heights of fame only to be tumbled headlong in a moment from that dazzling eminence. Carmagnola was at the very height of

fortune when clouds began to gather over his career.   Though
no idea of treachery was then imputed to him, he had been if
anything too zealous for his Duke, to whose service in the
meantime, as to that of a great and conquering prince, full of
schemes for enlarging his own territory and affording much
occupation for a brave soldiery, many other commanders had
flocked.   The enemies of Carmagnola were many.   Generals
whom he had beaten felt their downfall all the greater that
it had been accomplished by a fellow without any blood worth
speaking of in his veins ; and others whom it would have
pleased Philip to secure in his service were too proud to serve
under a man who had thus risen from the ranks.

The first sign which the doomed general received of his
failing favour was a demand from Philip for the squadron
of horsemen, 300 in number, who seem to have been Carmagnola's special troop, and for whom the Duke declared that
he had a particular use.   The reply of the general is at once
picturesque and pathetic.   He implored Philip not to take the
weapons out of the hands of a man born and bred in the midst
of arms, and to whom life would be bare indeed without his
soldiers.   As a matter of fact, it is to be presumed that this was
but the thin end of the wedge, and that other indignities were
prepared to follow.   The clique at Milan which was furthering
his downfall was led by two courtiers, Riccio and Lampugnano.
" Much better," says Bigli, the historian of Milan, who narrates
diffusely the whole course of the quarrel, " would it have
been for our State had such men as these never been born.
They kept everything from the Duke except what it pleased
him to learn.   And it was easy for them to fill the mind of
Philip with suspicions, for he himself began to wish that
Francesco Carmagnola should not appear so great a man."
Carmagnola received no answer to his remonstrance, and by
and by discovered, what is galling in all circumstances, and in
his especially so, that the matter had been decided by the
gossips of the Court, and that it was a conspiracy of his enemies
which was settling his fate.   Fierce and full of irritation, a man

who could never at any time restrain his masterful temper, and
still, no doubt, with much in him of the arrogant rustic whom
Facino could not make a captain of, lest he should at once
clutch at the baton, Carmagnola determined to face his enemies
and plead his own cause before his prince. The Duke was at
Abbiate-grasso, on the borders of Piedmont, a frontier fortress,
within easy reach of Genoa, where Carmagnola was governor :
and thither he rode with few attendants, no doubt breathing fire
and flame, and, in his consciousness of all he had done for Philip,
very confident of turning the tables upon his miserable assailants, and making an end of them and their wiles. His letters
had not been answered—no notice whatever had been taken of
his appeal; but still it seemed impossible to doubt that
Philip, with his trusty champion before him, would remember
all that had passed between them, and all that Francesco
had done, and do him justice. His swift setting out to put
all right, with an angry contempt of his assailants, but absolute
confidence in the renewal of his old influence as soon as
Philip should see him, might be paralleled in many a quarrel.
For nothing is so difficult as to teach a generous and impulsive
man that the friend for whom he has done too much may
suddenly become incapable of bearing the burden of obligation
and gratitude.

Arrived at Abbiate, he was about to ride over the bridge into
the castle, when he was stopped by the guards, whose orders
were to hinder his entrance. This to the commander-in-chief
was an extraordinary insult; but at first astonishment was the
only feeling Carmagnola evidenced. He sent word to Philip
that he was there desiring an audience, and waited with his
handful of men, the horses pawing the ground, their riders
chafing at the compulsory pause, which no one understood.
But instead of being then admitted with apologies and excuses,
as perhaps Carmagnola still hoped, the answer sent him was
that Philip was busy, but that he might communicate what he
had to say to Riccio. Curbing his rage, the proud soldier sent
another message to the effect that he had certain private matters

for the Duke's ear alone. To this no reply was given. The situation is wonderfully striking, and full of dramatic force. Carmagnola and his handful of men on one side of the bridge; the castle rising on the other with all its towers and bastions dark against the sky; the half-frightened yet half insolent guards trembling at their own temerity, yet glad enough to have a hand in the discomfiture of the rustic commander, the arrogant and high-handed captain, who of his origin was no better than they. The parley seems to have gone on for some time, during which Carmagnola was held at bay by the attendants, who would make him no answer other than a continual reference to Riccio, his well-known enemy. Then as he scanned the dark unresponsive towers with angry eyes, he saw, or thought he saw, the face of Philip himself at a loophole. This lit the smouldering fire of passion. He raised his voice—no small voice it may well be believed—and shouted forth his message to his ungrateful master. "Since I cannot speak before my lord the Duke," he cried, "I call God to witness my innocence and faithfulness to him. I have not been guilty even of imagining evil against him. I have never taken thought for myself, for my blood or my life, in comparison with the name and power of Philip." Then, "carried on in the insolence of his words," says the chronicle, "he accused the perfidious traitors, and called God to witness that in a short time he would make them feel the want of one whom the. Duke refused to hear."

So speaking Carmagnola turned his horse, and took his way towards the river. When the conspirators in the castle saw the direction he was taking, a thrill of alarm seems to have moved them, and one of them, Oldrado, dashed forth from the gate with a band of followers to prevent Carmagnola from crossing the Ticino, which was then the boundary of Savoy. But when he saw the great captain "riding furiously across the fields" towards Ticino, the heart of the pursuer failed him. Carmagnola would seem never to have paused to think—which was not the fashion of his time—but, carried along in headlong

impulse, wild with the thought of his dozen years of service, all
forgotten in a moment, did not draw bridle till he reached the
castle of the Duke of Savoy, his native prince, to whom he
immediately offered himself and his services, telling the story
of his wrong. Notwithstanding his fury, he seems to have
exonerated Philip,—a doubtful compliment, since he held him
up to the contempt of his brother potentate as influenced by the
rabble of his Court, "the singers, actors, and inventors of all
crimes, who make use of the labours of others in order to live
in sloth." Mere vituperation of Philip's advisers, however, was
not to the purpose, and Carmagnola artfully suggested to Duke
Amadeo certain towns more justly his than Philip's: Asti,
Alessandria, and others, which it would be easy to withdraw
from the yoke of Milan. It must have been difficult for a
fifteenth century prince to resist such an argument, but Amadeo,
though strongly tempted, was not powerful enough to declare
war by himself against the great Duke of Milan; and the fiery
visitor, leaving excitement and commotion behind him, continued his journey, making his way across a spur of the Pennine
Alps, by Trient and Treviso (but as secretly as possible, lest the
Swiss, whom he had beaten, should hear of his passage and rise
against him), till he reached Venice, to stir up a still more
effectual ferment there.

We are now brought back to our city, where for some time
past the proceedings of Philip, and the progress he was making,
especially the downfall of Genoa, had filled the Signoria with
alarm. The Venetians must have looked on with very mingled
feelings at the overthrow of the other republic, their own great
and unfailing enemy, with whom over and over again they had
struggled almost to the death, yet who could not be seen to fall
under the power of a conqueror with any kind of satisfaction.
The Florentines, too, had begun to stir in consternation and
amaze, and communications had passed between the two
great cities even in the time of the Doge Mocenigo, the predecessor of Foscari, who was the occupant of the ducal throne
at the time of Carmagnola's sudden appearance on the scene.

Old Mocenigo had not favoured the alliance with the Florentines. There is a long speech of his recorded by Sanudo which
reminds us of the pleadings in Racine's comedy, where the
sham advocates go back to the foundation of the world for their
arguments—and which affords us a singular glimpse of the
garrulous and vehement old man, who hated his probable successor, and the half of whose rambling discourse is addressed, it
would seem, personally to Foscari, then junior procurator, who
had evidently taken up the cause of the neighbouring republics.

"Our junior procurator (*procuratore giovane*), Ser Francesco Foscari,
Savio del Consiglio, has declared to the public (*sopra l'arringo*) all that
the Florentines have said to the Council and all that we have said to your
Excellencies in reply. He says that it is well to succour the Florentines,
because their good is our good, and, in consequence, their evil is our evil.
In due time and place we reply to this. Procuratore giovane : God created
and made the angelical nature, which is the most noble of all created
things, and gave it certain limits by which it should follow the way of
good and not of evil. The angels chose the bad way that leads to evil.
God punished them and banished them from Paradise to the Inferno, and
from being good they became bad. This same thing we say to the Florentines who come here seeking the evil way. Thus will it happen to us if we
consent to that which our junior procurator has said. But take comfort to
yourselves that you live in peace. If ever the Duke [of Milan] makes
unjust war against you, God is with you, Who sees all. He will so arrange
it that you shall have the victory. Let us live in peace, for God is peace ;
and he who desires war, let him go to perdition. Procuratore giovane : God
created Adam wise, good, and perfect, and gave him the earthly Paradise,
where was peace, with two commandments, saying : Enjoy peace with all
that is in Paradise, but eat not the fruit of a certain tree. And he was
disobedient and sinned in pride, not being willing to acknowledge that he
was merely a creature. And God deprived him of Paradise where peace
dwells, and drove him out and put him in war, which is this world, and
cursed him and all human generations. And one brother killed the other,
going from bad to worse. Thus it will happen to the Florentines for their
fighting which they have among themselves. And if we follow the counsel
of our junior procurator thus will it happen also to us. Procuratore giovane :
After the sin of Cain, who knew not his Creator nor did His will, God
punished the world by the flood, excepting Noah, whom He preserved.
Thus will it happen to the Florentines in their determination to have their
own way, that God will destroy their country and their possessions, and

they will come to dwell here, in the same way as families with their women and children came to dwell in the city of Noah, who obeyed God and trusted in Him. Otherwise, if we follow the counsel of our junior procurator our people will have to go away and dwell in strange lands. Procuratore giovane: Noah was a holy man elect of God, and Cain departed from God: the which slew Japhet (Abel ?) and God punished him: of whom were born the giants, who were tyrants and did whatever seemed good in their own eyes, not fearing God. God made of one language sixty-six, and at the end they destroyed each other, so that there remained no one of the seed of the giants. Thus will it happen to the Florentines for seeking their own will and not fearing God. Of their language sixty-six languages will be made. For they go out day by day into France, Germany, Languedoc, Catalonia, Hungary, and throughout Italy: and they will thus be dispersed, so that no man will be able to say that he is of Florence. Thus will it be if we follow the advice of our junior procurator. Therefore, fear God and hope in Him."

We can almost see the old man, with fiery eyes and moist mouth, stammering forth these angry maunderings, leaning across the council-table, with his fierce personal designation of the Procurator Giovane, the proud young man in his strength, whom not all the vituperations of old Mocenigo, or his warnings to the council, could keep out of the ducal chair so soon as death made it vacant. And there is something very curious in this confused jumble of arguments, so inconsequent, so earnest —the old man's love of peace and a quiet life mingled with the cunning of the aged mediæval statesman who could not disabuse his mind of the idea that the destruction of Florence would swell the wealth of Venice. In the latter part of the long, rambling discourse, mixed up with all manner of Scriptural parallels not much more to the purpose than those above quoted, the speaker returns to and insists upon the advantage to be gained by Venice from the influx of refugees from all the neighbouring cities. "If the Duke takes Florence," cries the old man, "the Florentines, who are accustomed to live in equality, will leave Florence and come to Venice, and bring with them the silk trade, and the manufacture of wool, so that their country will be without trade, and Venice will grow rich, as happened in the case of Lucca when it fell into the hands of a tyrant. The trade of Lucca and its wealth came to Venice, and Lucca became poor. Wherefore, remain in peace."

Romanin, always watchful for the credit of Venice, attempts to throw some doubt upon this wonderful speech, which, however, is given on the same authority as that which gives us old Mocenigo's report of the accounts of the republic and his words of warning against Foscari, which are admitted to be authentic. It gives us a remarkable view of the mixture of wisdom and folly, astute calculation of the most fiercely selfish kind, and irrelevant argument, which is characteristic of the age.

It was in the year 1421 that Mocenigo thus discoursed. He died two years later at the age of eighty, and the Procurator Giovane, whom he had addressed so fiercely, succeeded as the old man foresaw. He was that Francesco Foscari whose cruel end we have already seen, but at this time in all the force and magnificence of his manhood, and with a great career before him—or at least with a great episode of Venetian history, a period full of agitation, victory, and splendour before the city under his rule. When Carmagnola, in hot revolt, and breathing nothing but projects of vengeance, arrived within the precincts of the republic, a great change had taken place in the views of the Venetians. The Florentine envoys had been received with sympathy and interest, and as Philip's troops approached nearer and nearer, threatening their very city, the Venetian government, though not yet moved to active interference, had felt it necessary to make a protest and appeal to Philip, to whom they were still bound by old alliances made in Mocenigo's time, in favour of the sister republic. Rivalships there might be in time of peace; but the rulers of Venice could not but regard " with much gravity and lament deeply the adversity of a free people, determining that whosoever would retain the friendship of Venice should be at peace with Florence." The envoy or orator, Paolo Cornaro, who was sent with this protest, presented it in a speech reported by the chronicler Sabellico, in which, with much dignity, he enjoins and urges upon Philip the determination of the Republic. Venetians and Florentines both make

P

short work with the independence of others; but yet there is
something noble in the air with which they vindicate their own.

> "Nothing (says Cornaro) is more dear to the Venetians than freedom :
> to the preservation of which they are called by justice, mercy, religion,
> and every other law, both public and private, counting nothing more
> praiseworthy than what is done to this end. And neither treaties nor
> laws, nor any other reason, divine or human, can make them depart from
> this, that before everything freedom must be secured. And in so far as
> regards the present case, the Venetians hold themselves as much bound to
> bestir themselves when Florence is in danger as if the army of Philip was
> on the frontier of their own dominion ; for it becomes those who have
> freedom themselves to be careful of that of others : and as the republican
> forms of government possessed by Florence resemble greatly their own,
> their case is like that of those who suffer no less in the sufferings of their
> brethren and relations than if the misfortune was theirs. Nor is there
> any doubt that he who in Tuscany contends against freedom in every
> other place will do the same, as is the custom of tyrants—who have ever
> the name of freedom in abhorrence."

The speaker ends by declaring that if Philip carries on his
assaults against the Florentines, Venice, for her own safety, as
well as for that of her sister city, will declare war against him
as a tyrant and an enemy. "This oration much disturbed the
soul of Philip." But he was full of the intoxication of success,
and surrounded by a light-hearted Court, to whom victory had
become a commonplace. The *giovanotti dishonestissimi*, foolish
young courtiers who, from the time of King Rehoboam, have
led young princes astray, whose jeers and wiles had driven Carmagnola to despair, were not to be daunted by the grave looks
of the noble Venetian, whom, no doubt, they felt themselves
capable of laughing and flattering out of his seriousness.

The next scene of the drama takes place in Venice, to which
Philip sent an embassy to answer the mission of Cornaro, led by
the same Oldrado who had made that ineffectual rush after
Carmagnola from the castle gates, and who was one of his chief
enemies. An embassy from Florence arrived at the same time,
and the presence of these two opposing bands filled with interest
and excitement the City of the Sea, where a new thing was

received with as much delight as in Athens of old, and where
the warlike spirit was always so ready to light up. The keen
eyes of the townsfolk seized at once upon the difference so
visible in the two parties. The Milanese, ruffling in their fine
clothes, went about the city gaily, as if they had come for no
other purpose than to see the sights, which, says Bigli, who was
himself of Milan, and probably thought a great deal too much
fuss was made about this wonderful sea-city, seemed ridiculous
to the Venetians, so that they almost believed the Duke was
making a jest of them. The Florentines, on the contrary, grave
as was their fashion, and doubly serious in the dangerous position of their affairs, went about the streets "as if in mourning,"
eagerly addressing everybody who might be of service to them.
Sabellico gives a similar account of the two parties.

"There might then be seen in the city divers ambassadors of divers
demeanour," he says. "Lorenzo (the Florentine), as was befitting, showed
the sadness and humble condition of his country, seeking to speak with the
senators even in the streets, following them to their houses, and neglecting
nothing which might be to the profit of the embassy. On the other hand,
those of Philip, not to speak of their pomp, and decorations of many
kinds, full of hope and confidence, went gazing about the city so marvel-
lously built, such as they had never seen before, full of wonder how all these
things of the earth could be placed upon the sea. And they replied cheerfully to all who saluted them, showing in their faces, in their eyes, by all
they said, and, in short, by every outward sign of satisfaction, the prosperity
of their Duke and country."

The dark figure of the Florentine, awaiting anxiously the
red-robed senator as he made his way across the Piazza, or
hurrying after him through the narrow thoroughfares, while
this gay band, in all their finery, swept by, must have made
an impressive comment upon the crisis in which so much was
involved. While the Milanese swam in a gondola, or gazed at
the marbles on the walls, or here and there an early mosaic,
all blazing, like themselves, in crimson and gold, the ambassador, upon whose pleading hung the dear life of Florence,
haunted the bridges and the street-corners, letting nobody pass
that could help him. "How goes the cause to-day, illustrious

P 2

signor?" one can hear him saying. "What hope for my
country, *la patria mia?* Will the noble Signoria hear me
speak ? Will it be given me to plead my cause before their
Magnificences?" Or in a bolder tone, "Our cause is yours,
most noble sir, though it may not seem so now. If Philip sets
his foot on the neck of Florence, which never shall be while I
live, how long will it be, think you, before his trumpets sound
at Mestre over the marshes, before he has stirred your Istrians
to revolt ?" The senators passing to and fro, perhaps in the
early morning after a long night in the council-chamber, as
happened sometimes, had their steps waylaid by this earnest
advocate. The Venetians were more given to gaiety than their
brothers from the Arno, but they were men who before everything else cared for their constitution, so artfully and skilfully
formed—for their freedom, such as it was, and the proud
independence which no alien force had ever touched; and the
stranger with his rugged Tuscan features and dark dress, and
keen inharmonious accent, among all their soft Venetian talk,
no doubt impressed the imagination of a susceptible race.
Whereas the Milanese gallants, in their gaiety affecting to see
no serious object in their mission, commended themselves only
to the light-minded, not to the fathers of the city. And when
Carmagnola, the great soldier known of all men—he who had
set Philip back upon his throne as everybody knew, and won
so many battles and cities—with all the romantic interest of a
hero and an injured man, came across the lagoon and landed at
the Piazzetta between the fated pillars, how he and his scarred
and bearded men-at-arms must have looked at the gay courtiers
with their jests and laughter, who on their side could scarcely
fail to shrink a little when the man whose ruin they had
plotted went past them to say his say before the Signoria, in a
sense fatally different from theirs, as they must have known.

The speeches of these contending advocates are all given at
length in the minute and graphic chronicle. The first to
appear before the Doge and Senate was Lorenzo Ridolfi, the
Florentine, who conjoins his earnest pleading for aid to his own

State with passionate admonitions and warnings, that if Venice gives no help to avert the consequences, her fate will soon be the same. "Serene Prince and illustrious senators," he cries, "even if I were silent you would understand what I came here to seek.

"And those also would understand who have seen us leave Tuscany and come here in haste, ambassadors from a free city, to ask your favour, and help for the protection of our liberties, from a free people like yourselves. The object of all my speaking is this, to induce you to grant safety to my country, which has brought forth and bred me, and given me honour and credit—which if I can attain, and that you should join the confederation and friendship of the Florentines, and join your army with our Tuscans against the cruelest tyrant, enemy of our liberties, and hating yours, happy shall be my errand, and my country will embrace me with joy on my return. And our citizens, who live in this sole hope, will hold themselves and their city by your bounty alone to be saved from every peril. . . . . I tremble, noble Prince, in this place to say that which I feel in my soul : but because it is necessary I will say it. If you will not make this alliance with us, Philip will find himself able without help, having overthrown Florence, to secure also the dominion of Venice If it should be answered me that the Venetians always keep their promises and engagements, I pray and implore the most high God that, having given you goodness and faith to keep your promises, He would give you to know the arts and motives of this tyrant, and after discovering them, with mature prudence to restrain and overrule them. . . . That tyrant himself, who has so often broken all laws, both divine and human, will himself teach you not to keep that which he, in his perfidy, has not kept. But already your tacit consent gives me to understand that I have succeeded in convincing you that in this oration I seek not so much the salvation of my republic as the happiness, dignity, and increase of your own."

This speech moved the senators greatly, but did not settle the question, their minds being divided between alarm, sympathy, and prudence—fear of Philip on the one hand and of expense on the other—so that they resolved to hear Philip's ambassadors first before coming to any decision. Time was given to the orator of the Milan party to prepare his reply to Ridolfi, which he made in a speech full of bravado, declaring that he and his fellows were sent, not to make any league or peace with Venice, since their former treaties were still in full force, and any renewal was unnecessary between such faithful allies—but simply to salute the illustrious Signoria in Philip's name.

"But since these people, who have by nature the gift of speech, delicate and false, have not only to the Senate, but in the Piazza and by the streets, with pitiful lamentations, wept their fate, declaring that the war which they have carried on so badly was begun by Philip ; he desires to leave it to your judgment, not refusing any conditions which you may prescribe. What they say is false and vain, unheard-of things, such as they are accustomed to study in order to abuse your gravity, your constancy, the ancient laws of friendship, and all the treaties made with Philip. They bid you fear him and the increase of his power. But you know they are our enemies who speak. They tell you that kings hate the name of republics. . . . It is true that King Louis was a cruel enemy of the Venetian name, and all the house of Carrara were your enemies. But the Visconti, who for a hundred years have flourished in the noble duchy of Milan, were always friends of the Venetian Republic. . . . Philip has had good reasons to war against the Florentines, and so have all the Visconti. They ought to accuse themselves, their pride and avarice, not Philip, who is the friend of peace and repose, the very model of liberality and courtesy. Let them therefore cease to abuse and injure our noble Duke in your presence. Being provoked we have answered in these few words, though we might have said many more ; which are so true that they themselves (although they are liars) do not venture to contradict them."

This address did not throw much light upon the subject, and left the Senate in as much difficulty as if it had been an English Cabinet Council at certain recent periods of our own history. "Diverse opinions and various decisions were agitated among the senators. Some declared that it was best to oppose in open war the forces of Philip, who would otherwise deceive them with fair words until he had overcome the Florentines. Others said that to leap into such an undertaking would be mere temerity, adding that it was an easy thing to begin a war but difficult to end it." The Senate of Venice had, however, another pleader at hand, whose eloquence was more convincing. When they had confused themselves with arguments for and against, the Doge, whose views were warlike, called for Carmagnola, who had been waiting in unaccustomed inaction to know what was to happen to him. All his wrongs had been revived by an attempt made to poison him in his retreat at Treviso by a Milanese exile who was sheltered there, and who hoped by this good deed to conciliate Philip and purchase his recall—a man who, like Carmagnola, had married a Visconti, and perhaps had some private family hatred to quicken his patriotic zeal. The attempt had been unsuccessful, and the would-be assassin had paid for it by his life. But the result had been to light into wilder flame than ever the fire of wrong in the fierce heart of the great captain, whose love had been turned into hatred by the ingratitude of his former masters and friends. He appeared before the wavering statesmen, who, between their ducats and their danger, could not come to any decision, flaming with wrath and energy. " Being of a haughty nature, *una natura sdegnosa*, he spoke bitterly against Philip and his ingratitude and perfidy," describing in hot words his own struggles and combats, the cities he had brought. under Philip's sway, and the fame he had procured him, so that his name was known not only throughout all Italy, but even through Europe, as the master of Genoa. The rewards which Carmagnola had received, he declared proudly, were not rewards, but his just hire and no more. And now *quell' ingrato*, whom he had served so well, had not only wounded his heart and his good name, for the sake of a set of lying youths— *giovanotti dishonestissimi*—and forced him into exile, but finally had attempted to kill him. But yet he had not been without good fortune, in that he was preserved from this peril; and though he had lost the country in which he had left wife and children and much wealth, yet had he found another country where was justice, bounty, and every virtue—where every man got his due, and place and dignity were not given to villains! After this outburst of personal feeling, Carmagnola entered fully into the weightier parts of the matter, giving the eager senators to understand that Philip was not so strong as he seemed; that his money was exhausted, his citizens impoverished, his soldiers in arrears; that he himself, Carmagnola, had been the real cause of most of his triumphs; and that with his guidance and knowledge the Florentines themselves were stronger than Philip, the Venetians much stronger. He ended by declaring himself and all his powers at their service, promising not only to conquer Philip, but to increase the territory of the Venetians. Greater commanders they might have, and names more honoured, but none of better faith towards Venice, or of greater hatred towards the enemy.

Carmagnola's speech is not given in the first person like the others. By the time the narrative was written his tragic history was over, and the enthusiasm with which he was first received had become a thing to be lightly dwelt upon, where it could not be ignored altogether; but it is easy to see the furious and strong personal feeling of the man, injured and longing for revenge, his heart torn with the serpent's tooth of ingratitude, the bitterness of love turned into hate. So strong was the impression made by these hoarse and thrilling accents of reality that the doubters were moved to certainty, and almost all pronounced for war. At the risk of over-prolonging this report of the Venetian cabinet council and its proceedings, we are tempted to quote a portion of the speech of the Doge, in which the reader will scarcely fail to see on the contrary side some reflection or recollection of old Mocenigo's argument which had been launched at his successor's head only a few years before.

" There are two things in a republic, noble fathers, which by name and effect are sweet and gentle, but which are often the occasion of much trouble to the great and noble city—these are peace and economy. For there are dangers both distant and under our eyes, which either we do not see, or seeing them, being too much devoted to saving money, or to peace, esteem them little, so that almost always we are drawn into very evident peril before we will consider the appalling name of war, or come to manifest harm to avoid the odious name of expense. This fact, by which much harm and ruin has been done in our times, and which has also been recorded for us by our predecessors, is now set before us in an example not less useful than clear in the misfortunes of the Florentines, who, when they saw the power of Philip increasing, might many times have restrained it, and had many occasions of so doing, but would not, in order to avoid the great expense. But now it has come to pass that the money which they acquired in peace and repose must be spent uselessly ; and what is more to be lamented, they can neither attain peace, save at the cost of their freedom, nor put an end to their expenditure. I say, then, that such dangers ought to be considered, and being considered, ought to be provided for by courage and counsel. To guide a republic is like guiding a ship at sea. I ask if any captain, the sea being quiet and the wind favourable, ceases to steer the ship, or gives himself up to sleep and repose without thinking of the dangers that may arise, without keeping in order the sails, the masts, the cordage, or taking into consideration the sudden changes to which the sea is subject, the season of the year, by what wind and in what part of the sea lies his course, what depth of water and what rocks his vessel may encounter ? If these precautions are neglected, and he is assailed by sudden misfortune, does he not deserve to lose his ship, and with it everything ? A similar misfortune has happened to the Florentines, as it must happen to others who do not take precautions against future dangers to the republic. The Florentines (not to have recourse to another example) might have repressed and overcome the power of Philip when it was growing, if they had taken the trouble to use their opportunities. But by negligence, or rather by avarice, they refrained from doing so. And now it has come about that, beaten in war, with the loss of their forces, they are in danger of losing their liberty. And to make it worse, they are condemned everywhere, and instead of being called industrious are called vile, and held in good repute by none ; instead of prudent are called fools ; and instead of getting credit for their wariness are esteemed to be without intelligence. These evils, therefore, ought to be provided against when far off, which when near can cause such serious evil."

Words so plain and honest, and which are so germane to the matter, come to us strangely from under the gilded roofs of the ducal palace, and from the midst of the romance and glory of mediæval Venice. But Venice was the nation of shopkeepers in those days which England is said to be now, and was subject to many of the same dangers which menace ourselves—though wrath was more prompt, and the balance of well-being swayed more swiftly, both towards downfall and recovery, than is possible in our larger concerns.

"The energetic speech and great influence of the Doge, which was greater than that of any prince before him," says the chronicler (alas! though this was that same Francesco Foscari who died in downfall and misery, deposed from his high place), settled the matter. The league was made with the Florentines, war declared against the Duke of Milan, and Carmagnola appointed general of the forces. The Senate sent messengers, we are told, through all Italy to seek recruits, but in the meantime set in movement those who were ready ; while Carmagnola, like a valorous captain, began to contrive how he could begin the war with some great deed. It does not quite accord with our ideas that the first great deed which he planned was to secure the assassination of the Governor of Brescia and betrayal of that city, which is the account given by Sabellico. Bigli, however, puts the matter in a better light, explaining that many in the city were inclined to follow Carmagnola, who had once already conquered the town for Philip, who had always maintained their cause in Milan, and whose wrongs had thus doubly attracted their sympathy. The city was asleep, and all was still, when, with the aid from within of two brothers, *huomini di anima grande*, the wall was breached, and Carmagnola got possession of Brescia. "It was about midnight, in the month of March, on the last day of Lent, which is sacred to St. Benedict," when the Venetian troops marched into the apparently unsuspecting town. The scene is picturesque in the highest degree. They marched into the Piazza, the centre of all city life, in the chill and darkness of the spring night, and there, with sudden blare of trumpets and illumination of torches, proclaimed the sovereignty of Venice. It is easy to imagine the sudden panic, the frightened faces at the windows, the glare of the wild light that lit up the palace fronts, and showed the dark mass of the great cathedral rising black and silent behind, while the horses pawed the ringing stones of the pavement and the armour shone. The historian goes on to say: "Though at first dismayed by the clang of the trumpets and arms," the inhabitants, "as soon as they perceived that it was Carmagnola, remained quiet in their houses, except those who rushed forth to welcome the besiegers, or who had private relations with the general.

To face page 21°.

DOORWAY OF RUINED CHAPEL OF THE SERVI.

No movement was made from the many fortified places in the city." The transfer from one suzerain to another was a matter of common occurrence, which perhaps accounts for the ease and composure with which it was accomplished. This first victory, however, was but a part of what had to be done. The citadel, high above on the crown of the hill which overlooks the city, remained for some time unconscious of what had taken place below. Perhaps the Venetian trumpets and clang of the soldiery scarcely reached the airy ramparts above, or passed for some

SWORD HILT.

sudden broil, some encounter of enemies in the streets, such as were of nightly occurrence. The town was large, and rich, and populous upon the slopes underneath, surrounded with great walls descending to the plains—walls "thicker than they were high," with fortifications at every gate; and was divided into the old and new city, the first of these only being in Carmagnola's hands. It seems a doubtful advantage to have thus penetrated into the streets of a town while a great portion of its surrounding fortifications and the citadel above were still in other hands; but the warfare of those times had other laws than those with which we are acquainted. The fact that these famous fortifications were of little use in checking the attack is devoutly explained by Bigli as a proof that God was against them,—"because they were erected with almost unbearable expense and toil," "the very blood of the Brescians constrained by their former conqueror to accomplish this work, which was marvellous, no man at that time having seen the like." The Brescians themselves, he tells us, were always eager for change, and on the outlook for every kind of novelty, so that there was nothing remarkable in their quiet acceptance of, and even satisfaction in, the new sway. The reduction of the citadel was, however, a long and desperate task. The means employed by Carmagnola for this end are a little difficult to follow, at least for a lay reader. He seems to have surrounded the castle with an elaborate double work of trenches and palisades, with wooden towers at intervals; and wearing out the defenders by continued assault, as well as shutting out all chance of supplies, at last, after long vigilance and patience, attained his end. Brescia fell finally with all its wealth into the hands of the Venetians, a great prize worthy the trouble and time which had been spent upon it—a siege of seven months after the first night attack, which had seemed so easy.

This grave achievement accomplished, Carmagnola secured with little trouble the Brescian territory; most of the villages and castles in the neighbourhood, as far as the Lago di Garda, giving themselves up to the conqueror without waiting for any assault of arms. The tide of ill fortune seems to have been too much for Philip; and by the good offices of the Pope's legate, a temporary peace was made—at the cost, to the Duke, of Brescia, with all its territory, and various smaller towns and villages, together with a portion of the district of Cremona on the other bank of the Oglio, altogether nearly forty miles in extent. Philip, as may be supposed, was furious at his losses,— now accusing the bad faith of the Florentines, who had begun the war; now the avarice of the Venetians, who were not content with having taken Brescia, but would have Cremona too. The well-meant exertions of the legate, however, were of so little effect that before his own departure he saw the magistrates sent by the Venetians to take possession of their new property on the Cremona side driven out with insults, and Philip ready to take arms again. The cause of this new courage was to be found in the action of the people of Milan, who, stung in their pride by the national downfall, drew their purse-strings and came to their prince's aid, offering both men and money on condition that Philip would give up to them the dues of the city so that they might reimburse themselves. Thus the wary and subtle Italian burghers combined daring with prudence, and secured a great municipal advantage, while undertaking a patriotic duty.

It would be hopeless to follow the course of this long-continued, often-interrupted war. On either side there was a crowd of captains—many Italians, men of high birth and great possessions, others sprung from the people like Carmagnola: a certain John the Englishman, with a hundred followers, figured in the special following of the commander, like William the Cock in the train of Zeno. The great battles which bulk so largely in writing, the names and numbers of which confuse the reader who attempts to follow the entanglements of alliances and treacheries which fill the chronicle, were in most cases almost bloodless, and the prisoners who were taken by the victors were released immediately, "according to the usage of war," in order that they might live to fight another day, and so prolong and extend the profitable and not too laborious occupation of soldiering. Such seems to have been the rule of these endless combats. The men-at-arms in their complete mail were very nearly invulnerable. They might roll off their horses and be stifled in their own helmets, or at close quarters an indiscreet axe might hew through the steel, or an arrow find a crevice in the armour; but such accidents were quite unusual, and the bloodless battle was a sort of game which one general played against another, in ever renewed and changing combinations. The danger that the different bands might quarrel among themselves, and divided counsels prevail, was perhaps greater than any other in the composition of these armies.   In Philip's host, when the second campaign began, this evil was apparent.   Half-a-dozen captains of more or less equal pretensions claimed the command, and the wranglings of the council of war were not less than those of a village municipality.   On the other hand, Carmagnola, in his rustic haughtiness, conscious of being the better yet the inferior of all round him, his *anima sdegnosa* stoutly contemptuous of all lesser claims, kept perfect harmony in his camp, though the names of Gonzaga and Sforza are to be found among his officers. Even the Venetian commissioners yielded to his influence, Bigli says, with awe—though he hid his iron hand in no glove, but ruled his army with the arrogance which had been his characteristic from his youth up.   Already, however, there were suspicions and doubts of the great general, rising in the minds of those who were his masters.   He had asked permission more than once, even during the siege of Brescia, to retire to certain baths, pleading ill-health, a plea which it is evident the Signoria found it difficult to believe, and which raised much scornful comment and criticism in Venice.   These Carmagnola heard of, and in great indignation complained of to the Signoria: which, however, so far from supporting the vulgar plaints, sent a special commissioner to assure him of their complete trust and admiration.

The great battle of Maclodio or Macalo was the chief feature in Carmagnola's second campaign.   This place was surrounded by marshes, the paths across which were tortuous and difficult to find, covered with treacherous herbage and tufts of wood. Carmagnola's purpose was to draw the Milanese army after him, and bring on a battle if possible on this impracticable ground, which his own army had thoroughly explored and understood. Almost against hope his opponents fell into the snare, notwithstanding the opposition of the older and more experienced captains, who divined their old comrade's strategy.   Unfortunately, however, for the Milanese, Philip had put a young

Malatesta, incompetent and headstrong, whose chief recommendation was his noble blood, at the head of the old officers, by way of putting a stop to their rivalries. When the new general decided upon attacking the Venetians, his better instructed subordinates protested earnestly. "We overthrow Philip to-day," cried Torelli, one of the chiefs; "for either I know nothing of war, or this road leads us headlong to destruction; but that no one may say I shrink from danger, I put my foot first into the snare." So saying, he led the way into the marsh, but with every precaution, pointing out to his men the traps laid for them, and, having the good fortune to hit upon one of the solid lines of path, escaped with his son and a few of his immediate followers. Piccinino, another of the leaders, directed his men to turn their pikes against either friend or foe who stopped the way, and managed to cut his way out with a few of his men; but the bulk of the army fell headlong into the snare; the general, Malatesta, was taken almost immediately, and the floundering troops surrounded and taken prisoners in battalions.

Sabellico talks of much bloodshed, but it would seem to have been the innocent blood of horses that alone was shed in this great battle.

"Nearly five thousand horsemen, and a similar number of foot-soldiers, were taken—there was no slaughter," says Bigli; "the troops thus hemmed in, rather than be slain, yielded themselves prisoners. Those who were there affirm that they heard of no one being killed, extraordinary to relate, though it was a great battle. Philip's army was so completely equipped in armour that no small blow was needed to injure them; nor is there any man who can record what could be called a slaughter of armed men in Italy, though the slaughter of horses was incredible. This disaster was great and memorable," he adds, "for Philip—so much so that even the conquerors regretted it, having compassion on the perilous position of so great a Duke; so that you could hear murmurings throughout the camp of the Venetians against their own victory."

Were it not that the bloodless character of the combat involves a certain ridicule, what a good thing it would be could

we in our advanced civilisation carry on our warfare in this
innocent way, and take each other prisoners with polite regret,
only to let each other go to-morrow! Such a process would rob
a battle of all its terrors; and if in certain eventualities it were
understood that one party must accept defeat, how delightful
to secure all the pomp and circumstance of glorious war at so
easy a cost! There is indeed a great deal to be said in favour
of this way of fighting.

This great success was, however, the beginning of Carmagnola's evil fortune. It is said that he might, had he
followed up his victory, have pushed on to the walls of Milan
and driven Philip from his duchy. But no doubt this would
have been against the thrifty practices of the Condottieri, and
the usages of war. He returned to his headquarters after the
fight without any pursuit, and all the prisoners were set free.
This curious custom would seem to have been unknown to the
Venetian commissioners, and struck them with astonishment.
In the morning, after the din and commotion of the battle were
over, they came open-mouthed to the general's tent with their
complaint. The prisoners had in great part been discharged.
Was Carmagnola aware of it? "What then," cried those lay
critics, with much reason, "was the use of war? when all that
was done was to prolong it endlessly—the fighting men escap-
ing without a wound, the prisoners going back to their old
quarters in peace?" Carmagnola, ever proud, would seem to
have made them no reply; but when they had done he sent
to inquire what had been done with the prisoners, as if this
unimportant detail was unknown to him. He was answered
that almost all had been set free on the spot, but that about
four hundred still remained in the camp—their captors probably hoping for ransom. "Since their comrades have had so
much good fortune," said Carmagnola, "by the kindness of my
men, I desire that the others should be released by mine,
according to the custom of war." Thus the haughty general
proved how much regard he paid to the remonstrances of his
civilian masters. "From this," says Sabellico, "there arose

great suspicion in the minds of the Venetians. And there are many who believe that it was the chief occasion of his death." But no hint was given of these suspicions at the time ; and as Carmagnola's bloodless victory deeply impressed the surrounding countries, brought all the smaller fortresses and castles to submission, and, working with other misfortunes, led back Philip again with the ever-convenient legate to ask for peace, the general returned with glory to Venice, and was received apparently with honour and delight. But the little rift within the lute was never slow of appearing, and the jealous Signoria feasted many a man whom they suspected, and for whom, under their smiles and plaudits, they were already concocting trouble. The curious " usage of war," thus discovered by the Venetian envoys, is frankly accounted for by a historian, who had himself been in his day a Condottiere, as arising from the fear the soldiers had, if the war finished quickly, that the people might cry, "Soldiers, to the spade !"

A curious evidence of how human expedients are lost and come round into use again by means of that whirligig of time which makes so many revolutions, is to be found in Carmagnola's invention for the defence of his camp, of a double line of the country carts which carried his provisions, standing closely together—with three archers, one authority says, to each. Notwithstanding what seems the very easy nature of his victories, and the large use of treachery, it is evident that his military genius impressed the imagination of his time above that of any of his competitors. He alone, harsh and haughty as he was, kept his forces in unity. His greatness silenced the feudal lords, who could not venture to combat it, and he had the art of command, which is a special gift.

The peace lasted for the long period of three years, during which time Carmagnola lived in great state and honour in Venice, in a palace near San Eustachio which had been bestowed upon him by the State. His wife and children had in the former interval of peace been restored to him, and all seemed to go at his will. A modern biographer (Lomonaco), who does not cite any authorities, informs us that Carmagnola

Q

was never at home in his adopted city—that he felt suspicions
and unfriendliness in the air—and that the keen consciousness
of his low origin, which seems to have set a sharp note in his
character, was more than ever present with him here. "He
specially abhorred the literary coteries," says this doubtful
authority, "calling them vain as women, punctilious as boys,
lying and feigning like slaves,"—which things have been heard
before, and are scarcely worth putting into the fierce lips of
the Piedmontese soldier, whose rough accent of the north was
probably laughed at by the elegant Venetians, and to whom
their constant pursuit of novelty, their mental activity, politics,
and commotions of town life, were very likely nauseous and
unprofitable. He who was conversant with more primitive
means of action than speeches in the Senate, or even the discussions of the Consiglio Maggiore, might well chafe at so
much loss of time ; and it was the fate of a general of mercenaries, who had little personal motive beyond his pay, and what
he could gain by his services, to be distrusted by his masters.

The occasion of the third war is sufficiently difficult to discover. A Venetian cardinal—Gabriele Condulmero—had been
made Pope, and had published a bull, admonishing both lords
and people to keep the peace, as he intended himself to
inquire into every rising, and regulate the affairs of Italy.
This declaration alarmed Philip of Milan, to whom it seemed
inevitable that a Venetian Pope should be his enemy; and
thus, with no doubt a thousand secondary considerations on all
hands, the peninsula was once more set on fire. When it
became apparent that the current of events was setting
towards war, Carmagnola, for no given reason, but perhaps
because his old comrades and associates had begun to exercise
a renewed attraction, notwithstanding all the griefs that had
separated him from Philip, wrote to the Senate of Venice,
asking to resign his appointments in their service. This, however, the alarmed Signoria would by no means listen to.
They forced upon him instead the command in general of all
their forces, with 1,000 ducats a month of pay, to be paid
both in war and peace, and many extraordinary privileges. It

seems even to have been contemplated as a possible thing that
Milan itself, if Philip's powers were entirely crushed, as the
Venetians hoped, might be bestowed upon Carmagnola as a
reward for the destruction of the Visconti. Nevertheless, it is
evident that Carmagnola had by this time begun a correspondence with his former master, and received both letters and
messengers from Philip while conducting the campaign against
him. And that campaign was certainly not so successful, nor
was it carried on with the energy which had marked his
previous enterprises. He was defeated before Soncino, by
devices of a similar character to those which he had himself
employed, and here is said to have lost a thousand horses.
But that shedding of innocent blood was soon forgotten in the
real and terrible disaster which followed.

The Venetians had fitted out not only a land army, but,
what ought to have been more in consonance with their
habits and character, an expedition by sea under the Admiral
Trevisano, whose ships, besides their crews, are said to have
carried 10,000 fighting men, for the capture of Cremona. The
fleet went up the Po to act in concert with Carmagnola in
his operations against that city. But Philip on his side had
also a fleet in the Po, though inferior to the Venetian, under
the command of a Genoese, Grimaldi, and manned in great
part by Genoese, the hereditary opponents and rivals of Venice.
The two generals on land, Sforza and Piccinino, then both in
the service of Philip—men whose ingenuity and resource had
been whetted by previous defeats, and who had thus learned
Carmagnola's tactics—amused and occupied him by threatening his camp, which was as yet imperfectly defended, *piutosto
alloggiamento che ripari*: but in the night stole away, and under
the walls of Cremona were received in darkness and silence
into Grimaldi's ships, and flung themselves upon the Venetian
fleet. These vessels, being sea-going ships, were heavy and
difficult to manage in the river—those of their adversaries
being apparently of lighter build ; and Grimaldi's boats seem
to have had the advantage of the current, which carried them
" very swiftly " against the Venetians, who, in the doubtful

dawn, were astonished by the sight of the glittering armour
and banners bearing down upon them with all the impetus of
the great stream. The Venetian admiral sent off a message
to warn Carmagnola; but before he could reach the river-
bank, the two fleets, in a disastrous jumble, had drifted out
of reach. Carmagnola, roused at last, arrived too late, and,
standing on the shore, hot with ineffectual haste, spent his
wrath in shouts of encouragement to his comrades, and in
cries of rage and dismay as he saw the tide of fortune drifting on, carrying the ships of Philip in wild concussion against
the hapless Venetians. When things became desperate,
Trevisano, the admiral, got to shore in a little boat, and fled,
carrying with him the treasure of 60,000 gold pieces, which
was one of the great objects of the attack. But this was
almost all that was saved from the rout. Bigli says that
seventy ships were taken, of which twenty-eight were ships of
war; but in this he is probably mistaken, as he had himself
described the fleet as one of thirty ships. "The slaughter,"
he adds, "was greater than any that was ever known in Italy,
more than 2,500 men being said to have perished, in witness
of which the Po ran red, a great stream of blood, for many
miles." A few ships escaped by flight, and many fugitives,
no doubt, in boats and by the banks, where they were assailed
by the peasants, who, taking advantage of their opportunity,
and with many a wrong to revenge, killed a large number.
Such a disastrous defeat had not happened to Venice for many
a day.

The Venetian historian relates that Carmagnola received the
warning and appeal of the admiral with contempt—"as he was
of a wrathful nature, *di natura iraconda*, and with a loud voice
reproved the error of the Venetians, who, despising his counsel,
refused the support to the army on land which they had given
to their naval expedition; nor did he believe what the messengers told him, but said scornfully that the admiral, fearing
the form of an armed man, had dreamt that all the enemies in
their boats were born giants." This angry speech, no doubt,
added to the keen dissatisfaction of the Venetians in knowing

that their general remained inactive on the bank while their
ships were thus cut to pieces. The truth probably lies between the two narratives, as so often happens; for Carmagnola
might easily express his hot impatience with the authorities
who had refused to be guided by his experience, and with the
admiral who took the first unexpected man in armour for a
giant, when the messengers roused him with their note of alarm
in the middle of the night, and yet have had no traitorous
purpose in his delay. He himself took the defeat profoundly
to heart, and wrote letters of such distress, excusing himself, that
the senators were compelled in the midst of their own trouble
to send ambassadors to soothe him—"to mitigate his frenzy,
that they might not fall into greater evil, and to keep him at
his post"—with assurances that they held him free of blame.
It is evident, we think, that the whole affair had been in direct
opposition to his advice, and that, instead of being in the wrong,
he felt himself able to take a very high position with the ill-
advised Signoria, and to resent the catastrophe which, with
greater energy on his part, might perhaps have been prevented
altogether. The Venetians avenged the disaster by sending a
fleet at once to Genoa, where, coursing along the lovely line of
the eastern Riviera, they caught in a somewhat similar way the
Genoese fleet, and annihilated it. But this is by the way.

Carmagnola, meanwhile, lay like Achilles sullen in his tent.
Philip himself came in his joy and triumph to the neighbourhood, but could not tempt the disgusted general to more than a
languid passage of arms. An attempt to take Cremona by
surprise, made by one of his officers, a certain Cavalcabó, or as
some say by Colleoni, seemed as if it might have been crowned
with success had the general bestirred himself with sufficient
energy—"if Carmagnola had sent more troops in aid." As it
was, the expedition, being unsupported, had to retire. If he
were indeed contemplating treachery, it is evident that he had
a great struggle with himself, and was incapable of changing
his allegiance with the light-hearted ease of many of his
contemporaries. He lay thus sullen and disheartened in his
leaguer even when spring restored the means of warfare, and

though his old enemy Piccinino was up and stirring, picking up here and there a castle in the disturbed precincts of the Cremonese. "The marvel grew," cries Sabellico, "that Carmagnola let these people approach him, and never moved."

The Signoria, in the meantime, had been separately and silently turning over many thoughts in their mind on the subject of this general who was not as the others, who would not be commanded nor yet dismissed, too great to be dispensed with, too troublesome to manage. Ever since the memorable incidents of the battle of Maclodio, doubts of his good faith had been in their minds. Why did he liberate Philip's soldiers if he really wished to overthrow Philip? It was Philip himself —so the commissioners had said in their indignation—whom he had set free; and who could tell that the treachery at Soncino was not of his contriving, or that he had not stood aloof of set purpose while the ships were cut in pieces? Besides, was it not certain that many a Venetian had been made to stand aside while this northern mountaineer, this rude Piedmontese, went swaggering through the streets, holding the noblest at arm's-length? A hundred hidden vexations came up when some one at last introduced his name, and suddenly the senators with one consent burst into the long-deferred discussion for which every one was ready.

"There were not a few," says Sabellico, "who, from the beginning, had suspected Carmagnola. These now openly in the Senate declared that this suspicion not only had not ceased but increased, and was increasing every day ; and that, except his title of commander, they knew nothing in him that was not hostile to the Venetian name. The others would not believe this, nor consent to hold him in such suspicion until some manifest signs of his treachery were placed before them. The Senate again and again referred to the Avogadori the question whether such a man ought to be retained in the public service, or whether, if convicted of treachery, he ought to be put to capital punishment. This deliberation, which lasted a very long time, ought to demonstrate how secret were the proceedings of the Senate when the affairs of the country were in question, and how profound the good faith of the public counsellors. For when the Senate was called together for this object, entering into counsel at the first lighting of torches, the consultation lasted till it was full day. Carmagnola himself was in Venice for some time while it was proceeding ; and going one morning to pay his respects to the Doge, he met him coming out of the council-chamber to the palace, and with much cheerfulness asked whether he ought to bid him good morning or good evening, seeing he had not slept since supper. To whom that prince replied, smiling, that among the many serious matters which had been talked of in that long discussion, nothing had been oftener mentioned than his (Carmagnola's) name But in order that no suspicion might be awakened by these words, he immediately turned the conversation to other subjects. This was nearly eight months before there was any question of death ; and so secret was this council, holding everything in firm and perpetual silence, that no suggestion of their suspicions reached Carmagnola. And though many of the order of the senators were by long intimacy his friends, and many of them poor, who might have obtained great rewards from Carmagnola had they betrayed this secret, nevertheless all kept it faithfully."

There is something grim and terrible in the smiling reply of the Doge to the man whose life was being played for between these secret judges, that his name had been one of those which came oftenest uppermost in their discussions. With what eyes must the splendid Venetian in his robes of state, pale with the night's watching, have looked at the soldier, erect and cheerful, *con fronte molto allegra*, who came across the great court to meet him in the first light of the morning, which, after the dimness of the council-chamber and its dying torches, would dazzle the watcher's eyes ? The other red-robed figures, dispersing like so many ghosts, pale-eyed before the day, did they glance at each other with looks of baleful meaning as the unsuspicious general passed with many salutations and friendly words and greetings—"Shall it be good even or good morrow, illustrious gentlemen, who watch for Venice while the rest of the world sleeps ?" Would there be grace enough among the secret councillors to hurry their steps as they passed him, or was there a secret enjoyment in Foscari's *double entendre*—in that fatal smile with which he met the victim ? The great court which has witnessed so much has rarely seen a stranger scene.

At what time this curious encounter can have happened it is difficult to tell—perhaps on the occasion of some flying visit to his family, which Carmagnola may have paid after laying up his

army in winter quarters after the fashion of the time. The
Signoria had sent messengers to remonstrate with him upon his
inaction to no avail; and that he still lingered in camp doing
little or nothing added a sort of exasperation to the impatience
of the city, and gave their rulers a justification for what they
were about to do. The Venetian senators had no thought of
leaving their general free to carry over to Philip the help of his
great name in case of another war. Carmagnola's sword thrown
suddenly into the balance of power, which was so critical in
Italy, might have swayed it in almost any conceivable direction
—and this was a risk not to be lightly encountered. Had he
shaken the dust from his feet at Mestre, and, instead of embark-
ing upon the lagoon, turned his horse round upon the beach
and galloped off, as he had done from Philip's castle, to some
other camp—the Florentines', perhaps, or his own native Duke
Amadeo of Savoy—what revolutions might happen? He had
done it once, but the magnificent Signoria were determined that
he should not do it again. Therefore the blow, when finally
resolved upon, had to be sharp and sudden, allowing no time for
thought. Thanks to that force of secrecy of which the historian
brags, Carmagnola had no thought of any harm intended to
him. He thought himself the master of the situation—he to
whom only a year before the rulers of Venice had sent a deputation to soothe and caress their general, lest he should throw
up his post. Accordingly, when he received the fatal message
to return to Venice in order to give his good masters advice as
to the state of affairs, he seems to have been without suspicion
as to what was intended. He set out at once, accompanied by
one of his lieutenants, Gonzaga, the lord of Mantua, who had
also been summoned to advise the Signoria, and rode along the
green Lombard plains in all the brilliancy of their spring ver-
dure, received wherever he halted with honour and welcome.
When he reached the Brenta he took boat; and his voyage
down the slow-flowing stream, which has been always so dear
to the Venetians, was like a royal progress. The banks of the
Brenta bore then, as now, long lines of villas, inhabited by all
that was finest in Venice; and such of the noble inhabitants

as were already in *villeggiatura*, "according to their habit,"
Sabellico says, received him, as he passed, *con molta festa*. And
so he went to his fate.   At Mestre he was met by an escort of
eight gentlemen from Venice—those, no doubt, to whom the
historian refers as bound to him by long intimacy, who yet
never breathed to him a word of warning.   With this escort he
crossed the lagoon, the towers and lofty roofs of Venice rising
from out the rounded line of sea, his second home, the country
of which he had boasted, where every man received his due.

How did they talk with him, those silken citizens who knew
but would not by a look betray whither they were leading their
noble friend ?   Would they tell him the news of the city, what
was thought of the coming peace, what intrigues were afloat,
where Trevisano, the unlucky admiral, had gone to hide his
head in his banishment ? or would the conversation flow on the
last great public show, or some rare conceit in verse, or the fine
fleet that followed the *Bucentoro* when last the Serenest Prince
took the air upon the lagoon ?   But Carmagnola was not
lettered, nor a courtier, so that such subjects would have little
charm for him.   When the boats swept past San Stai, would
not a waving scarf from some balcony show that his wife and
young daughter had come out to see him pass, though well
aware that the business of the Signoria went before any in-
dulgence at home ?   Or perhaps he came not by Canereggio
but up the Giudecca, with the wind and spray from the sea
blowing in his face as he approached the centre of Venetian life.
He was led by his courtier-attendants to the palace direct—the
senators having, as would seem, urgent need of his counsel.   As
he entered the fatal doors, those complacent friends, to save
him any trouble, turned back and dismissed the retainers,
without whom a gentleman never stirred abroad, informing
them that their master had much to say to the Doge, and
might be long detained.

Here romance comes in with unnecessary aggravations of the
tragic tale, relating how, not finding the Doge, as he had expected, awaiting him, Carmagnola turned to go to his own house,
but was stopped by his false friends, and led, on pretence of

being shown the nearest exit, another gloomy way—a way that led through bewildering passages into the prisons. No sentimental Bridge of Sighs existed in these days. But when the door of the strong-room which was to be his home for the rest of his mortal life was opened, and the lively voices of his conductors sank in the shock of surprise and horror, and all that was about to be rushed on Carmagnola's mind, the situation is one which requires no aid of dramatic art. Here, in a moment, betrayed out of the air and light, and the freedom which he had used so proudly, this man, who had never feared the face of men, must have realised his fate. At the head of a great army one day, a friendless prisoner the next, well aware that the light of day would never clear up the proceedings against him, or common justice, such as awaits a poor picker and stealer, stand between him and the judges whose sentence was a foregone conclusion. Let us hope that those intimates who had accompanied him thus far slunk away in confusion and shame from the look of the captive. So much evil as Carmagnola had done in his life—and there is no reason to suppose, and not a word to make us believe, that he was a sanguinary conqueror, or abused the position he held—must have been well atoned by that first moment of enlightenment and despair.

During the thirty days that followed, little light is thrown upon Carmagnola's dungeon. He is swallowed up in the darkness, "examined by torture before the Secret Council," a phrase that chills one's blood—until they have the evidence they want, and full confirmation in the groans of the half-conscious sufferer of all imagined or concocted accusations. Sabellico asserts that the proof against him was "in letters which he could not deny were in his own hand, and by domestic testimony," whatever that may mean; and does not mention the torture. It is remarkable that Romanin, while believing all this, is unable to prove it by any document, and can only repeat what the older and vaguer chronicler says. The points of the accusation were these," Sabellico adds: "succour refused to Trevisano, and Cremona saved to Philip by his treacherous abstinence." The fact, however, is more simply stated by Navagero before the

trial, that "the Siguoria were bent on freeing themselves" from
a general who had apparently ceased to be always victorious—
after the excellent habit of republics, which was to cut off the
head of every unsuccessful leader—thus effectually preventing
further failure, on his part at least.

Carmagnola was not a man of words. Yet he might have
launched with his dying breath some ringing defiance to catch
the echoes, and leave in Venetian ears a recollection, a watchword of rebellion to come. The remorseless Council thought of
this, with the vigilance and subtle genius which inspired all the
proceedings of their secret conclave; and when the May morning dawned which was to be his last, a crowning indignity was
added to his doom. He was led out *con uno sbadocchio in bocca*,
gagged, "in order that he might not speak" to the Piazzetta,
now so cheerful and so gay, which then had the most dreadful
associations of any in Venice. "Between the columns," the
blue lagoon, with all its wavelets flinging upward their countless gleams of reflection in the early sun; the rich-hued sails
standing out against the blue; the great barges coming serenely
in, as now, with all their many-coloured stores from the Lido
farms and fields,—the gondolas crowding to the edge of the
fatal pavement, the populace rushing from behind. No doubt
the windows of the ducal palace, or so much of the galleries
as were then in existence, were crowded with spectators too.
Silent, carrying his head high, like him of whom Dante writes
who held great Hell itself in despite—*sdeynoso* even of that gag
between his lips—the great soldier, the general whose praises
had rung through Venice, and whose haughty looks had been
so familiar in the streets, was led forth to his death. By that
strong argument of the axe, unanswerable, incontestable, the
Signoria managed to *lilcrarsi* of many an inconvenient servant
and officer, either unsuccessful or too fortunate. Carmagnola
had both of these faults. He was too great, and for once he
had failed. The people called "*Sventura! Sventura!*" "Misfortune! Misfortune!" in their dark masses, as they struggled
to see the wonderful sight. Their sympathies could scarcely
be against the victim on that day of retribution; and perhaps,

had his voice been free to speak to them, they might have
thought of other things to shout, which the Signoria had been
less content to hear.

Thus ended the great Carmagnola, the most famous of all
Italian soldiers of fortune. Over one of the doors of the noble
church of the Frari there has hung for generations a coffin
covered with a pall, in which it was long supposed that his
bones had been placed, suspended between heaven and earth
per infamia, as a romantic Custode says. This, however, is one
of the fables of tradition. He was buried in San Francesco
delle Vigne (not the present church), whence at a later period
his remains were transferred to Milan. His wife and daughter,
or daughters, were banished to Treviso with a modest pension,
yet a penalty of death registered against them should they
break bounds—so determined, it is evident, were the Signoria
to leave no means by which the general could be avenged. And
what became of these poor women is unknown. Such unconsidered trifles drop through the loopholes of history, which has
nothing to do with hearts that are broken or hopes that cannot
be renewed.

COFFIN IN THE CHURCH OF THE FRARI.

CHAPTER IV.

BARTOLOMMEO COLLEONI.

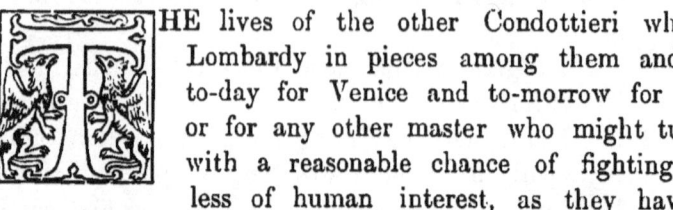HE lives of the other Condottieri who tore Lombardy in pieces among them and were to-day for Venice and to-morrow for Milan, or for any other master who might turn up with a reasonable chance of fighting, have less of human interest, as they have less of the tragic element in their lives, and less of what we may call modern characteristics in their minds than the unfortunate general who ended his days "between the columns," the victim of suspicion only, leaving no proof against him that can satisfy posterity. If Carmagnòla was a traitor at all, he was such a one as might be the hero of an analytical drama of our own day, wavering between truth and falsehood, worked upon by old associations and the spells of relenting affection, but never able to bring himself to the point of renouncing his engagements or openly breaking his word. Such a traitor might be in reality more dangerous than the light-hearted deserter who went over with his lances at a rousing gallop to the enemy. But modern art loves to dwell upon the conflicts of the troubled mind, driven about from one motive or object to another, now seized upon by the tender recollections of the past, and a longing for the sympathy and society of the friends of his youth, now sternly called back by the present duty which requires him to act in the service of their enemy.

It is difficult to realise this nineteenth century struggle as going on under the corslet of a mediæval soldier, a fierce illiterate general, risen from the ranks, ferocious in war and arrogant in peace, according to all the descriptions of him. But there is nothing vulgar in the image that rises before us as we watch Carmagnola lying inactive on those devastated plains, letting his fame go to the winds, paralysed between the subtle wooings of old associations, the horror of Philip's approaching ruin wrought by his hands—of Philip who had been his playfellow when they were both youths at Pavia, the cousin, perhaps the brother, of his wife—and the demands of the alien masters who paid him so well, and praised him so loudly, but scorned with fine ridicule his rough military ways. Philip had wronged him bitterly, but had suffered for it : and how was it possible to keep the rude heart from melting when the rage of love offended had passed away, and the sinner pleaded for forgiveness ? Or, who could believe that the woman by his side, who was a Visconti, would be silent, or that she could see unmoved her own paternal blazon sinking to the earth before the victorious Lion of the Venetians ? The wonder is that Carmagnola did not do as at one time or another every one of his compeers did—go over cheerfully to Philip, and thus turn the tables at once. Some innate nobility in the man, who was not as the others were, could alone have prevented this very usual catastrophe. Even if we take the view of the Venetian Signoria, that he was in his heart a traitor, we must still allow the fact, quite wonderful in the circumstances, that he was not so by any overt act—and that his treachery amounted to nothing more than the struggle in his mind of two influences which paralysed and rendered him wretched. The ease with which he fell into the snare laid for his feet, and obeyed the Signoria's call, which in reality was his death-warrant, does not look like a guilty man.

The others were all of very different mettle. Gonzaga, Marquis of Mantua, who with a few generations of forefathers behind him, might have been supposed to have learned the laws of honour better than a mere Savoyard trooper, went over without

To face page 239.

COLLEONI.

a word, at a most critical moment of the continued war, yet died in his bed comfortably, no one thinking of branding him with the name of traitor. Sforza acted in the same manner repeatedly, without any apparent criticism from his contemporaries, and in the end displaced and succeeded Philip, and established his family as one of the historical families of Italy. None of these men seem to have had any hesitation in the matter. And neither had the lesser captain who has so identified himself with Venice that when we touch upon the mainland and its wars, and the conquests and losses of the republic, it is not possible to pass by the name of Colleoni. This is not so much for the memory of anything he has done, or from any characteristics of an impressive nature which he possessed, as from the wonderful image of him which rides and reigns in Venice, the embodiment of martial strength and force unhesitating, the mailed captain of the middle ages, ideal in a tremendous reality which the least observant cannot but feel. There he stands as in iron—nay, stands not, but rides upon us, unscrupulous, unswerving, though his next step should be on the hearts of the multitude, crushing them to pulp with remorseless hoofs. Man and horse together, there is scarcely any such warlike figure left among us to tell in expressive silence the tale of those days when might was right, and the sword, indifferent to all reason, turned every scale. Colleoni played no such emphatic part in the history of Venice as his great leader and predecessor. But he was mixed up in all those wonderful wars of Lombardy, in the confusion of sieges, skirmishes, surprises ever repeated, never decisive, a phantasmagoria of moving crowds, a din and tumult that shakes the earth, thundering of horses, cries and shouts of men, and the glancing of armour, and the blaze of swords, reflecting the sudden blaze of burning towns, echoing the more terrible cries of sacked cities. From the miserable little castello, taken again and again, and yet again, its surrounding fields trampled down, its poor inhabitants drained of their utmost farthing, to such rich centres as Brescia and Verona, which lived for half their time shut up within their walls, besieged by one army or the other, and spent

the other half in settling their respective ransoms, changing
their insignia, setting up the Lion and Serpent alternately upon
their flags, what endless misery and confusion, and waste of
human happiness!   But the captains who changed sides half-a-
dozen times in their career, and were any man's men who would
give them high pay and something to fight about, pursued their
trade with much impartiality, troubling themselves little about
the justice or injustice of their cause, and still less, it would
appear, about any bond of honour between themselves and their
masters.   Colleoni alone seems to have had some scrupulousness
about breaking his bond before his legal time was up.   The
others do not seem to have had conscience even in this respect,
but deserted when it pleased them, as often as not in the middle
of a campaign.

Bartolommeo Colleoni, or Coglioni, as his biographer calls
him, was born in the year 1400, of a family of small rustic
nobility near Bergamo, but was driven from his home by a
family feud, in the course of which his father was displaced
from the fortress which he seems to have won in the good old
way by his spear and his bow—by a conspiracy headed by his
own brothers.   This catastrophe scattered the children of Paolo
Colleoni, and threw into the ranks of the free lances (which
probably, however, would have been their destination in any
case) his young sons as soon as they were old enough to carry
a spear.   The first service of Bartolommeo was under the
Condottiere Braccio, in the service of the Queen of Naples,
where he is said by his biographer, Spino, to have acquired, from
his earliest beginnings in the field, singular fame and reputation.
It is unfortunate that this biographer, throughout the course of
his narrative, adopts the easy method of attributing to Colleoni
all the fine things done in the war, appropriating without scruple
acts which are historically put to the credit of his commanders.
It is possible, no doubt, that he is right, and that the young
officer suggested to Gattamelata his famous retreat over the
mountains, and to the engineer who carried it out the equally
famous transport overland to the Lago di Garda of certain

galleys to which we shall afterwards refer. Colleoni entered the
service of Venice at the beginning of Carmagnola's first campaign,
with a force of forty horsemen, and his biographer at once
credits him on the authority of an obscure historian with one
of the most remarkable exploits of that war, the daring seizure
of a portion of the fortifications of Cremona, before which
Carmagnola's army was lying. He was at least one of the little
party which executed this feat of arms.

"Bartolommeo, accompanied by Mocimo da Lugo, and by Cavalcabue,
the son of Ugolino, once Lord of Cremona, both captains in the army, the
latter having friends in the city, approached the walls by night, with great
precaution, and on that side where they had been informed the defences
were weakest, placed their ladders. Bartolommeo was the first, *con intrepi-
dissimo animo*, to ascend the wall and to occupy the tower of San Luca,
having killed the commander and guards. News was sent at once to
Carmagnola of this success, upon which, had he, according to their advice,
hastened to attack, Cremona without doubt would have fallen into the
hands of the Venetians."

The young adventurers held this tower for three days, as
Quentin Durward, or the three Mousquetaires of Dumas might
have done—but finally were obliged to descend as they had
come up, and return to the army under cover of night, with
nothing but the name of a daring feat to reward them—though
that, no doubt, had its sweetness, and also a certain value in
their profession. The curious complication of affairs in that
strange distracted country, may be all the more clearly realised,
if we note that one of the three and most probably the leader
of the band was a Cremonese, familiar with all the points of
vantage in the city, and the son of its former lord, with no
doubt partisans, and a party of his own, had he been able to
push his way out of the Rocca to the interior of the city. Thus
there was always some one, who even in the subjection of his
native place to the Republic, may have hoped for a return of his
own family, or at least for vengeance upon the neighbouring
despot which had cast it out.

We hear of Colleoni next in a rapid night march to Bergamo,
which was the original home of his own race, and which was

R

threatened by the Milanese forces under Piccinino. Knowing the city to be without means of defence, though apparently still in a state of temporary independence, Colleoni proposed to his commanders to hurry thither and occupy and prepare it for the approaching attack, with the condition, however, that the affairs of the city, *le cose de Bergamaschi*, at least within the walls, should receive no damage—another consolatory gleam of patriotism in the midst of all the fierce selfishness of the time. With his usual promptitude, and what his biographer calls *animosità*, impetuosity, he rushed across the country while Piccinino was amusing himself with the little independent castles about, "robbing and destroying the country, having given orders that whatever could not be carried away should be burned, so that in a very short time the villages and castles of the valleys Callepia and Trescoria were reduced to the semblance and aspect of a vast and frightful solitude." Colleoni had only his own little force of horsemen and three hundred infantry, and had he come across the route of the Milanese would have been but a mouthful to that big enemy. But he carried his little band along with such energy and inspiration of impetuous genius, that they reached Bergamo while still the foe was busy with the blazing villages: and had time to strengthen the fortifications and increase both ammunition and men before the approach of Piccinino, who, finally repulsed from the walls of the city in which he had expected to find an easy prey and harbour for the stormy season—and exposed to that other enemy, which nobody in those days attempted to make head against, the winter with its chilling forces of rain and snow—streamed back disconsolate to Milan *al suo Duca*, who probably was not at all glad to see him, and expected with reason that so great a captain as Piccinino would have kept his troops at the expense of Bergamo, or some other conquered city, until he could take the field again, instead of bringing such a costly and troublesome following home.

We cannot, however, follow at length the feats which his biographer ascribes to Colleoni's *animosità* and impetuous spirit, which was combined, according to the same authority, with a prudence and foresight "above the captains of his time."

One of these was the extraordinary piece of engineering by which a small fleet, including one or two galleys, was transported from the Adige to the Lago di Garda over the mountain pass, apparently that between Mori and Riva. Near the top of the pass is a small lake called now the Lago di Loppio, a little mountain tarn, which afforded a momentary breathing space to the workmen and engineers of this wonderful piece of work. The galleys, "two of great size and three smaller," along with a number of little boats which were put upon carts, were dragged over the pass, with infinite labour and pains, and it was only in the third month that the *armata*, the little squadron painfully drawn down hill by means of the channel of a mountain stream, found its way to the lake at last. This wonderful feat was the work, according to Sabellico, of a certain Sorbolo of Candia. But the biographer of Colleoni boldly claims the idea for his hero, asserting with some appearance of justice that the fathers of Venice would not have consented to such a scheme upon the word of an altogether unknown man, who was simply the engineer who carried it out. It was for the purpose of supplying provisions to Brescia, then closely besieged, that this great work was done. Sabellico gives a less satisfactory but still more imposing reason. "It was supposed," he says, "that the intention of the Venetian Senators was rather to encourage the Brescians, than for any other motive, as they were aware that these ships were of no use, the district being so full of the enemy's forces that no one could approach Brescia, and great doubts being entertained whether it would be possible to retain Verona and Vicenza." On the other hand, Spino declares that the *armata* fulfilled its purpose and secured the passage of provisions to Brescia. It was, at any rate, a magnificent way of keeping the beleaguered city, and all the other alarmed dependencies of Venice, in good heart and hope.

None of our historians have, however, a happy hand in their narratives of these wars. They are given in endless repetitions,

R 2

and indeed were without any human interest, even that of
bloodshed, an eternal see-saw of cities taken and retaken, of
meaningless movements of troops, and chess-board battles
gained and lost.   One of the greatest of these, in which Colleoni
was one of the leaders against Sforza, who led the troops of
Milan, bore a strong resemblance to that battle of Maclodio, in
which Carmagnola won so great but so unfortunate a victory.
Sforza had established himself, as his predecessor had done,
among the marshes; and although at the first onset the Venetians had the best of it, their success was but momentary, and
the troops were soon wildly flying and floundering over the
treacherous ground.   Colleoni, who led the reserve and who
made a stand as long as he could, escaped at last on foot, Sanudo
says, who writes the woful news as it arrives at the fifteenth
hour of the 15th of September, 1448. "The Proveditori Almoro
Donato and Guado Dandolo were made prisoners," he says,
"which proveditori were advised by many that they ought to
fly and save themselves, but answered that they would rather
die beside the ensigns than save themselves by a shameful
flight.   And note," adds the faithful chronicler, "that in this
rout *only one* of our troops was killed, the rest being taken
prisoners and many of them caught in the marshes." The flight
of the mercenaries on every side, while the two proud Venetians
stood by their flag, perhaps the only men of all that host who
cared in their hearts what became of St. Mark's often triumphant lion, affords another curious picture in illustration of surely
the strangest warfare ever practised among men.

"But not for this," Sanudo goes on, "was the Doge discouraged, but
came to the Council with more vigour than ever, and the question was
how to reconstruct the army, so that *having plenty of money* they should
establish the camp again as it was at first."

Thus Venetian pride and gold triumphed over misfortune.
The most energetic measures were taken at once with large
offers of pay and remittances of money, and the broken bands
were gradually re-gathered together.   Sforza, after his victory,

pushed on, taking and ravaging everything till he came once more to the gates of Brescia, where again the sturdy citizens prepared themselves for a siege. In the meantime pairs of anxious Proveditori with sacks of money went off at once to every point of danger; 30,000 ducats fell to the share of Brescia alone. At Verona, these grave officials "day and night were in waiting to enrol men, and very shortly had collected a great army by means of the large payments they made."

While these tremendous efforts were in the course of making, once more the whole tide of affairs was changed as by a magician's wand. The people of Milan had called Sforza back on their duke's death, but had held his power in constant suspicion, and were now seized with alarm lest, flushed with victory as he was, he should take that duke's place—which was indeed his determination. They seized the occasion accordingly, and now rose against his growing power, "desiring to maintain themselves in freedom." Sforza no sooner heard of this than he stopped fighting, and by the handy help of one of the Proveditori who had been taken in the battle of the marshes, and who turned out to be a friend of his secretary Simonetta, made overtures of peace to Venice, which were as readily accepted. So that on the 18th of October of the same year, little more than a month after the disastrous rout above recorded, articles of peace were signed, by which the aid of 4,000 horsemen and 2,000 foot were granted to Sforza, along with a subsidy of 13,000 ducats a month, according to Sanudo, though one cannot help feeling that an extra cypher must have crept into the statement. Venice regained all she had lost; and the transformation scene having thus once more taken place, our Colleoni among others, so lately a fugitive before the victorious Milanese, settled calmly down in his saddle once more as a lieutenant of Sforza's army, as if no battle nor hostility had ever been.

A curious domestic incident appears in the midst of the continued phantasmagoria of this endless fighting. The Florentines, more indifferent to consistency than the Venetians,

and always pleased to humiliate a sister state, not only supported Sforza against the Milanese, but presumed to remonstrate
with the Signoria when after a time, getting alarmed by his
growing power, they withdrew from their alliance with him.
This was promptly answered by a decree expelling all Florentine
inhabitants from Venice, and forbidding them the exercise of
any commercial transactions within the town. Shortly before, King Alfonzo of Naples had made the same order in
respect to the Venetians in his kingdom. These arbitrary acts
probably did more real damage than the bloodless battles which
with constant change of combinations were going on on every
side.

The remaining facts of Colleoni's career were few. Notwithstanding a trifling backsliding in the matter of aiding Sforza,
he was engaged as Captain General of the Venetian forces in
1455, and remained in this office till the term of his engagement was completed, which seems to have been ten years. He
then, Sanudo tells us, " treated with Madonna Bianca, Duchess of
Milan " (Sforza being just dead) " to procure the hand of one of
her daughters for his son. But the marriage did not take place,
and he resumed his engagements with our Signoria." It is
difficult to understand how this proposal could have been made,
as to all appearance Colleoni left no son behind him, a fact which
is also stated in respect to most of the generals of the time—a
benevolent interposition of nature one cannot but think for
cutting off that seed of dragons. The only other mention of
him in the Venetian records is the announcement of his death,
which took place in October, 1475, in his castle of Malpaga,
surrounded by all the luxury and wealth of the time. He was
of the same age as the century, and a completely prosperous
and successful man, except in that matter of male children with
which, his biographer naïvely tells us, he never ceased to attempt
to provide himself, but always in vain. He left a splendid
legacy to the Republic which he had served so long—with
aberrations, which no doubt were by that time forgotten—no
less than 216,000 ducats, Sanudo says, besides arms, horses, and

other articles of value. The grateful Signoria, overwhelmed by such liberality, resolved to make him a statue with a portion of the money. And accordingly, there he stands to this day, by the peaceful portals of San Zanipolo ready at any moment to ride down any insolent stranger who lifts a finger against Venice. Appropriately enough to such a magnificent piece of work it is not quite clear who made it, and it is impossible to open a guide-book without lighting upon a discussion as to how far it is Verocchio's and how far Leopardi's. He of the true eye at all events had a large hand in it, and never proved his gift more completely than in the splendid force of this wonderful horseman. The power and thorough-going strength in him has impressed the popular imagination, as it was very natural they should, and given him a false importance to the imaginative spectator. It is a great thing for a man when he has some slave of genius either with pen or brush or plastic clay to make his portrait. Sforza was a much greater general than Colleoni, but had no Verocchio to model him. Indeed our Bartolommeo has no pretensions to stand in the first rank of the mediæval condottieri. He is but a vulgar swordsman beside Carmagnola, or Sforza or Piccinino. But perhaps from this fact he is a better example than either of them of the hired captains of his time.

The possessions of Venice were but little increased by the seventy years of fighting which ensued after Carmagnola had won Brescia and Bergamo for her, and involved her in all the troubles and agitations of a continental principality. She gained Cremona in the end of the century, and she lost nothing of any importance which had been once acquired. But her province of terra firma cost her probably more than it was worth to her to be the possessor even of such fertile fields and famous cities. The unfailing energy, the wealth, the determined purpose of the great Republic were, however, never more conspicuous than in the struggle which she maintained for the preservation of the province. She had the worst of it in a great number of cases, but the loss was chiefly to her purse and her vanity. The

pawns with which she played that exciting game were not of
her own flesh and blood. The *largo pagamento* with which she
was prepared was always enough to secure a new army when
the other was sped, and notwithstanding all her losses at sea
and in the East, and the idleness which began to steal into the
being of the new generation, she was yet so rich and overflowing
with wealth that her expenditure abroad took nothing from the
lavish magnificence of all her festivals and holidays at home.
Her ruler during all the period at which we have here hurriedly
glanced was Francesco Foscari, he against whom his predecessor
had warned the Signoria as a man full of restlessness and
ambition, whose life would be a constant series of wars. Never
did prediction come more true; and though it seems difficult to
see how, amid all the stern limits of the doge's privileges, it
could matter very much what his character was, yet this man, in
the time of his manhood and strength must have been able,
above others, to influence his government and his race. The
reader has already seen amid what reverses this splendid and
powerful ruler, after all the conflicts and successes in which he
was the leading spirit, ended his career.

POZZO.

PART III.—THE PAINTERS.

CHAPTER I.

THE THREE EARLY MASTERS.

T is one of the favourite occupations of this age to trace every new manifestation of human genius or force through a course of development, and to prove that in reality no special genius or distinct and individual impulse is wanted at all, but only a gradual quickening, as might be in the development of a grain of corn or an acorn from the tree. I am not myself capable of looking at the great sudden advances which, in every department of thought and invention, are made from time to time, in this way. Why it should be that in a moment by the means of two youths in a Venetian house, not distinguishable in any way from other boys, nor especially from the sons of other poor painters, members of the *scuola* of S. Luca, which had long existed in Venice, and produced dim pictures not without merit—the art of painting should have sprung at once into the noblest place, and that nothing which all the generations have done since with all their inventions and appliances, should ever have bettered the Bellini, seems to me one of those miraculous circumstances with which the world abounds, and which illustrate this wayward, splendid, and futile humanity better than any history of development could do.

The art of painting had flourished dimly in Venice for long. The love of decorative art seems indeed to have been from its very beginning characteristic of the city. Among the very earliest products of her voyages, as soon as the infant state was strong enough to have any thought beyond mere subsistence, were the beautiful things from the East with which, first the churches, and then the houses were adorned. But the art of painting, though its earliest productions seem to have been received with eagerness and honour, lingered and made little progress. In Murano—where glass-making had been long established, and where fancy must have been roused by the fantastic art, so curious, so seemingly impossible of blowing liquid metal into forms of visionary light, like bubbles, yet hard, tenacious, and clear—the first impulse of delineation arose, but came to no remarkable success. There is much indeed that is beautiful in the pictures of some of these dim and early masters amidst the mists of the lagoons. But with the Bellini the pictorial art came like Athene, full arrayed in maturity of celestial godhood, a sight for all men. It is a doubtful explanation of this strange difference to say that their father had foregathered in the far distance, in his little workshop, with Donatello from Florence, or studied his art under the instructions of Gentile da Fabriano. The last privilege at least was not special to him, but must have been shared with many others of the devout and simple workmen who had each his little manufactory of Madonnas for the constant consumption of the Church. But when Jacopo Bellini with his two sons came from Padua and settled near the Rialto, the day of Venice, so far as the pictorial art is concerned, had begun. They sprang at once to a different standing-ground altogether, as far beyond the work of their contemporaries as Dante was above his. No theory has ever explained to the human intelligence how such a thing can be. It is; and in the sudden bound which Genius takes out of all the trammels of the ordinary—an unaccountable, unreasonable, inimitable initiative of its own—arise the epochs and is summed up the history of Art.

It must have been nearly the middle of the fifteenth century when the Bellini began to make themselves known in Venice. Mediæval history does not concern itself with dates in respect to such humble members of the commonwealth, and about the father, Jacopo, it is impossible to tell how long he lived or when he died. .He was a pupil, as has been said, of Gentile da Fabriano, and went with him to Florence in his youth, and thus came in contact with the great Tuscan school and its usages; and it is known that he settled for some time at Padua, where his sons had at least a part of their education, and where he married his daughter to Andrea Mantegna: therefore the school of Padua had also something to do with the training of these two young men: but whether they first saw the light in Venice, or when the family returned there, it is not known. Jacopo, the father, exercised his art in a mild mediocre way, no better or worse than the ordinary members of the *scuola*. Probably his sons were still young when he returned to the Rialto, where the family house was: for there is no indication that Gentile or Giovanni were known in Padua, nor can we trace at what period it began to be apparent in Venice that Jacopo Bellini's modest workshop was sending forth altar-pieces and little sacred pictures such as had never before been known to come from his hand. That this fact would soon appear in such an abundant and ever-circulating society of artists, more than usually brought together by the rules of the *scuola* and the freemasonry common to artists everywhere, can scarcely be doubted: but dates there are few. It is difficult even to come to any clear understanding as to the first great public undertaking in the way of art—the decoration of the hall of the Consiglio Maggiore. It was begun, we are told, in the reign of Marco Cornaro, in the middle of the previous century: but both the brothers Bellini were engaged upon it when they first come into sight, and it seems to have given occupation to all the painters of their age. Kugler mentions 1456 as the probable date 'of a picture of Giovanni Bellini: but though this is conjectural, Bellini (he signs himself *Juan* in the receipt

preserved in the Sala Margherita at the Archivio, which is occasionally altered into Zuan in the documents of the time) would
at that date be about thirty, and no doubt both he and his brother
were deep in work and more or less known to fame before that
age.

It was not till a much later period, however, that an event
occurred of the greatest importance in the history of art—the
arrival in Venice of Antonello of Messina, a painter chiefly, it
would seem, of portraits, who brought with him the great discovery of the use of oil in painting which had been made by Jan
von Eyck in Bruges some time before. Antonello had got it,
Vasari says, from the inventor himself; but a difficulty of dates
makes it more probable that Hans Memling was the Giovanni di
Bruggia whose confidence the gay young Sicilian gained, perhaps
by his lute and his music and all his pleasant ways. Antonello
came to Venice in 1473, and was received as a stranger, especially a stranger with some new thing to show, seems to have
always been in the sensation-loving city. But when they first saw
his work, the painter brotherhoods, the busy and rising *scuole*,
received a sensation of another kind. Up to this time the only
known medium of painting had been distemper, and in this
they were all at work, getting what softness and richness they
could, and that *morbidezza*, the melting roundness which the
Italians loved, as much as they could, by every possible con-
trivance and exertion out of their difficult material. But the
first canvas which the Sicilian set up to show his new patrons
and professional emulators, was at once a revolution and a
wonder. Those dark and glowing faces which still look at us
with such a force of life, must have shone with a serene
superiority upon the astonished gazers who knew indeed how
to draw from nature and find the secret of her sentiment and
expression as well as Antonello, but not how to attain that
lustre and solidity of texture, that bloom of the cheek and light
in the eye which were so extraordinarily superior to anything
that could be obtained from the comparatively dry and thin
colours of the ancient method. This novelty created such a

To face page 252.

GATEWAY OF THE ABBAZIA DELLA MISERICORDIA.

flutter in the workshops as no wars or commotions could call
forth. How could that warmth and glow of life be got upon a
piece of canvas? One can imagine the painters gathering, discussing in storms of soft Venetian talk and boundless argument,
the Vivarini hurrying over in their boats from Murano and every
lively *cena* and moonlight promenade upon the lagoon apt in a
moment to burst into tempests of debate as to what was this
new thing. And on their scaffoldings in the great hall of the
palazzo, where they were dashing in their great frescoes, what a
hum of commotion would run round. How did he get it, that
light and lustre, and how could they discover what it was, and
share the benefit?

The story which is told by Ridolfi, but which the historians
of a more critical school reject as fabulous, is at all events in no
way unlikely or untrue to nature, or the eager curiosity of the
artists, or Venetian ways. These were the days, it must be recol-
lected, when craftsmen kept the secret of their inventions and discoveries jealously to themselves, and it was a legitimate as well as
a natural effort, if one could, to find them out. The story goes that
Giovanni Bellini, by this time at the head of the painters in
Venice, the natural and proper person to take action in any such
matter, being unable to discover Antonello's secret by fair means,
got it by what we can scarcely call foul, though it was a trick.
But the trick was not a very bad one, and doubtless among men
of their condition might be laughed over as a good joke when
it was over. What Bellini did, "feigning to be a gentleman,"
was to commission Antonello to paint his portrait—an expedient
which gave him the best opportunity possible for studying the
stranger's method. If it were necessary here to examine this
tale rigorously, we should say that it was highly unlikely so
distinguished a painter as Bellini could be unknown to the
new comer, who must, one would think, have been eager to
make acquaintance on his first arrival with the greatest of
Venetian artists. But at all events it is a picturesque incident.
One can imagine the great painter "feigning to be a gentleman,"
seating himself with a solemnity in which there must have been

a great deal of grim humour, in the sitter's chair—he had put
on "the Venetian toga" for the occasion, Ridolfi says, evidently
something different from the usual garb of the artist, and no
doubt felt a little embarrassment mingling with his professional
sense of what was most graceful in the arrangement of the
unaccustomed robe.   But this would not prevent him from
noting all the time, under his eyelids, with true professional
vision, the colours on the palette, the vials on the table, the
sheaf of brushes—losing no movement of the painter, and quick
to note what compound it was into which he dipped his pencil
—"osservando Giovanni che di quando in quando intengeva il
pennello nell' oglio di lin, venne in cognizione del modo,"
"seeing him dip his brush from time to time in oil" which
perhaps was the primitive way of using the new method.   One
wonders if Antonello ever finished the portrait, if it was he who
set forth the well-known image of the burly master with his
outspreading mop of russet hair; or if the Venetian after a
while threw off his toga, and with a big laugh and roar of good-
humoured triumph announced that his purpose was served and
all that he wanted gained.

There is another version of the manner in which Antonello's
secret was discovered in Venice.   Of this later story it is Vasari
who is the author.   He, on his side, develops out of the dim
crowd of lesser artists a certain Domenico Veniziano who was
the first to make friends with the Sicilian.   Antonello, for the
love he bore him, communicated his secret, Vasari says, to this
young man, who for a time triumphed over all competitors; but
afterwards coming to Florence was in his turn cajoled out of the
much-prized information by a Florentine painter, Andrea del
Castegna, who, envious of Domenico's success, afterwards waylaid
him, and killed him as he was returning from their usual evening
diversions.   This anecdote has been taken to pieces as usual by
later historians jealous for exactness who have discovered that
Domenico of Venice outlived his supposed murderer by several
years.   Vasari is so very certain on the point however, that we
cannot help feeling that something of the kind he describes,

some assault must have been made, a quarrel perhaps sharper than usual, an attempt at vengeance for some affront, though it did not have the fatal termination which he supposes.

Vasari, however, in telling this story affords us an interesting glimpse of the condition of Venice at the period. Politically, it was not a happy moment. While the Republic exhausted her resources in the wars described in our last chapters, her dominion in the East, as well as her trade, had been greatly impaired. The Turk, that terror of Christendom, had cruelly besieged and finally taken several towns and strong places along the Dalmatian coast: he had been in Friuli murdering and ravaging. The interrupted and uncertain triumphs of the terra-firma wars, were but little compensation for these disasters, and the time was approaching when Venice should be compelled to withdraw from many more of her Eastern possessions, leaving a town here, an island there, to the Prophet and his hordes. But within the city it is evident nothing of the kind affected the general life of pleasure and display and enjoyment that was going on. The doges were less powerful, but more splendid than ever; the canals echoed with song and shone with gay processions; the great patrician houses grew more imposing and their decorations more beautiful every day. The ducal palace had at last settled, after many changes, into the form we now know: the great public undertaking which was a national tribute to the growing importance of art, was being pushed forward to completion: and though the great Venetian painters, like other painters in other ages, seem to have found the state a shabby paymaster, and to have sometimes shirked and always dallied in the execution of its commissions, yet no doubt public patronage was at once a sign of the quickened interest in art, and a means of increasing that interest.

The frescoes in the Hall of the Great Council were in full course of execution when the Sicilian Antonello with his great secret came to seek his fortune in the magnificent and delightful city of the seas—a place where every rich man was the artist's patron, and every gentleman a dilettante, and a new triumphant

day of art was dawning, and the streets were full of songs and
pleasure, and the studios of enthusiasm, and beauty and delight
were supreme everywhere : notwithstanding that, in the silence,
to any one who listened, the wild and jangled bells might almost
be heard from besieged cities that were soon no longer to be Venetian, calling every man to arms within their walls, and appealing
for help to heaven and earth.   Such vulgar external matters do
not move the historian of the painters, and are invisible in his
record.   The account of Antonello is full of cheerfulness and
light.   "Being a person much given to pleasure he resolved to
dwell there for ever, and finish his life where he had found a
mode of existence so much according to his mind.   And when
it was understood that he had brought that great discovery from
Flanders, he was loved and caressed by those magnificent
gentlemen as long as he lived."   His friend Domenico is also
described as "a charming and attractive person who delighted
in music and in playing the lute : and every evening they found
means to enjoy themselves together" (*far buon tempo*—literally,
have a good time, according to the favourite custom of our
American cousins) "serenading their sweethearts ; in which
Dominico took great delight."   Thus the young painters lived,
as still in Venice the young and gay, as far as the habits of a
graver age permit, love to live—roaming half the night among
the canals or along the silvery edge of the lagoon, intoxicated
with music and moonlight and the delicious accompaniment of
liquid movement and rhythmic oars ; or amid the continual
pageants in the piazza, the feast of brilliant colour and delightful
groups which made the painters wild with pleasure ; or with a
cluster of admiring and splendid youths at every hand caressed
and flattered by all that was noblest in Venice.   We scarcely
think of this high-coloured and brilliant life as the proper background for those early painters, whose art, all the critics tell us,
derives its excellence from their warmer faith and higher moral
tone ; but we have no reason to believe that any great social
revolution took place between the day of the Bellini and Carpaccio, and that of Titian.   Vasari's description, corroborated as

it is by many others, refers to a period when the Bellini were in the full force of life. Nor are we led to suppose that they were distinguished by special devotion, or in any way separated from their class. Venice had never been austere, but always gay. There was the light and glow of a splendid careless exuberant life in her very air, a current of existence too swift and full of enjoyment to be subdued even by public misfortunes which were distant, and intensified by the wonderful spring, superior to every damping influence, of a new and magnificent development of art.

The two Bellini lived and laboured together during their father's lifetime, but when he died, though never losing their mutual brotherly esteem and tender friendship, separated, each to his own path. Giovanni, the youngest but greatest, continued faithful to the subjects and methods in which he had been trained, and which, though all the habits of the world were changing, still remained most perfectly understood and acceptable to his countrymen. The Divine Mother and Child, with their attendant saints and angels, were the favourite occupation of his genius. He must have placed that sweet and tender image over scores of altars. Sometimes the Virgin Mother sits, simple and sweet, yet always with a certain grandeur of form and natural nobility, not the slim and childish beauty of more conventional painters, with her Child upon her knees: sometimes enthroned, holding the Sacred Infant erect, offering Him to the worship of the world: sometimes with reverential humility watching Him as He sleeps, attended on either side by noble spectator figures, a little court of devout beholders, the saints who have suffered for His sake; often with lovely children seated about the steps of her throne, piping tenderly upon their heavenly flutes, thrilling the chords of a stringed instrument, with a serious sweetness and abstraction, unconscious of anything but the infant Lord to whom their eyes are turned. No more endearing and delightful image could be than that of these angel children. They were a fashion of the age, growing in the hands of Florentine Botticelli into angelic youths, gravely

S

meditating upon the wonders they foresaw. In Rafael, though so much later, they are more divine, like little kindred gods, waiting in an unspeakable awe till the great God should be revealed; but in Bellini more sweet and human, younger, all tender interest and delight, piping their lovely strains if perhaps they might give Him pleasure. One cannot but conclude that he who painted these children at the foot of every divine group in twos and threes, small exquisite courtiers of the Infant King, first fruits of humanity, must have found his models in children who were his own, whose dimpled, delightful limbs were within reach of his kiss, and whose unconscious grace of movement and wondering sweet eyes were before him continually. The delightful purity and gravity, and at the same time manliness, if we may use such a word, of these pictures, is beyond expression. There is no superficial grace or ornament about them, not even the embrace and clinging together of mother and child, which in itself is always so touching and attractive, the attitude of humanity which perhaps has a stronger and simpler hold on the affections than any other. Bellini's Madonna, raising the splendid column of her throat, holding her head high in a noble and simple abstraction, offers not herself but her Child to our eager eyes. She too is a spectator, though blessed among women in holding Him, presenting Him to our gaze, making of her own perfect womanhood His pedestal and support, but all unconscious that prayer or gaze can be attracted to herself, in everything His first servant, the handmaid of the Lord. The painter who set such an image before us could scarcely have been without a profound and tender respect for the woman's office, an exquisite adoration for the Child.

While the younger brother kept in this traditional path, giving to it all the inspiration of his manly and lofty genius, his brother Gentile entered upon a different way. Probably he too began in his father's workshop with mild Madonnas; but ere long the young painter must have found out that other less sacred yet noble subjects were better within his range of power. His fancy must have strayed away from the primitive unity of the sacred

group into new combinations, compositions of wider horizon and
more extended plan. The life that was round him with all its
breadth and rich variety must have beguiled him away from the
ideal. The pictures he has left us set Venice before us in the
guise she then wore, as no description could do. In the two
great examples which remain in the Venetian Accademia there
is a sacred motive : they are chapters in the story of a miraculous holy cross. In one, the sacred relic is being carried across
the piazza, attended by a procession of wonderful figures in
every magnificence of white and red, and gilded canopy and
embroidered mantle. And there stands S. Marco in a softened
blaze of gold and colour, with all the fine lines of its high houses
and colonnades, the Campanile not standing detached as now,
but forming part of the line of the great square ; and in the
midst, looking at the procession, or crossing calmly upon their
own business, such groups of idlers and busy men, of Eastern
travellers and merchants, of gallants from the Broglio, with here
and there a magistrate sweeping along in his toga, or a woman
with her child, as no one had thought of painting before. We
look, and the life that has been so long over, that life in which
all the offices and ceremonies of religion occupy the foreground,
but where nothing pauses for them, and business and pleasure
both go on unconcerned, rises before us. The Venice is not
that Venice which we know ; but it is still most recognisable,
most living and lifelike. No such procession ever sweeps now
through the great piazza ; but still the white mitres and
glistening copes pour through the aisles of S. Marco, so that the
stranger and pilgrim may still recognise the unchangeable ac-
companiments of the true faith. The picture is like a book,
more absolutely true than any chronicle, representing not only
the looks and the customs of the occasion, but the very scene.
How eagerly the people must have traced it out when it first
was made public, finding out in every group some known faces,
some image all the more interesting because it was met in the
flesh every day ! Is that perhaps Zuan Bellini himself, with his
hair standing out round his face, talking to his companions

s 2

about the passing procession, pointing out the curious effects of
light and shade upon the crimson capes and birettas, and watching while the line defiles with its glimmer of candles and sound
of psalms against the majestic shadow of the houses? Still
more characteristic is the other great picture. The same procession, but more in evidence, drawn out before us with the
light in their faces as they wind along over the bridge, with
draperies hung at every window and the women looking out, at
every opening one or two finely ornamented heads in elaborate
coiffes and hoods; while along the Fondamenta, on the side of
the canal, a row of ladies in the most magnificent costumes,
pilgrims or votaries kneeling close together, with all their ornaments—jewelled necklaces and coronets, and light veils of
transparent tissue through which the full matronly shoulders
and countenances appear unobscured—look on, privileged spectators, perhaps waiting to follow in the procession. It is a
curious instance of the truth of the picture that this is no file
of youthful beauties such as a painter would naturally have
chosen, but, with scarcely an exception, consists of buxom and
full-blown mothers with here and there a child thrust in between. It is said by tradition that the first of those figures, she
with the crown, is Catherine Cornaro, the ex-queen of Cyprus,
probably come from her retirement at Asolo to view the procession and see a little life and gaiety, as a variation on the
cultured retirement of that royal villa. The object of the
picture is to show how the cross, which has fallen into the canal
by much pushing and crowding of the populace, floats upright
in the water and is miraculously rescued by its guardian in full
priestly robes, notwithstanding the eager competition of all
manner of swimmers in costumes more handy for the water who
have dashed in on every side; but this, though its pious
purpose, is not its most interesting part.

It is difficult as has been said to find any guidance of dates
in the dimness of distance, in respect to matters so unimportant
as pictures: and accordingly we are unable to trace the progress
of the decoration in the Great Hall. It was delayed by many

CLOISTERS OF THE ABBAZIA.

causes, the indifference of the Signoria and the lukewarm interest
of the painters. Gentile Bellini received permission from the
Signoria to go to the East in 1479, and is there described
as engaged on the restoration of a picture in this magnificent
room, originally painted or begun by his namesake (or, as we
should say in Scotland, his name-father—Jacopo Bellini having
named his eldest son after his master) Gentile da Fabriano—a
work which the magnificent Signoria consider his brother
Giovanni may well be deputed to finish in his place. Nor is
it more easy to discover what the principle was which actuated
the Signoria in selecting for the decoration of the hall that
special historical episode which is so problematical, and of which
even Sanudo says, doubting, that "if it had not happened our
good Venetians would never have had it painted"—a somewhat
equivocal argument. The pertinacity with which the same
subjects were repeated three times—first by the earliest masters,
then, in the full glory of art by all the best of the Bellini generation and by that of Titian: and at last in the decay of that
glory, after the great fire, by the Tizianellos and Vecellini, the
successors of the great painters departed, whose works remain—
is very curious. Perhaps something even in the apocryphal
character of this great climax of glory and magnificence for
Venice, may have pleased the imagination and suggested a
bolder pictorial treatment, with something of allegorical meaning, which would have been less appropriate to matters of pure
fact and well-authenticated history. And no doubt the people
who thronged to look at the new pictures believed it all
entirely, if not the great gentlemen in their crimson robes,
the senators and councillors who selected these scenes as the
most glorious that could be thought of in the history of the
city : how Venice met and conquered the naval force of
Barbarossa and made her own terms with him, and reconciled
the two greatest potentates of the world, the pope and the
emperor, was enough to fill with elation even the great
Republic. And the authority of fact and document was but
little considered in those stormy days.

The subject on which Gentile Bellini was at work when he left Venice was the naval combat between the Doge iani and Prince Otto, son of Barbarossa, which ended in the completest victory; while that allotted to Giovanni Bellini was the voyage in state of the same Doge Ziani to fetch with all splendour from the Carità the pope who was there in hiding under a guise of excessive humility—as the cook of that convent. At the period identified thus by his brother's departure Giovanni Bellini must have been over fifty, so that his promotion did not come too soon. It is not, however, till a much later period that we obtain the next glimpse authentic and satisfactory of his share of the great public work, in which there were evidently many lapses and delays for which the painters were to blame, as well as weary postponements from one official's term of power to another. Early in the next century, however, in 1507, in some pause of larger affairs, the Council seems to have been seized with a sudden movement of energy, and resolved that it would be no small ornament to their hall if three pictures begun by the late Alvise Vivarini could be finished, along with other two, one of which was not even begun, "so that the said hall might be completed without the impediments which have hitherto existed." It would almost seem to be the pictures confided to the Bellini which were in this backward condition, for the Signoria makes an appeal over again to "the most faithful citizen our Zuan Bellini" to bestir himself. But the negligent painter must by this time have been eighty or more, and it was evidently necessary that he should have help in so great an undertaking. His brother had died that year a very old man, and a younger brotherhood was coming to light. And here we find what seems the first public recognition of another name which is closely connected with those of the Bellini in our minds, and to which recent criticism has allotted even a higher place than theirs. The noble senators or councillors, suddenly coming out of the darkness for this object, appear to us for a moment like masters of the ceremonies introducing a new immortal. "Messer Vector, called Scarpazza," is the

assistant whom they designate for old Zuan Bellini, along with
two names unknown to fame, " Messer Vector, late Mathio," and
" Girolamo, painter," no doubt a novice whose reputation was
yet to win.   Carpaccio was to have five ducats a month for his
work ; the other, Messer Vector, four ; Girolamo, the youth, only
two—" and the same are to be diligent and willing in aid of the
said Ser. Zuan Bellini in painting the aforesaid pictures, so that
as diligently and in as little time as is possible they may be
completed."   A warning note is added in Latin (perhaps to
make it more solemn and binding) of the conditions above set
forth—in which it is " expressly declared" that the little band
of painters bind themselves to work "continuously and every
day"—*laborare de continuo et omni die.*   This betrays an inclination on the part of the painters to avoid the public work
which it is amusing to see.   Let us hope the Signoria succeeded
in getting their orders respected : no absences to finish a
Madonna or Saint Ursula which paid better, perhaps both in
fame and money ; no returning to the public service when
private commissions failed ; no greater price for what may be
called piece-work, for specially noble productions ; but steady
labour day by day at four or five ducats a month as might be,
with the pupil-journeyman to clean the palettes and run the
errands !   In Venice, as in other places, it is clear that the state
service was not lucrative for art.

Six years after, we find the work still going on, and another
workman is added.   " In this council it was decided that Tiziano,
painter [*pytor*], should be admitted to work in the hall of
the Great Council with the other painters, without, however,
any salary, except the agreed sum which has usually been
given to those who have painted here, who are Gentile and
Zuan Bellini and Vector Scarpazza.   This Tiziano to be the
same."   It will strike the reader with a certain panic to see
with what indifference these great names are bandied about as
if they were the names of a set of decorators : one feels an
awed desire to ask their pardon !   But not so the great Ten,
who held the lives and fortunes of all Venetians in their hands.

About the date when old Bellini was thus conjured to
complete or superintend the completion of the wanting pictures,
another painter from a very different region—from a landward
town fortified to its ears and full of all mediæval associations,
in the middle of Germany—came to Venice. The high peaked
roofs and picturesque turrets of Nuremburg were not more
unlike the rich and ample façades of the Venetian palaces, or
the glow and glory of Venetian churches, than was the sober
life of the Teuton unlike the gay and genial existence of the
Venetians. Albert Dürer found himself in a southern paradise.
He gives the same account of that Venetian life at first hand
as Vasari does in his historical retrospect. He finds himself
among a crowd of pleasant companions ; players on the lute, so
accomplished and sensitive that their own music makes them
weep: and all, great and small, eager to see, to admire, to
honour the great artist. " Oh, how I shall freeze after this
sunshine ! Here I am a gentleman, at home only a dependant,"
he cries, elated, yet cast down by the difference, and to think
that all these fine Italian lords think more highly of him than
his bourgeois masters in Nuremburg. Sanbellini, he tells his
friends, has come to see him, the venerable old man—very old,
but still the best painter of them all, and a good man, as everybody says : and from this master he receives the sweetest
praise, and a commission to paint something for him for which
he promises to pay well. Old Zuan Bellini, with his vivacious
Venetian ways, and the solemn German, with his long and serious countenance, like a prophet in the desert—what a contrast
they must have made ! But they had one language between
them at least, the tongue which every true artist understands,
the delightful secret freemasonry and brotherhood of art.

It was when he had arrived at this venerable age, over eighty,
but still coming and going about these pictures in the great
hall, and alert to hear of and visit the stranger from Germany
who brought the traditions of another school to Venice—that
Bellini painted his last or almost last picture, so touching in
its appropriateness to his great age and concluding life, the old

St. Jerome in San Giovanni Grisostomo, seated high upon a
solitary mount with a couple of admiring saints below. Perhaps
he had begun to feel that old age needs no desert, but is always
solitary even in the midst of all pupils and followers. He did
not die till he was ninety. It was the fashion among the
painters of Venice to live to old age. Among other works for
the great hall, it is understood that Bellini painted many
portraits of the doges, of which one remains, familiar to us all,
the picture now in our National Gallery of that wonderful old
man with his sunken eyes of age, so full of subtle life and power,
the portrait which forms the frontispiece of this volume. History
bears no very strong impression of the character of Leonardo
Loredan. He held the realm of state bravely at a time of great
trial: but the office of doge by this time had come to be of
comparatively small importance to the constitution of Venice ;
however, of all the potent doges of Venetian chronicles, he
alone may be said to live for ever. With all these thinkings,
astute yet humorous, which are recorded in his eyes, and his
mouth scarcely sure whether to set with thin lips in the form
it took to pronounce a fatal sentence, or to soften into a smile,
this dry and small, yet so dignified and splendid old man,
remains the impersonation of that mysterious and secret
authority of the republic by which, alas ! the doges suffered
more than they enjoyed. The painter is said in his *momens
perdus* to have painted many portraits—among others that
Imagine celeste shining like the sun, which made Bembo,
though a cardinal, burst into song :—

> " Credo che il mio Bellin con la figura,
>   T'habbia dato il costume anche di lei,
>   Che m'ardi s'io ti mira, e pur tu sei,
>   Freddo smalto a cui gionse alta ventura."

In the meantime the elder brother, Gentile, had met with
adventures more remarkable. In the year 1479, as has been
noted, the Signoria commissioned him to go to Constantinople
at the request of the sultan, who had begged that a painter
might be sent to exhibit his powers, or—as some say—who had

seen a picture by one of the Bellini carried thither among the
stores of some Venetian merchant, and desired to see how such
a wonderful thing could be done.   This is, we may point out by
the way, a thing well worthy of remark as a sign of the wonderful
changes that had taken place in the East without seriously
altering the long habit of trade, and the natural alliance, in
spite of all interruptions, between buying and selling communities. Even within these simple pages we have seen the Venetians
fighting and struggling, making a hundred treaties, negotiating
long and anxiously for charters and privileges from the Greek
empire in the capital of the East, then helping to destroy
that imperial house, seizing the city, setting up a short-lived
Latin empire, making themselves rich with the spoils of Constantinople.   And now both these races and dynasties are swept
away, and the infidel has got possession of the once splendid
Christian city, and for a time has threatened all Europe, and
Venice first of all.   But the moment the war is stopped, however short may be the truce, and however changed the circumstances, trade indomitable has pushed forward with its cargoes,
sure that at least the Turk's gold is as good as the Christian's,
and his carpets and shawls perhaps better, who knows ?   There
is nothing so impartial as commerce so long as money is to
be made.   Scutari had scarcely ceased to smoke when Gentile
Bellini was sent to please the Turk, and prove that the republic
bore no malice.   One can imagine that the painter went, not
without trepidation, among the proud and hated invaders who
had thus changed the face of the earth.   The grim monarch
before whom Europe trembled received him with courtesy and
favour, and Gentile painted his portrait, and that of his queen—
no doubt some chosen member of the harem whom the Venetian
chose to represent as the sharer of Mahommed's throne.

The portrait of the sultan, formally dated, has been brought
back to Venice, after four hundred years and many vicissitudes,
by Sir Henry Layard.   It represents no murderous Turk, but a
face of curious refinement, almost feeble, though full of the
impassive calm of an unquestioned despot.   The Venetian as

To face page 266.

PORTRAIT OF SULTAN : GENTILE BELLINI.

the story goes had begun to be at his ease, cheered, no doubt, by the condescension of the autocrat before whom all prostrated themselves, but who showed no pride to the painter, and by the unanimous marvelling surprise, as at a prodigy, of all beholders, when a horrible incident occurred. He would seem to have gone on painting familiar subjects notwithstanding the inappropriateness of his surroundings, and had just finished the story of John the Baptist "who was reverenced by the Turks as a prophet." But when he exhibited the head of the Baptist on the charger to the sultan, that potentate began to criticise, as a man who at last finds himself on familiar ground. He told the painter that his anatomy was wrong, and that when the head was severed from the body, the neck disappeared altogether. No doubt with modesty, but firmly, the painter would defend his work, probably forgetting that the sultan had in this particular a much greater experience than he. But Mahommed was no man to waste words. He called a slave to him on the spot, and whether with his own ready sword or by some other hand, swept off in a trice the poor wretch's head, that the painter might be no longer in any doubt as to the effect. This horrible lesson in anatomy was more than Gentile's nerves could bear, and it is not wonderful that from that moment he never ceased his efforts to get his dismissal, "not knowing," says Ridolfi "whether some day a similar jest might not be played on him." Finally he was permitted to return home with laudatory letters and the title of Cavalière, and a chain of gold of much value round his neck. The Venetian authorities either felt that a man who had risked so much to please the sultan and keep up a good understanding with him was worth a reward, or they did not venture to neglect the recommendation of so great a potentate—for they gave the painter a pension of 200 ducats a year for his life. And he was in time to resume his pencil in the great hall where Ridolfi gives him the credit of five of the pictures, painted in great part after his return. All this no doubt splendid series was destroyed a hundred years after by fire; but as has been already noted, the subjects were repeated in the subsequent pictures which still exist, although these, with the exception of one by Tintoretto and one by Paolo Veronese, were executed by less remarkable hands.

Gentile Bellini died in 1507 at the age of eighty, his brother nearly ten years after : they were both laid with so many others of their brotherhood in the great church of San Giovanni e Paolo, where the traveller may see their names upon the pavement in all humility and peace.

ANGEL FROM CARPACCIO.

The nearest to these two brothers in the meaning and sentiment of his work is Victor Carpaccio. His place would almost seem to lie justly between them. He is the first illustrator of religious life and legend in Venice, as well as the most delightful story-teller of his time, the finest poet in a city not given to audible verse. The extreme devotion which Mr. Ruskin has for this painter has perhaps raised him to a pedestal which is slightly

To face page 269.

URSULA RECEIVING HER BRIDEGROOM: FROM CARPACCIO.

factitious—at least so far as the crowd is concerned, who follow the great writer without comprehending him, and are apt to make the worship a little ridiculous. But there is enough in the noble series of pictures which set forth the visionary life of St. Ursula to justify a great deal of enthusiasm. No more lovely picture was ever painted than that which represents the young princess lying wrapped in spotless slumber, seeing in her dream the saintly life before her and the companion of her career, the prince, half knight, half angel, whose image hovers at the door. The wonderful mediæval room with all its slender antique furniture, the soft dawn in the window, the desk where the maiden has said her prayers, the holy water over her head, form a dim harmonious background of silence and virgin solitude. And what could surpass the profound and holy sleep, so complete, so peaceful, so serene in which she lies, lulled by the solemn sweetness of her vision, in which there is no unrest as of earthly love always full of disquiet, but a soft awe and stillness as of great tragic possibilities foreseen. The other pictures of the series may be more rich in incident and expression, and have a higher dramatic interest, but the sleep of Ursula is exquisite, and goes to every heart.

The San Giorgio in the little church of the Slavs, detaches itself in a similar way from all others, and presents to the imagination a companion picture. Ursula has no companion in her own story that is so worthy of her as this St. George. Her prince is only a vision, he is absorbed in her presence, a shadow, whom the painter has scarcely taken the trouble to keep of one type, or recognisable throughout the series. But the San Giorgio of the Schiavoni remains in our thoughts, a vision of youthful power and meaning, worthy to be that maiden's mate. No sleep for him, or dreams. He puts his horse at the dragon with an intent and stern diligence as if there were (as truly there was not) no moment to lose, no breath to draw, till his mission had been accomplished. A swift fierceness and determination is in every line of him : his spear, which seems at first on the wrong side of the horse, is so on purpose to get a stronger lever-

age in the tremendous charge. The dragon is quite a poor
creature to call forth all that force of righteous passion; but we
think nothing of its abject meanness, all sympathy and awe
being concentrated in the champion's heavenly wrath and inspiration of purpose. We do not pretend to follow the great
critic who has thrown all his own tender yet fiery genius into
the elucidation of every quip and freak of fancy in this elaborate mediæval poem. The low and half lighted walls of the
little brown church, which bears a sort of homely resemblance

HEAD OF ST. GEORGE.

to an English Little Bethel, enshrine for us chiefly this one
heroic semblance, and no more: and we do not attempt to
discuss the painting from any professional point of view. But
we are very sure that this knight and maiden, though they never
can belong to each other, will find their places in every sympathetic soul that sees them, together—George charging down in
abstract holy wrath upon the impersonation of sin and evil,
Ursula dreaming of the great, sad, yet fair life before her, the
pilgrim's journey, and the martyr's palm.

The lives of the saints were the popular poetry of Christendom, catholic and universal beyond all folk-lore and folks-lieder, before even the limits of existing continental nations were formed. All the elements of romance, as well as that ascetic teaching and doctrine of boundless self-sacrifice which commends itself always to the primitive mind as the highest type of religion, were to be found in these primitive tales, which are never so happy as when taking the youngest and fairest and noblest from all the delights of life, and setting them amid the mediæval horrors of plague and destitution. Carpaccio's saints, however, belong to even an earlier variety of the self-devoted, the first heroes of humanity. It is for the faith that they contend and die; they are the ideal emissaries of a divine religion but newly unveiled and surrounded by a dark and horrible infidel world which is to be converted only by the blood of the martyrs; or by mysterious forms of evil, devouring dragons and monsters of foul iniquity, who must be slain or led captive by the spotless warriors in whom there is nothing kindred to their rapacious foulness. Perhaps it is because of the vicinity of Venice to the East, and of the continual conflict with the infidel which Crusades and other enterprises less elevated had made more familiar than any other enemy to the imagination of the city of the sea, that Carpaccio's story-telling is all of this complexion. The German painter from over the Alps had his dreams of sweet Elizabeth with the loaves in her lap which turned to roses, and the leper whom she laid in the prince's bed, when our Venetian conceived his Ursula forewarned of all that must follow, leaving home and father to convert the heathen, or that strenuous grave St. George, with stern fierce eyes aflame, cutting down the monster who was evil embodied.

These were the earliest of all heroic tales in Christendom, and Carpaccio's art was that of the minstrel-historian as well as the painter. He knew how to choose his incidents and construct his plot like any story-teller, so that those, if there were any, in Venice who did not care for pictures might still be caught by the interest of his tale, and follow breathless, the fortunes of the royal maiden, or that great episode of heroic adventure which has made so many nations choose St. George as their patron saint. Gentile Bellini had found out how the aspect of real life and all its accessories might be turned to use in art, and how warm was the interest of the spectators in the representation of the things and places with which they were most familiar; but Carpaccio made a step beyond his old master when he discovered that art was able, not only to make an incident immortal, but to tell a story, and draw the very hearts of beholders out of their bosoms, as sometimes an eloquent friar in the pulpit, or story-teller upon the Riva, with his group of entranced listeners, could do. And having made this discovery, though it was already the time of the Renaissance and all the uncleanly gods of the heathen, with all their fables, were coming back, for the diversion and delight of the licentious and the learned, this painter sternly turned his back upon all these new-fangled interests, and entranced all Venice, though she loved pleasure, and to pipe and sing and wear fine dresses and flaunt in the sunshine, with the story of the devoted princess and her maiden train, and with St. George, all swift and fierce in youthful wrath, slaying the old dragon, the emblem of all ill, the devouring lust and cruelty, whose ravages devastated an entire kingdom and devoured both man and maid.

But of the man who did this we know nothing, not even where he was born or where he died. He has been said to belong to Istria because there has been found there a family of Carpaccio, among whom, from time immemorial, the eldest son has been called Victor or Vettore : but that this is the painter's family is a matter of pure conjecture. The diligent researches of Signor Molmenti, who has done so much to elucidate Venetian manners and life, has found in the archives of a neighbouring state, a letter, perhaps the only intelligible trace of Carpaccio as an ordinary mortal and not an inspired painter, which is in existence. It affords us no revelation of high meaning or purpose, but only a homely view of a man with no greater pretensions than those of an honest workman living on his earnings, reluctant to lose a commission, and eager to recommend himself to a liberal and well-paying customer. It shows him upon no elevation of poetic meaning such as we might have preferred to see; but after all, even in heroic days, there was nothing contrary to inspiration in selling your picture and commending yourself as much as was in you, to who would buy. And it is evident that Carpaccio had much confidence in the excellence of the work he had to sell, and felt that his wares were second to none. The letter is addressed to the well-known amateur and patron of artists, he who was the first to make Titian's fortune, Francesco Gonzaga, Lord of Mantua.

"ILLUSTRISSIMO SIGNOR MIO,

"Some days ago a person unknown to me, conducted by certain others, came to me to see a *Jerusalem* which I have made, and as soon as he had seen it, with great pertinacity insisted that I should sell it to him, because he felt it to be a thing out of which he would get great content and satisfaction. Finally we made a bargain by mutual agreement, but since then I have seen no more of him. To clear up the matter I asked those who had brought him, among whom was a priest, bearded and clad in grey, whom I had several times seen in the hall of the Great Council with your highness: of whom asking his name and condition I was told that he was Messer Laurentio, painter to your illustrious highness—by which I easily understood where this person might be found, and accordingly I direct these presents to your illustrious highness to make you acquainted with my name as well as with the work in question. First, signor mio, I am that painter by whom your illustrious highness was conducted to see the pictures in the great hall, when your illustrious highness deigned to ascend the scaffolding to see our work, which was the story of Ancona, and my name is Victor Carpatio. Concerning the *Jerusalem* I take upon me to say that in our times there is not another picture equal to it, not only for excellence and perfection, but also for size. The height of the picture is twenty-five feet, and the width is five feet and a half, according to the measure of such things, and I know that of this work Zuane Zamberti has spoken to your sublimity. Also it is true, and I know certainly, that the aforesaid painter belonging to your service has carried away a sketch incomplete and of small size which I am sure will not be to your highness's satisfaction. If it should please your highness to submit the picture first to the inspection of some judicious men, on a word of guarantee being given to me it shall be at your highness's disposal. The work is in distemper on canvas, and it can be rolled round a piece of wood without any detriment. If it should please you to desire it in colour, it rests with your illustrious highness to command, and to me with profoundest study to

T

execute. Of the price I say nothing, remitting it entirely to your illustrious highness, to whom I humbly commend myself this fifteenth day of August, 1511, at Venice.   "Da V. Subl. humilo. Servitore,

"VICTOR CARPATHIO, *Pictore.*"

Whether the anxious painter got the commission, or if his sublimity of Mantua thought the humble missive beneath his notice, or if the *Jerusalem* was ever put into colour *cum summo studio,* will probably never be known; but here he appears to us, a man very open to commissions, eager for work, probably finding the four ducats a month of the Signoria poor pay, and losing no opportunity of making it up.   But though the painter is anxious and conciliatory, he does not deceive himself as to the excellence of his work.   He takes upon him to say that there is no better picture to be had in his time, and gives the measure of it with simplicity, feeling that this test of greatness at least must be within his correspondent's capacity.   And one cannot but remark with a smile how this old demi-god of art in the heroic age was ready to forward his picture to the purchaser rolled round a piece of wood, as we send the humble photograph nowadays by the post!   How great a difference! yet with something odd and touching of human resemblance too.

Of the great painters of the following generation who raised the Venetian school to the height of glory, almost all who were born subjects of the republic passed through the studio of the Bellini.   The historians tell us how young Giorgio of Castel Franco awoke a certain despite in the breast of his master by his wonderful progress and divination in the development of art—seizing such secrets as were yet to discover, and conjuring away a certain primitive rigidity which still remained in the work of the elders: and how young Tiziano, from his mountain village, entered into the method of his fellow-pupil, and both together carried their mystery of glorious colour and easy splendid composition to its climax in Venice.   But the feeling and criticism of the present age, so largely influenced by Mr. Ruskin, are rather disposed to pass that grand perfection by, and return with devotion to the simple splendour of those three early masters who are nearer to the fountain-head, and retain a more absolute reality and sincerity in their work. Gentile Bellini painting behind and around his miracle the genuine Venice which he saw, a representation more authentic and graphic than any that history can make: and Carpaccio giving life and substance to the legends which embodied literature and poetry and the highest symbolical morals to the people—express the fact of every-day life and the vision and the faculty divine of a high and pure imagination, with a force and intensity which are not in their more highly-trained and conventionally perfect successors. And as for the third, in some respects the noblest of the three—he whose genius sought no new path, who is content with the divine group which his homely forefathers had drawn and daubed before him, but which it was his to set forth for the first time in Venice in all the lustre of the new method of colour which he and his successors carried to such glow and splendour that all that is most brilliant in it is called Venetian —where shall we find a more lovely image of the Mother and the Child than that which he sets before us, throned in grave seclusion in the Frari, humbly retired behind that window in the Accademia, shining forth over so many altars in other places, in a noble and modest perfection ? The angel children sounding their simple lutes, looking up with frank and simple childish reverence, all sweet and human, to the miraculous Child, have something in them which is as much beyond the conventional cherubic heads and artificial ornamented angels of the later art as heaven is beyond earth, or the true tenderness of imagination beyond the fantastic inventions of fiction. And if Rafael in our days must give way to Botticelli, with how much greater reason should Titian in the height of art, all earthly splendour and voluptuous glow, give place to the lovely imaginations of old Zuan Bellini, the father of Venetian art!

CHAPTER II.

HE day of art had now fully risen in Venice. The dawning had been long, progressing slowly through all the early efforts of decoration and ornament, and by the dim religious light of nameless masters, to the great moment in which the Bellini revealed themselves, making Venice splendid with the sunrise of a new faculty, entirely congenial to her temperament and desires. It would almost appear as if the first note, once struck, of a new departure in life or in art, was enough to wake up in all the regions within hearing the predestined workers, who but for that awaking might have slumbered for ever, or found in other fields an incomplete development. While it is beyond the range of human powers to determine what cause or agency it is which enables the first fine genius—the Maker who in every mode of creative work is like the great priest of the Old Testament, without father and without mother—to burst all bonds and outstep all barriers, it is comparatively easy to trace how, under his influence and by the stimulus of a sudden new impulse felt to be almost divine, his successors may spring into light and being. Nothing to our humble thinking explains the Bellini : but the Bellini to a certain extent explain Titian and all the other splendours to come.

When the thrill of the new beginning had gone through all the air, mounting up among the glorious peaks and snows, to Cadore on one side, and over the salt-water country and marshy plains on the other to Castel Franco, two humble families had each received the uncertain blessing of a boy, who took to none of the established modes of living, and would turn his thoughts neither to husbandry, nor to such genteel trades as became the members of a family of peasant nobility, but dreamed and drew with whatsoever material came to their hands upon walls or other handy places. At another epoch it is likely enough that parental force would have been employed to balk, for a time at least, these indications of youthful genius: but no doubt some of the Vecelli family, the lawyer uncle or the soldier father, had some time descended from his hill-top to the great city which lay gleaming upon the edge of those great plains of sea that wash the feet of the mountains, and had seen some wonderful work in church or senate-chamber, which made known a new possibility to him, and justified in some sort the attempts of the eager child. More certainly still a villager from the Trevisano, carrying his rural merchandise to market, would be led by some gossip in the Erberia to see the new Madonna in San Giobbe, and ask himself whether by any chance little Giorgio, always with that bit of chalk in his fingers, might come to do such a wonder as that if the boy had justice done him? They came accordingly with beating hearts, the two little rustics, each from his village, to Zuan Bellini's *bottega* in Rialto to learn their art. The mountain boy was but ten years old—confided to the care of an uncle who lived in Venice; but whether he went at once into the head-quarters of the art is unknown, and unlikely, for so young a student could scarcely have been far enough advanced to profit by the instructions of the greatest painter in Venice. It is supposed by some that he began his studies under Zuccato, the mosaicist, or some humbler instructor. But all this would seem mere conjecture. Vasari, his contemporary and friend, makes no mention of any preliminary studies, but places the boy at once under Giovanni Bellini. Of the young Barbarella from Castel Franco the same story is told. He too was brought to Venice by his father and placed under Bellini's instruction. Messrs. Crowe and Cavalcasella have confused these bare but simple records with theories of their own respecting the influence of Giorgione upon Titian, which is such, they think, or thought, as could only have been attained by an elder over a younger companion, whereas all the evidence goes to prove that the two were as nearly as possible the same age, and that they were fellow pupils, perhaps fellow apprentices, in Bellini's workshop. We may, however, find so much reason for the theory as this, that young Tiziano was in his youth a steady and patient worker, following all the rules and discipline of his master, and taking into his capacious brain everything that could be taught him, awaiting the moment when he should turn these stores of instruction to use in his own individual way; whereas young Giorgio was more masterful and impatient, and with a quicker eye and insight (having so much less time to do his work in) seized upon those points in which his genius could have full play. Vasari talks as if this brilliant youth with all the fire of purpose in his eyes had blazed all of a sudden upon the workshop in which Bellini's pupils laboured—Titian among them, containing what new lights were in him in dutiful subordination to the spirit of the place—"about the year 1507," with a new gospel of colour and brightness scattering the clouds from the firmament. Ridolfi, on the other hand, describes him as a pupil whom the master looked upon with a little jealousy, "seeing the felicity with which all things were made clear by this scholar. And certainly," adds the critic in his involved and ponderous phraseology, "it was a wonder to see how this boy added to the method of Bellini (in whom all the beauties of painting had seemed conjoined) such grace and tenderness of colour, as if Giorgione, participating in that power by which Nature mixes human flesh with all the qualities of the elements, harmonised with supreme sweetness the shadow and the light, and threw a delicate flush of rose tints upon every member through which the blood flows."

Giorgione, with his bolder impulse and that haste which we

perceive to have been so needful for his short life, is more apparent than his fellow student in these early years. When he came out of Bellini's workshop, his apprenticeship done, he roamed a little from *bottega* to *bottega*, painting now a sacred picture for an oratory or chapel, now a marriage chest or cabinet. "Quadri di devotione, ricinti da letto, e gabinetti," says Ridolfi—not ashamed to turn his hand to anything there might be to do. Going home afterwards to his village, he was received—the same authority informs us—with enthusiasm, as having made himself a great man and a painter, and commissions showered upon him. Perhaps it was at Castel Franco, amid the delight and praise of his friends, that the young painter first recognised fully his own powers. At all events, when he had exhausted their simple applauses and filled the village church and convent with his work, he went back to Venice, evidently with a soul above the *ricinti da letto*, and launched himself upon the world. His purse was no doubt replenished by the work he had done at home, a number of the wealthy neighbours having had themselves painted by little Giorgio—an opportunity they must have perceived that might not soon recur. But it was not only for work and fame that he returned to Venice. He was young, and life was sweet, sweeter there than anywhere else in all the world, full of everything that was beautiful and bright. He took a house in the Campo San Silvestro, opposite the church of that name, not far from the Rialto, in the midst of all the joyous companions of his craft; and "by his talent and his pleasant nature," drawing round him a multitude of friends, lived there amid all the delights of youth—*dilettandosi suonar il liuto*—dividing his days between the arts. No gayer life nor one more full of pleasure could be; his very work a delight, a continual crowd of comrades, admiring, imitating, urging him on, always round him, every man with his *canzone* and his picture, and all ready to fling them down at a moment's notice, and rush forth to swell the harmonies on the canal, or steal out upon the lagoon in the retirement of the gondola, upon some more secret adventure. What hush there would be of all the laughing commentaries when a fine patrician in his sweeping robes was seen approaching across the *campo*, a possible patron : what a rush to the windows when, conscious perhaps of all the eyes upon her, but without lifting her own, some lovely Madonna wrapped in her veil, with her following of maidens, would come in a glory of silken robes and jewels out of the church door ! " Per certo suo decoroso aspetto si detto Giorgione," says Ridolfi, but perhaps the word *decoroso* would be out of place in our sense of it—for his delightsome presence rather and his pleasant ways. The Italian tongue still lends itself to such caresses, and is capable of making the dear George, the delightful fellow, the beloved of all his companions, into Giorgione still.

And amid all this babble of lutes and laughter, and all the glow of colour and flush of youth, the other lad from the mountains would come and go, no less gay perhaps than any of them, but working on, with that steady power of his, gathering to himself slowly but with an unerring instinct the new principles which his comrade, all impetuous and spontaneous, made known in practice rather than in teaching, making the blood flow and the pulses beat in every limb he drew. Young Tiziano had plodded through the Bellini system without making any rebellious outbreak of new ideas as Giorgione had done, taking the good of his master, so far as that master went, but with his eyes open to every suggestion, and very ready to see that his comrade had expanded the old rule, and done something worth adopting and following in this joyful splendid outburst of his. It was in this way no doubt, that the one youth followed the other, half by instinct, by mingled sympathy and rivalry, by the natural contagion of a development more advanced than that which had been the starting point of both—confusing his late critics after some centuries into an attempt to prove that the one must have taught the other, which was not necessary in any formal way. Titian had ninety years to live, and Nature worked in him at leisure, while Giorgione had but a third of that time, and went fast, flinging about what genius

OUT OF THE GRAND CANAL.

To face page 251.

and power of instruction there was in him with careless
liberality, not thinking whether from any friendly comrade
about him he received less than he gave. Perhaps the same
unconscious hurry of life, perhaps only his more impetuous
temper induced him, when work flagged and commissions were
slow of coming in, to turn his hand to the front of his own
house and paint that, in default of more profitable work. It
was no doubt the best of advertisements for the young painter.
On the higher story in which most probably he lived, he covered
the walls with figures of musicians and poets with their lutes,
and with groups of boys, the *putti* so dear to Venice, as well
as *altre fantasie*, and historic scenes of more pretension which
were the subject of " a learned eulogy by Signor Jacopo Pighetti,
and a celebrated poem by Signor Paolo Vendramin," says Ridolfi.
The literary tributes have perished, and so have the frescoes,
although the spectator may still see some faded traces of
Giorgione's *putti* upon the walls of his house; but they answered
what no doubt was at least one of their purposes by attracting
the attention of the watchful city, ever ready to see what
beautiful work was being done. It was at this moment that
the Fondaco de' Tedeschi, the German factory so to speak, on
the edge of the Grand Canal, was re-building, a great house
wanting decoration. The jealous authorities of the republic,
for some reason one fails to see, had forbidden the use of archi-
tectural ornamentation in the new building, which, all the same,
was their own building, not the property of the Germans. Had
it belonged to the foreigner there might have been a supposable
cause in the necessity for keeping these aliens down, and
preventing any possible emulation with native born Venetians.
We can only suppose that this was actually the reason, and
that, even in the house which Venice built for them, these
traders were not to be permitted to look as fine or feel as
magnificent as their hosts and superiors. But a great house
with four vast walls, capable of endless decoration, and nothing
done to them, would probably have raised a rebellion in the
city, or at least among the swarms of painters on the other

side of the Rialto, gazing at it with hungry eyes. So it was
conceded by the authorities that this square undecorated house,
a singularly uninteresting block of buildings to stand on such
a site, should be painted at least to harmonise it so far with its
neighbours. It is not to be supposed that this was the first
piece of work on which Titian had been engaged. No doubt
he had already produced his tale of Madonnas, with a few
portraits to make him known. But he steps into sight for the
first time publicly when we hear that the wall on the land
side, the street front, of the building was allotted to him, while
the side toward the canal was confided to Giorgione. Perhaps the
whole building was put into Giorgione's hands, and part of the
work confided by him to his comrade; at all events they divided
it between them. Every visitor to Venice is aware of the faint
and faded figure high up in the right-hand corner, disappearing,
as all its neighbouring glories have disappeared, which is the
last remnant of Giorgione's work upon the canal front of this
great gloomy house. Of Titian's group over the great doorway
in the street there remains nothing at all : the sea breezes and
the keen air have carried all these beautiful things away.

In respect to these frescoes, Vasari tells one anedote, which
is natural and characteristic, and may indicate the point at
which these two young men detached themselves, and took
each his separate way. He narrates how "many gentlemen,"
not being aware of the division of labour, met Giorgione on the
evening of the day on which Titian had uncovered a portion of
his work, and crowded round him with their congratulations,
assuring him that he had never done anything so fine, and that
the front towards the Merceria quite excelled the river front !
Giorgione was so indignant, *sentiva tanto sdegno*, at this unlucky
compliment, that until Titian had finished the work and it had
become well known which portion of it was his, the sensitive
painter showed himself no more in public, and from that
moment would neither see Titian nor acknowledge him as a
friend. Ridolfi tells the same story, with the addition that it
was a conscious mistake made maliciously by certain comrades

who feigned not to know who had painted the great Judith over the door.

This is not a history of the Venetian painters, nor is it necessary to follow the life and labours of these two brilliant and splendid successors of the first masters in our city. Whether it was by the distinct initiative of Giorgione in painting his own house that the habit of painting Venetian houses in general originated, or whether it was only one of the ever increasing marks of luxury and display, we do not pretend to decide. At all events it was an expedient of this generation to add to the glory of the city, and the splendid aspect which she bore. The nobler dignity of the ancient architecture had already been partially lost, or no longer pleased in its gravity and stateliness the race which loved colour and splendour in all things. A whole city glowing in crimson and gold, with giant forms starting up along every wall, and sweet groups of cherub boys tracing every course of stone, and the fables of Greece and Rome taking form upon every façade, must have been no doubt a wonderful sight. The reflections in the Grand Canal as it flowed between these pictured palaces must have left little room for sky or atmosphere in the midst of that dazzling confusion of brilliant tints and images. And every *campo* must have lent its blaze of colour, to put the sun himself to shame. But we wonder whether it is to be much regretted that the sun and the winds have triumphed in the end, and had their will of those fine Venetian houses. Among so many losses this is the one for which I feel the least regret.

It is recorded among the expenses of the republic in December, 1508, that 150 ducats were paid to Zorzi da Castel Franco for his work upon the Fondaco, in which, according to this businesslike record, Victor Carpaccio had also some share: but this is the only indication of the fact, and the total disappearance of the work makes all other inquiry impossible.

By this time, however, Giorgione's brief and gay life was approaching its end. That stormy, joyous existence, so full of work, so full of pleasure, as warm in colour as were his pictures, and pushed to a hasty perfection all at once without the modesty of any slow beginning, ended suddenly as it had begun. Vasari has unkindly attributed his early death to the disorders of his life ; but his other biographers are more sympathetic. Ridolfi gives two different accounts, both popularly current : one that he caught the plague from a lady he loved : the other, that being deserted by his love he died of grief, *non trovando altro remedio*. In either case the impetuous young painter, amid his early successes—more celebrated than any of his compeers, the leader among his comrades, the only one of them who had struck into an individual path, developing the lessons of Bellini —died in the midst of his loves and pleasures at the age of thirty-four, not having yet reached the *mezzo del cammin di nostra vita*, which Dante had attained when his great work began.

This was in the year 1511, only three years after the completion of his work at the Fondaco, and while old Zuan Bellini was still alive and at work, in his robust old age, seeing his impetuous pupil out. It was one of the many years in which the plague visited Venice, carrying consternation through the gay and glowing streets. It is said that Giorgione was working in the hall of the Great Council, among the other painters, at the picture in which the emperor is represented as kissing the pope's foot, at the time of his death. At all events he had lived long enough to make his fame great in the city, and to leave examples of his splendid work in many of the other great cities of Italy, as well as in his own little *borgo* at Castel Franco, where still they are the pride and glory of the little town.

It would almost seem as if it were only after the death of Giorgione that Titian began to be estimated at his just value. The one had given the impulse, the other had received it, and Vasari does not hesitate to call Titian the pupil of his contemporary, though not in the formal sense attached to the word by modern writers, notwithstanding the fact that they were of the same age. Ridolfi's formal yet warm enthusiasm for the painter " to whom belongs perpetual praise and honour, since he has become a light to all those who come after him,"

assigns to Giorgione a higher place than that which the spectator of to-day will probably think justified. His master,
Bellini, appeals more warmly to the heart; his pupil, Titian,
filled a much greater place in the world and in art. But "it is
certain," says the historian and critic of the sixteenth century,
with a double affirmation, " that Giorgio was without doubt the
first who showed the good way in painting, fitting himself
(*approssimandosi*) by the mixture of his colours to express with
facility the works of nature, concealing as much as possible the
difficulties to be encountered in working, which is the chief
point; so that in the flesh tints of this ingenious painter the
innumerable shades of grey, orange, blue, and other such colours
customarily used by some, are absent. . . . . The artificers who
followed him, with the example before them of his works,
acquired the facility and true method of colour by which so
much progress was made."

The works of Giorgione, however, are comparatively few : his
short life, and perhaps the mirth of it, the sounding of the lute,
the joyous company, and all the delights of that highly-coloured
existence restrained the splendid productiveness which was characteristic of his art and age. And yet perhaps this suggestion
does the painter injustice; for amid all those diversions, and the
ceaseless round of loves and festivities, the list of work done is
always astonishing. Many of his works, however, were frescoes,
and the period in which he and Titian were, as Mr. Ruskin
says, house painters, was the height of his genius. The sea air
and the keen *tramontana* have thus swept away much that was
the glory of the young painter's life.

The moment at which Titian appears publicly on the stage,
so to speak, of the great hall, called to aid in the work going on
there, was not till two years after the death of his companion.
Whether Giorgione kept his hasty word, and saw no more of
him after that unfortunate compliment about the Judith over
the doorway of the Fondaco, we are not told: but it was not
until after the shadow of that impetuous youthful genius had
been removed, that the other, the patient and thoughtful, who

had not reached perfection in a burst, but by much consideration and comparison and exercise of the splendid faculty of
work that was in him, came fully into the light.   Messrs. Crowe
and Cavalcasella make much of certain disputes and intrigues
that seem to have surrounded this appointment, and point out
that it was given and withdrawn, and again conferred upon
Titian, according as his friends or those of the older painters
were in the ascendant in the often-changed combinations of
power in Venice.   Their attempt to show that old Zuan
Bellini, the patriarch of the art, schemed against his younger
rival, and endeavoured to keep him out of state patronage are
happily supported by no documents, but are merely an inference
from the course of events, which show certain waverings and
uncertainties in the bargain between the Signoria and the
painter.   The manner in which this bargain was made, and in
which the money was provided to pay for the work of Titian
and his associates, is very characteristic and noticeable.   After
much uncertainty as to what were the intentions of the Signoria,
the painter received an invitation to go to Rome through
Pietro Bembo, which, however *bonâ fide* in itself, was probably
intended to bring matters to a crisis, and show the authorities,
who had not as yet secured the services of the most promising
of all the younger artists then left in Venice, that their decision
must be made at once.   Titian brings the question before them
with much firmness—will they have him or not? must he turn
aside to the service of the pope instead of entering that of the
magnificent Signoria, which, " desirous of fame rather than of
profit," he would prefer? Pressing for a decision, he then sets forth
the pay and position for which he is willing to devote his powers
to the public service.   These are; the first brokership that
shall be vacant in the Fondaco de' Tedeschi, " irrespective of all
promised reversions of such patent," and the maintenance of
two pupils as his assistants, to be paid by the Salt Office, which
also is to provide all colours and necessaries required in their
work.   The curious complication of state affairs which thus
mixes up the most uncongenial branches, and defrays the expenses

of this, the supremest luxury of the state, out of the tarry purse
of its oldest and rudest industry, is very remarkable: and the
bargain has a certain surreptitious air, as if even the magnificent
Signoria did not care to confess how much their splendours cost.
If our own Government, ashamed to put into their straightforward budget the many thousands expended on the purchase of
the Blenheim Madonna, had added it in with the accounts of
the Inland Revenue, it would be an operation somewhat similar. But such balancings and mutual compensations, robbing
Peter to pay Paul, were common in those days. The brokership, however, is about as curious an expedient for the pay of a
painter as could be devised. The German merchants were forbidden to trade without the assistance of such an official, and
the painter of course fulfilled the duties of the office by deputy.
It affords an amazing suggestion indeed to think of old Bellini,
or our magnificent young Titian, crossing the Rialto by the side
of some homely Teuton with his samples in his pocket, to drive
a noisy bargain in the crowded piazza round San Giacomo where
all the merchants congregated. But the expedient was perfectly
natural to the times in which they lived, and indeed such resources have not long gone out of use even among ourselves.

Titian's proposal was accepted, then modified, and finally
received and established, with the odious addition that the
broker's place to be given to him was not simply the first
vacancy, but the vacancy which should occur at the death of
Zuan Bellini, then a very old man, and naturally incapable of
holding it long. This brutal method of indicating that one day
was over, and another begun, and of pushing the old monarch
from his place, throws an unfavourable light upon the very
pushing and practical young painter, who was thus determined
to have his master's seat.

When Bellini died in 1516, it is gratifying to know that there
was still some difficulty about the matter, other promises apparently having been made, and other expectations raised as to the
vacant brokership. Finally, however, Titian's claim was allowed,
and he entered into possession of the income about which he

had been so eager. He then established himself at San Samuele, abandoning, it would seem, the old centre of life at the Rialto where all the others had been content to live and labour. It was like a migration from the business parts of the town to those of fashion, or at least gentility: and perhaps this change showed already a beginning of pretension to the higher social position which Titian, in his later days at least, evidently enjoyed. They were noble in their rustic way up at Cadore, and he who was presently to stand before kings probably assumed already something more of dignity than was natural to the sons of painters, or to the village genius who is known to posterity only by his Christian name.

Another day had now dawned upon the studios and work-shops. The reign of the Bellini was over and that of Titian had begun. Of his contemporaries and disciples we cannot undertake any account. The nearest in association and influence to the new master was the gentle Palma, with all the silvery sweetness of colour which so far as the critics know he had found for himself in his village on the plains, or acquired some-how by the grace of heaven, no master having the credit of them. Some of these authorities believe that, from this modest and delightful painter, Titian, all acquisitive, gained something too, so much as to be almost a pupil of the master who is so much less great than himself. And that is possible enough, for it is evident that Titian, like Molière, took his goods where he found them, and lost no occasion for instruction, whoever supplied it. He was at all events for some time much linked with Palma, whose daughter was long supposed to be the favourite model of both these great painters. The splendid women whom they loved to paint, and who now stepped in, as may be said, into the world of fancy, a new and radiant group, with the glorious hair upon which both these masters expended so much skill, so that "every thread might be counted," Vasari says, represent, as imagination hopes, the women of that age, the flower of Venice at her highest perfection of physical magnificence. So at least the worshipper of Venice believes, finding in those

grand forms and in their opulence of colour and natural endow-
ment something harmonious with the character of the race and
time. From the same race, though with a higher inspiration,
Bellini had drawn his Madonnas, with stately throats like
columns and a noble amplitude of form. There is still much
beauty in Venice, but not of this splendid kind. The women

GROUP OF HEADS: GENTILE BELLINI.

have dwindled if they were ever like Violante. But she and
her compeers have taken their place as the fit representatives of
that age of splendour and luxury. When we turn to records
less imaginative, however, the ladies of Venice appear to us
under a different guise. They are attired in cloth of gold, in
brocaded silks and velvets, with cords, fringes, pendents and

U

embroidery in gold, silver, pearls, and precious stones, " even their shoes richly ornamented with gold," Sanudo tells us: but they are feeble and pale, probably because of their way of living, shut up indoors the greater part of their time, and when they go out, tottering upon heels so high that walking is scarcely possible, and the unfortunate ladies in their grandeur have to lean upon the shoulders of their servants (or slaves) to avoid accident. Their heels were at least half the Milanese *braccio* in height (more than nine inches), says another authority. Imagination refuses to conceive the wonderful lady who lives in Florence, the *Bella* of Titian, in all her magnificent apparel, thus hobbling on a species of stilts about the streets, supported by one of those grinning negroes whose memory is preserved in the parti-coloured figures in black and coloured marble which pleased the taste of a later age. Such, however, were the shoes worn in those very days of Bellini and Carpaccio which the great art critic of our time points out as so much nobler than our own, even pausing in his beautiful talk to throw a little malicious dart aside at modern English (or Scotch) maidens in high-heeled boots. The nineteenth century has not after all deteriorated so very much from the fifteenth, for the veriest Parisian abhorred of the arts has never yet attempted to poise upon heels half a *braccio* in height.

These jewelled clogs however, which if memory does not deceive us are visible on the floor in Carpaccio's picture of the two Venetian ladies in the Museo Correr, so much praised by Mr. Ruskin, were part of the universal ornamentation of the times. The great wealth of Venice showed itself in every kind of decorative work, designed in some cases rather by skill than by common sense. The Venetian houses were not only painted without, throwing abroad a surplus splendour to all the searching of the winds, but were all glorious within as in the Psalms. The furniture carved and gilded, the curtains made of precious stuff, the chimney-pieces decorated with the finest pictures, the beds magnificent with golden embroidery and brocaded pillows, the very sheets edged with delicate work in gold thread.

When Giorgione opened his studio, setting up in business so to speak, he painted wardrobes, spinning wheels, and more particularly chests, the wedding coffers of the time, of which so many examples remain: and—a fact which takes away the hearer's breath—when Titian painted that noble pallid Christ of the Tribute money, he did it, oh heavens! on a cabinet, a fact which, though the cabinet was in the study of Alfonso of Ferrara, strikes us with a sensation of horror. Only a prince could have his furniture painted with such a work; but no doubt in Titian's splendid age there might be many *armari, armoires*—aumries as they were once called in Scotland—with bits of his youthful work, and glowing panels painted by Giorgione on the mantelpieces to be found in the Venetian houses. This was the way of living of the young painters, by which they came into knowledge of the world. Perhaps the doors of the wardrobe in a friend's house, or the panels over the fireplace, might catch the eye of one of the Savii, now multiplied past counting in every office of the state, who would straightway exert himself to have a space in the next church allotted to the young man to try his powers on: when if there was anything in him he had space and opportunity to show it, and prove himself worthy of still higher promotion.

It would seem, however, that Titian was not much appreciated by his natural patrons during all the beginning of his career. There is no name of fondness for him such as there was for Giorgio of Castel Franco. Was it perhaps that these keen Venetians, who, notwithstanding that failure of religious faith with which they are suddenly discredited, and which is supposed to lie at the root of all decadence in art, had still a keen eye and insight for the true and real, perceived that in the kind of pictures they most desired something was wanting which had not been wanting either in the Madonnas of Bellini or the saints of Carpaccio—a something higher than manipulation, more lovely than the loveliest colour of the new method? These sacred pictures might be beautiful, but they were not divine. The soul had gone out of them. That purity and

wholesome grace which was in every one of old Zuan's Holy
Families had stolen miraculously out of Titian, just as it had
stolen miraculously in, no one knowing how, to the works of
the elder generation. If this was the case indeed it was an
effect only partially produced by the works of the young
master, for his portraits were all alight with life and meaning,
and in other subjects from his hand there was no lack of truth
and energy. Whatever the cause might be, it is clear however
that he was not popular, though the acknowledged greatest of
all the younger painters. It was only the possibility of seeing
his services transferred to the pope that procured his admission
to the privileges of state employment: and it was after his
fame had been echoed from Ferrara and Bologna and Rome,
and by the great emperor himself—the magnificent patron who
picked up his brush, and with sublime condescension declared
that a Titian might well be served by Cæsar—that the more
critical and fastidious Venetians, or perhaps it might only be
the more prejudiced and hardly-judging, gave way to the
strong current of opinion in his favour, and began to find him
a credit to Venice. As soon as this conviction became general
the tide of public feeling changed, and the republic became
proud of the man who, amid all the disasters that began to
disturb her complacence and interrupt her prosperity, had done
her credit and added to her fame.

It is evident however that even when he finally got his
chance, and painted, for the church of the Frari, the magnificent
Assumption which occupies now a kind of throne in the Accademia as if in some sort the sovereign of Venice, doubts
pursued him to the end of his work. Fra Marco Jerman or
Germano, the head of the convent, who had ordered it at his own
expense and fitted it when completed into a fine framework of
marble for the high altar, had many a criticism to make during
the frequent anxious visits he paid to the painter at his work.
Titian was troubled indeed by all the ignorant brethren
coming and going, *molestato dalle frequenti visite loro,* and by
il poco loro intendimento, their small understanding of the

necessities of art. They were all of the opinion that the Apostles in the foreground were too large, *di troppo smisurata grandezza*, and though he took no small trouble to persuade them that the figures must be in proportion to the vastness of the space and the position which the picture was to occupy, yet nevertheless the monks continued to grumble and shake their heads, and make their observations to each other under their hoods, doubting even whether the picture was good enough to be accepted at all, after all the fuss that had been made about it, and the painter-fellow's occupation of their church itself as his painting room. The ignorant are often the most difficult to please. But the condition of the doubting convent, with no confidence in its own judgment, and a haunting terror lest Venice should sneer or jeer when the picture was uncovered, is comprehensible enough. Titian, it is evident, had not even now attained such an assured position as would justify his patrons in any certainty of the excellence of his work. He was still on his promotion, with no settled conviction in the minds of the townsfolk as to his genius and power. No doubt the brethren all thought that their *guardiano* had done a rash thing in engaging him, and Fra Marco himself trembled at the thought of the mistake he might perhaps have made. It was not until the emperor's envoy, already it is evident a strong partisan of Titian, and bringing to his work an eye unclouded by local prepossessions, declared that the picture was a marvellous picture, and offered a large sum if they would give it up, in order that he might send it to his master, that the *frati* began to think it might be better perhaps to hold by their bargain. "Upon which offer," says Ridolfi, "the fathers in their chapter decided, after the opinion of the most prudent, not to give up the picture to any one, recognising finally that art was not their profession, and that the use of the breviary did not convey an understanding of painting."

It is curious to find that Vasari makes no particular note of this picture except to say that it cannot be well seen (that is in its original position in the Frari), and that Marco Sanudo, in

recording its first exhibition, mentions the frame as if it was a
thing quite as important as the picture.   Such is the vagueness
of contemporary opinion.   It seems at all events to have been
the first picture of Titian's which at all struck the imagination
of his time.   By this time, however, he had begun to be courted
by foreign potentates, and it is evident that his hands were
very full of commissions, and that some shiftiness and many of
the expedients of the dilatory and unpunctual were in his
manner of dealing with his patrons, to whom he was very
humble in his letters, but not very faithful in his promises.
And now that he has reached the full maturity of power, Titian
unfolds to us a view, not so much of Venice, as of a corrupt and
luxurious society in Venice, which is of a very different character from the simplicities of his predecessors in art.   Even
young Giorgione's gay dissipations, his love of lute and song,
his pretensions to gallantry and finery, *mischiante sempre amore*
with all his doings, have a boyish and joyous sweetness, in
comparison with the much more luxurious life in which we
now find his old companion, the vile society of the Aretino
who flattered and intrigued for him, and led Titian, too, not
unwilling, to intrigue and flatter and sometimes betray.
Perhaps at no time had there been much virtue and purity
to boast of in the career of the painter who had half forced
the Signoria into giving him his appointment, and seized upon
old Zuan Bellini's office before he was dead : then dallied
with the work he seemed so eager to undertake, and left it
hanging on hand for years.   But the arrival of Pietro Aretino
in Venice seems to have been the signal for the establishment
there of a society such as the much-boasted Renaissance of
classical learning and art seems everywhere to have brought
with it, shaming the ancient gods which were thus proved so
little capable of re-inspiring mankind.   There is no one in all
the sphere of history and criticism who has a good word to say
of Aretino.   He was the very type of the base-born adventurer,
the hanger-on of courts, the entirely corrupt and dazzlingly clever
parasite, whose wit and cunning and impudence and unscrupu-

lousness, his touch of genius and cynical indifference to every
law and moral restraint, gave him a power which it is very
difficult to understand, but impossible to deny. That such a
man should be able to recommend the greatest painter of the
day to the greatest potentate, Titian to Charles V., is amazing
beyond description, but it would seem to have been directly or
indirectly the case. Aretino had an immense correspondence
with all the cultured persons of his time, and in the letters
which were a sort of trade to him, and by which he kept
himself and his gifts and pretensions before the great people
who ministered to his wants, he had it in his power to spread
the fame of a friend, and let the dukes and princes know—the
young men who were proud of a correspondent so clever and
wise and learned in all depravity as well as all the sciences of
the beautiful; and the old men who liked his gossip and his
·pungent comments, and thought they could keep a hold upon
the world by such means—that here was another accomplished vassal ready to serve their pleasure. How such a
mixture of the greatest and the basest is practicable, and how
it has so often happened that the lovers of every beautiful art
should be in themselves so unbeautiful, so low in all the true
loveliness of humanity, while so sensitive to its external refinements, is a question of far too much gravity and intricacy to be
discussed here. Titian found a better market for his Venuses
and Ariadnes among the Hellenised elegants of the time, at
the courts of those splendid princes who were at the summit of
fashion and taste, and a far more appreciative audience (so to
speak) than he ever found at home for the religious pictures
which his countrymen felt to be without any soul, beautiful
though their workmanship might be.

In another region of art, however, he was now without a
rival. The splendid power of portraiture, in which no painter
of any age has ever surpassed him, conducted him to other
triumphs. It was this which procured him the patronage of
Charles V., who not only sat to him repeatedly, but declared
him to be the only painter he would care to honour, and called

him an Apelles, and all the other fine things of that classical
jargon which was so conventional and so meaningless.   Certainly nothing can be more magnificent than the portraits with
which Titian has helped to make the history of his age.   The
splendour of colour in them is not more remarkable than that
force of reality and meaning which is so wanting in his smooth
Madonnas, so unnecessary to his luxurious goddesses.   The men
whom Titian paints are almost all worthy to be senators or
emperors : no trifling coxcomb, no foolish gallant, ever looks
out upon us from his canvas, but a series of noble personages
worthy their rank and importance in the world.   It is difficult
to overrate the power which has this fine effect.   Even in the
much discussed decorative tableau of the Presentation, with
its odious old woman and her eggs, which are *tanto naturale*
according to the vulgar, the group of gentlemen at the foot of
the stair are noble every one, requiring no pedigree.   It was
only just that in recompense of such a power the great
emperor should have ennobled Titian and made him Cavalier
and Count Palatine and every other splendid thing.   Such
rewards were more appropriate in his case than they would
have been in almost any other.   It was in his power to confer
the splendour they loved upon the subjects of his pencil, and
hand them down to posterity as if they all were heroes and
philosophers.   The least the emperor could do was to endow the
painter with some share of that magnificence which he bestowed.

And when we look back upon him where he still reigns in
Venice, it is not with any thought of his matronly Madonna
among her cherubs, notwithstanding all the importance which
has been locally given to that imposing composition, any more
than, when we turn to the magnificent picture painted for the
same church, the altar-piece of the Pesaro chapel, known as the
Madonna of the Pesaro family, it is the sacred personages who
attract our regard.   In vain is the sacred group throned on
high : the Virgin with her Child is without significance, no
true Queen of Heaven, with no mission of blessing to the
world ; but the group of Venetian nobles beneath, kneeling in

proud humility, their thoughts fixed on the grandeur of their
house and the accomplishment of their aims, like true sons of
the masterful republic—not negligent of the help that our
Lady and the saints may bestow if properly propitiated, and
snatching a moment accordingly to lay their ambitions and
keen worldly desires distinctly before her and her court—live
for ever, genuine representatives of one of the most powerful
civilisations of the mid-ages, true men of their time. And with
a surprise of art, a sudden human gleam of interest, an appeal
to our kindred and sympathy which it is impossible to with-
stand, there looks out at us from the canvas a young face
careless of all, both the Madonna and the family, a little weary
of that senseless kneeling, a little wondering at the motive of
it, seeking in the eyes of the spectator some response more
human, full of the abstraction of youth, to which the world is
not yet open, but full of dreams. If our practical, money-
making, pleasure-loving painter had found in his busy life any
time for symbols, we might take this beautiful face as a
representation of that new undeveloped life seen only to be
different from the old, which, with a half weariness and half
disdain of the antiquated practices of its predecessors, kneels
there along with them in physical subordination but mental
superiority, not sufficiently awakened to strain against the curb
as yet, with opposition only nascent, an instinctive separation
and abstraction rather than rebellion of thought. But Titian,
we may be sure, thought of none of these things. He must
have caught the look, half protest, half appeal, that the tired
youth (at the same time partially overawed by his position)
turned towards him as he knelt: and with the supreme perception of a great artist of meanings more than he takes the
trouble to fathom, save for their effect, have secured the look,
for our admiration and sympathy evermore.

In the full maturity of his age and fame, Titian removed
from his dwelling at San Samuele, where he had lived amid his
workshops midway between the two centres of Venetian life,
the Rialto and the Piazza, to a luxurious and delightful house

in San Cassiano, on that side of Venice which faces Murano and
the wide lagoon with all its islands.   There is no trace to be
found now of that home of delights.   The water has receded,
the banks have crept outward, and the houses of the poor now
cover the garden where the finest company in Venice once
looked out upon one of the most marvellous scenes in the world.
The traveller may skirt the bank and linger along the lagoon
many a day without seeing the sea fog lift, and the glorious line
of the Dolomite Alps come out against the sky.   But when
that revelation occurs to him he will understand the splendour
of the scene, and why it was that the painter chose that house,
looking out across the garden and its bosquets upon the marvellous line of mountains coming sheer down as appears to the
water's edge, soaring clear upward in wild yet harmonious
variety of sharp needles and rugged peaks, here white with
snow, there rising in the sombre grandeur of the living rock,
glistening afar with reflections, the lines of torrents, and every
tint that atmosphere and distance give.   When the atmosphere,
so often heavy with moisture and banked with low-lying cloud,
clears, and the sun brings out triumphantly like a new discovery
that range of miraculous hills, and the lurid line of the lagoon
stretches out and brims over upon the silvery horizon, and the
towers of Torcello and Burano in the distance, with other
smaller isles, stand up out of the water, miraculous too, with no
apparent footing of land upon which to poise themselves, the
scene is still beautiful beyond description, notwithstanding the
frightful straight lines of red and white wall which enclose San
Michele, the burial place of Venice, and the smokes and high
chimneys of the Murano glassworks.   The walls of San Michele
did not exist in Titian's day : but I wonder whether Mr. Ruskin
thinks there was no smoke over Murano even in the ages of
primal simplicity and youth.

There is nothing now but a crowd of somewhat dilapidated
houses in these inferior parts of the city, sadly mean and common on close inspection, amid the bewildering maze of small
streets through which the traveller is hurried now to see what

is left (which is nothing) of the house of Titian: and very squalid along the quays of the Fondamenta Nuova, with obvious signs everywhere that this is the back of the town, and freed from all necessity for keeping up appearances. In Titian's day it was a retired suburban quarter, with green fields edging the level shore, and stretching on each side of that garden in which grew the trees, and over which shone the sky which formed the back-ground of the great Peter Martyr, the picture which was burnt in 1867 and which everybody is free to believe was Titian's *chef d'œuvre*. Here the painter gathered his friends about him, and supped gaily in the lovely evenings, while the

GROUP OF HEADS: GENTILE BELLINI.

sun from behind them shot his low rays along the lagoon, and caught a few campaniles here and there gleaming white in the dim line of scarcely visible country at the foot of the hills. If the sun were still too high when the visitors arrived there was plenty to see in the house, looking over the pictures with which it was crowded, the wonderful glowing heads of dukes and emperors, great Charles in all his splendour, or, more splendid still, the nymphs and goddesses without any aid of ornament, which were destined for all the galleries in Europe. A famous grammarian from Rome, Priscian by name, in the month of August, 1540, describes such a party, the *convives* being Aretino,

("a new miracle of nature"), Sansovino the architect of San
Marco, Nardi the Florentine historian, and himself. "The
house," he says,

> "Is situated in the extreme part of Venice on the sea, and from it one
> sees the pretty little island of Murano and other beautiful places. This
> part of the sea, as soon as the sun went down, swarmed with gondolas,
> adorned with beautiful women, and resounding with the varied harmony
> and music of voices and instruments which till midnight accompanied our
> delightful supper, which was no less beautiful and well arranged than
> copious and well provided. Besides the most delicate viands and precious
> wines there were all those pleasures and amusements that were suited to the
> season, the guests and the feast."

While they were at their fruit letters arrived from Rome, and
there suddenly rose a discussion upon the superiority of Latin
to Italian, very exciting to the men of letters—though the
painters no doubt took it more quietly, or looked aside through
the trees to where the wonderful silvery gleaming of the sea
and sky kept light and life in the evening landscape, or a snowy
peak revealed itself like a white cloud upon the grey: while
the magical atmosphere, sweet and cool with the breath of night
after·the fervid day, a world of delicious space about them,
thrilled with the soft rush of the divided water after every
gondola, the tinkle of the oar, the subdued sounds of voices
from the lagoon, and the touching of the lute. Round the
table in the garden the sounds of the discussion were perhaps
less sweet: but no doubt the Venetian promenaders, taking
their evening row along the edge of the lagoon, kept as close to
the shore as courtesy permitted, heard the murmur of the
talk with admiration, and pointed out where Messer Tiziano
the great painter feasted and entertained his noble guests in
the shade.

For doubtless Titian, Knight, Count Palatine, with jewelled
collar and spurs at heel, was by this time a personage who drew
every eye, notwithstanding that the Signoria were but little
pleased with him, and after a hundred fruitless representations
about that picture in the great hall, took the strong step at
last of taking his brokership from him, and calling upon him in

MURANO AND SAN MICHELE.

To face page 348.

the midst of his careless superiority to refund the money which
he had been drawing all these years in payment of work which he
had never executed.   This powerful appeal made him set aside
his royal commissions for a time and complete the picture in
the hall, which was that of a battle, very immaterial to any one
now, as it perished with all the rest in the fire.   This, however,
was a most effectual way of recalling the painter to his duties,
for he never seems throughout his life to have had enough of
money, though that indeed is not an unusual case.   His letters
to his patrons are, however, full to an undignified extent with
this subject.   The emperor had granted him a certain income
from the revenues of Naples, which however turned out a very
uncertain income, and is the subject of endless remonstrance
and appeals.   To the very end of his life there is scarcely one
of his letters in which the failure of this, or of a similar grant
upon Milan, or of some other mode in which his royal and
imperial patrons had paid for their personal acquisitions by
orders upon somebody else's treasury, is not complained of.
Titian it would seem eventually got his money, but not without
a great deal of trouble, fighting for it strenuously by every means
that could be thought of.   And he pursued his labours cease-
lessly, producing pictures of every kind, a Christ one day, a
Venus the next, with a serene impartiality.   Anything is to be
got from Titian for money, says the envoy of King Philip after
the great days of Charles are over.   He pleads for a benefice
for his son who is a priest, for the enforcement of his claims
upon state revenues because of the betrothal of his daughter,
and because he is growing old, and for a number of reasons,
always eager to have the money at any cost.   "He is old and
therefore avaricious," says Philip's ambassador.   But to the last
he could paint his Venuses, though coarsely, and in the midst
of all these studies from the nude suddenly would produce a
Last Supper, credited once more among so many, by the
busy coteries and critics, as likely to be Titian's best.

At the same time this great and celebrated painter, who
thought no harm to fleece the dukes, and to insist upon their
money, and, had alas! forgot, it seems, the honour and glory

of being Titian, and aimed at a rich man's substance and estimation—this magnificent Venetian, with his feudal powers and
title, never forgot little Cadore among the hills, towards which
his windows looked, and where his kindred dwelt.   There is a
letter extant from his cousin, another Titian, but so different,
thanking him for his good offices, which among all those letters
about money is a refreshment to see.   The Tiziano of the village regrets deeply to have been absent when his "all but
brother" the great Titian, he whose name was known over all
the world, visited Cadore, and therefore to have been prevented
from "making proper return for all we owe you, in respect of
numerous proofs of friendship shown to our community at large,
and in special to our envoys, for all of which you may be
assured we have a grateful memory."   He then informs his
kinsman that two citizens have been appointed as orators or
spokesmen of the city to the Signoria of Venice, and implores
for them Titian's "favour and assistance, which must ensure
success."   "My son Vecello," continues the writer, "begs you
to give him your interest in respect of the place of San
Francesco, and this by way of an exchange of services, as I am
ready at all times to second your wishes and consult your convenience": and finally requests to know when the money is
to be paid "which you so courteously lent to the community."
"In conclusion we beg of you to command us all: and should
this exchange of services be carried out on both sides it will be
a proof of the utmost kindness and charity, in which it is our
wish that God should help you for many years."

It would be curious to imagine what the little highland
borgo could do for Titian in exchange for his kindnesses.   He
painted them a picture at a later date for which they paid him
in a delightful way, granting him a piece of land upon which he
built a cottage. This house was pitched on a marvellous mount
of vision on the side of one of those magnificent hills, so that his
dwelling above and his home below must have exchanged visions,
so to speak, in the vast space of blue that lay between.

But notwithstanding all this glory and honour, there were
critics in his own craft and a prevailing sentiment underneath

the admiration extorted from Venice, which detracted a little from the fame of Titian. The common people would not love his goddesses, though the princes adored them. The commonalty, with a prejudice which no doubt shows their ignorance, yet has its advantages, never out of Greece approves the nude, whatever connoisseurs may say. And the ambassadors were wanting in respect, yet true to fact, when they said that for money anything could be got from the great painter who never had enough for his needs. Another criticism, which would have affected him more than either of these, was that of some of his great rivals in art, who with all their admiration had still something to find fault with in the method of his work. When Titian visited Rome it was the good fortune of Vasari, who had already some acquaintance with him, to show him the great sights of that capital of the world. And one day while Titian was painting his portrait of the pope, Messer Giorgio the good Florentine, accompanied by a great countryman of his, no less a personage than Michel Angelo, paid the Venetian painter a visit at his studio in the Belvedere, where they saw the picture of Danae under the rain of gold, a wonderful piece of colour and delicate flesh-painting, which they applauded greatly. But afterwards, as they came away talking together in their grave Tuscan style, the great master of design shook his serious head while he repeated his praises. What a pity, *che peccato !* that these Venetian painters did not learn to draw from the beginning and had not a more thorough method of teaching—for, said he, " if this man were aided by art, and laws of design, as he is by nature, and by his power of counterfeiting life, no one could attain greater excellence than he, having such a noble genius and such a fine and animated manner of working." In almost the same words Sebastian del Piombo lamented to Messer Giorgio the same defect: which certainly must have been Vasari's opinion too, or his friends would not have remarked it so freely. But they all allowed that he was *il piu bello e maggiore imitatore della Natura* that had ever been seen : and perhaps this was praise enough for one man.

He lived till ninety, a splendid, successful, prosperous, but not very elevated or noble life, working on till the very end, not from necessity, or from any higher motive, but apparently from a love of gain, and tradesmanlike instinct against refusing any order, as well as no doubt from a true love of the beautiful art, to which his life had been devoted from childhood up. The boy of ten who had come down from his mountains to clean Zuan Bellini's palette, and pick up the secrets of the craft in his *bottega* before he was old enough for serious teaching, had a

long career from that beginning until the day when he was carried to the Frari in hasty state, by special order of the Signoria, to be buried there against all law and rule, while the other victims of the plague were taken in secret to out-lying islands and put into the earth out of the way, in the hideous panic which that horrible complaint brought with it. But never during all this long interval, three parts of a century, had

HEAD FROM TITIAN'S TOMB: BELIEVED TO BE
F. PAOLO SARPI.

he given up the close pursuit of his art. And what changes during that time had passed over Art in Venice! The timid *tempera* period was altogether extinct—the disciples of the old school all gone : and of the first generation which revolutionised the Venetian *bottegas*, and brought nature and the secret of lustrous modern colour, and ease and humanity into Art, none were left. Bellini and Carpaccio and all the throng of lesser masters had been swept away in the long inevitable procession of the generations. And their principles had been carried into the sensuous brilliancy of a development which loved colour and the dimpled roundness of flesh, and the beauty which is of the body rather than the mind. When Titian began, his teachers and masters applied all their faculties to the setting forth of a noble ideal, of perfect devotion and purity of manhood and womanhood, with the picturesque clothing and sentiment of their century,

yet consecrated by some higher purpose, something in which all
the generations should sympathise and be of accord. When he
ended, the world was full of images lovely in their manner, in which
the *carnagione* of the naked limbs, the painting of a dimple, were
of more importance than all the emotions that touch the soul.
It is none of our business to make moral distinctions between
the one method and the other. This was the result in Venice
of that new inspiration which the older painters had first
turned to every pious and noble use. And it was Titian in his
love of beauty, in his love of money, in his magnificent faculty
of work and adaptability to the wishes of the time that brought
it about. His associates of youth all dropped from him, the
gentle Palma, now called il Vecchio, dying mid-way in the
career of the robuster companion, as Giorgione had fallen at its
beginning. In his long life and endless labours, as well as in his
more persevering and steady power, Titian, whatever hints and
instructions he may have taken, as his later prosaic biographers
suggest from each of them, outdid them both. And there can
be no doubt that he still stands above them all, at least in the
general estimation, dwelling in a supremacy of skill and strength
upon the side of the deep flowing stream that divides Venice,
dominating everything that came after him, like the white
marble mountain of the Salute, but never learning the heavenly
secret of the elder brotherhood who first instructed his youth.

There are some picturesque anecdotes of Titian which everybody knows, as for instance that of the astounding moment
in which the painter having dropped a brush, great Charles, the
lord of so many kingdoms, a Spaniard and accustomed to the
utmost rigidity of etiquette, the Roman Emperor at the apex
of human glory, made the hair stand on end of every courtly
beholder by picking it up. "Your servant is unworthy of such
an honour," said Titian, in words that might have been addressed
to something divine. "A Titian is worthy to be served by Cæsar,"
replied his imperial majesty, not undervaluing the condescension, as perhaps a friendly English prince who had acted on
impulse, or a more light-hearted Frenchman with the *de rien*

of exquisite courtesy, might have done. Charles knew it was an incident for history, and conducted himself accordingly. There is a prettier and more pleasant suggestion in the scene recorded by Ridolfi, which describes how Titian, while painting Alfonso of Este, the Duke of Ferrara, was visited by Ariosto with the *divino suo poema* in his pocket, which he was still in the course of writing—who read aloud his verses for the delight of both sitter and painter, and afterwards talked it over, and derived much advantage from Titian's criticisms and remarks, which helped him "in the description of landscapes and in setting forth the beauty of Alcina, Angelica, and Bradamante." "Thus," Ridolfi adds, "Art held the office of mute poetry, and poetry of painting eloquent."

KNOCKER.

CHAPTER III.

TINTORETTO.

HEN Titian was at the height, or rather approaching the height, of his honours, a certain little dyer, or dyer's son, a born Venetian, from one of the side canals where the *tintori* are still by times to be seen, purple-limbed from the dye-houses, was brought to his studio. The lad had daubed with his father's colours since he could walk, tracing figures upon the walls and every vacant space, and no doubt with his *spirito stravagante* making himself a nuisance to all his belongings. Robusto, the father, was a man of sense, no doubt, and saw it was vain to strive against so strong a natural impulse : besides, there was no reason why he should do so, for he had no position to forfeit, and the trade of a painter was a prosperous trade, and not one to be despised by any honest citizen. We are not told at what age young Jacopo, the *tintorettino*, the little dyer, came into the great painter's studio. But he was born in 1512, and if we suppose him to be fifteen or so, no doubt that would be the furthest age which he was likely to have reached before being set to his apprenticeship by a prudent Venetian father. The story of his quickly interrupted studies there is told by Ridolfi with every appearance of truthfulness.

"Not many days after, Titian came into the room where his pupils worked, and seeing at the foot of one of the benches certain papers upon which figures were drawn, asked who had done them. Jacopo, who was the author of the same, afraid to have done wrong, timidly said that they were from his hand. Titian perceiving from these beginnings that the boy would probably become a great man, and give him trouble in his supremacy of art, had no sooner gone up stairs and laid aside his mantle than he called Girolamo, his pupil (for in human breasts jealousy works like a canker), to whom he gave orders to send Jacopo away.'

"Thus," adds Ridolfi, "without hearing the reason, he was left without a master." The story is an ugly one for Titian: though it is insinuated of other masters that they have regarded the progress of their pupils with alarm, there has been no such circumstantial account of professional jealousy in the very budding of youthful powers. Vasari, who was a contemporary of both, and a friend of Titian, though he does not mention this incident, gives in his sketch of the younger painter a picture which accords in every respect with Ridolfi's detailed biography, though the criticism of Vasari has all the boldness of a contemporary, and that lively, amused appreciation with which a calm looker-on beholds the eccentricities of a passionate genius which he admires but cannot understand. Tintoretto's violence and extravagance had become classical by Ridolfi's time. They were still half ridiculous, a thing to talk about with shrugged shoulders and shaken head, in the days when Messer Giorgio of Florence had the story told to him, or perhaps saw with his own eyes the terrible painter rushing with the force of a giant at his work.

"In the same city of Venice," says Vasari, suddenly bursting into this lively narrative in the midst of the laboured record of a certain Battista Franco who was nobody, "there lived and lives still a painter called Jacopo Tintoretto, full of worth and talent, especially in music and in playing divers instruments, and in other respects amiable in all his actions : but in matters of art, extravagant, capricious, swift and resolute ; and the most hot-headed (*il piu terribile cervello*) that ever has taken painting in hand, as may be seen in all his works and in the fantastic composition which he puts together in his own way, different from the use and custom of other

Palazzo Camello
Venezia
25. Nov. 1877.

To face page 358.

PALAZZO CAMELLO : HOUSE OF TINTORETTO.

painters, surpassing extravagance with new and capricious inventions, and strange whims of intellect, working on the spur of the moment and without design, almost as if Art was a mere pleasantry. Sometimes he will put forth sketches as finished pictures, so roughly dashed in that the strokes of the brush are clearly visible, as if done by accident or in defiance rather than by design and judgment. He has worked almost in every style, in fresco, in oil, portraits from nature, and at every price : in such a way that according to their different modes, he has painted and still paints the greater number of pictures that are executed in Venice. And as in his youth he showed much understanding in many fine works, if he had known the great principle which there is in nature, and aided it with study and cool judgment, as those have done who have followed the fine methods of their predecessors, and had not, as he has done, abandoned this practice, he would have been one of the best painters who have ever been known in Venice—not that it should be understood by this that he is not actually a fine and good painter, of a vivid, fanciful, and gracious spirit."

How this swift, imperious, masterful genius was formed, Ridolfi tells us with much more detail than is usual, and with many graphic touches, himself waking up in the midst of his somewhat dry biographies with a quickened interest, and that pleasure in coming across a vigorous, original human being amid so many shadows which none but a writer of biographical sketches can fully know. No one of all our painters stands out of the canvas like the dyer's son, robust as his name, a true type, perhaps the truest of all, of his indomitable race. When he was turned out of Titian's studio, "every one may conceive," says Ridolfi, "what disgust he felt in his mind."

"But such affronts become sometimes powerful stimulants to the noble spirit, and afford material for generous resolutions. Jacopo, excited by indignation, although still but a boy, turned over in his mind how to carry on the career he had begun—and not allowing himself to be carried away by passion, knowing the greatness of Titian, whose honours were predicted by all, he considered in every way how, by means of studying the works of that master, and the relievos of Michel Angelo Buonarotti, reputed father of design, he might become a painter. Thus, with the help of these two divine lights, whom Painting and Sculpture have rendered so illustrious in modern times, he went forward towards his desired end ; well advised to provide himself with secure escort to point out the path to him in difficult passages. And in order not to deviate from his proposed course he inscribed the laws which were to regulate his studies upon the walls of the cabinet in which he pursued them, as follows :—

"IL DESEGNO DI MICHEL ANGELO, E'L COLORITO DI TITIANO.

"Upon this he set himself to collect from all quarters, not without great expense, casts of ancient marbles : and procured from Florence the miniature models done by Daniele Volterrano from the figures upon the tombs of the Medici, in San Lorenzo in that city : that is, the Aurora, the Twilight, the Day and the Night, of which he made a special study, making drawings of them from every side, and by the light of a lamp, in order, by the strong shadows thrown from this light, to form in himself a powerful and effective manner.   In the same way, every arm, hand, and torso which he could collect he drew over and over again on coloured paper with charcoal, in water-colours, and every other way in which he could teach himself what was necessary for the uses of art. . . . Nor did he give up copying the pictures of Titian, upon which he established an excellent method of colour, so that many things painted by him in the flower of his age retain all the advantages of that style, to which he added those of much observation from his continual studies, and thus following the traces of the best masters, advanced with great steps towards perfection."

We need not follow Ridolfi in his detailed account of all the experiments of the self-instructed painter—how he "departed from the study of nature alone, which for the most part produces things imperfect, not conjoining, except rarely, all the parts of corresponding beauty"; how he improvised for himself a course of anatomy; how he forestalled the lay figures of modern times by models of wax and plaster, upon which he hung his draperies; how he arranged his lights, both by day and night, so as to throw everything into bold relief. His invention seems to have been endless: in his solitary workshop, without the aid of any master, the young man faced by himself all the difficulties of his art, and made for himself many of the aids which the ingenuity of later ages has been supposed to contrive for the advantage of the student. Nor did he confine himself to his studio, or to those endless expedients for seeing his models on every side, and securing the effect of them in every light.

"He also continued, in order to practise himself in the management of colour to visit every place where painting was going on—and it is said that, drawn by the desire of work, he went with the builders to Cittadella, where round the rays of the clock he painted various fanciful matters, solely to relieve his mind of some of the innumerable thoughts that filled it. He went much about also among the painters of lower pretensions who worked in the piazza of San Marco on the painters' benches, to learn their method too."

The painters' benches, *le banche per depintori*, were, as Ridolfi tells us in another place, under the porticoes in the Piazza, where, according to an ancient privilege granted by the Senate, the poorer or humbler members of the profession plied their trade, painting on chests and probably other articles of furniture "histories, foliage, grotesques, and other bizarre things." They would seem to have worked in the open air, unsheltered save by the arches of the colonnade, where now tourists sip their ices, and gossiping politicians congregate; and to have sold their wares as they worked, a lowly but not unprofitable branch of an already too much followed profession. The *depintori da banche* seem to have been a recognised section of artists, and such a painter as Schiavone was fain by times in his poverty, we are told, to get a day's work from a friend of this humble order. The dyer's son, it is evident, had no such need. He went but to look on, to watch how they got those bold effects which told upon the *cassettone* for a bourgeois bride, or the finer ornamentation of the coffer which was to inclose the patrician lady's embroideries of gold. He scorned no instruction where-ever he could find it, this determined student, whom Titian had refused to teach.

And it adds a new feature to that ancient Venice which was so like, yet unlike, the present city of the sea, to behold thus clearly in the well-known scene the painters on their benches, with their long panels laid out for sale, and admiring groups lingering in their walk to watch over the busy artist's shoulder the progress he was making, or to cheapen the fine-painted lid of a box which was wanted for some approaching wedding. The new porticoes were not yet quite completed, and the chippings of the stones, and all the dust of the mason's work, must have disturbed the painters, who were of too little account to trouble Sansovino, the fine architect, who was then piling up the Procuratie Nuove in those dignified masses, over the heads of all the gay and varied life going on below.

"In those days," adds Ridolfi, "which may be called the happy days of painting, there abounded in Venice many youths of fine genius, who, full of talent, made great progress in art, exhibiting in emulation one with another the result of their labours in the Merceria in order to know the opinions of the spectators : where also Tintoretto with his inventions and fancies did not fail to show the effects which God and nature had worked in him. And among the things which he thus exhibited were two portraits, one of himself with a relievo in his hand, the other of his brother playing the harp, represented by night with such tremendous force, *con si terribile maniera*, that every beholder was struck with amazement: at sight of which a gentle bystander, moved by the sight of so much poetic rapture, sung thus :—

"'Si Tinctorettus noctes sic lucet in umbris
Exorto faciet quid radiante Die ?'

"He exhibited also in Rialto a history with many figures, the fame of which reached the ears of Titian himself, who, going up to it in haste, could not contain his praises, though he wished no good to his despised scholar : genius (*la virtu*) being of that condition that even when full of envy it cannot withhold praise of true merit though in an enemy."

With all this, however, Tintoretto did not prosper in the exercise of his profession. He got no commissions like the other young men. The cry was all for Palma Vecchio, for Pordenone, for Bonifazio, says Ridolfi, perhaps not too exact in his dates : but above all for Titian, who received most of the commissions of importance. Titian himself, however, was at the probable time referred to, about 1530, the earliest date at which Tintoretto could possibly match himself against the elder painters, much pressed by Pordenone, to whom the Senate were anxious to hand over his uncompleted work. In short, it is evident that the brotherhood of Art was already suffering from too much competition. The dyer's energetic son, who seems to have had no pinch of necessity forcing him to paint *cassettoni* like the other poor painters, moved heaven and earth, with the high-handed vigour which pecuniary independence gives, to get work for himself, and to make himself known. If it was work which did not pay, no matter ; the

Palazzo Camello
Venezia
20 Nov. 1877. R.Holmes.

To face page 312.

PALAZZO CAMELLO : HOUSE OF TINTORETTO.

determined painter took it in hand all the same: and to poor churches in need of decoration his advent would be a god-send. Whether it was an organ that wanted painting, or the front of a house, or an altar-piece for a little out-of-the-way chapel, he was ready for all. On one occasion a house which was being built near the Ponte dell' Angelo seemed to him to afford a fitting opportunity for the exhibition of his powers. He addressed himself accordingly to the builders—with whom it seems to have been the interest of the painters to keep a good understanding, and who were often intrusted with the responsibility of ordering such frescoes as might be required—who informed him that the master of the house did not want any frescoes painted. But Tintoretto, intoxicated no doubt with the prospect of that fine fair wall all to himself, to cover as he would, "determined in one way or another to have the painting of it," and proposed to the master mason to paint the house for nothing, for the price of the colours merely. This offer being submitted to the proprietor was promptly accepted, and the painter had his way.

Something of the same kind happened, according to Ridolfi, in a more serious undertaking at the church of the Madonna dell' Orto. With his many thoughts "boiling in his fruitful brain," and with an overwhelming desire to prove himself the boldest painter in the world, he suddenly proposed to the prior of this convent to paint the two sides of the chief chapel behind the great altar. The frescoed house-fronts are visible no longer, but the two vast pictures in this chapel remain to tell the tale. The spaces were fifty feet in height, and the prior laughed at the mad suggestion, thinking that for such a work the whole year's income of the convent would scarcely be enough: and without taking any notice of the proposal bade the painter good day. But Tintoretto, taking no heed of this dismissal, went on to say that he would ask nothing for the work, but only the cost of the material, giving his own time and labour as a gift. These words made the prior pause: for who could doubt that to have two such huge illustrations, superior to all

aroround, without paying anything for them, would be balm to
any Venetian's thoughts ? Finally the bargain was made and
the work begun, the painter flinging himself upon it with all
his strength. The two great pictures, one representing the
Return of Moses after receiving the Tablets of the Law, to find
that all Israel was worshipping the golden calf, the other the
Last Judgment were promptly executed, and still remain,
gigantic, to the admiration of all spectators. The fame of
this strange bargain ran through the city, and attracted the
attention of all classes. The critics and authorities shook their
heads and lamented over the decay of art which had to resort
to such measures. "But little cared Tintoretto for the discussions of the painters, proposing to himself no other end
than self-satisfaction and glory—little useful as these things
are."

Both Vasari and Ridolfi concur in the story of a certain
competition at the school of San Rocco, in which Tintoretto
was to contend with Schiavone, Salviati and Zucchero for the
ornamentation of a portion of the ceiling. While the others
prepared drawings and designs, this tremendous competitor had
the space measured, and with all his fire of rapid execution, in
which nobody could touch him—so that Vasari says, when the
others thought he had scarcely begun, he had already finished
—set to work to paint a picture of the subject given. When the
day of the competition arrived he conveyed his canvas to the
spot, and had it secretly fixed up in its place and covered—and
after the other competitors had exhibited their drawings he,
to the consternation of all, snatched away the linen which
covered his picture, and revealed it completed. A great uproar,
as might be supposed, arose. What the feelings of his rivals
were, seeing this march which he had stolen upon them, may
be imagined : but the authorities of the *confraternità*, solemnly
assembled to sit upon the merits of the respective designs, were
no less moved. They told him with indignation that they had
met to inspect designs and choose one which pleased them for
after-execution, not to have a finished picture thrust upon them.

To which Tintoretto answered that this was his method of de-
signing, that he could not do otherwise, and that designs and
models ought to be so executed, in order that no one should be
deceived as to their ultimate effect; and finally, that if they did
not wish to pay him he willingly made a present of the picture
to the saint. "And thus saying," adds Vasari, "though there
was still much opposition, he produced such an effect that the
work is there to this day." Ridolfi, enlarging the tale, describes
how the other painters, stupefied by the sight of so great a
work executed in so few days and so exquisitely finished,
gathered up their drawings and told the fraternity that they
withdrew from the competition, Tintoretto by the merit of his
work having fairly won the victory. Notwithstanding which
the heads of the corporation still insisted that he should take
away his picture, declaring that they had given him no commission to paint it, but had desired only to have sketches submitted
to them that they might give the work to whoever pleased
them best. When, however, he flung the picture at their
heads, so to speak, and they found themselves obliged to keep
it, whether they liked or not (for they could not by their law
refuse a gift made to their saint) milder counsels prevailed, and
finally the greater part of the votes were given to Tintoretto,
and it was decided that he should be paid a just price for his
work. He was afterwards formally appointed to do all that
was necessary for the future adornment of the *scuola*, and
received from the society a grant of a hundred ducats yearly
for his whole life, he on his side binding himself to paint a
picture for them every year."

This proceeding proves the justice of what Vasari says, always
with a certain half-amusement. "These works and many others
which he left behind him were done by Tintoretto so rapidly, that
when others scarcely believed him to have begun he had finished :
and the wonderful thing was that though he adopted the most
extravagant methods in the world to secure commissions yet
when he failed to do so by interest or friendship he was
ready to sacrifice all gain and give his work at a small price, or

for nothing, so as to force its acceptance, in order that one way or other he should succeed in getting the work to do."

Ridolfi adds that the Scuola of San Rocco when completed became in itself a sort of Accademia,

"The resort of the studious in painting, and in particular of all the foreigners from the other side of the Alps who came to Venice at that time : Tintoretto's works serving as examples of composition, of grace, and harmony of design, of the management of light and shade, and force and freedom of colour : and in short of all that can be called most accurate and can most exhibit the gifts of the ingenious Painter."

The pilgrim from beyond the Alps who follows his predecessors into the echoing halls of San Rocco, can judge for himself still of the great works thus eulogised, and see the picture which Tintoretto fixed upon the roof while his rivals prepared their drawings, and which he flung as it were, at the brotherhood when they demurred. His footsteps are all over Venice, in almost every church and wherever pictures are to be seen— from the great *Paradiso* in the Council Hall, the greatest picture in one sense in the world, down to the humblest chapels, parish churches, sacristies, there is scarcely an opportunity which he has neglected to make himself seen and known. According to the evidence of the historians of art, Titian never forgave the boy whose greatness he had foreseen, and there is at least one subject, that of the Presentation, which the two painters have treated with a certain similarity, with what one cannot but feel must, in the person of the younger at least, have been an intended rivalry. These two splendid examples of art remain, if not side by side, as the pictures of Turner hang beside the serene splendour of the Claudes in our own National Gallery, yet with an emulation not dissimilar, which in some minds will always militate against the claims of the artist whose aim is to prove that he is the better man. The same great critic who has been the live-long champion of Turner against the claims of his long dead rival, has in like manner espoused those of the later master in Venice. And in respect to these particular pictures they are, we believe, a sort of test of art-understanding by which the Illuminati judge the capacity of the less instructed according to the preference they give. However that may be, Tintoretto's greatness, the wonderful sweep and grandeur which his contemporaries call *stravagante*, the lavish power with which he treats every subject, nothing too great, too laborious, for his hand, cannot fail to impress the beholder. He works like a giant, flinging himself abroad " upon the wings of all the winds:" with something of the immortal Bottom in him, determined to do the lion too, at which a keen observer like Vasari cannot but smile: and yet no clown but a demi-god, full of power, if also full of emulation and determination to be the best. But the man is still more remarkable than his work, and to the lover of human nature more interesting, an ideal Venetian, rather of the fifteenth than of the sixteenth century, in his imperious independence and self-will and resolution to own no master. All the arrogance of the well-to-do citizen is in him; he who will take the wall of any man and will not yield a jot or tittle of his own pretensions for the most splendid gallant, or the greatest genius in Christendom: one who is not to be trifled with or condescended to—nor will submit to any parleying about his work or undervaluing of his manhood. No fine patrician, no company even of his townsfolk he was resolved should play patron to him. He did not require their money—one large ingredient in such a character: he could afford to do without them, to fling his pictures at their heads if need were, to execute their commissions for love or, at least, for glory, not for their pay, or anything they could do for him : but all the same not to be shut out from any competition that was going, not to be thrust aside by the foolish preference of the employer for any other workman, determined that he, and he only should have every great piece of work there was to do.

Ridolfi who lingers upon every incident with the pleasure of an enthusiast and who is entirely on Tintoretto's side against Titian and all his fine company of critics, tells how the painter once inquired with the *naïveté* of an ignorance which he was

rather proud to show of all court practices and finery—what was
the meaning of a certain act which he saw performed by king
Henry of France on the occasion of his visit to Venice·
Tintoretto had made up his mind to paint a portrait of the
king, with a sort of republican sentiment, half admiration,
half contempt, for that strange animal, and in order to do this
threw aside his toga (which his wife had persuaded him to wear,
though he had no real right to that patrician garment) and,
putting on the livery of the doge, mingled in the retinue by
which his majesty was attended, and hung about in the ante-
chambers, marking the king's individuality, his features and
ways—until his presence and object were discovered, and he was
admitted to have a formal sitting.   The painter observed that
from time to time certain personages were introduced to the
king, who touched them lightly on the shoulder with his sword,
adding divers ceremonies.   What did it mean, he asked with
simplicity, probably somewhat affected, as the courtier-chamber-
lain, who was his friend, approached him in all the importance
of office ? The Polonius of the moment explained with pompous
fulness, and added that Tintoretto must prepare to go through
the same ceremony in his own person, since the king intended
to make a knight of him. Ridolfi says that the painter modestly
declined the honour—more probably strode off with sturdy contempt and a touch of unrestrained derision, very certain that
whatever Titian and the others might think, no king's touch
upon his shoulder, or patent of rank conferred, could make any
difference to him !

And notwithstanding that all the historians are anxious to
record as a set-off against these wild ways, the fact that he was
very amiable in his private life, and fond of music, and to
suonare il liuto, here is a little story which makes us feel that
it must have been somewhat alarming, if he had any grievance
against one, to be left alone with Tintoretto.   On some occasion
not explained, the painter met Pietro Aretino, the infamous but
much-courted man of letters, who was the centre of the fine
company, the friend of Titian, the representative of luxury and

To face page 318.

THE COURTYARD OF PALAZZO CAMELLO.

corruption in Venice; and invited him to his house, under pretence of painting his portrait.

"When Aretino had come in and disposed himself to sit, Tintoretto with much violence drew forth a pistol from under his vest. Aretino, in alarm, fearing that he was about to be brought to account, cried out, 'What are you doing, Jacopo?' 'I am going to take your measure,' said the other. And beginning to measure from the head to the feet, at last said sedately, 'Your height is two pistols and a half.' 'Oh, you mad fellow,' cried the other, recovering his courage. But Aretino spoke ill of Tintoretto no more."

Perhaps it is the absence of what we may call the literary faculty in these great painters that makes their appeal so much more exclusively to the connoiseur in art, to the critic qualified to judge on technical and classical grounds, to the expert in short—than to the amateur who seeks in pictures and in books the sympathy of humanity, the fine suggestion which rouses the imagination, the touch that goes to the heart. The earlier masters perhaps in all regions (after they have a little surmounted the difficulties of pictorial expression) possess this gift in higher development than their successors who, carrying art to its perfection of design and colour, not unusually leave the heart and the imagination of the spectator altogether out of the reckoning. The Bellini and Carpaccio are all strong in this impulse which is common to poet and storyteller, whether in the graver paths of history, or in the realms of fiction. They appeal to something in us which is more than the eye: they never lose touch of human sentiment, in the Venetian streets all full of a hundred histories, in the legends of love and martyrdom which are of universal potency, in the sweetest ideal of life, the consecrated women and children. Ursula wrapped in maiden sleep, with the winged Angel-Knight touching the sweet edge of her dreams: or throned in a simple majesty of youth and sacred purity and love divine, the Mother holding up to men and Angels the Hope and Saviour of mankind: or with a friendly glow of sympathetic nature diffused all around, the group of neighbours gazing at the procession in the piazza, the women kneeling on the edge of the water-way to see the sacred relic go by.   Such visions do not come to us from the magnificence of Titian, or the gigantic power, *stravagante*, of Tintoretto. A few noble heads of senators are all that haunt our memory, or enter into our friendship from the hand of the latter painter: and even they are too stern sometimes, too authoritative and conscious of their dignity that we should venture to employ such a word as friendship.   Titian's senators are more suave, and he leaves us now and then a magnificent fair lady to fill us with admiration—but, except one or two of such fine images, how little is there that holds possession of our love and liking, and, as we turn away, insists on being remembered !   Not anything certainly in the great Assumption, splendid as it is, and perfect as it may be.   Light, shade, colour, science and beauty are all there, but human feeling has been left out in the magnificent composition.   I return for my part with a great and tender pleasure to the silence and vast solemnity of the Frari where that one young serious face in the great Pesaro picture, looks out of the canvas suddenly, wistfully, asking the meaning of many things, into the spectator's heart—with a feeling that this is about the one thing which the great Titian has ever said to me.

It is impossible and unnecessary for us, standing in the place of the unlearned, to go into full detail of the painters of Venice, or discuss the special qualities of Cima in all his silvery sweetness, or the gentle Palma, or the bolder Pordenone, or the long list of others who through many glowing and beautiful pieces of painting, conducted art from perfection to decay.   The student knows where to find all that can be said on the subject which has indeed produced an entire literature of its own.   When all is said that can be said about the few inaccurate dates, and mistaken stories, with which he is credited, Messer Giorgio of Florence, the graphic and delightful Vasari, remains always the best guide.   But, alas, he was not a Venetian, and his histories of the painters of Venice are generally modified by the reflection, more or less disguised, that if they had but had the luck to be Florentines they might have been great : or at least must have been much greater—even the great Titian himself.

We have ventured to speak of some of the works of Titian as decorative art. The productions of the last great painter whose name will naturally recur to every lover of Venice, the splendid and knightly Paul Veronese, claim this character still more distinctively—as if the great republic, unapproachable in so many ways, had seized a new splendour, and instead of tapestries or humbler mural adornments, had contented herself with nothing less than the hand of genius to ornament her walls. These wonderful halls and balconies, those great banquets spread as upon a more lordly dais of imagination and exquisite skill, those widening vistas of columns and balustrades thronged with picturesque retainers, the tables piled with glowing fruit and vessels of gold and silver, in a mimic luxury more magnificent than any fact, transport the spectator with a sense of greatness, of wealth, of width and space, and ever beautiful adornments, which perhaps impairs our appreciation of the art of the painter in its purer essence. No king ever enlarged and furnished and decorated his palace like the Veronese: the fine rooms in which these pictures are hung are but antechambers to the grander space which opens beyond in the painter's canvas. It is scarcely enough, though magnificent in its way, to see them hanging like other pictures in a gallery, among the works of other masters—for then their purpose is lost, and half their grandeur. The *Marriage of Cana* is but a picture in the Louvre : but in Venice, as we walk into such a presence and see the splendid party serenely banqueting, with the sky opening into heavenly blue behind them, the servants bringing in the courses, appearing and disappearing behind the columns, the carpet flung in all its Oriental wealth of colour upon the cool semi-transparence of the marble steps, the room of which this forms one side, is transformed for ever. Were it the humblest chamber in the world it would be turned into a palace before our eyes. Never were there such noble and princely decorations: they widen the space, they fill the far-

Y

withdrawing anterooms with groups worthy the reception of a king. Mr. Ruskin gives a lively account, from the records of Venice, of how Messer Paolo was had up before the Inquisition, no less, on the charge of having introduced unbecoming and undignified figures, negro pages, and even little dogs, into pictures meant for the church—where, indeed, such details were no doubt out of place. But Paul of Verona was not the man to paint religious pictures, having no turn that way. He is a painter for palaces, not for churches. Mind of man never devised presence chamber or splendid hall that he could not have rendered more splendid. Notwithstanding the prominence of the negro pages, and many an attendant beside, his lords of the feast are all the finest gentlemen, his women courtly and magnificent. It is the best of company that sits at that table, whether the wine is miraculous or only the common juice of the grape : even should the elaboration of splendid dress be less than that which Titian loves. The effect is a more simple one than his, the result almost more complete. So might the walls of heaven be painted, the vestibules and the corridors : still leaving, as poor Florentine Andrea sighs in Mr. Browning's poem, "four great walls in the New Jerusalem" for a higher emulation,

> "For Leonard, Rafael, Agnolo, and me"

to try their best upon.

The fashion of fresco painting on the outsides of the houses still continued, and was largely practised also by Paolo Veronese : but let us hope that the far more splendid internal decoration supplied by his pictures had some effect, along with the good sense native to the Venetians and their sound practical faculty, in putting an end to so great a waste of power and genius as these outside pictures proved. They were already fading out by Paolo's time, sinking into pale shadows of what they had been, those pictured images with which Giorgione and young Titian had made the ugly German factory for a moment glorious : and the art which had been so superb in their hands had sunk also to the execution of pictured colonnades and feigned architecture such as still lingers about Italy, not to any one's advantage. Upon such things as these, false perspectives and fictitious grand façades with imitation statues in unreal relief, even Paolo spent much of his time, though he could do so much better. And thus the fashion wore itself into poverty and decadence, as fashions have a way of doing, going out in ridicule as well as in decay.

KNOCKER: PALAZZO DA PONTE

PART IV.— MEN OF LETTERS.

CHAPTER I.

THE GUEST OF VENICE.

OTHING can be more difficult to explain than the manner in which the greater gifts of human genius are appropriated — to some regions lavishly, to some scarcely at all, notwithstanding that the intellectual qualities of the race may be as good, possibly indeed may reach a higher average in the one neglected than in the one favoured. We fear that no theory that has ever been invented will suffice to explain why the great form of Dante, like a mountain shadowing over the whole peninsula, should have been given to Florence, and nothing to Venice, not so much as a minor minstrel to celebrate the great deeds of the republic which was the most famous and the greatest of all Italian republics, and which maintained its independence when all its rivals and sisters lost theirs. Petrarch, too, was a Florentine by origin, only not born there because of one of the accidents of her turbulent history. Boccaccio, the first of Italian story-tellers, belonged to the same wonderful city. But to Venice on her seas, with the charm of a great poem in every variation of her aspect, with the harmonies of the sea in her very streets, not one. We have to find her reflected in the mild eyes of a temporary visitor, in the learned and easy yet formal talk of the friendly Canon, half French, half Italian, who, all the vagaries of his youth over, came, elderly and famous, and never without an eye to his own comfort and interests, to visit the great Mistress of the Seas, taking refuge there, "in this city, true home of the human race," from trouble and war and pestilence outside. The picture given by Dom Francesco, the great poet, laureate of all the world, the friend of kings and princes, is in some ways very flattering to our city. He was received with great honour there as everywhere, and found himself in the centre of an enlightened and letter-loving society. But his residence was only temporary, and, save Petrarch, no poet of a high order has ever associated himself with the life of Venice, much less owed his birth or breeding to her. The reader will not fail to recollect another temporary and recent visitor, whose traces are still to be seen about Venice, and whose record remains, though not such as any lover of poetry would love to remember, in all the extravagance and ostentatious folly natural to the character of Lord Byron: but that was in the melancholy days when Venice had almost ceased to be. Save for such visitors and for certain humble breathings of the nameless, such as no homely village is entirely without, great Venice has no record in poetry. Her powerful, vigorous, subtle, and imaginative race have never learned how to frame the softest dialect of Italy, the most musical of tongues, into any linked sweetness of verse. The reason is one which we cannot pretend to divine, and which no law of development or natural selection seems capable of accounting for.

Petrarch was not only a poet, but a patriot in the larger sense of the word—a sense scarcely known in his day. Perhaps the circumstance that he was an exile from his birth, and that his youth had been sheltered in a neighbouring country, from which he could see in all the force of perspective the madness of those Italian states which spent all their strength in tearing each other in pieces, had elevated him to that pitch of enlightenment, unknown to the fierce inhabitants of Genoa, Venice, and

Florence, each determined to the death that his own city should be the first. Petrarch is worthy of a higher niche for this than for his poetry, a civic wreath above his laurel. His first appearance in connection with Venice is in a most earnest and eloquent letter addressed to his friend Andrea Dandolo, the first serious chronicler of Venice, and a man learned in all the knowledge of the time, whom the poet, who probably had made acquaintance with the noble Venetian at learned Padua, or in some neighbouring court or castle whither scholars and wits loved to resort, addresses with an impassioned pleading for peace. One of the endless wars with Genoa was then beginning, and Petrarch adduces every argument, and appeals to every motive—above all, "Italian as I am," to the dreadful folly which drives to arms against each other

"the two most powerful peoples, the two most flourishing cities, the two most splendid stars of Italy, which, to my judgment, the great mother nature has placed here and there, posted at the doorway of the Italian race. Italians for the ruin of Italians invoke the help of barbarous allies," he adds. "And what hope of aid can remain to unhappy Italy when, as if it were a small matter to see her sons turn against her, she is overrun also by strangers called by them to he'p in the parricide?"

But not even the enlightened Dandolo, the scholar-doge, thought of Italy in those days, and though the poet's protest does not seem to have alienated his friend, it was entirely without avail. Two years after, in 1353, an embassy, of which Petrarch was one of the principal members, was sent from Milan on the part of the Visconti to attempt to negotiate a peace. This was not his first visit to Venice, and it cannot have been an agreeable one. One of the chroniclers indeed says that much as Doge Andrea loved the poet, and strong as was the attraction of such a visitor to a man of his tastes, the occasion was so painful that he refused to see Petrarch. It does not seem, however, that this was the case, for the poet, in a subsequent letter to Dandolo, reminds the doge of his visit and its object. After two battles—after the Hellespont and the Ionian sea had twice been reddened by such a lake of blood

as might well extinguish the flames of cruel war—"as mediator
of peace, I was sent by our greatest among great Italians to
you, the most wise of all the doges, and to your citizens. Such
and so many things I said in the council over which you presided, such and so many in your private rooms, as must still
remain in your ears. But all was in vain: for neither your
great men, nor, what was more wonderful, yourself, could be
moved by any salutary counsel or just prayer—the impetuosity
of war, the clamour of arms, the remains of ancient hatred
having closed the way." The letter in which Petrarch repeats
this fruitless attempt at mediation was written in May, 1354,
a year after, and still with the same object. The Venetians
had been conquerors on the first occasion, but the fortune of
war had now turned, and in September of the same year Doge
Andrea died, just before one of those final and crushing defeats
which Venice over and over again had to submit to from
Genoa, without ever ceasing to seize the first opportunity of
beginning again.

It was not, however, till several years after that it occurred
to the much-wandering poet to fix his habitation in Venice.
This was in the latter portion of Petrarch's life. Romance
and Laura had long departed out of it. He was already the
crowned poet, acknowledged the greatest, and, save for an occasional sonnet or two, cultivated divine poetry no more. He was
a person of ease and leisure, much courted by the most eminent
persons in Europe, accustomed to princely tables and to familiar
intercourse with every magnate within reach, accustomed, too,
to consider his own comfort and keep danger and trouble at a
distance. Disorder and war and pestilence drove him from one
place to another—from Milan to Padua, from Padua to Venice.
He had fulfilled many dignified missions as ambassador to
various courts, and he was not a man who could transfer himself from one city to another without observation. It would
seem that when, driven by the fear of the plague, and by the
horror of those continued conflicts which were rending Italy from
day to day—that Italy which he was almost alone in considering

as one country—he turned his eyes towards Venice, it was with
some intention of making it his permanent home : for the preliminary negotiations into which he entered show a desire to
establish himself for which he does not seem to have taken any
such precautions before.   One of the best known of all facts in
the history of literature is that the poet left his library to the
republic, and the unworthy manner in which that precious
bequest was received.   But it has not been noted with equal
distinctness that the prudent poet made this gift, not as a
legacy because of his love for Venice, which is the light in
which it has generally been regarded, but as an offer of eventual
advantage in order to procure from the authorities a fit lodging
and reception for himself.   This, however, is the true state of
the case.   He puts it forth in a letter to his friend and agent
Benintendi, the chancellor of the republic, in whose hands it
would seem he had placed his cause.   A certain plausible
and bland insistence upon the great benefit to Venice of a
public library, of which the poet's books should be the foundation, discreetly veils the important condition that the poet's
own interests should be served in the meantime.

"If the effort succeeds," he says, "I am of opinion that your posterity
and your republic will owe to you, if not their glory, yet at least the
opening of the way to glory. And oh !" he adds piously, "if it had but
been thought of when the commonwealth was governed by that most holy
spirit to whom, as you who knew him well will understand, it would have
afforded so much delight. For my part, I do not doubt that even in the
heavens he is glad of our design, and anxiously awaits its success. I believe
also that, looking down lovingly without a grudge, it will greatly please
him, having himself earned such glory and honour as no other Venetian
doge did before him, that the glory of instituting a public library should
have been reserved for the fourth of his successors, a man also so excellent,
a noble doge and zealous of the public good."

This invocation of the sainted shade of Andrea Dandolo, the
much-lamented doge, to sanctify an effort the immediate object
of which was the acquisition of a handsome house for Dom
Francesco the poet, has a flavour of Tartuffe, or at least of

Pecksniff, which may make the reader smile. It was however a perfectly legitimate desire, and no doubt Petrarch's books were valuable, and the suggestion of a public library an admirable thing : and it was to the credit of the republic that the bargain was at once made, and the poet got his house, a palace upon the Riva degli Schiavoni—the Palazzo delle due Torri, now no longer in existence, but which is commemorated by an inscription upon the house which replaces it. It was situated at the corner of the Ponte del Sepolcro. In the curious illumination, taken from a manuscript in the Bodleian Library, which the reader will find at the head of a preceding chapter, the two towers are visible, rising from among the picturesque roofs, over the quay from which the Eastern merchants, the Poli, are to be seen setting out upon their voyage.

This was in the year 1362. He had visited Venice in his youth when a student at Bologna. He had returned in the fulness of his fame as the ambassador of the Prince of Milan to negotiate peace with Genoa, though the attempt was vain. He was now approaching his sixtieth year, full of indignation and sorrow for the fate of his country, denouncing to earth and heaven the horrible bands of mercenaries who devastated Italy, bringing rapine and pestilence—and for his own part intent upon finding a peaceful home, security, and health. His letters afford us a wonderfully real glimpse of the conditions of the time. In one of them, written soon after his settlement in Venice, to an old friend, he defends himself for having fallen into the weakness of age, the *laudator temporis acti*. He reviews in this epistle the scenes in which his youth and that of his friend were passed, the peace, the serenity, the calm of these early days, comparing them with the universal tumult and misery of the existing time; denying that the change was in himself or his ideas, and painting a dismal picture of the revolution everywhere—the wars, the bands of assassins and robbers let loose on the earth, the universal wretchedness. "This same city," he adds, "from which I write, this Venice which by the farsightedness of her citizens and by the advantage of her natural position appears more powerful and tranquil than any other part of the world, though quiet and serene, is no longer festive and gay as she once was, and wears an aspect very different from that prosperity and gladness which she presented when first I came hither with my tutor from Bologna." But these words are very different from the phrases he employs in speaking of other cities. Venice, as has been seen in previous chapters, had trouble enough with the mercenary armies of the time when they were in her pay : but she was safe on her sea margin with the wide lagoons around her, unapproachable by the heavy-mailed troopers who might appear any day under the walls of a rich inland city and put her to sack or ransom. With all the force of his soul the poet loathed these barbarous invaders, the terror of his life and the scourge of Italy, into whose hands the Italian states themselves had placed weapons for their own destruction ; and it is with a sense of intense repose and relief that he settles down in his stately house looking out upon the wide harbour, upon San Giorgio among its trees, and the green line of the Lido, and all the winding watery ways, well defended by fort and galley, which led to the sea. The bustle of the port under his windows, the movement of the ships, would seem at once to have caught, with the charm of their novelty and wonder, his observant eyes. Shortly after his settlement on the Riva he wrote a letter full of wise and serious advice to another friend, who had been appointed secretary to the Pope—an office not long before offered to himself. But in the very midst of his counsels, quoting Aristotle on the question of art, he bursts forth into comment upon *la nautica*, to which, he says, "after justice, is owing the wonderful prosperity of this famous city, in which, as in a tranquil port, I have taken refuge from the storms of the world. See," he cries, "the innumerable vessels which set forth from the Italian shore in the desolate winter, in the most variable and stormy spring, one turning its prow to the east, the other to the west; some carrying our wine to foam in British cups, our fruits to flatter the palates of the Scythians, and, still more hard of credence, the

To face page 330.

COURTYARD. SIDE CANAL.

wood of our forests to the Egean and the Achaian isles; some
to Syria, to Armenia, to the Arabs and Persians, carrying oil and
linen and saffron, and bringing back all their diverse goods
to us."

"Let me persuade you to pass another hour in my company. It was
the depth of night and the heavens were full of storm, and I, already
weary and half asleep, had come to an end of my writing, when suddenly
a burst of shouts from the sailors penetrated my ear. Aware of what these
shouts should mean from former experience, I rose hastily and went up to
the higher windows of this house, which look out upon the port. Oh,
what a spectacle, mingled with feelings of pity, of wonder, of fear, and of
delight! Resting on their anchors close to the marble banks which serve
as a mole to the vast palace which this free and liberal city has conceded
to me for my dwelling, several vessels have passed the winter, exceeding
with the height of their masts and spars the two towers which flank my
house. The larger of the two was at this moment—though the stars were
all hidden by the clouds, the winds shaking the walls, and the roar of the
sea filling the air—leaving the quay and setting out upon its voyage.
Jason and Hercules would have been stupefied with wonder, and Tiphys,
seated at the helm, would have been ashamed of the nothing which won
him so much fame. If you had seen it, you would have said it was no ship
but a mountain swimming upon the sea, although under the weight of its
immense wings a great part of it was hidden in the waves. The end of the
voyage was to be the Don, beyond which nothing can navigate from our
seas; but many of those who were on board, when they had reached that
point, meant to prosecute their journey, never pausing till they had
reached the Ganges or the Caucasus, India and the Eastern Ocean. So
far does love of gain stimulate the human mind. Pity seized me, I
confess, for these unfortunates, and I perceived how right the poet was
who called sailors wretched. And being able no longer to follow them
with my eyes into the darkness, with much emotion I took up my pen
again, exclaiming within myself, 'Oh, how dear is life to all men, and in
how little account they hold it!'"

It is evident that the beginning of his stay in Venice was
very agreeable to the poet. He had not been long established
in the palace of the two towers when Boccaccio, like himself
seeking refuge from the plague and from the wars, came to visit
him, and remained three months, enjoying the calm, the lovely
prospect, the wonderful city, and, what was still more, the
learned society which Petrarch had already gathered around

him. The scholars and the wits of those days were sufficiently
few to be known to each other, and to form a very close and
exclusive little republic of letters in every centre of life. But in
Venice even these learned personages owned the charm of the
locality, and met not only in their libraries among their books,
or at the classic feasts, where the gossip was of Cicero and Cato,
of Virgil and of Ovid, and not of nearer neighbours—where every
man had his classical allusion, his quotations, his talk of Helicon
and Olympus—but on the soft and level waters, the brimming
wide lagoon, like lesser men. When Petrarch invites the great
story-teller of Florence to renew his visit, he reminds him of
those "elect friends" with whom he had already made acquaintance, and how the dignified Benintendi, though devoted to public
business all day, yet in the falling of the evening, with light-
hearted and friendly countenance, would come in his gondola
to refresh himself with pleasant talk from the fatigues of the
day. "You know by experience," he says, "how delightful
were those nocturnal rambles on the sea, and that conversation
enlightened and sincere." To think of Boccaccio stepping forth
with Petrarch upon the Riva, taking a boat in those soft
summer nights, *in sul far della sera*, in the making of the
evening, when the swift shadows fell across the glimmering
distance, and the curves of the lagoon caught the first touches
of the moonlight, comes upon us with a delightful contrast, yet likeness to the scenes more associated with their
names. The fountain of Vaucluse and Laura's radiant image,
the gardens and glades of the *Decameron*, with all their youths
and maidens, were less suitable now to the elderly poets than
that talk of all things in earth and heaven, which in the dusk,
upon the glistening levels of the still water, two friendly gondolas, softly gliding on in time, would pass from one to another
in interchanges sometimes pensive, sometimes playful, in gentle
arguments long drawn out, and that mutual comparison of the
facts of life and deductions from them which form the conversation of old men. There were younger companions, too, like
that youth of Ravenna of whom Petrarch writes, "whom you

do not know, but who knows you well, having seen you in
this house of mine, which, like all that belongs to me, is yours,
and, according to the use of youth, watched you daily," who
would join the poets in their evening row, and hang about the
gondola of the great men to catch perhaps some word of
wisdom, some classical comparison: while, less reverential, yet
not without a respectful curiosity, the other boats that skimmed
across the lagoon would pause a minute to point out, the lover
to his lady, the gondolier to his master, the smooth and urbane
looks of him who had been crowned at Rome the greatest of
living poets, and the Florentine at his side, the romancer of his
age—two such men as could not be equalled anywhere, the
guests of Venice. No doubt neither lute nor song were wanting
to chime in with the tinkle of the wave upon the boats and
the measured pulsation of the oars. And as they pushed forth
upon the lagoon, blue against the latest yellow of the sunset
would rise the separate cones and peaks of the Euganeans,
amongst which lay little Arqua, still unnoted, where the laureate
of the world was to leave his name for ever. The grave discussions of that moment to come, of the sunset of life, and how
each man endured or took a pensive pleasure in its falling
shadows, would be dismissed with a smile as the silvery
ferro glided slowly round like a swan upon the water, and the
pleased companions turned to where the two towers rose over
the bustling Riva, and the lighted windows shone, and the
table was spread. "*Vieni dunque invocato*," says the poet as
he recals these delights to the mind of his friend. "The
gentle season invites to where no other cares await you but
those pleasant and joyful occupations of the muses, to a house
most healthful, which I do not describe because you know it."
It is strange, however, to remember that these thoughtful old
men in the reflective leisure of their waning years are the lover
of Laura and the author of the *Decameron*.

On another occasion the poet puts before us a picture of a
different character, but also full of interest. It is on the 4th
of June, 1364, a memorable day, and he is seated at his window

with a friend, looking out over the *ampio mare*, the full sea which spreads before him. The friend was one of his oldest and dearest companions, his schoolfellow, and the comrade of his entire life, now Archbishop of Patras, and on his way to his see, but pausing to spend the summer in that most healthful of houses with the happy poet. The two old friends, newly met, sat together looking out upon that lively and brilliant scene as they talked and exchanged remembrances, when their conversation was disturbed by a startling incident.

"Suddenly and without warning there rose upon our sight one of those long vessels which are called galleys, crowned with green branches, and with all the force of its rowers making for the port. At this unexpected sight we broke off our conversation, and felt a hope springing in our hearts that such a ship must be the bearer of good news. As the swelling sails drew near the joyful aspect of the sailors became visible, and a handful of young men, also crowned with green leaves and with joyous countenances, standing on the prow, waving flags over their heads, and saluting the victorious city as yet unaware of her own triumph. Already from the highest tower the approach of a strange ship had been signalled, and not by any command, but moved by the most eager curiosity, the citizens from every part of the town rushed together in a crowd to the shore. And as the ship came nearer and everything could be seen distinctly, hanging from the poop we perceived the flag of the enemy, and there remained no doubt that this was to announce a victory."

A victory it was, one of the greatest which had been gained by Venetian arms, the re-capture of Candia ·(Crete) with little bloodshed and great glory to the republic—though it is somewhat difficult to understand Petrarch's grand assumption that it was the triumph of justice more than of Venice which intoxicated the city with delight. He rises into ecstatic strains as he describes the rejoicings of the triumphant state.

"What finer, what more magnificent spectacle could be than the just joy which fills a city, not for damage done to the enemy's possessions or for the gains of civic rivalry such as are prized elsewhere, but solely for the triumph of justice? Venice exults; the august city, the sole shelter in our days of liberty, justice, and peace, the sole refuge of the good, the only port in which, beaten down everywhere else by tyranny and war, the ships of those men who seek to lead a tranquil life may find safety and restoration : a city rich in gold but more rich in fame, potent in strength but more in virtue, founded upon solid marble, but upon yet more solid foundations of concord and harmony—and, even more than by the sea which girds her, by the prudent wisdom of her sons defended and made secure. Venice exults, not only over the regained sovereignty of Crete, which, howsoever great in antique splendour, is but a small matter to great spirits accustomed to esteem lightly all that is not virtue : but she exults in the event with good reason, and takes pleasure in the thought that the right is victorious—that is to say, not her proper cause alone, but that of justice."

It is clear from this that the triumph in the air had got into the poet's head, and the great contagion of popular enthusiasm had carried him away. He proceeds to relate, as well as " the poverty of my style and my many occupations " will permit, the joyful progress of the thanksgivings and national rejoicing.

" When the orators landed and recounted everything to the Great Council, every hope and anticipation were found to fall short of the truth ; the enemy had been overcome, taken, cut to pieces, dispersed in hopeless flight : the citizens restored to freedom, the city subdued ; Crete brought again under the ancient dominion, the victorious arms laid down, the war finished almost without bloodshed, and glory and peace secured at one blow. When all these things were made known to the Doge Lorenzo, to whose greatness his surname of Celso [1] agrees perfectly, a man distinguished for magnanimity, for courtesy, and every fine virtue, but still more for piety towards God and love for his country—well perceiving that nothing is good but that which begins with heaven, he resolved with all the people to render praise and homage to God ; and accordingly, with magnificent rites through all the city, but specially in the basilica of San Marco Evangelista, than which I know nothing in the world more beautiful, were celebrated the most solemn thanksgivings which have ever taken place within the memory of man ; and around the temple and in the piazza a magnificent procession, in which not only the people and all the clergy, but many prelates from foreign parts, brought here by curiosity, or the great occasion, or the proclamation far and near of these great ceremonies, took part. When these demonstrations of religion and piety were completed, every soul turned to games and rejoicings."

Our poet continues at length the record of these festivities, especially of those with which the great festival terminated,

[1] *Eccelso*, excellent.

two exercises of which he cannot, he says, give the Latin name,
but which in Italian are called, one *corsa*, a race, the other
giostra, a tournament.   In the first of these, which would seem
to have been something like the ancient riding at the ring,
no strangers were allowed to compete, but only twenty-four
Venetian youths of noble race and magnificently clad, under
the direction of a famous actor, Bombasio by name (from whence,
we believe, " Bombast "), who arranged their line in so delightful
a manner that one would have said it was not men who rode but
angels who flew, " so wonderful was it to see these young men,
arrayed in purple and gold, with bridle and spurs, restraining
at once and exciting their generous steeds, which blazed also in
the sun with the rich ornaments with which their harness was
covered."   This noble sight the poet witnessed in bland content
and satisfaction, seated at the right hand of the doge, upon a
splendid balcony shaded with rich and many-tinted awnings,
which had been erected over the front of San Marco behind
the four bronze horses.   Fortunate poet! thus throned on high
to the admiration of all the beholders, who crowded every
window and roof and portico, and wherever human footing was
to be found, and filled every corner of the piazza so that there
was not room for a grain of millet—an " incredible, innumerable crowd," among which was no tumult or disorder of
any kind, nothing but joy, courtesy, harmony, and love!   It is
curious to note that among the audience were certain " very
noble English personages, in office and kindred near to the King
of England," who, " taking pleasure in wandering on the vast
sea," faithful to the instincts of their race, had been attracted
by the news of these great rejoicings.   Among all the splendours of Venice there is none which is more attractive to the
imagination than this grand tournay in the great piazza, at
which the mild and learned poet in his black hood and gown,
half clerical and always courtly, accustomed to the best of company, sat by the side of the doge in his gold-embroidered
mantle, with all that was fairest in Venice around, and gazed
well pleased upon the spectacle, not without a soothing sense

To face page 336.

CAMPO DI S. VIO.

that he himself in the ages to come would seem amid all the purple and gold the most notable presence there.

In the year 1366, when Petrarch had been established for about four years in Venice, an incident of a very different kind occurred to disturb his peace, and did, according to all the commentaries, so seriously disturb it, and offend the poet so deeply, that when he next left the city it was to return no more. Among the stream of visitors received by him with his usual bland courtesy in the palace of the two towers, were certain young men whom the prevailing fashion of the time had banded together in a pretence of learning and superior enlightenment, not uncommon to any generation of those youthful heroes whose only wish it is that their fathers were more wise. Four in particular, who were specially given to the study of such Greek philosophy as came to them broken by translators into fragments fit for their capacity, had been among the visitors of the poet. Deeply affronted as Petrarch was by the occurrence which followed, he was yet too magnanimous to give their names to any of his correspondents: but he describes them so as to have made it possible for commentators to hazard a guess as to who they were. "They are all rich: and all studious by profession, devouring books, notwithstanding that the first knows nothing of letters: the second little: the third not much: the fourth, it is true, has no small knowledge, but has it confusedly and without order." The first was a soldier, the second a merchant (*simplex mercator*), the third a noble (*simplex nobilis*), the fourth a physician. A mere noble, a mere merchant—significant words !—, a soldier, and one who probably led them with his superior science and information, the only one who had the least claim to be called a philosopher, the young professional to whom no doubt those would-be learned *giovinastri* looked up as to a shining light. They were disciples of Averrhoës—or most likely it was the young physician who was so, and whose re-interpretation charmed the young men: and by consequence, in that dawn of the Renaissance, they were all infidels, believers in Aristotle and nothing else. Petrarch himself narrates with much *naïveté* the method he employed with one of these irreverent and disdainful youths. The poet, in his argument with the young unbeliever, had quoted from the New Testament a saying of an apostle.

" 'Your apostle,' he replied, 'was a mere sower of words, and more than that, was mad.' 'Bravo!' said I, 'oh, philosopher. These two things have been laid to the charge of other philosophers in ancient times ; and of the second Festus, the Governor of Syria, accused him whom I quote. But if he was a sower of words, the words were very useful, and the seed sown by him, and cultivated by his successors and watered by the holy blood of martyrs, has grown into the great mass of believers whom we now see.' At these words he smiled, and 'Be you, if you like it, a good Christian,' he said : 'I don't believe a word of all that : and your Paul and Augustine and all the rest whom you vaunt so much, I hold them no better than a pack of gossips. Oh, if you would but read Averrhoës! then you would see how much superior he is to your fable-mongers.' I confess that, burning with indignation, it was with difficulty that I kept my hands off that blasphemer. 'This contest with heretics like you,' I said, 'is an old affair for me. Go to the devil, you and your heresy, and come no more here.' And taking him by the mantle with less courtesy than is usual to me, but not less than his manners deserved, I put him to the door."

This summary method of dealing with the young sceptic is not without its uses, and many a serious man wearied with the folly of youthful preachers of the philosophy fashionable in our day, which is not of Aristotle or Averrhoüs, might be pardoned for a longing to follow Petrarch's example. Perhaps it was the young man described as *simplex nobilis* who, indignant, being thus turned out, hurried to his comrades with the tale: upon which they immediately formed themselves into a bed of justice, weighed Petrarch in the balance, and found him wanting. "A good man, but ignorant," was their sentence after full discussion— *dabben uomo, ma ignorante.* The mild yet persistent rage with which the poet heard of this verdict, magnanimous, restraining himself from holding up the *giovinastri* to the contempt of the world, yet deeply and bitterly wounded by their boyish folly, is very curious. The effect produced upon Lord Tennyson and Mr. Browning at the present day by the decision of a tribunal made up of, let us say, a young guardsman, a little lord, a millionaire's heir, led by some young professional writer or scientific authority, would be very different. The poets and the world would laugh to all the echoes, and the *giovinastri* would achieve a reputation such as they would little desire. But the use of laughter had not been discovered in Petrarch's days, and a poet crowned in the Capitol, laureate of the universe, conscious of being the first man of letters in the world, naturally did not treat these matters so lightly. He talks of them in his letters with an offended dignity which verges upon the comic. "Four youths, blind in the eyes of the mind, men who consider themselves able to judge of ignorance as being themselves most ignorant—*si tengono competenti a giudicare della ignoranza perchè son essi ignorantissimi*—attempting to rob me of my fame, since they well know that they can never hope for fame in their own persons," he says: and at last, in the bitterness of his offence, Venice herself, the hospitable and friendly city, of which he had lately spoken as the peaceful haven and refuge of the human spirit, falls under the same reproach. In every part of the world, he says, such a sentence would be received with condemnation and scorn: "except perhaps in the city where it was given forth, a city truly great and noble, but inhabited by so great and so varied a crowd that many therein take men without knowledge for judges and philosophers." And when the heats of summer came, sending him forth on the round of visits which seems to have been as necessary to Petrarch as if he had lived in the nineteenth century, the offended poet did not return to Venice. When his visits were over he withdrew to Arqua, on the soft skirts of the Euganean hills, where all was rural peace and quiet, and no presumptuous *giovinastri* could trouble him more.

This incident, however, would seem to point to an element of tumult and trouble in Venice, to which republics seem more dangerously exposed than other states. It was the insults of the *giovinastri*, insolent and unmannerly youths, which drove Marino Faliero to his doom not very many years before.

And Petrarch himself implores Andrea Dandolo, the predecessor
of that unfortunate doge, to take counsel with old men of experience, not with hot-headed boys, in respect to the Genoese
wars. The youths would seem to have been in the ascendant,
idle—for it was about this period that wise men began to
lament the abandonment at once of traditional trade and of
the accompanying warlike spirit among the young patricians,
who went to sea no more, and left fighting to the mercenaries—
and luxurious, spending their time in intrigues on the Broglio
and elsewhere, and taking upon them those arrogant airs which
make aristocracy detestable. A Dandolo and a Contarini are
in the list (supposed to be authentic) of Petrarch's assailants,
and no doubt the support of fathers in the Forty or the Ten
would embolden these idle youths for every folly. Their
foolish verdict would by this means cut deeper, and Petrarch,
like the old doge, was now sonless, and had the less patience
to support the insolence of other people's boys. He retired
accordingly from the ignoble strife, and on his travels, as he
says, having nothing else to do, on the banks of the Po, began
his treatise on "the ignorance of himself and many others"—
de sui ipsius et multorum ignorantia, which was, let us hope, a
final balsam to the sting which the *giovinastri*, unmannerly
and presumptuous lads, had left in his sensitive mind.

The books which he had offered to the republic as the
foundation of a public library were left behind, first in the
hands of a friend, afterwards in the charge of the State. But
Venice at that time had other things to do than to think of
books, and these precious manuscripts were placed in a small
chamber on the terrace of San Marco, near the four great horses
of the portico—and there forgotten. Half a century later the
idea of the public library revived : and this was confirmed by the
legacy made by Cardinal Bessarione of all his manuscripts in
1468—a hundred years after the gift of Petrarch ; but nearly
two centuries more had passed, and the splendid Biblioteca de
San Marco had come into being, a noble building and a fine
collection, before it occurred to some stray citizens and scholars

to inquire where the poet's gift might be. Finally, in 1634, the little room was opened, and there was discovered—a mass of damp decay, as they had been thrown in nearly three centuries before—the precious parchments, the books which Petrarch had collected so carefully, and which he thought worthy to be the nucleus of a great public library. Some few were extracted from the mass of corruption, and at last were placed where the poet had intended them to be. But this neglect will always remain a shame to Venice. Perhaps at first the *giovinastri* had something to do with it, throwing into contempt as of little importance the gift of the poet—a suggestion which has been made with more gravity by a recent librarian, who points out that the most valuable of Petrarch's books remained in his possession until his death, and were sold and dispersed at Padua after that event. So that it is possible, though the suggestion is somewhat ungenerous, that after all the loss to humanity was not so very great. At all events there is this to be said, that Petrarch did not lose by his bargain, though Venice did. The poet got the dignified establishment he wanted—a vast palace, as he himself describes it, in which he had room to receive his friends and from which he could witness all the varied life of Venice. He had not, we think, any great reason to complain—he had received his equivalent. His hosts were the losers by their own neglect, but not the poet.

It was but a short episode in his learned and leisurely and highly successful life; but it is the only poetical association we have with Venice. He shows us something of the cultured society of the time, with its advantages and its drawbacks, a society more "precious" than original, full of commentaries and criticisms, loving conversation and mutual comparison and classical allusion, not so gay as the painters of an after age, with less inclination to *suonar il liuto*, or indeed introduce anything which could interfere with that talk which was the most beloved of all entertainments. Boccaccio, one cannot but feel, must have brought something livelier and more gay with him when he was one of those who sat at the high windows of the

Palazzo delle due Torri and looked out upon all the traffic of the port, and the ships going out to sea. But the antechambers of the poet were always crowded as if he had been a prince, the doge ever ready to do him honour, and all the great persons deeply respectful of Dom Francesco, though the young ones might scoff, not without a smile aside from their fathers, at the bland laureate's conviction of his own greatness.

No other poet has ever illustrated Venice. Dante passed through the great city and did not love her, if his supposed letter on the subject is real—at all events brought no image out of her except that of the pitch boiling in the Arsenal, and the seamen repairing their storm-beaten ships. Nameless poets no doubt there were whose songs the mariners bellowed along the Riva, and the maidens sang at their work. The following anonymous relic is so pure and tender that, though far below the level of a laureated poet, it may serve to throw a little fragrance upon the name of poetry in Venice, so little practised and so imperfectly known. It is the lament of a wife for her husband gone to the wars—*alla Crociata in Oriente*—a humble Crusader-seaman no doubt, one of those perhaps who followed old Enrico Dandolo, with the cross on his rough cap, ignorant of all the wiles of statesmanship, while his wife waited wistfully through many months and years.

> " Donna Frisa, in your way,
> You give me good advice, to lay
> By this grieving out of measure,
> Saying to see me is no pleasure,
> Since my husband, gone to war,
> Carried my heart with him afar ;
> But since he's gone beyond the sea
> This alone must comfort me.
> I have no fear of growing old,
> For hope sustains and makes me bold
> While I think upon my lord :   .
> In him is all my comfort stored,
> No other bearing takes my eye,
> In him does all my pleasure lie,

Nor can I think him far, while he
Ever in love is near to me.
Lone in my room, my eyes are dim,
Only from fear of harm to him.
Nought else I fear, and hope is strong
He will come back to me anon ;
And all my plaints to gladness rise,
And into songs are turned my sighs,
Thinking of that good man of mine ;
No more I wish to make me fine,
Or look into the glass, or be
Fair, since he is not here to see.
In my chamber alone I sit,
The *festa* may pass, I care not for it,
Nor to gossip upon the stairs outside,
Nor from the window to look, nor glide
Out on the balcony, save 't may be
To gaze afar, across the sea,
Praying that God would guard my lord
In Paganesse, sending His word
To give the Christians the victory,
And home in health and prosperity
To bring him back, and with him all
In joy and peace perpetual.

" When I make this prayer I know
All my heart goes with it so
That something worthy is in me
My lord's return full soon to see.
All other comforts I resign.
Your way is good, but better mine,
And firm I hold this faith alone :
The women hear me, but never one
Contradicts my certitude,
For I hold it seemly and good,
And that to be true and faithful
To a good woman is natural ;
Considering her husband still,
All his wishes to fulfil,
And with him to be always glad,
And in his presence never sad.

" Thus should there be between the two
No thought but how pleasure to do,
She to him and he to her,

This their rivalry : nor e'er
Listen to any ill apart,
But of one mind be, and one heart.
He ever willing what she wills,
She what his pleasure most fulfils.
With never quarrel or despite,
But peace between them morning and night.
This makes a goodly jealousy
To excel in love and constancy.
And thus is the pilgrim served aright,
From eve to morn, from day to night."

CHAPTER II.

HE first development of native literature in Venice, and indeed the only one which attained any greatness, was History. Before ever poet had sung or preacher discoursed, in the early days when the republic was struggling into existence, there had already risen in the newly-founded community and among the houses scarcely yet to be counted noble, but which had begun to sway the minds of the fishers and traders and salt-manufacturers of the marshes, annalists whose desire it was to chronicle the doings of that infant state, struggling into existence amid the fogs, of which they were already so proud. Of these nameless historians the greater number have dropped into complete oblivion ; but they have furnished materials to many successors, and in some cases their works still exist in codexes known to the learned, affording still their quota of information, sometimes mingled with fable, yet retaining here and there a vigorous force of life which late writers more correct find it hard to put into the most polished records. To all of these Venice was already the object of all desire, the centre of all ambition. Her beauty, the splendour of her rising palaces, the glory of her churches, is their subject from the beginning ; though still the foundations were not laid of that splendour and glory which has proved the enchantment of later ages. This city was the joy of the whole earth, a wonder and

witchery to Sagornino in the eleventh century as much as to
Molmenti in the nineteenth ; and before the dawn of serious
history, as well as with all the aid of state documents and
critical principles in her maturity, the Story of Venice has been
the great attraction to her children, the one theme of which no
Venetian can ever tire. It would be out of our scope to give
any list of these early writers. Their name is Legion—and
any reader who can venture to launch himself upon the
learned, but chaotic, work of the most serene Doge Marco
Foscarini upon Venetian literature, will find himself hustled on
every page by a pale crowd of half-perceptible figures in every
department of historical research. The laws, the church, the
trade of Venice, her money, her ceremonials and usages, the
speeches of her orators, her treaties with foreign Powers, her
industries—in all of these by-ways of history are crowds of busy
workers, each contributing his part to that one central object of
all—the glory and the history of the city, which was to every
man the chief object in the world.

It was, however, only in the time of Andrea Dandolo, the
first man of letters who occupied the doge's chair, the friend of
Petrarch and of all the learned of his time, that the artless
chronicles of the early ages were consolidated into history. Of
Andrea himself we have but little to tell. His own appearance
is dim in the far distance, only coming fairly within our vision
in those letters of Petrarch already quoted, in which the learned
and cultivated Scholar-Prince proves himself, in spite of every
exhortation and appeal, a Venetian before all, putting aside the
humanities in which he was so successful a student, and the
larger sympathies which letters and philosophy ought to bring—
with a sudden frown over the countenance which regarded with
friendly appreciation all the other communications of the poet
until he permitted himself to speak of peace with Genoa, and to
plead that an end might be put to those bloody and fratricidal
wars which devastated Italy. Dandolo, with all his enlightenment, was not sufficiently enlightened to see this, or to be able
to free himself from the prejudices and native hostilities of his

CANAREGGIO.

state. He thought the war with Genoa just and necessary, while Petrarch wrung his hands over the woes of a country torn in pieces; and instead of responding to the ideal picture of a common prosperity such as the two great maritime rivals might enjoy together, flamed forth in wrath at the thought even of a triumph which should be shared with that most intimate enemy. The greater part of his reign was spent in the exertions necessary to keep up one of these disastrous wars, and he died in the midst of defeat, with nothing but ill news of his armatas, and Genoese galleys in the Adriatic, pushing forward, perhaps, who could tell? to Venice herself. "The republic within and without was threatened with great dangers," says Sabellico, at the moment of his death, and he was succeeded by the ill-fated Faliero, to show how distracted was the state at this dark period. Troubles of all kinds had distinguished the reign of the learned Andrea. Earthquakes, for which the philosophers sought strange explanations, such as that they were caused by "a spirit, bound and imprisoned underground," which, with loud noises, and often with fire and flame, escaped by the openings and caverns; and pestilence, which Sabellico believes to have been caused by certain fish driven up along the coast. Notwithstanding all these troubles, Dandolo found time and leisure to add a sixth volume to the collections of laws already made, and to compile his history—a dignified and scrupulous, if somewhat brief and formal, narrative of the lives and acts of his predecessors in the ducal chair. The former writers had left each his fragment, Sagornino, for instance, dwelling chiefly upon Venice under the reign of the Orseoli, to the extent of his personal experiences. Dandolo was the first to weave these broken strands into one continuous thread. He had not only the early chronicles within his reach, but the papers of the state and those of his own family, which had already furnished three doges to the republic, and thus was in every way qualified for his work. It is remarkable to note through all the conflicts of the time, through the treacherous stillness before the earthquake and the horrified clamour after, through the fierce exultation of victory and the dismal gloom of defeat, and amid all those troubled ways where pestilence and misery had set up their abode, this philosopher—doctor of laws, the first who ever sat upon that throne—the scholar and patron of letters, distracted with all the cares of his uneasy sway, yet going on day by day with his literary labours, laying the foundation firm for his countrymen, upon which so many have built. How Petrarch's importunities about these dogs of Genoese, perpetual enemies of the republic, as if, forsooth, they were brothers and Christian men! must have fretted him in the midst of his studies. What did a poet-priest, a classical half-French man of peace, know about such matters? The same language! Who dared to compare the harsh dialect these wretches jabbered among themselves with the liquid Venetian speech? The same country! As far different as east from west. They were no brethren, but born enemies of Venice never to be reconciled; and in this faith the enlightened doge, the philosopher and sage, reigned and died.

After Dandolo there seems to have been silence for about half a century, though no period was without its essays in history: a noble patrician here and there, a monk in his leisure, an old soldier after his wars were over, making each his personal contribution, to lie for the greater part unnoted in the archives of his family or order. But about the end of the fourteenth century there rose a faint agitation among the more learned Venetians as to the expediency of compiling a general history upon the most authentic manuscripts and records, which should be given forth to the world with authority as the true and trustworthy history of Venice. There was perhaps no one sufficiently in earnest to press the matter, nor had they any writer ready to take up the work. But no doubt it was an excellent subject on which to debate when they met each other in the public places whither patricians resorted, and where the wits had their encounters. Oh, for a historian to write that great book! The noble philosophers themselves were too busy with their legislations, or their pageants, or their classical studies,

to undertake it themselves, and it was difficult to find any one
sufficiently well qualified to fill the office which it was their intention should be that of a public servant encouraged and paid by
the state. During the next half century there were a great many
negotiations begun, but never brought to any definite conclusion,
with sundry professors of literature, especially one Biondo, who had
already written much on the subject. But none of them came
to any practical issue. The century had reached its last quarter,
when the matter was summarily and by a personal impulse taken
out of the noble dilettanti's hands. Marco Antonio Sabellico,
a native of Vicovaro, among the Sabine hills, and one of the
most learned men and best Latinists of his day, had been drawn
to Venice probably by the same motives which drew Petrarch
thither: the freedom of its society, the hospitality with which
strangers were received, and the eager welcome given by a race
ambitious of every distinction, but not great in the sphere of
letters, to all who brought with them something of that envied
fame. How it was that he was seized by the desire to write a
history of Venice, which was not his own country, we are not
told. But it is very likely that he was one of those men of
whom there are examples in every generation, for whom Venice
has an especial charm, and who, like the occasional love-thrall
of a famous beauty, give up their lives to her praise and service,
hoping for nothing in return. He might, on the other hand, be
nothing more than an enterprising author, aware that the patrons
of literature in Venice were moving heaven and earth to have a
history, and taking advantage of their desire with a rapidity and
unexpectedness which would forestall every other attempt. He
was at the time in Verona, in the suite of the Captain of that
city, Benedetto Trivigiano, out of reach of public documents, and
naturally of many sources of information which would have been
thrown open to an authorised historian. He himself speaks of
the work of Andrea Dandolo as of a book which he had heard
of but never seen, though it seems incredible that any man
should take in hand a history of Venice without making himself
acquainted with the only authoritative work existing on the

subject. Neither had he seen the book of Jacopo Zeno, upon
the work and exploits of his grandfather Carlo, which is the
chief authority in respect to so important an episode as the war
of Chioggia. And he wrote so rapidly that the work was completed in fifteen months, "by reason of his impatience," says Marco
Foscarini. Notwithstanding these many drawbacks, Sabellico's
history remains among the most influential, as it is the most
eloquent, of Venetian histories. It is seldom that a historian
escapes without conviction of error in one part or another of his
work, and Sabellico was no exception to the rule. The learned
of the time threw themselves upon him with all the heat of
critics who have never committed themselves by serious production in their own persons. They accused him of founding
his book upon the narratives of the inferior annalists, and neglecting the good—of transcribing from contemporaries, and above all
of haste, an accusation which it is impossible to deny. "But,"
says Foscarini, "the thirst for a general history was such that
either these faults were not discovered, or else by reason of the
unusual accompaniment of eloquence, to which as to a new thing
the attention of all was directed, they passed unobserved." The
eager multitude took up the book with enthusiasm, although
the critics objected : and though Sabellico was in no manner
a servant of the state, and had never had the office of historian
confided to him, "the Senate, perceiving the general approval,
and having rather regard to its own greatness than to the real
value of the work, settled upon the writer two hundred gold
ducats yearly, merely on the score of gracious recompense."
This altogether disposes, as Foscarini points out, of the spiteful
imputation of "a venal pen," which one of his contemporaries
attributed to Sabellico : but at the same time he is careful to
guard his readers from the error of supposing that the historian
had the privileges and position of a functionary chosen by the
state.

The learned doge is indeed very anxious that there should be
no mistake on this point, nor any undue praise appropriated to
the first historian of Venice. All foreign historians, he says,

take him as the chief authority on Venice, and quote him continually; not only so, but the writers who immediately succeeded him did little more than repeat what he had said, and the most learned among them had no thought of any purgation of his narrative, but only to add various particulars, in the main following Sabellico, for which reason they are to be excused who believe that they find in him the very flower of ancient Venetian history: but yet he cannot be justly so considered. Foscarini cites various errors in the complicated history of the Crusades, respecting which it is allowed, however, that the ancient Venetian records contain very little information: and such mistakes as that on a certain occasion Sabellico relates an expedition as made with the whole of the armata, while Dandolo fixes the number at thirty galleys—not a very important error. When all has been said, however, there is little doubt that as a general history full in all the more interesting details, and giving a most lifelike and graphic picture of the course of Venetian affairs, with all the embassies, royal visits, rebellions, orations, sorrows, and festivities that took place within the city, together with those events more difficult to master that were going on outside, the history of Sabellico is the one most attractive and interesting to the reader, and on all general events quite trustworthy. The original is in Latin, but it was put into the vulgar tongue within a few years after its publication, and was afterwards more worthily translated by Dolce in a version which contains much of the force and eloquence of the original.

After this another long interval elapsed in which many patrician writers one after another, whose names and works are all recorded by Foscarini, made essays less or more important, without, however, gaining the honourable position of historian of the republic: until at last the project for establishing such an office was taken up in the beginning of the sixteenth century for the benefit of a young scholar, noble but poor, Andrea Navagero. He was the most elegant Latin writer in Italy, Foscarini says; indeed, the great Council of Ten themselves have put their noble hands to it that this was the case. "His

style was such as, by agreement of all the learned, had not its
equal in Italy or out of it," is the language of the decree by
which his appointment was made. Being without means he
was about to leave Venice to push his fortune elsewhere
by his talents, "depriving the country of so great an ornament"—a conclusion "not to be tolerated." To prevent such
an imputation upon the state, the Council felt themselves bound
to interfere, and appointed Navagero their historian, to begin
over again that authentic and authorised history which Sabellico
had executed without authority. The chances probably are that
the young and accomplished scholar had friends enough at court
to make a strong effort for him, to liberate him from the alarming possibility, so doubly sad for a Venetian, of being "confined
within the boundaries of private life"—and that the authorities
of the state bethought themselves suddenly of a feasible way of
providing for him by giving him this long thought of but
never occupied post. They were no great judges of literature,
more especially of Latin, their own being of the most atrocious
description, but they were susceptible to the possible shame
of allowing a scholar who might be a credit to the republic to
leave Venice in search of a living.

Young Navagero thus entered the first upon the post of
Historian of Venice, which he held for many years without
producing anything to justify the Council in their choice. It
was probably intended only as a means of providing for him
pending his introduction into public life : for we find a number
of years after a letter from Bembo congratulating him on his
appointment as ambassador to Spain, "the first thing which you
have ever asked from the country," and prophesying great things
to follow. He was appointed historian in 1515, but it is not
till fifteen years after that we hear anything of his history, and
that in the most tragical way. In 1530 he was sent on an
embassy to France, and carried there with him certain manuscripts, the fruit of the intervening years—ten books, it is said,
of the proposed story of Venice. But he had not been long in
Paris when he fell ill and died. And shortly before his death

—on the very day, one writer informs us—he threw his papers into the fire with his own hands and destroyed the whole. Whether this arose from dissatisfaction with his work, or whether it was done in the delirium of mortal sickness, no one could tell. Foscarini quotes from an unpublished letter of Cardinal Valiero some remarks upon this unfortunate writer, in which he is described as one who was never satisfied with moderate approval from others, and still less capable of pleasing himself. This brief and tragic episode suggests even more than it tells. Noble, ambitious, and poor, probably of an uneasy and fastidious mind—for he is said on a previous occasion to have burnt a number of his early productions in disgust and discouragement—the despondency of sickness must have overwhelmed a sensitive nature. The office to which he had been promoted was still in the visionary stage : the greatest things were expected of the new historian of the republic, a work superseding all previous attempts. Sabellico, who had gone over the same ground in choicest Latin, was still fresh in men's minds ; and, still more alarming, another Venetian, older and of greater weight than himself, Marino Sanudo, one of the most astonishing and gifted of historical moles, was going on day by day with those elaborate records which are the wonder of posterity, building up the endless story of the Republic with details innumerable—a mine of material for other workers, if too abundant and minute for actual history. Ser Andrea was no doubt well aware of the keen inspection, the criticism sharpened by a sense that this young fellow had been put over the heads of older men, which would await his work ; and his own taste had all the fastidious refinement of a scholar, more critical than confident. When he found himself in a strange country, though not as an exile but with the high commission of the republic—sick, little hopeful of ever seeing the beloved city again, his heart must have failed him altogether. These elaborate pages, how poor they are apt to look in the cold light darkened by the shadow of the grave ! He would think perhaps of the formidable academy in the Aldine work-

shops shaking their heads over his work, picking out inaccu-
racies—finding perhaps, a danger more appalling still to every
classical mind, something here and there not Ciceronian in
his Latin. Nothing could be more tragic, yet there is a lingering touch of the ludicrous too, so seldom entirely absent from
human affairs. To tremble lest a solecism should be discovered
in his style when the solemnity of death was already enveloping
his being ! Rather finish all at one stroke, flinging with his
feverish dying hands the work never corrected enough, among
the blazing logs, and be done with it for ever. Amid all the
artificial fervour of Renaissance scholarship and the learned
chatter of the libraries, what a tragic and melancholy scene !

The critics are careful to indicate that this is not the same
Andrea Navagero who wrote the chronicle bearing that name,
and whose work is of the most commonplace description. It is
confusing to find the two so near in time, and with nothing to
identify the second bearer of the name except that he writes
in indifferent Italian (Venetian), and not in classic Latin, and
that his book was given to the public while the other Andrea,
lo Storico, was still only a boy. The only productions of the
historian so called, though nothing of his history survives, seem
to have been certain Latin verses of more or less elegance.

A very much more important personage in his time, as in the
value of the extraordinary collections he left behind him, was
the diarist and historian already referred to, Marino Sanudo.
He too, we may remark in passing, is apt to be confused with
an elder writer of the same name, Marino Sanudo, called Torsello,
who wrote on the subject of the Crusades, and on many other
matters more exclusively Venetian, something like a hundred
and fifty years before, in the middle of the fourteenth century.
The younger Sanudo (or Sanuto) was born in 1466, of one of
the most noble houses in Venice, and educated in all the erudition of his time. He was of such a precocious genius that
between his eleventh and fourteenth years he corresponded with
the most eminent scholars of the day, and gave the highest
hopes of future greatness. Even in that early age the dominant

passion of his life had made itself apparent, and he seems already
to have begun the collection of documents and the record of
daily public events. At the age of eight it would appear the
precocious historian had already copied out with his own small
hand the fading inscriptions made by Petrarch under the series
of pictures, *anticchissimi*, the first of all painted in the Hall of
the Great Council. Sanudo himself announces that he did
this, though without mentioning his age : but the anxious care
of Mr. Rawdon Brown, so well known among the English
students and adorers of Venice, points out that these pictures
were restored and had begun to be repainted in 1474, during
the childhood of his hero. There could be nothing more characteristic and natural, considering the after life of the man,
than this youthful incident, and it adds an interest the more
to the hall in which so often in latter days our historian mounted
the tribune, *in renga*, as he calls it, and addressed the assembled
parliament of Venice—to call before us the small figure, tablets
in hand, his childish eyes already sparkling with observation, and
that historical curiosity which was the inspiration of his life—
copying before they should altogether perish the inscriptions
under the old pictures which told the half-fabulous triumphant
tale of Barbarossa beaten and Venice victrice. The colours
were no doubt fading, flakes of the old distemper peeling off and
a general ruin threatened, before the Senate saw it necessary to
renew that historical chronicle. When we remember Sanudo's
humorous, only half-believing note on the subject years after,
"that if the story had not been true our brave Venetians would
not have had it painted," it gives a still more delightful glow
of smiling interest to the image of the little Marino, no doubt
with unwavering faith in his small bosom and enthusiasm for
his city, taking down, to the awe of many an unlearned contemporary, the fading legends written by the great poet, a
record at once of the ancient glories of Venice and of her
illustrious guest.

He was seventeen, however, and eager in all the exercises of
a Venetian gentleman when he went with his elder cousin Marco

Sanudo, who had been appointed one of the Auditors or Syndics
of Terra-firma, to Padua in the spring of 1483. The brilliant
cavalcade rode from Fusina by the banks of the Brenta, then
as now a line of villas, castellos, hospitable houses, where they
were received with great honour and pomp—and visited everything that was remarkable in the city. *Visto tutto*, is the
youth's record wherever he went: and there can indeed be
no doubt that in all his journeys the young Marino saw and
noted everything—the circumstances of the locality, the scenery,
the historical occurrences—all that is involved in the external
aspect of a place which had associations both classical and contemporary. The characteristics of his time are very apparent
in all his keen remarks and inspections. He is told, he says,
that Padua has many bodies of the saints, and in this respect
is second only to Rome—but the only sacred relic in which he
is specially interested is the *corpo e vero osse* of Livy, to which
he refers several times, giving the epitaph of the classical historian at full length. Strangely enough, at an age when the art
of painting was growing to its greatest development in Venice,
no curiosity seems to have been in the young man's curious
mind, nor even any knowledge of the fact that the chapel of
the Arena had been adorned by the great work of a certain
Giotto, though that is the chief object now of the pilgrim who
goes to Padua. That beautiful chapel must have been in its
fullest glory of colour and noble art; but there is no evidence
that our cavalier had so much as heard of it, though he spies
every scrap of marble on the old bridges, and carefully quotes
epigrams and verses about the city, and records every trifling
circumstance. "The markets are Tuesday, Thursday, and Fri-
day." "There are forty parish churches, and four hospitals,"
&c., &c.—but not a word of the then most famous pictures in
the world.

This is the *Itinerario in Terra-firma*, which is the first of the
young author's works. It is full of the sprightly impulses of a
boy, and of a boy's pleasure in movement, in novelty, in endless
rides and expeditions, tempered by now and then a day in which

the Syndic *data audientia per toto el jorno*, his young cousin
sitting no doubt by his side more grave than any judge, to hide
the laugh always lurking at the corners of his mouth : *data
benigna audientia*, he says on one occasion, perhaps on one of
those May days when he rode off with a cavalcade of his friends
through that green abundant country to the village or castello
where lived the queen of his affections "that oriental jewel
(Gemma), that lovely face which I seem to have always before
me, inspiring me with many songs for my love." "Oh me!
Oh me!" he cries in half-humorous distraction, "I am going
mad! Let me go and sing more than ever. Long before this
I ought to have been in love. Fain would I sing of the goddess,
my bright Gemma, whose lovely countenance I ever adore. and
who has made me with much fear her constant servant." Gemma
shines out suddenly like a star only in this one page of the
Itinerario. Perhaps he exhausted his boyish passion in constant
rides to Rodigio or Ruigo, where the lady lived, and in his songs,
of which the specimens given are not remarkable. But the
sentiment is full of delightful youthful extravagance : and the
aspect of the young man gravely noting everything by the instinct of his nature, gallopping forth among his comrades—one
of whom he calls Pylades—some half-dozen of them, a young
Cornaro, a Pisani, the bluest blood in Venice—scouring the
country, to see the churches, the castles and palaces, and everything that was to be seen, and Gemma above all, mingles with
charming ease and inconsistency the dawning statesman, the
born chronicler, the gallant boyish lover. Sometimes the cavalcade counted forty horsemen, sometimes only three or four. The
Itinerario is a mass of information, full of details which Professor
R. Fulin, its latest editor, considers well worth the while of the
patriotic Venetian of to-day. "To compare our provinces at
four centuries distance with their present state is certainly curious,
and without doubt useful also," he says—but the glimpses between the lines of that sprightly youthful company is to us who
are less seriously concerned, still more interesting. "We have
before our eyes," adds the learned professor, "a boy—but a boy

who begins to bear very worthily the name of Marino Sanudo."
It somewhat disturbs all Marino's commentators, however, that,
though his education had been so good and classical references
abound in his writings, yet his style is never so elevated as his
culture.   It is indeed very disjointed, entirely unstudied, prolix,
though full of an honest simplicity and straightforwardness
which perhaps commends itself more to the English taste than
to the Italian.   In his after life Sanudo's power of production
seemed indeed endless.   Besides his published works, he left
behind him fifty-six volumes of his diary, chiefly of public events,
a record day by day of all the news that came to Venice, and
all that happened there.   It was by the loving care of the
Englishman already referred to, Mr. Rawdon Brown, a kindred
spirit, that portions of those wonderful diaries were first given
to the world.   They are now in course of publication, a mass
of minute and inexhaustible information, from the first aspect
of which I confess to have shrunk appalled.   This sea of facts,
of picturesque incidents, of an eye-witness's sketches, and the
reports of an immediate actor in the scenes described—affords
to the careful student an almost unexampled guide, and assistance to the understanding of the years between 1482 and 1533,
from Sanudo's youth to the end of his life.

The *Vitæ Ducum*, from which we have already quoted largely,
is full of the defects of style which were peculiar to this volumi-
nous writer : they are charged with repetitions and written without regard to any rules of composition or prejudices of style—
but their descriptions are often exceedingly picturesque in
unadorned simplicity, and the reflections of popular belief and
the report of the moment give often, as the reader will observe
on turning back to our earlier chapters, an idea of the manner
in which an incident struck the contemporary mind which is
exceedingly instructive, even though as often happens, it cannot
be supported by documents or historical proof.   To my thinking
it is at least quite as interesting to know what account was
given among the people of a great event, and how it shaped
itself in the general mind, as to understand the form it takes in

To face page 358.

CLOISTERS OF S. GREGORIO.

the archives of the country when it has fallen into perspective and into the inevitable subordination of individual facts to the broader views of history. At the same time Sanudo's story, while keeping this popular character, is supported by the citation of innumerable public documents to which he had access in his character of politician and magistrate: so that the essentially different characteristics of the legendary and the documentary history are combined in this loosely written, quaintly expressed, most real and interesting chronicle. The work is said to have been composed by Sanudo between his eighteenth and his twenty-seventh year. The garrulous tone and rambling narrative are more like an old man than a young one: but it is evident that the instinct of the chronicler, the minute and constant observation, the ears open and eyes intent upon everything small and great which could be discussed, with a certain absence of discrimination between the important and the unimportant which is the characteristic defect of these great qualities, was in him from the beginning of his career.

The great printer, Aldus, dedicated one of his publications to Sanudo in the year 1498, when our Marino was but thirty-two— in which already mention is made as of completed works of the *Magistratus Urbis Venetae*, the *Vitis Principium*, and the *De Bello Gallico*, all then ready for publication "both in Latin and the vulgar tongue, that they may be read by learned and unlearned alike." From this it is apparent that Sanudo had also already begun his wonderful diaries, the collection of his great library, and the public life which would seem in its many activities incompatible with these ceaseless toils. He followed all these pursuits however through the rest of his life. His diaries became the greatest storehouses of minute information perhaps existing in the world: his library was the wonder of all visitors to Venice: and the record of his own acts and occupations chronicled along with everything else in his daily story of the life of the city, shows a perpetual activity which takes away the beholder's breath. His speeches in the Senate, generally recorded as "*Io Marin Sanudo contradixi*," were

numberless.   He was employed in all kinds of public missions
and work.   He was in succession a Signore di Notte, a Savio
degli Ordini, one of the Pregadi, one of the Zonta, a member of
the Senate, Avvogadore : exercising the functions of magistrate,
member of Parliament, statesman—and taking a part in all
great discussions upon state affairs whether in the Senate or in
the great Council.   He was, as Mr. Rawdon Brown, using the
terms natural to an Englishman, describes, almost always in
opposition—"contradicting," to use his own expression ; and for
this reason was less fortunate than many obscure persons whose
only record is in his work.   Again and again he has to tell us
that the votes are given against him, that he comes out last
in the ballot, that for a time he is no longer of the Senate, and
excluded from public office.   But he never loses heart nor
withdraws from the lists.   " *Io Marino Sanudo è di la Zonta*,"
he describes himself, always proud of his position and eager to
retain, or recover it when lost.   A man of such endless industry,
activity of mind and actions, universal interest and intelligence,
would be remarkable anywhere and at any time.

His first entry into public life was in March, 1498—" a day
to be held in eternal memory :" a few months later he was
elected Senator, and passed through various duties and offices,
always actively employed.   The first break in this busy career
he records on the 1st April, 1503 :—

"Having accomplished my term of service in the Ordini (Savii degli Ordini),
in which I have had five times the reward of public approbation, and having
passed out of the college, I now determine that, God granting it, I will let
no day pass without writing the news that comes from day to day, so that
I may the better, accustoming myself to the strict truth, go on with my true
history, which was begun several years ago.   Seeking no eloquence of
composition, I will thus note down everything as it happens."

This retirement however does not last long : for within a
few months we read :—

"Having been, in the end of September, without any application on my
part, or desire to re-enter, elected by the grace of the fathers of the Senate,

in a council of the Pregadi, for the sixth time, Savio degli Ordini, I have decided not to refuse office for two reasons. First, because I desire always to do what I can for the benefit of our republic ; the second, because my former service in the college was always in times of great tribulation during the Turkish war, in which I endured no little fatigue of mind. But now that peace with the Turk has been signed, as I have recorded in the former book, I find myself again in the college in a time of tranquillity ; therefore, with the Divine aid, following my first determination, I will describe here day by day the things that occur, the plain facts, leaving for the moment every attempt at an elaborate style aside."

Other notices of a similar kind follow at intervals. Now and then there occur gaps, and on several occasions Marino puts on a little polite semblance of being rather pleased than otherwise when these occur; but gradually as the tide of public life seizes him, becomes more and more impatient of exclusion, and ceases to pretend that he likes it, or that it suits him. His time of peace did not last long. The league of Cambrai rose like a great storm from west and south and north, threatening to overwhelm the republic, which, as usual in such great dangers, was heavy with fears, and torn with intrigues within, when most seriously threatened from without. Sanudo tells us of an old senator long retired from public life for whom the doge sent in the horror of the first disasters, and who, beginning to weep, said to his wife, " Give me my cloak. I will go to the Council to say four words, and then die." The troubled Council, where every man had some futile expedient to advise, a change of the Proveditori, or the sending of a new commissioner to the camp of the defeated, is put before us in a few words. Sanudo himself was strongly in favour of two things—that the doge himself should take the field, and that an embassy should be sent to the Turk to ask for help. He gives a melancholy description of the great Ascension Day, the holiday of the year, which fell at this miserable moment when the forces of the republic were in full rout, retreating from point to point.

"17 May, 1509.—It was Ascension Day (La Sensa), but there was nothing but weeping. No visitors were to be heard of, no one was visible in the

Piazza ; the fathers of the college were broken down with trouble, and still more our doge, who never spoke, but looked like a dead man. And much was said for this last time of sending the doge in person to Verona, to encourage cur army and our people there, and to send five hundred gentlemen with his Serenity, at their own expense. Thus the talk went in the Piazza and on the benches of the Pregadi, but those of the College (of Senators) took no action, nor did the doge offer himself. He said, however, to his sons and dependants, 'The doge will do whatever the country desires' At the same time he is more dead than alive ; he is seventy-three. Thus those evil days go on ; we see our own ruin, and do nothing to prevent it. God grant that what I proposed had been done. I had desired to re-enter as a Savio degli Ordini, but was advised against it, and now I am very sorry not to have carried out my wish, to have procured five or six thousand Turks, and sent a secretary or ambassador to the Sultan ; but now it is too late."

Sanudo's project of calling in the Turks, their ancient enemies to help them against the league of Christian princes, seemed a dangerous expedient, but it must be remembered that the republic was in despair. The poor old doge, who was more dead than alive, yet ready to do whatever the country wished, was Leonardo Loredano, whose portrait is so notable an object in our own National Gallery, and forms our frontispiece. In the midst of all these troubles, however, while the Venetian statesmen were making anxious visits to their nearest garrison, and reviewing and collecting every band they could get together, the familiar strain of common life comes in with such a paragraph as the following :—

"17 *July*, 1509.—On the way to my house I met a man having a beautiful Hebrew Bible in good paper, value twenty ducats, who sold it to me as a favour for one marzello : which I took to place it in my library."

We are unable to say what was the value of a marzello : but it is evident that he got his Bible a great bargain, taking in this case a little permissible advantage of the troubles of the time.

There is something calming and composing to the mind in a long record like this extending over many years. There occurs the episode of a great war, of many privations, misfortunes, and

bereavements, such as seem to cover the whole world with
gloom: but we have only to turn a few pages, however agitated, however moving may be the record, and we find the
state, the individual sufferer, whosoever it may be, going on
calmly about the ordinary daily businesses of life, and the
storm gone by. These storms and wars and catastrophes are
after all but accidents in the calmer career which fills all
the undistinguished nights and days, only opening here and
there to reveal one which is full of trouble, which comes and
departs again. History, indeed, makes more of these episodes
than life does, for they are her milestones by which to guide
her path through the dim multitude of uneventful days. Our
historian, however, in his endless record, gives the small events
of peace almost as much importance as the confusion and excitement of the desperate moment when Venice stood against
all Europe, holding her own.

Sanudo's public life was one of continual ups and downs. He
would seem to have been a determined Conservative, opposing
every innovation, though at the same time, like many men of
that opinion, exceedingly daring in any suggestion that approved itself to his mind; as for instance in respect to asking aid
from the Turks, which was not a step likely to commend itself
to a patriot of his principles. And he would not seem to have
been very popular even among his own kindred, for there are
various allusions to family intrigues against him, as well as to
the failure of his hopes in respect to elections and appointments.
But that extraordinarily limited intense life of the Venetian
oligarchy, a world pent up within a city, with all its subtle
trains of diplomacy, determined independence, on its own side,
and equally determined desire to have something to say in every
European imbroglio, was naturally a life full of intrigue, of perpetual risings and fallings, where every man had to sustain
discomfiture in his day, and was ready to trip up his neighbour
whenever occasion served. Marino's inclination to take in all
matters a side of his own was not a popular quality, and it
is evident that like many other obstinate and clear-sighted

protesters, he was often right, often enough at least to make him
an alarming critic and troublesome disturber of existing parties, being at all times, like the smith of Perth, for his own
hand. " I, Marino Sanudo, moved by my conscience, went to
the meeting and opposed the new proposals," *andai in renga et
contradixi a questo modo nove*, is a statement which is continually
recurring. And as the long list of volumes grows, there is a
preface to almost every new year, in which he complains,
explains, defends his actions, and appeals against unfavourable judgments, sometimes threatening to relinquish his toils,
taking them up again, consoling himself by the utterance
of his complaint. On one occasion he thanks God that notwithstanding much illness he still remains able " to do something
in this age in honour of the eternal majesty, and exaltation of
the Venetian State, to which I can never fail, being born in that
allegiance, for which I would die a thousand times if that could
advantage my country, notwithstanding that I have been beaten,
worn out, and evil entreated in her councils."

" In the past year (1522) I have been dismissed from the Giunta (Zonta),
of which two years ago I was made a member : but while I sat in that
Senate I always in my speeches did my best for my country, with full
honour from the senators for my opinions and judgment, even when against
those of my colleagues. And this is the thing that has injured me, for had
I been mute, applauding individuals as is the present fashion, letting things
pass that are against the interest of my dearest country, acting contrary to
the law, as those who have the guidance of the city permit to be done,
even had I not been made Avvogadore, I should have been otherwise treated.
But seeing all silent, my conscience pushing me to make me speak, since
God has granted me good utterance, an excellent memory, and much knowledge of things, having described them for so many years, and seen all the
records of public business, it seemed to me that I should sin against myself
if I did not deliver my opinion in respect to the questions discussed,
knowing that those who took the other side complained of being opposed,
because they hoped to reap some benefit from the proposals in question.
But I caring only for the public advantage, all seemed to me nothing in
comparison with the good of my country. . . . I confess that this repulse
has caused me no small grief, and has been the occasion of my illness : and
if again I was rejected in the ballot for the past year it was little wonder,
seeing that many thought me dead, or so infirm that I was no longer good

for anything, not having stirred from my house for many months before. But the Divine bounty has still preserved me, and, as I have said, enabled me to complete the diary of the year ; for however suffering I was I never failed to record the news of every day which was brought to me by my friends, so that another volume is finished. I had some thought of now giving up this laborious work, but some of my countrymen who love me say to me, 'Marin, make no mistake, follow the way you have begun, remember *moglie e magistrato è del ciel destinato*' (marriages and magistrates are made in heaven)."

In another of these many prefaces, Sanudo reflects that he has now attained his fifty-fifth year, and that it is time to stop this incessant making of notes, and to set himself to the work of polishing and setting forth in a more careful style, and in the form of dignified history his mass of material, " being now of the number of the Senators of the Giunta and engaged in many cares and occupations : "—

" But I am persuaded by one who has a right to command, by the noble lord Lorenzo Loredano, procurator, son of our Most Serene Prince, who many times has exhorted me not to give up the work which I have begun, saying that in the end it will bring me glory and perpetual fame ; and praying me at least to continue it during the lifetime of his Serene father, who has been our doge for nineteen years, who has been in many labours for the republic, and having regained a great part of all that had been lost in the late great and terrible war, now waits the conclusion of all things, being of the age of eighty-four. He cannot be expected to live long, although of a perfect constitution, lately recovered from a serious illness, and never absent from the meetings of the Senate or Council, or failing in anything that is for the benefit of the State. For these reasons I have resolved not to relinquish the work which I have begun, nor to neglect that which I know will be of great use to posterity, the highest honour to my country, and to myself an everlasting memorial."

Thus our chronicler over and over again persuades himself to continue and accomplish what it was the greatest happiness and first impulse of his life to do.

It was when the great war against the League was over, and all returned in peace to their usual occupations, Sanudo to the library which he was gradually making into one of the wonders of Venice, and to his still more wonderful work, that the Senate executed that job—if we may be allowed the word—and elected young Navagero, because he was so poor, to the office, heretofore only an imagination, of Historian of the Republic. Marino was nearly fifty, and still in the full heat of political life, giving his opinion on every subject, " contradicting " freely, and taking nothing for granted, when this appointment was made ; and there is no doubt that to be passed over thus for so much younger and less important a man must have been a great mortification for the indefatigable chronicler of every national event. He speaks with a certain quiet scorn in one place of *Messer Andrea Navagero stipendiate pubblico per scrivere la Historia.* Nor was this the only wrong done him, for the successor appointed to Navagero, after a long interval of time, it would appear, was another man with opportunities and faculties much less appropriate than his own, the learned dilettante Pietro Bembo, afterwards cardinal. Bembo had spent the greater part of his life out of Venice, in Rome at the court of the Pope, where he filled some important offices ; at Padua, which was his home in his later years ; at the court of Mantua at the period when that court was the centre of cultivation and fine sentiment. Indeed we find only occasional traces of him at Venice ; though one of his first works was about the fantastic little court of Queen Catherine Cornaro, at Asolo, a small Decameron, full of the unreal prettiness, the masques, and posturing, and versifications of the time. It was to this man that in the second place the office of historian was given over the head of our Marino ; nor was this the only vexation to which he was exposed. One of the documents quoted by Mr. Rawdon Brown is a letter from Bembo, an appeal to the doge to compel Sanudo to open to him the treasures of his collection, one of the most curious demands perhaps that was ever made. It is dated from Padua, the 7th August, 1531, and shows that not even for the writing of the history did this official of the Senate remove his dwelling to Venice.

" Serene Prince, my lord always honoured. Last winter, when I was in Venice I saw the histories of Messer Marin Sanudo, and it appeared to me that they were of a quality, though including much that is unnecessary, to give me light on an infinite number of things needful for me in carrying out the work committed to my hands by your Serenity. I begged of him to allow me to read and go over these as might be necessary for my work ; to which he replied that these books were the care and labour of his whole life, and that he would not give the sweat of his brow to any one. Upon which I went away with the intention of doing without them, though I did not see how it would be possible. Now I perceive that if I must see the public letters of your Serenity in order to understand many things contained in the books of the Senate, which are very necessary for the true understanding of the acts of this illustrious Dominion, this labour will be a thing impossible to me, and if possible, would be infinite. Wherefore I entreat your Serenity to exercise your authority with Messer Marin to let me have his books in my own hands according as it shall be necessary, pledging myself to return them safe and unhurt."

Perhaps it was the visible invidiousness of this appeal, the demand upon a man who had been passed over, for the use of his collections in the execution of a work for which he was so much better qualified than the actual holder of the office, which shamed the Senate at last into according to Marino a certain recompense for his toil. Mr. Rawdon Brown makes it evident that this allowance or salary came very late in the life of the neglected historian. The Council of Ten gave him a hundred and fifty ducats a year as an acknowledgment of the existence of his books, "which I vow to God," he says, "is nothing to the great labour they have cost me." It is but a conjecture, but it does not seem without probability, that the rulers of the Republic may have been shamed into bestowing this provision by Bembo's peevish appeal, and that mollified by the grant, Marino permitted the use of his *sudori*, the sweat of his brow, the labour of his life to the official historian, whose work even Foscarini, dry himself to the utmost permissible limit of aridity, confesses to be very dry, and which possesses nothing of the charm of natural animation and verisimilitude which is in Sanudo's rough, confused, and often chaotic narrative.

This wonderful work was carried on till the year 1533, and finally filled fifty-six large volumes, the history of every day being brought down to within two years and a half of the author's death. He left this extraordinary collection to the republic in a will dated 4th December, 1533, immediately after the close of the record.

"I desire and ordain that all my books of the history and events of Italy, written with my own hand, beginning with the coming of King Charles of France into Italy, books bound and enclosed in a book-case, to the number of fifty-six, should be for my illustrious Signoria, to be presented to them by my executors, and placed wherever it seems to them good by the Heads of the Council of Ten, by which excellent Council an allowance of a hundred and fifty ducats a year was made to me, which I swear before God is nothing to the great labour I have had.

"Also I will and ordain that all my other printed books, which are in my great study down-stairs, and those manuscripts which are in my book-cases (*Armeri*, Scottice, Aumries) in my chamber, which are more than six thousand five hundred in number, which have cost me a great deal of money, and are very fine and genuine, many of them impossible to replace : of which there is an inventory marked with the price I paid for each (those which have a cross opposite the name I sold in the time of my poverty), I desire my executors that they should all be sold by public auction. And I pray my Lords Procurators, or Gastaldi, not to permit these books to be thrown away, especially those in manuscript which are very fine and have cost me a great deal, as will be seen in the inventory ; and those in boards and the works printed in Germany have also cost me no small sum. And I made so much expenditure in books because I wished to form a library in some monastery, or to find a place for some of them in the library of S. Marco ; but this library I no longer believe in, therefore I have changed my mind and wish everything to be sold—which books are now of more value than when I bought them, having purchased them advantageously in times of famine, and having had great bargains of them. Wherefore Messer Zanbatista Egnazio and Messer Antonio di Marsilio, seeing the index will be able to form an estimate, and not allow them to be thrown away as is the custom."

This resolution was taken because the new library of S. Marco so long promised to the Venetians, had not yet been begun ; and the old collector loving his books as if they had been his children, had evidently lost heart and faith in any undertaking of this kind being carried out in Venice. No doubt he had heard of the legacy made by Petrarch two hundred years before to the republic, and how it had disappeared, if not that the rotting remains of the poet's bequest still lay in the chamber on the roof of S. Marco, where they had been thrown with a carelessness which looks very much like contempt, and as if the busy city had no time for such vanities. The sale of his books would at least pay his creditors and be an inheritance for the nephews who had taken the place of children to him, yet were not too grateful for his care. The fifty-six volumes in the great oak press however profited scarcely more than Petrarch's gift from being placed in the custody of the tremendous Ten. They were deposited somewhere out of reach of harm it is to be supposed after the author's death, but were so completely lost sight of that the conscientious Foscarini makes as little account of Marino Sanudo, as if he had been but a mere chronicler of the lives of certain doges, with a wealth of documentary evidence indeed, but no refinement of style nor special importance as a chronicler. It was not till the year 1805 that these books were found, in the Royal Library at Vienna, got there nobody knows how in some accident of the centuries. They are now being printed in all their amplitude as has been already said, a mine of incalculable historical wealth.

During the whole time of their composition Sanudo was a public official and magistrate, taking the most active part in all the business of his time. And he was also a collector filling his library with everything he could find to illustrate his work, from the great *mappamondo*, which was one of the chief wonders of his study, down to drawings of costumes, and of the animals and flowers of those subject provinces of Venice which he had visited in his gay youth, where he had found his first love, and which, in later days, he had seen lost and won again. "The illustrious strangers who visited Venice in these days went away dissatisfied unless they had seen the Arsenal, the jewels of S. Marco, and the library of Sanudo." On one occasion he himself tells of a wandering prince who sent to ask if he might see this collection, and above all its owner; but Marino was out of humour or tired of illustrious visitors, and refused to receive him. Some of these visitors, quoted by the learned Professor Fulin, have left records of their visits, and of how they came

B B

out of the modest house of the historian stupefied with wonder and admiration. "Stupefied certainly," adds the Professor, "was that gentleman of Vicenza, Federico da Porto, who exclaims in his poem on the subject, 'He who would see the sea, the earth, and the vast world, must seek your house, O learned Marino !'"

"Sanudo had indeed collected a series, marvellous for his time, of pictures (whether drawn, painted, or engraved we cannot now ascertain), in which were represented not only the different forms of the principal European nations, but the ethnographical varieties of the human race in the old world, and also in the new, then recently discovered. Da Porto continues as follows :—

> "Then up the stairs you lead us, and we find
> A spacious corridor before us spread,
> As if it were another ocean full
> Of rarest things ; the wall invisible
> With curious pictures hid—no blank appears,
> But various figures, men of every guise ;
> A thousand unaccustomed scenes we see.
> Here Spain, there Greece, and here the apparel fair
> Of France ; nor is there any land left out.
> The new world, with its scarce known tribes, is there.
> Nor is there any place so far remote
> That does not send some envoy to your walls,
> Or can refuse to show its wonders there."

A great picture of Verona, where Marino had filled the office of Camerlengo, and where the uncle who stood to him in place of a father was Captain, seems to have been a special attraction, and is celebrated by many visitors in very bad Latin. We are obliged to admit that the description of the collection sounds very much like that of a popular museum, and does not at all resemble the high art which we should expect from such a connoisseur nowadays. But probably the things with which we should fill our shelves and niches were the merest commonplaces to Sanudo, to whom the different fashions of men, and their dresses and their ways, and their dwellings (his own youthful *Itinerario* is illustrated by sketches of towns and houses and fortifications, in the style of the nursery), would be infinitely

more interesting than those art products of his own time, which
form our delight. His books, however, were the most dear of
all; and the glimpses we have of the old man seated among his
ancient tomes, so carefully catalogued and laid up in these great
wooden *armeri*, no doubt rich with carving, and for one of which
a nineteenth century collector would give his little finger, though
they are not worth thinking of, mere furniture to Marino—is
most interesting and attractive. With what pleasure he must
have drawn forth his pen when he came in from the council,
having happily delivered himself of a *lungo e perfetta renga*, to
put it all down—how he held out against the payment of the
magistrates, for example, and contradicted every *modo novo:* or
when sick and infirm himself, the quiet of the study was broken
by one after another visitor in toga or scarlet gown, fresh from
the excitements of the contest, recounting how, at the fifteenth
hour, has come a messenger with news from the camp, or a
galley all adorned with green bearing the report of a victory!
The old man with his huge book spread out, his ink-horn always
ready, his every sense acute, his mind filled with parallel cases,
with a hundred comparisons, and that delightful conviction that
it was not only for the benefit of the *carissima patria*, but for
his own eternal fame and glory, that he continued page by page
and day by day—furnishes us with a picture characteristically
Venetian, inspired by the finest instincts of his race. He was no
meek recluse or humble scribe, but a statesman fully capable of
holding his own, and with no small confidence in his own opinion;
yet the glory of Venice is his motive above all others, and the
building up of the fame of the city for whose benefit he would
die a thousand times, as he says, and for whose honour he continues day after day and year after year, his endless and tardily
acknowledged toils. Would it have damped his zeal, we wonder,
could he have foreseen that his unexampled work should drop
into oblivion, after historians such as the best informed of doges,
Marco Foscarini, knowing next to nothing of him—till suddenly
a lucky and delighted student fell upon those great volumes in
the Austrian Library; and all at once, after three centuries and

more, old Venice sprang to light under the hand of her old chronicler, and Marino Sanudo with all his pictures, his knick-nacks, his brown rolls of manuscript and dusty volumes round him, regained, as was his right, the first place among Venetian historians—one of the most notable figures of the mediæval world.

Sanudo died in 1539, at the age of seventy-three, poor, as would seem from his will, in which, though he has several properties to bequeath, he has to commit the payment of his faithful servants, especially a certain Anna of Padua, who has nursed and cared for him for twenty years ["who is much my creditor, for I have not had the means to pay her, though she has never failed in her service"] to his executors as the first thing to be done, *primo et ante omnium*, after the sale of his effects. But he would seem to have had anticipations of a satisfactory conclusion to his affairs, since he orders for himself a marble sepulchre, to be erected in the Church of S. Zaccaria, with the following inscription :—

NE TU HOC DESPICE QUOD VIDES SEPULCHRUM
SEU SIS ADVENA, SEU URBANUS,
OSSA SUNT HIC SITA
MARINI SANUTI LEONARDI FILII
SENATORIS CLARISSIMI,
RERUM ANTIQUARUM INDAGATORIS
HISTORIE VENETORUM EX PUBLICO DECRETO
SCRIPTORIS SOLERTISSIMI.
HOC VOLUI TE SCIRE, NUNC BENE VADE,
VALE.

Some time afterwards, however, the old man, perhaps losing heart, finding his books and his curiosities less thought of than he had hoped, gives up the marble sarcophagus so dear to his age, and bids them bury him where he falls, either at S. Zaccaria with his fathers, or at S. Francisco della Vigna where his mother lies, he no longer cares which : but he still clings to his epitaph, the *eterna memoria* with which he had comforted himself through all his toils. Alas ! it has been with his bodily remains

To face page 372.

GATEWAY OF S. GREGORIO.

as for three centuries with those of his mind and spirit. No one knows where the historian lies. His house, with his *stemma*, the arms of the Ca' Sanudo, still stands in the parish of S. Giacomo dell'Orio, behind the Fondaco dei Turchi, an ancient house, once divided into three for the use of the different branches of an important family, now fallen out of all knowledge of the race, and long left without even a stone to commemorate Marino Sanudo's name. This neglect has now been remedied, but not by Venice, by the loving care of Mr. Rawdon Brown, the first interpreter and biographer of this long-forgotten name. The municipality of Venice are fond of placing *Lapide* on every point of vantage, but the anxious exhortations of our countryman did not succeed in inducing the then authorities to give this tribute to their illustrious historian.

Since that period however his place in his beloved city has been fully established, and it is pleasant to think that it was an Englishman who was the first to claim everlasting remembrance, the reward which he desired above all others for the name of Marino Sanudo, of all the historians of Venice the greatest, the most unwearied, and the best.

CHAPTER III.

ALDUS AND THE ALDINES.

N the end of the fifteenth century, when all the arts were coming to their climax, notwithstanding the echoes of war and contention that were never silent, and in the midst of which the republic had often hard ado to hold her own, Venice suddenly became the chief centre of literary effort in Italy, or we might say, at that moment, in the world. Her comparative seclusion from actual personal danger, defended as she was like England by something much more like a "silver streak" than our stormy Channel, had long made the city a haven of peace, such as Petrarch found it, for men of letters; and the freedom of speech, of which that poet experienced both the good and evil, naturally attracted many to whom literary communion and controversy were the chief pleasures in life. It was not however from any of her native *literati* that the new impulse came. A certain Theobaldo Mannucci, or Manutio, familiarly addressed, as is still common in Italy, as Messer or Ser Aldo, born at the little town of Bassiano near Rome, and consequently calling himself Romano, had been for some time connected with the family of the Pii, princes of Carpi, as tutor. The dates are confused and the information uncertain at this period of his career. One of his earlier biographers, Manni, introduces Aldo's former pupil as a man able to enter into literary discussions and take a part in the origination of great plans, whereas Renouard, the accomplished author of the *Annales de l'Imprimerie des Aldes*, speaks

of Alberto as a boy, precocious, as was not unusual to the time, but still in extreme youth, when the new turn was given to his preceptor's thoughts. The natural conclusion from the facts would be, that having completed his educational work at Carpi, Aldo had gone to Ferrara to continue his studies in Greek, and when driven away by the siege of that city had taken refuge with Count Giovanni Pico at Mirandola, and from thence, in company with that young and brilliant scholar, had returned to his former home and pupil—where there ensued much consultation and many plans in the intervals of the learned talk between these philosophers, as to what the poor man of letters was now to do for his own living and the furtherance of knowledge in Italy. Probably the want of text-books, the difficulty of obtaining books of any kind, the incorrectness of those that could be procured, the need of grammars, dictionaries, and all the tools of learning, which would be doubly apparent if the young Alberto, heir of the house, was then in the midst of his education, led the conversation of the elders to this subject. Count Pico was one of the best scholars of his time, very precocious as a boy and in his maturity still holding learning to be most excellent; and Messer Aldo was well aware of all the practical disadvantages with which the acquisition of knowledge was surrounded, having been himself badly trained in the rules of an old-fashioned "Doctrinale," "a stupid and obscure book written in barbarous verse." Their talk at last would seem to have culminated in a distinct plan. Aldo was no enterprising tradesman or speculator bent on money-making. But his educational work would seem to have been brought to a temporary pause, and in the learned leisure of the little principality, in the fine company of the princely scholars who could both understand and help, some lurking desires and hopes no doubt sprang into being. To fill the world with the best of books, free from the blemishes of incorrect transcription, or the print which was scarcely more trustworthy—what a fine occupation, better far than the finest influence upon the mind of one pupil, however illustrious! The scheme would grow, and one detail after another would be added in the conversation which must have become more and more interesting as this now exciting project shaped itself. We can hardly imagine that the noble house in which the scheme originated, and the brilliant visitor under whose auspices it was formed, did not promise substantial aid in an undertaking which the learned tutor had naturally no power of carrying out by himself; and when all the other preliminaries were settled, Venice was fixed upon as the fit place for the enterprise. Pico was a Florentine, Aldo a Roman, but there seems to have existed no doubt in their minds as to the best centre for this great scheme.

The date of Aldo's settlement in Venice is uncertain, like many other facts in this obscure beginning. His first publication appeared in 1494, and it was in 1482 that he left Ferrara to take shelter in the house of the Pii. It would seem probable that he reached Venice soon after the later date, since in his applications to the Senate for the exclusive use of certain forms of type he describes himself as for many years an inhabitant of the city. Manni concludes that he must have been there towards 1488, or rather that his preparations for the establishment of his Stamperia originated about that time. He did not however begin at once with this project, but established himself in Venice as a reader or lecturer on the classical tongues, "reading and interpreting in public for the benefit of the noble and studious youth of the city the most renowned Greek and Latin writers, collating and correcting those manuscripts which it was his intention to print." He drew around him while engaged in this course of literature all that was learned in Venice. Senators, students, priests, whoever loved learning, were attracted by his already well-known fame as a fine scholar, and by the report of the still greater undertaking on which he was bent when a favourable moment should arise. No doubt Aldo had been furnished by his patrons with the best of introductions, and friends and brethren flocked about him, so many that they formed themselves into a distinct society—the *Neacademia* of Aldo—a collection of eager scholars all ready to help, all conscious of the great need, and what we should call in modern parlance the wonderful opening for a great and successful effort. Sabellico, the learned and eloquent historian, with whose new work Venice was ringing; Sanudo, our beloved chronicler, then beginning his life-long work ; Bembo, the future cardinal, already one of the fashionable semi-priests of society, holding a canonicate ; the future historian who wrote no history, Andrea Navagero, but he in his very earliest youth; another cardinal, Leandro, then a barefooted friar : all crowded about the new classical teacher. The enthusiasm with which he was received seems to have exceeded even the ordinary welcome accorded in that age of literary freemasonry to every man who had any new light to throw upon the problems of knowledge. And while he expounded and instructed, the work of preparation for still more important labours went on. It is evident that he made himself fully known, and even became an object of general curiosity, one of the personages to be visited by all that were on the surface of Venetian society—and that the whole of Venice was interested and entertained by the idea of the new undertaking. Foreign printers had already made Venice the scene of their operations, the Englishman Jenson and the Teutons from Spires having begun twenty or thirty years before to print Venezia on the title-pages of their less ambitious volumes. But Aldo was no mere printer, nor was his work for profit alone. It was a labour of love, an enterprise of the highest public importance, and as such commended itself to all who cared for education or the humanities, or who had any desire to be considered as members or disciples of that highest and most cultured class of men of letters, who were the pride and glory of the age.

The house of Aldus is still to be seen in the corner of the Campo di San Agostino, not far from the beautiful Scuola di S. Giovanni Evangelista, which every stranger visits. It was a spot already remarkable in the history of Venice, though the ruins of the house of that great Cavaliere, Bajamonte Tiepolo, must have disappeared before Aldus brought his peaceful trade

to this retired and quiet place—far enough off from the centres
of Venetian life to be left in peace one would have thought.
But that this was not the case, and that his house was already a
great centre of common interest, is evident from one of the
dedicatory epistles to an early work addressed to Andrea
Navagero, in which Aldus complains with humorous seriousness
of the many interruptions from troublesome visitors or correspondents to which he was subject.   Letters from learned men,
he says, arrive in such multitudes that were he to answer them
all it would occupy him night and day.   Still more importunate
were those who came to see him, to inquire into his work:

"Some from friendship, some from interest, the greater part because
they have nothing to do—for then ' Let us go,' they say, ' to Aldo's.'   They
come in crowds and sit gaping—

"' Non missura cutem, nisi plena cruoris hirudo.'

I do not speak of those who come to read to me either poems or prose,
generally rough and unpolished, for publication, for I defend myself from
these by giving no answer or else a very brief one, which I hope nobody
will take in ill part, since it is done, not from pride or scorn, but because
all my leisure is taken up in printing books of established fame.   As for
those who come for no reason, we make bold to admonish them in classical
words in a sort of edict placed over our door—' WHOEVER YOU ARE, Aldo
requests you, if you want anything, ask it in few words and depart,
unless, like Hercules, you come to lend the aid of your shoulders to the
weary Atlas.   Here will always be found in that case something for you to
do, however many you may be.' "

This affords us a whimsical picture of one of the commonest
grievances of busy persons, especially in literature.   No doubt
the idlers who said to each other, " Let us go to Aldo's "
considered themselves to be showing honour to literature, as
well as establishing their own right to consideration, when they
went all that long way from the gaieties of the Piazza or the
lively bottegas and animation of the Rialto to the busy workshops
in that retired and distant Campo, where it might be their
fortune to rub shoulders with young Bembo steeped in Greek,
or get into the way of Sanudo, or be told sharply to ask no
questions by Aldo himself: let us hope they were eventually

frightened off by the writing over the door. The suggestion however that they should help in the work was no form of speech, for Aldo's companions and friends not only surrounded him with sympathy and intelligent encouragement, but diligently worked with him, giving him the benefit of their varied studies and critical experience—collating manuscripts and revising proofs with a patience and continuous labour of which the modern printer, even in face of the most illegible "copy," could form no idea. For the manuscripts from which they printed were in almost all instances incorrect and often imperfect, and to develop a pure text from the careless or fragmentary transcripts which had perhaps come mechanically through the hands of ignorant scribes—taking from each what was best, and filling up the gaps, was a work which required great caution and patience, as well as intelligence and some critical power.

The first work published by Aldus, true to his original purpose, was the Greek grammar of Constantine Lascaris, conveyed to him, as he states in his preface, by Bembo and another young man of family and culture, "now studying at Padua." Bembo it is well known had spent several years in Sicily with Lascaris studying Greek, so that it would seem natural that he should be the means of communication between the author and publisher. This is the first work with a date, according to the careful Renouard, which came from the new press. A small volume of poetry, but without date, the *Musæus*, competes with this book for the honour of being the first published by Aldus; but it would not seem very easy to settle the question, and the reader will not expect any bibliographical details in this place. The work went on slowly, the first two years producing only five books one of which was Aristotle—the first edition ever attempted in the original Greek. In this great undertaking Aldus had the assistance of two editors, Alexander Bondino and Scipione Fortiguerra, scholars well known in their time, one calling himself Agathemeron, the other Carteromaco, according to their fantastic fashion, and both now entirely unknown by either appellation. It was dedicated to Alberto Pio of Carpi, the young prince with whom and whose training the new enterprise was so much connected. It is not to be supposed that publishing of this elaborate kind, so slow, so elaborately revised, so difficult to produce, could have paid even its own expenses, at least at the beginning. It is true that the printer had a monopoly of the Greek, which he was the first to introduce to the world. No competing editions pressed his Aristotle: he had the limited yet tolerably extensive market—for this new and splendid work would be emphatically, in the climax of Renaissance enthusiasm and ambition, one which no prince who respected himself, no cardinal given to letters, or noble dilettante could be content without—in his own hands. And the poor scholars who worked in his studio, some of them lodging under his roof, with *instancabili confronti de' codici migliori*, collation of innumerable manuscripts according to the careful "judgment of the best men in the city, accomplished not only in both the classical languages but in the soundest erudition"— would probably have but small pay for their laborious toils. But under the most favourable circumstances the aid of his wealthy patrons was no doubt indispensable to Aldo in the beginning of his career.

Nor was the costly work of editing his only expense. From the time when the scholar took up the new trade of printer, it is evident that a new ambition rose within him: not only the best text, but the best type occupied his mind. The Lascaris, Renouard tells us, was printed in "*caractère Latin un peu bizarre*"—of which scarcely any further use was made. For some time indeed each successive volume would seem to have been printed in another and another form of type, successive essays to find the best, which is another proof of the anxiety of Aldus that his work should be perfect. Not content with the ordinary Roman character with which Jenson in Venice and the other printers had already found relief from the ponderous dignity of the Black Letter, he set himself to invent a new type. The tradition is that the elegant handwriting of Petrarch, so fine and clear, was the model chosen for this invention which was received with enthusiasm at the moment. It was founded by Francesco of Bologna, and called at first Aldino, after its inventor, and then Italic. No one who knows or possesses books in this graceful and beautiful type will doubt that it is the prettiest of all print; but after a little study of these beautiful pages, without the break or relief of a single paragraph, all flowing on line after line, the reader will probably succumb half blinded and wholly confused, and return with pleasure to the honest every-day letters, round and simple, of the Roman type. A copy of the *Cortigiano*, one of the best known of old Italian books, lies before us at this moment, with the delicate Aldine mark, the anchor and dolphin, on the title-page. Nothing could be more appropriate to the long unending dialogue and delightful artificial flow of superfine sentiment and courtly talk, than the charming minute and graceful run of the letters, *corsivo*, like a piece of the most beautiful penmanship. No reader could possibly wish to read the *Cortigiano* straight through at one or a dozen readings; but were the subject one of livelier interest, or its appeal to the heart or intellect a deeper one, the head would soon ache and the eyes swim over those delightful pages. In the enthusiasm of invention Aldus himself describes his new type as " of the greatest beauty, such as was never done before," and appeals to the Signoria of Venice to secure to him for ten years the sole right to use it—kindly indicating to the authorities at the same time the penalty which he would like to see attached to any breach of the privilege.

"I supplicate that for ten years no other should be allowed to print in cursive letters of any sort in the dominion of your Serenity, nor to sell books printed in other countries in any part of the said dominion, under pain to whoever breaks this law of forfeiting the books and paying a fine of two hundred ducats for each offence, which fine shall be divided into three parts, one for the officer who shall convict, another for the *Pietà*, the third for the informer : and that the accusation be made before any officer of this most excellent city before whom the informer may appear."

Aldus secured his privilege from a committee (if we may use so

modern a word) of counsellors, among whom is found the name of
a Sanudo, cousin of our Marino, who himself, according to a note
in his diary, seems to have prepared the necessary decree. But
the essential over-delicacy of the type was its destruction. It
continued in use for a number of years, during which many
books were printed in it : but after that period dropped into
the occasional usage for emphasis or distinction which we still
retain—though our modern Italics, no doubt the natural successors and descendants of the invention of Aldus, are much
more commonplace and not nearly so beautiful.

It is pretty to know however that the first Italian book
published in this romantic and charming form was the poems of
Petrarch, *Le Cose Volgari di Messer Francesco Petrarcha*, edited
with great care by Bembo, " who," writes a gentleman of Pavia
to the illustrious lady, Isabella, Duchess of Mantua, " has
printed the Petrarch from a copy of the verses written in
Petrarch's own hand, which I have held in mine, and which
belongs to a Paduan. It is esteemed so much that it has been
followed letter by letter in the printing with the greatest diligence." The book is described on the title-page as " taken from
the very handwriting of the Poet," and not only the year but
the month of the date, July, 1501, carefully given. Renouard
tells a charming story of a copy he had seen, inscribed from one
fond possessor to another, through three or four inheritances,
avec une sorte d'idolatrie, and which contained at the end a
sonnet in the handwriting of Pietro Bembo :

> " Se come qui la fronte onesta e grave
>   Del sacro almo Poeta
>   Che d'un bel Lauro colse eterna palma
>   Cosi vedessi ancor lo spirto e l'alma :
>   Stella si chiara e lieta,
>   Diresti, certo il ciel tutto non ave.

> " Tu che vieni a mirar l'onesta e grave
>   Sembianza del divin nostro Poeta,
>   Pensa, s'in questa il tuo desio s'acqueta,
>   Quanto fu il veder lui dolce e soave."

Lorenzo of Pavia (the same man apparently who visited Carpaccio on behalf of Gonzaga, the husband of Isabella, and saw that painter's picture of Jerusalem) secured a copy of this true amateur's book, printed with such love and care "on good paper, very clear and white and equal, not thick in one part and thin in another, as are so many of those you have in Mantua," as a "rare thing, which, like your Ladyship, has no paragon" for Duchess Isabella.

After this fine beginning however there followed darker days. In 1506 Aldus had to leave Venice to look after properties lost or in danger, a troubled enterprise which he sweetened as he could by his usual search after manuscripts and classical information. In the month of July of that year an accident happened to him which affords us an interesting glimpse of the scholar-publisher. He was riding along with his servant, who was a Mantuan, but under sentence of banishment from that princedom, returning to Asola, where his family were, from a prolonged journey through Lombardy. The pair rode along quietly enough, though there were fightings going on round about—in short stages, ever ready to turn aside to convent or castle where codexes might be found, or where there was some learned chaplain or studious friar who had opinions on the subject of Aristotle or Virgil to be consulted—when suddenly, as they crossed the Mantuan frontier, the guards who had been set to watch for certain suspected persons, started forth to seize the passengers. The servant, terrified, fled, thinking that he was the object of their suspicions, and his master was seized and made prisoner, his precious papers taken from him, and himself shut up in the house of the official who had arrested him. Aldus immediately wrote to the prince of Mantua, himself an amateur of the arts, stating his hard case. His servant's foolish flight had aroused all manner of suspicions, and perhaps the old manuscripts which formed his baggage strengthened the doubts with which he was regarded. He writes thus with modest dignity, explaining his position :—

"I am Aldo Manutio Romano, privileged to call myself of the family of the Pii by my patron Alberto of Carpi, who is the son-in-law of your illustrious Highness—and am and have always been your humble servant, as is my lord whom I naturally follow.   At present, in consequence of my undertaking as a printer of books, I dwell in Venice.   Desiring to print the works of Virgil which hitherto have been very imperfectly rendered, correctly and according to the best texts, I have sought through all Italy and beyond : and in person I have gone over almost all Lombardy to look for any manuscripts of these works that may be found.   On my way back to Venice, passing by your Highness's villa at Casa Romana, and having with me Federico de Ceresara, my servant, who is a native of and banished from these parts, he took fright when your Highness's guards seized his bridle, and, striking his horse with his feet, fled outside the boundaries of your Highness's territory.   Having got to the other side of the frontier he sent back his horse : for which cause I am retained here with my horses and goods, both those which my servant carried and those which I myself had. And this is the third day that I am detained here, to the great injury of my business, and I intreat your Highness to be pleased to command Messer Joanpetro Moraro, in whose house I am, to permit me to proceed upon my journey, and to restore to me my horses and my goods.   As I am illustrating the works of Virgil, who was a Mantuan, it appears to me that I do not deserve evil treatment in Mantua, but rather to be protected."

Two days after Aldus was compelled to write again, having received no answer; but on the 25th of July, when his detention had lasted a week, he was liberated with Gonzaga's apologies and excuses.   He did not like the incident, complaining bitterly of the shame of being incarcerated; but it forms an interesting illustration in history to see him, with all his precious papers in his saddle-bags, and his consciousness of a name as well known as their masters', answering the interrogatories of the guards, appealing to the prince, who could not mistake, though these ignorant men-at-arms might do so, who Aldo Manutio was.

Among the various assistants whom Aldus employed during these first busy years, and whom his biographer, Manni, calls *correttori della Stamperia*, figured, among others, a man more illustrious than any yet mentioned—Erasmus of Rotterdam, *uomo d'ampia e spaziosa fama*.   It is said that Erasmus wrote from Bologna to propose for publication his collection of Adages, a proposal which was received eagerly by Aldus; but when

To face page 384.

NEAR SAN BIAGIO.

the philosopher came to Venice, he shared at first the fate of those unfortunates who were warned by the placard over the door of the Stamperia to state their business quickly and be gone. When Aldus knew however who his visitor was, he hurried from his workshop and his proofs to receive with honour a guest so welcome. The Dutchman would seem to have entered his house at once as one of his recognised assistants. The famous Scaliger, in a philippic directed against Erasmus, declares that when he found refuge there, he ate for three and drank for many without doing the work of one; but such amenities are not unknown among scholars any more than among the ignorant. Perhaps the heavier Teuton always seems to exceed in these respects amid the spare living and abstemious sobriety of Italians. Erasmus himself allows that after the publication of his *Proverbs* he had worked with Aldus on the comedies of Terence and Plautus and the tragedies of Seneca—not the loftiest perhaps of classical works—" in which," he says, " I think that I have happily restored some passages with the support of ancient manuscripts. We left them with Aldus," he adds, " leaving to his judgment the question of publication." This work never seems to have been published by the elder Aldus, so that perhaps Erasmus' indignant denial afterwards of ever having done any work of correction, except upon his own book, may after all be reconcilable with the above statements.

The busy house on its quiet Campo, with all the bustle of Venice distant—not even the measured beat of the oars on the canal, most familiar of sounds, to disturb the retired and tranquil square: but all the hum of incessant work within, the scholars withdrawn in silent chambers out of the way of the printing presses, poring over their manuscripts, straining after a better reading, a corrected phrase, with proofs sent from one to another, and the master most busy of all, giving his attention now to a new form, now to an old manuscript—how strange a contrast it offers to the gay and animated life, the intrigues, the struggles, the emulations, outside! No doubt the Stamperia had its conflicts too. Ser Marino stepping round in his senator's robes from the Ca' Sanudo not far off, would not meet perhaps

C C

without a jibe the youngster Navagero, who had been named
to the post of historian over his head; nor could the poor Italian
scholars refrain from remarks upon the big appetite and slow
movements of that Dutch Erasmus, whose reputation has proved
so much more stable than their own.   But these jealousies are
small in comparison with the struggles of the council chamber,
the secret tribunals, the betrayals, the feuds and frays that went
on everywhere around them.   When the Neacademia met upon
its appointed days, and the learned heads were laid together,
and the talk was all of Virgil and Ovid, of Plato and Aristotle,
how full of an inspiring sense of virtue, and work that was for
the world, was that grave assembly!   When Aldus wrote his
preface to the grammar of Lascaris, which was his first publication, he declares himself to have determined to devote his life
to the good of mankind, for which great end, though he might
live a life much more congenial to him in retirement, he had
chosen a laborious career.   They were all inspired with the
same spirit, and toiled over obscure readings and much corrected
proofs with the zeal of missionaries, bringing new life and light
to the dark place.   "Everything is good in these books," says
the French critic Renouard.   "Not only for their literary merit,
most of them being the greatest of human works, but also in
the point of view of typographical excellence, they are un-
surpassed."   Neither rival nor imitator has reached the same
height—even his sons and successors, though with the aid of
continually improving processes, never attained the excellence
of Aldo *il Vecchio*, the scholar-printer, the first to devote
himself to the production of the best books in the best way, not
as a mercantile speculation, but with the devout intention of
serving the world's best interests, as well as following his own
cherished tastes, and working out the chosen plan of his life.

It is one remarkable sign of the universal depression and
misery that Aldus and his studio and all his precious manuscripts disappeared during the troubled years of the great
Continental war in which all the world was against Venice.   In
1510, 1511, and 1512, scarcely any book proceeded from his
press.   The painters went on with their work, and notwith-

standing the misery and fear in the city the statesmen, councillors, all public officials, were more active and occupied than ever. Had Venice possessed a great poet, he would not in all probability have been put to silence even by the terrible and unaccustomed distant roar upon the mainland, of the guns. But the close and minute labours of the literary corrector and critic were not compatible with these horrible disturbances. Even in the height of the Renaissance men were indifferent to fine Latin and fine Greek and the most lovely varieties of type, in the vehemence of a national struggle for life.

After the war Aldus returned to his work with renewed fervour.

"It is difficult," says Renouard, "to form an idea of the passion with which he devoted himself to the reproduction of the great works of ancient literature. If he heard of the existence anywhere of a manuscript unpublished, or which could throw a light upon an existing text, he never rested till he had it in his possession. He did not shrink from long journeys, great expenditure, applications of all kinds ; and he had also the satisfaction to see that on all sides people bestirred themselves to help him, communicating to him, some freely, some for money, an innumerable amount of precious manuscripts for the advantage of his work. Some were even sent to him from very distant countries, from Poland and Hungary, without any solicitation on his part."

It is not in this way however that the publisher, that much-questioned and severely criticised middleman, makes a fortune. And Aldus died poor. His privileges did not stand him in much stead, copyright, especially when not in books but in new forms of type, being non-existent in his day. In France and Germany, and still nearer home, his beautiful Italic was robbed from him, copied on all sides, notwithstanding the protection granted by the Pope and other princes as well as by the Venetian Signoria. His fine editions were printed from, and made the foundation of foreign issues which replaced his own. How far his princely patrons stood by him to repair his losses there seems no information. His father-in-law, Andrea of Asola, a printer who was not so fine a scholar, but perhaps more able to cope with the world, did come to his aid, and his son Paolo Manutio, and his grandson Aldo *il Giovane*, as he is called, succeeded him in turn ; the first with kindred ambition and aim at excellence, the latter perhaps with aims not quite so high. We cannot further follow the fortunes of the family, nor of the highly cultured society of which their workshops formed the centre. Let us leave Aldo with all his aids about him, the senators, the school-masters, the poor scholars, the learned men who were to live to be cardinals, and those who were to die as poor as they were famous : and his learned Greek Musurus, and his poor student from Rotterdam, a better scholar perhaps than any of them —and all his idle visitors coming to gape and admire, while our Sanudo swept round the corner from S. Giacomo dell' Orio, with his vigorous step and his toga over his shoulders, and the young men who were of the younger faction came in, a little contemptuous of their elders and strong in their own learning, to the meeting of the Aldine academy and the consultation on new readings. The Stamperia was as distinct a centre of life as the Piazza, though not so apparent before the eyes of men.

Literature ran into a hundred more or less artificial channels in the Venice of the later centuries : it produced countless works upon the antiquities of the city, often more valuable than interesting : it brightened into the laughter, the quips and quirks of Goldoni ; it produced charming verses, pastorals, descriptions of pageants and feasts : but never has risen into any of the splendour which is the dower of the neighbour Republic, the proud and grave Tuscan city. The finest of literary memo-ries for Venice is that of the Aldine Stamperia, where for once there was a printer-publisher who toiled and spent his life to fill the world with beautiful books, and hold open to all men the gates of learning—" all for love and nothing for reward."

I had hoped to have introduced as the last in this little gallery of Venetians a personage more grave and great, a figure unique in the midst of this ever-animated, strong, stormy, and restless race. He should have stood in his monastic robe, the Theologian of Venice : he too, like every other of her sons, for his city against every power, even those of Church and Pope. But Fra Paolo is too great to come in at the end without due space and perspective about him. The priest who forestalled with his

quick-flashing genius half the discoveries of his time, who
guessed what it meant when the golden lamp with its red
glimmer swayed as it hung in the splendid gloom of San Marco,
before ever Galileo had put that heresy forth; who divined how
the blood made its way through our veins before Harvey; who
could plan a palace and sway a senate, as well as defy a pope;
who was adored by his order and worshipped by his city, yet
almost murdered at his own door—is perhaps of all Venetians
the one most worthy of study and elucidation. It is only natural,
according to the common course of human events, that he should
therefore be left out. The convent of Fra Paolo lies in ruins,
his grave, just over the threshold of that funereal place, is shown
with a grudge by the friar at San Michele, who probably knows
little of him save that he was in opposition to the Holy See.
To us at the present moment, as to so many in his city, Fra Paolo
must continue to be only a name.

The critics of recent days have had much to say as to the
deterioration of Venice in her new activity, and the introduction
of alien modernisms in the shape of steamboats and other new
industrial agents into her canals and lagoons. But in this
adoption of every new development of power Venice is only
proving herself the most faithful representative of the vigorous
republic of old. Whatever prejudice or even angry love may
say, we cannot doubt that the Michiels, the Dandolos, the
Foscari, the great rulers who formed Venice, had steamboats
existed in their day, serving their purpose better than their
barges and *peati*, would have adopted them without hesitation,
without a thought of what any critics might say. The wonderful
new impulse which has made Italy a great power has justly put
strength and life before those old traditions of beauty which
made her not only the "woman-country" of Europe, but a sort
of Odalisque trading upon her charms rather than the nursing
mother of a noble and independent nation. That in her recoil
from that somewhat degrading position she may here and there
have proved too regardless of the claims of antiquity, we need
not attempt to deny: the new spring of life in her is too genuine

aud great to keep her entirely free from this evident danger. But it is strange that any one who loves Italy and sincerely rejoices in her amazing resurrection should fail to recognise how venial is this fault.

And we are glad to think that the present Venetians have in no respect failed from the love entertained by their forefathers for their beautiful city. The young poet of the lagoons, whose little sonnet I have placed on the title-page of this book, blesses in his enthusiasm not only his Venice and her beautiful things, but in a fervour at which we smile yet understand, the sirocco which catches her breath, and the hoarseness which comes of her acquaintance with the seas. But he and his fellow-townsmen have happily learned the lesson which the great Dandolo could not learn, nor Petrarch teach, that Venice, glorious in her strength and beauty, is but a portion of a more glorious ideal still—of Italy for the first time consolidated, a great Power in Europe and in the world.

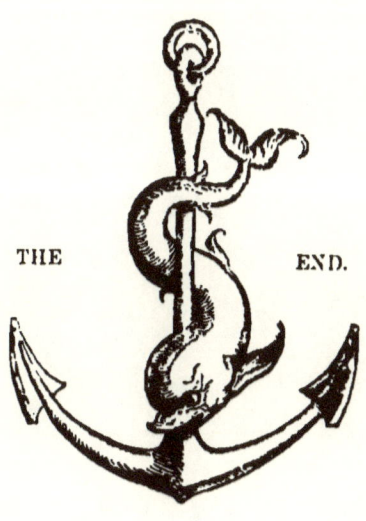

THE   END.

RICHARD CLAY AND SONS,
LONDON AND BUNGAY.

www.ingramcontent.com/pod-product-compliance
Lightning Source LLC
Chambersburg PA
CBHW022028110726
47901CB00006B/1694